THE FUTURE
HOMEMAKERS
OF AMERICA

Laurie Graham

HARPER PERENNIAL
London, New York, Toronto and Sydney

Harper Perennial
An imprint of HarperCollins*Publishers*
1 London Bridge Street
London SE1 9GF

www.harperperennial.co.uk

This edition published by Harper Perennial 2006

Previously published in paperback by Fourth Estate in 2002

First published in Great Britain in 2001

A catalogue record for this book
is available from the British Library

ISBN-13 978-0-00-723407-3

Typeset in Monotype Fournier by
Rowland Phototypesetting Ltd, Bury St Edmunds, Suffolk
Printed and bound by CPI Group (UK) Ltd, Croydon, CR0 4YY

MIX
Paper from
responsible sources
FSC
www.fsc.org FSC C007454

For my own hardy perennials
Bridget, Liz, Rachel, Trish and Vivvy

THE FUTURE
Homemakers
OF AMERICA

We were down at the commissary, just for something to do, me and Lois, pushing Sandie in her stroller. Breath puffing out like smoke every time we laughed and just hanging there in the air. The cold hadn't killed the scent of the beet harvest, though. All my born days, I never knowed such a sickly smell.

'I swear,' she said, loud as you please, 'this place is colder than a gravedigger's ass.' Lois always did have a mouth on her.

'Uh-oh,' she said, 'here comes the Pie-Crust Queen.'

And sure enough, there was Betty running after us, flagging us to wait till she could catch her breath and tell us the big story.

'Peggy!' she said, gasping and wheezing and hanging on to my arm. 'Have you heard the terrible news?'

When your husband flies F-84s, sitting up there on 3,000 gallons of jet fuel, cruising – now *there*'s a word – cruising at 510mph, hoping to get his tail waxed by some Russki so he can be Jock-of-the-Week back at the base, there's only one kind of Terrible News, but we both knew, me and Lois, that it wasn't that.

That kinda news comes quiet, on flannel feet. The base chaplain brings it to your door, and the CO's wife follows through with a few brisk words about courage and dignity. After that, you better hope you got some friends. Some squadron wives to take turns answering your phone and feeding your kids and keeping you from falling into a thousand pieces.

When Terrible News comes to married quarters, there's no pulling down of blinds. Military don't hold with closing the drapes. Word gets round, but you'd never know, looking in from outside, that anything was happening, because heck, if air force wives went around yelling 'Have you heard?' the whole thing could run out of control. Next thing you know, every girl on the base'd be out there screaming, 'His poor wife! His poor orphaned children! It's so tragic. It's unbearable. But I'm okay. *I'*m okay. It's not me. Not this time!' And that would never do.

Still, I guess we both missed a beat. Terrible news?

'His Majesty King George of England,' she said, 'died in his sleep at Sandring Ham Palace.'

Betty always had a thing about royalty, clipping photos, pasting them in her albums, specially anything about that Princess Margaret, or the royal babies.

'Princess Margaret had tea with General and Mrs Eisenhower,' she told us one time. 'She was fifteen minutes late, but it wasn't her fault. They had angel-food cake and dainty little sandwiches, but the princess probably didn't do cake, watching her lovely figure an' all. She wore a yellow shirt and the cutest black dirndl skirt.'

'Well, I'll be dirndled.' Lois was always taking the rise out of Betty, but she took it in good part. When you're in a hole you gotta stick together and USAF Drampton was a hole, no two ways.

I knew Betty from way back, at Topperwein High, Class of '42. I was captain of the softball team and she was president of Future Homemakers, stuffing toy bears for needy children and selling lunch-boxes for Healthful Living Week. We really didn't run with the same crowd. But then she married Ed Gillis and I married Vern Dewey which made us both 96th Bomber Wing wives. By the time we were posted from Travis, Texas, to some frozen salt-marsh, East Anglia, next stop Siberia, we were blood-sisters, near enough. Never would have thought I'd be so glad of Betty's everlasting cheerfulness. That's homesickness for you.

'He was found by a servant,' she said. 'That'd be a footman or a pageboy, taking him his coffee. Imagine. He'd put down the tray, all beautiful silver and jewels, and say, "Good morning, sire" and ba-boom, the king's dead.'

The Daily Telegraph

No. 30,139 THURSDAY, FEBRUARY 7, 1952 and Morning Post Printed in LONDON and MANCHESTER Price 2d.

DEATH OF KING GEORGE VI

EACEFULLY IN SLEEP AT SANDRINGHAM

LAST WALK IN GROUNDS ON PREVIOUS EVENING

NEW QUEEN ON WAY HOME: PROCLAMATION TO-MORROW

PEERS AND M.P.s TAKE OATH: MR. CHURCHILL TO BROADCAST

HIS MAJESTY KING GEORGE VI DIED IN HIS SLEEP AT NDRINGHAM HOUSE IN THE EARLY HOURS OF YESTERDAY RNING. A SERVANT FOUND HIM DEAD IN BED AT 7.30 A.M. ANNOUNCEMENT FROM SANDRINGHAM, REPEATED IN A ECIAL ISSUE OF THE LONDON GAZETTE LAST NIGHT, SAID:

The King, who retired last night in his usual health, passed peacefully away in his sleep early this morning.

Princess Elizabeth, who accedes to the Throne, was informed of her her's death while she was at the Royal hunting lodge near Nyeri, in aya. Later she left by air for London, where she is due at 4.30 p.m. day.

The Privy Council met at 5 p.m. last night to decide on the Accession clamation. This will be read at St. James's Palace, at Temple Bar and the steps of the Royal Exchange in the City to-morrow.

Mr. Churchill will broadcast on all B.B.C. wavelengths at 9.15 p.m. ight for 15 minutes.

ST WALK IN GROUNDS

The King, who was 56, was born at Sandringham. During his last stay ere, he was out on Tuesday morning and afternoon and appeared to be in od health. In the evening he walked in the grounds.

Queen Elizabeth and Princess Margaret accompanied him when he went to ndringham last Friday. On the previous day he had gone to London Airport see his elder daughter and the Duke of Edinburgh leave for Nairobi.

Queen Mary was informed at Marlborough House of her son's death. The ke of Gloucester, who was at his home at Barnwell Manor, Northants, went Sandringham on hearing the news. He will go to London Airport to meet the een to-day.

The Princess Royal was told at St. James's Palace. She cancelled her visit Switzerland, where she was to have received treatment for fibrositis.

O CABINET MEETINGS

The Prime Minister and Sir David Maxwell Fyfe, Home Secretary, were given news by telephone. A Cabinet meeting was held in the morning and again he afternoon.

All business in the House of Commons and the House of Lords was sus- ded. Each Chamber met formally for two minutes and then adjourned il after the Accession Privy Council, when M.P.s and Peers began to take the h of allegiance to the new monarch. The meeting of the Parliamentary bour Party was adjourned before any discussion had started.

All the cinemas were closed yesterday, and the Lord Chamberlain directed t theatres should be shut for the day and also on the day of the funeral of King. B.B.C. programmes were cancelled except for news bulletins and ather forecasts.

There will be a restricted programme from to-day until after the funeral, date of which has not yet been fixed.

All sport stopped except for the four Football Association Cup-ties. Satur- 's Rugby Union international between England and Ireland at Twickenham been postponed. Football League and Rugby League fixtures will be played arranged. National Hunt racing will not be resumed until after the funeral.

WDS AT PALACE

As soon as the news became known, a crowd began to gather outside Buck- ham Palace and was there most of the day. A servant was seen to lower all blinds of the Palace in the morning. Ambassadors were calling throughout day to sign the visitors' book as an official expression of their sorrow.

Mr. Churchill issued a message from 10, Downing-street last night asking t there should be no public gathering at London Airport when the Queen ves from Kenya. He expressed the hope that her return should be as quiet ossible.

No official announcement was made in Australia regarding the tour which Queen and the Duke of Edinburgh were to have begun on Mar. 1, but Mr. roak, Acting Prime Minister of New Zealand, spoke of the "deep disappoint- t which will be felt at the cancellation of the visit."

The King was to have left Portsmouth on Mar. 11 on a cruise with the en and Princess Margaret in H.M.S. Vanguard to restore his health after his ration in September. He had planned to hold an investiture at Buckingham ace on Feb. 27.

King George and Queen Elizabeth were crowned in Westminster Abbey on 12, 1937. The new Queen will be the first to be proclaimed since Queen oria's accession 115 years ago. The Heir to the Throne is now Prince rles, the Queen's three-year-old son.

T END LIGHTS WITCHED OFF

EET LAMPS ONLY

West End of London was [illegible] night by the lack of [illegible] theatre and cinema signs [illegible] entertainment were [illegible] from light from a few [illegible] and even restaurants [illegible] street [illegible]

[illegible] some theatres [illegible] in view for pur- [illegible] tickets [illegible] performances.

[illegible] none of the advertising signs were in [illegible] The fountains in [illegible] been playing and flood- [illegible] off. But for a few [illegible] for hours of traffic [illegible] deserted.

[illegible] cancelled [illegible] and cabarets.

STOCKBROKERS STOP DEALING

CITY MARKETS CLOSE

By Our City Editor

In the City the news of the King's death brought all business to a standstill. On the Stock Exchange when the announcement was made over the tape no further attempt was made to do any trading.

Mr. John Braithwaite, the chairman, immediately summoned a special meeting of the Stock Exchange Council. Just after 11.30 it was announced: "In consequence of the death of His Majesty the King, the Stock Exchange will be closed at 12 noon today. It is announced that there shall be no dealings after that time."

Similar steps were taken regarding practically all the other leading City markets. On the Baltic members held a special service.

POLICE PREPARE CEREMONIAL PLAN

SIR H. SCOTT'S RECALL

Daily Telegraph Reporter

Sir John Nott-Bower, Acting Commissioner of the Metropolitan Police, was notified of the King's death by the Home Office. Immediately telephone messages were sent to Sir Harold Scott, the Commissioner, who was on leave in Somerset, and to Assistant Commissioner P. A. Margetson, who is in charge of ceremonial at Scotland Yard, and had also started his leave.

At a conference on their return plans for police arrangements for ceremonies concerning the King's death and the Accession of the Queen in London were discussed. Arrangements were completed for the return of the Queen to London to-day.

Extra police and wireless cars were sent to Buckingham Palace and the Mall last night.

A recent portrait of His Majesty King George VI.

LYING IN STATE ON MONDAY

PARLIAMENT TO SEND CONDOLENCES

BY OUR POLITICAL CORRESPONDENT

Parliament is expected to meet on Monday for Addresses of condolence to the Queen and the Royal Family on the death of the King to be moved in both Houses. Lords and Commons will then adjourn until Tuesday, Feb. 19.

The body of the King will lie in state in Westminster Hall from Monday until the day fixed for the funeral.

These arrangements are provisional until the wishes of the new Queen regarding her father's funeral are made known on her return.

Meanwhile Members of the House of Commons will take the oath to the Queen, a process which began last night and will continue to-day and to-morrow.

Mr. Churchill will broadcast to the nation to-night at 9 o'clock.

The Government and the Governments of Commonwealth countries all continue in office under the Demise of the Crown Act, 1901, which laid down that the position of all who held office under the Crown would not be affected by the monarch's death. No seals will be surrendered or letters patent cancelled, but Ministers will kiss hands and take the oath.

Parliament itself continues in being until the end of its normal term or until dissolved by the new sovereign under the provisions of the Representation of the People Act, 1867.

To-day's Supplement

With this issue THE DAILY TELEGRAPH *presents an eight-page Memorial Supplement of the life of King George VI and his Queen, and of the new Queen.*

Other news consequent on the death of the King is on Pages 5, 7, and 9.

MR. VINCENT MASSEY

Mr. Vincent Massey, Governor-General designate of Canada, who was due to leave Tilbury by sea to-morrow, cancelled his passage to Canada and will leave later.

LATE NEWS

Broadcasting: Page 4, Column 8

7.30 a.m. DISCOVERY BY SANDRINGHAM SERVANT

FROM OUR SPECIAL CORRESPONDENT

SANDRINGHAM, Wednesday.

It was 7.30 this orning when the King was found dead in his bed at Sandringham House. He had died as he slept.

A short while before he retired after a family dinner party last night the King took a last walk in the grounds around the house. The evening was calm and quiet, and he was looking forward to going out shooting to-day.

This morning a servant who carried in the King's usual morning cup of tea could not rouse him. Immediately help was summoned and the Queen was told.

A message was sent calling for Dr. Ansell, in the village of Wolferton, three miles away, and the doctor drove along the road that winds through the Royal estate.

When he arrived at the house and was taken to the King's room, there was nothing he could do.

No blinds were drawn over the windows of this favourite home of the King. Smoke from the first fires hung limp in the still morning air. No announcement was posted on the wrought-iron gates of the main drive.

BELOVED AS SQUIRE

In the district around the estate, where the King was beloved more as the squire than the monarch, people went about their everyday tasks. Gamekeepers prepared for a day's shooting with the King and a party.

The first news that many had of his death was when they heard

(Continued on P. 2, Col. 4)

"SHOCK" FOR QUEEN MARY

REMAINING AT HOME

The news was conveyed to Queen Mary at Marlborough House some time before the official announcement was made. "The news came as a great shock to her," said a member of her staff. It is understood that Queen Mary will remain in her own home and will not undertake the journey to Sandringham.

The Princess Royal, at St. James's Palace, was told by telephone from Buckingham Palace. Her planned visit to Switzerland, because of an attack of fibrositis, has been cancelled.

The Duke of Gloucester was at Barnwell Manor, Northamptonshire, and was on the point of leaving to fulfil engagements in London when the news reached him. He immediately cancelled his visit to London and made arrangements to go at once to Sandringham.

The Duchess of Kent arrived back at Northolt Airport last night on a B.E.A. Viking from Munich, where she has been visiting her sister. She was driven to her residence, Coppins, Iver, Bucks. Photographers were requested not to take pictures of the Duchess leaving the plane.

The 16-year-old Duke of Kent is expected to return to England from his Swiss school at Gstaad within a day or two. Princess Alexandra, daughter of the Duchess of Kent, was told at Heathfield School, Ascot.

DR. FISHER

The Archbishop of Canterbury, Dr. Fisher, is prevented by illness from attending the meetings of the Privy Council. He is still in bed with bronchitis. A statement from Lambeth Palace said that, owing to the Archbishop's indisposition, the Bishop of Norwich, Dr. Herbert, as Clerk of the Closet and Bishop of the diocese in which Sandringham is situated, is in touch with the Royal family officially and pastorally.

COMPLICATION COULD NOT BE FORESEEN

BY OUR MEDICAL CORRESPONDENT

Comfort must be taken by the Royal Family and nation that His Majesty died in his sleep without pain.

Lumbar sympathectomy, performed three years ago for circulatory failure in his leg, gave evidence of arterial disease, and it is probable that the main artery of the body, the aorta, and the branches it gives to the heart called the coronary arteries, were also likewise hardened and narrowed.

This condition can cause clotting known as coronary thrombosis, which stops the heart. Death in these cases is sometimes immediate and painless.

Looking back, we also have the unrelenting course of the King's lung trouble which resulted in resection. The same structural changes, probably a malignant growth reported as being in the lung, can occur in the brain as a secondary complication. Such changes are often without symptoms until a fatal haemorrhage or clotting reveals their presence and doctors X-ray the chest, in many cases of brain disease with this in view.

SUDDEN CONDITIONS

It is possible that such a trouble may have been the actual cause of death. Another possible cause is clotting in the pulmonary circulation, a complication of resection more usually met in the immediate post-operative period.

All these conditions are sudden and, though recognised, the date or the fact that they will occur cannot be foreseen.

To-day's Weather

GENERAL INFERENCE: Anti-cyclone expected to be centred to S.W. of British Isles. Many parts of England, Wales, Ireland and S. Scotland will have mainly fine weather. There may, however, be a little rain in some S. districts of England at first. In N. and Central Scotland there will be bright periods and squally showers.

LONDON, S.E., S.W. ENGLAND: Moderate S.W. to W. winds; mainly fine, but possibly cloudy at first with a little rain or drizzle.

E. ENGLAND, E., W. MIDLANDS, WALES AND MON.: Light or moderate W. winds; mainly fine.

N.E. ENGLAND, S.E., MID SCOTLAND: Fresh or perhaps strong W. winds; long bright periods, chance of a few showers.

S.W. SCOTLAND, ISLE OF MAN, N.E., N.W. IRELAND: Fresh or moderate W. winds; long bright periods, chance of a few showers.

W., N.W., N.E. SCOTLAND, ORKNEY AND SHETLAND: Fresh or strong W. winds; squally showers and bright periods.

S.E., S.W. IRELAND: Light or moderate variable winds; mainly fine apart from some mist and fog patches early.

IRISH SEA: Fresh or strong W. to N.W. winds; showers and bright intervals; visibility mainly good; sea moderate to rough.

TO-MORROW'S OUTLOOK: Probably fine in many E. districts; rain may spread to many W. and N. areas from Atlantic.

STORM DELAYS QUEEN'S PLANE TWO HOURS

ROYAL PARTY FLEW TO JOIN AIRLINER AT UGANDA

NAIROBI, Wednesday.

Queen Elizabeth and the Duke of Edinburgh left Entebbe, Uganda, in their Argonaut aircraft, Atalanta, to-night after being delayed more than two hours by a tropical thunderstorm.

They had flown to Entebbe in a light aircraft from the Royal Lodge at Nyeri, Kenya, on the first stage of their return to London.

On the home flight they will stop at El Adem Royal Air Force station in Libya, and were due to reach London Airport at 4.30 G.M.T. to-morrow if they had not been delayed.

NEWS BROKEN BY DUKE

BORE IT LIKE A QUEEN

From FRANK HARVEY,
Daily Telegraph Special Correspondent
NYERI, Kenya, Wednesday.

News that she had become Queen came to Princess Elizabeth at Sagana Lodge, the wedding gift house here in which she and her husband were spending a brief holiday.

The news of the King's death was broken to her by the Duke of Edinburgh. She stood it bravely, "like a Queen," it was stated.

First news of the death came from Mr. Granville Roberts, correspondent of the East African Standard. He was at lunch in the Outspan Hotel here when the telephone message reached him from his Nairobi office.

He informed Sir Leslie Charteris, the Princess's secretary, and then telephoned the news to Lt.-Cmdr. Parker, the Duke of Edinburgh's equerry, at the lodge. Sir Leslie suggested that confirmation be obtained before the Princess was told.

SHOCK TO BRITONS

The King's death came as a bitter shock to the handful of British subjects in this remote hotel. News of the death coincided with a most unusual storm for this time of the year. It had been the usual sunny morning but by lunch-time clouds gathered thickly over Mount Kenya, and distant rumblings of thunder were heard.

Despite the tragic circumstances, [illegible] smiled and waved [illegible] people when they [illegible] stage of the [illegible]

NEWS HEARD BY MEN IN KOREA

101-GUN SALUTE

From Our Special Correspondent
SEOUL, Thursday.

The news of the death of the King shocked and stunned the British troops in Korea. It was not heard until late in the evening over the local radio station. At first it was not believed.

But the official news given by divisional headquarters was sent round the units by courier jeep by telephone. When the news was at last accepted there was silence among the tents in the snow frozen hills.

At 11 a.m. to-morrow there will be a 101-gun salute by each artillery unit in the division at their present positions, followed by a 21-gun salute in honour of the new Queen. They will fire live ammunition as no blank is available.

PROCLAMATION OF QUEEN ELIZABETH II

DAILY TELEGRAPH REPORTER

Princess Elizabeth succeeded to the Throne from the moment that her father, King George VI, died in his sleep yesterday morning. In the midst of informal holiday surroundings in the heart of Kenya, she became England's seventh reigning Queen.

Because of the unprecedented absence of the Sovereign's heir 4,000 miles away in the Commonwealth the young Queen's accession was formally proclaimed in her absence at a meeting of the Privy Council at St. James's Palace yesterday evening.

The public proclamation, with its ancient traditional heraldry, will be made by the Garter King-of-Arms, Sir George Bellew, at St. James's Palace to-morrow. He will stand on the balcony overlooking Friary Court accompanied by the other Kings-of-Arms, the Heralds and the Pursuivants in their brilliant uniforms.

After a fanfare from the State trumpeters, Garter King-of-Arms will unroll the parchment and proclaim that the Queen is, "with one voice and consent of tongue and heart our only lawful and rightful liege lord." Last night workmen were busy erecting scaffolding for the ceremony.

TO SUMMON PRIVY COUNCIL

One of the first acts of the young Queen when she arrives home from her hurried flight will be to summon a second meeting of the Privy Council. This may take place this evening or to-morrow. She will address the Council and will make the accession declaration, which includes these words:

"I do solemnly and sincerely, in the presence of God, profess, testify and declare that I am a faithful Protestant and that I will, according to the true intent of the enactments which secure the Protestant succession to the Throne of my realm, uphold and maintain the said enactments to the best of my powers according to law."

The Queen will also take the oath relating to the security of the established Church in Scotland.

Only after the Privy Council has proclaimed the new Sovereign and renewed its oath of allegiance can Parliament assemble to take a fresh oath. The urgency with which this

(Continued on P. 8, Col. 6)

CROWNING MAY BE 1953

The coronation of the Queen may not take place until the summer of 1953, if it follows the precedent of King George V.'s death in January, 1936. Then, there was a period of nine months' mourning, and King Edward VIII's coronation was fixed for May, 1937. Following the abdication the date for the ceremony remained unchanged, and King George VI and Queen Elizabeth were crowned on May 12, 1937.

Gayle Jackson was parked, waiting for us.

'Y'all wanna come back to my place?' she said. 'Get a coffee or something?' Time hung heavy for Gayle, poor kid, stuck out in a rental waiting for her darling Okey to come home.

Lois said, 'Sure. You won't mind if I bring along something, give it a little *lift*?' She had a liquor bag hanging from the back of Sandie's stroller.

Gayle's face lit up. I guess there always was that weakness in her.

Betty said, 'Honey, did you hear? About the king?'

'He's dead,' Lo chipped in. 'Ba-boom.'

'Course,' Betty said, 'it had to be a servant found him, not the queen. They'd have separate bedrooms. Kings and queens always do.'

'Jeez,' Gayle said. 'How come?'

'Why, because they have such palatial homes, of course!' We relied on Betty for that kind of inside information. 'They have separate closets, separate everything.'

Sounded fine to me.

'And poor Princess Elizabeth is thousands of miles away in Africa, having the news broke to her by her courtiers. She's just going to have to pack her bags and fly right back here and get coronated.'

She leaned down to rub Sandie's frozen little cheeks. 'Hi, sweetie pie. Have I been ignoring you today? My, you're so cold. Lois, is this child warm enough?'

Sandie gave Betty a big smile. 'Told,' she said. 'Digger's ass.'

So we all headed down to Gayle's place, and Audrey came in from next door, for coffee and a little something from Lois's bottle, just to warm us through and wish the old king God speed. Even Betty came along and that didn't happen too often, on account of Ed keeping her on a short tether. Betty was allowed to go any place she liked, as long as it was the PX, the chapel or the school gate.

'I'm just fine,' she always said. 'If Ed Gillis is happy, Betty Gillis is happy. Anyways, I don't have time for gallivanting. My babies keep me busy. Caring for my home and my babies.' Her babies were Deana and Sherry, but she included Ed too, for some reason we could never fathom, so that made three whining brats, leaving their skivvies for her to pick up and generally giving her the runaround.

Gayle and Audrey were off-base, on account of they didn't have kids. The rest of us were in quarters. They weren't much more than cabins, with flat asphalt roofs, but at least we had each other. At least inside that perimeter fence we were one Nation, under God, indivisible, with Liberty and Justice for all.

Audrey didn't seem to mind being outside. She was of a pioneering disposition. They could have put her in a mule wagon and she'd have made the best of things.

'When in Rome,' she always said.

Well, when in *Rome*, maybe, but not when you've been posted to the asshole of the universe.

Lois said, 'Aud, you're wasted here. Can't they send you some place you'd have to live in a pup tent? I may just have a word to the CO's wife. See if they got any mutinies need putting down. Any prairie fires need extinguishing.'

The rentals were just outside Drampton, in a place called Smeeth. It wasn't a town. Just a couple of places growing sugar beet and a pumping station, supposed to keep the river moving along. It was called The Drain and it ran higher'n the roadway, which didn't seem natural to me. I hoped and prayed that pumping station never broke down. Been me quartered there, I'd never have dared turn my back on it. I wouldn't have slept nights for fear of waking up drowned.

Where they were, looked like one house but it was two, back to back, holding each other up but only just. Every house out there had that look about it, sagging in the middle, crouched down, like the sky was too much for it. They had a whole lot of sky in Norfolk, England.

Audrey and Lance were in one side of this broke-back house, Gayle and Okey were in the other, and oh how Gayle longed for a baby. A baby, and quarters, with steam heating and a Frigidaire.

'Next year,' Okey said, 'next year.'

They seemed like a pair of skinny kids, playing house. Her with her ponytail and her bobbysocks. Him with his crewcut.

Gayle put on the coffee and Audrey fetched a kitchen stool from her place, Gayle and Okey not having much in the way of seating.

'Right, this king?' Lois said.

'*The* king.' Betty put her straight.

'Whatever. They'll have a fancy funeral for him, right? With a big parade and everything. And it'll be in London, huh? Because he's the king.'

'Well, I guess.'

'And where exactly is London?'

Audrey said it was in the south-east. Fact was, though, none of us had seen the sun since the day we landed, so that didn't help much. Get to the base gate, we still wouldn't know whether to turn left or right.

'Anyone else thinking what I'm thinking?' Lois was looking excited, jiggling Sandie up and down on her knee. 'We go, girls. We go. Find London, see the parade, then have some fun. See a new movie, or a show. Find ourselves some top-hole toffs, what-ho, treat a girl to dinner, dontcher know.'

Betty said much as she'd love to go and pay her respects, Ed'd never allow it. For starters, who'd look after Sherry and Deana? 'And Crystal,' she said to me, 'who'd mind her?' She was looking to me to stop her building up any silly hopes. When it came to playing the mommy card, showing how you just had to rein yourself in once you had kids, Betty always turned to me for back-up because you sure as hell couldn't rely on Lois.

Gayle said, 'I will.' Her love of children extended even as far as Deana Gillis. Deana was in third grade. Sherry, Betty's youngest, was in first grade, same as my Crystal. Well, they should have been, except nobody ever heard of grade school in England. In elementary school there they just had names like Miss Boyle's Class, Mrs Warley's Class, Miss Jex's Class. Crystal's reading and writing seemed to be coming along okay. Still, every night I prayed we weren't ruining our child's education. Wrecking her future just so's her daddy could save their English asses from the Red Menace.

'And what about little Sandie?' Betty now felt she had a watertight case. I could tell because she wasn't furrowing her brow quite so deep. 'You can't drag a tiny tot thousands of miles,' she said. 'Not even knowing where you're going to. Do you realise, they don't even have enough food out there? I'm sorry, Lois, but it'd be just too crazy for words.'

Audrey said, 'Well, I guess that's the kinda attitude opened up the West.'

She never had a lot of patience with Betty. Besides, even I knew nothing's thousands of miles away in England. You keep going, it won't be long before you run outta country.

Then Gayle piped up. She said, 'I'll look after all of them. I don't mind not going. I never even heard of this king.'

Betty said, 'No. It's a wild and irresponsible idea.'

'Hey . . .' Lois was pepping up her coffee from the bottle. Those little red patches were breaking out over her cheekbones. 'Hey,' she said, 'I could care less. You're the royalty freak. I can go to London any damn time I please.' And everything went quiet, 'cept for Sandie, crying with the hot-aches, thawed her little fingers out too fast against the wood-stove.

Gayle said, 'Okey's Mom mailed me the new McCall's pattern book. Anyone want a look at it? There's a real easy pattern for a bolero.' And she ran upstairs to get it. I whispered to Audrey, 'Blessed are the peacemakers.'

'Mm-mm,' she said, 'and the dressmakers.'

I took Sandie on my lap, tried to rub her hands better, and Betty squared away the bottle of Jim Beam behind a cushion; hoping Lois might forget it, I daresay.

2

We were just finishing up dinner, Crystal wriggling in her chair, wanting to get down and play, Vern waving his fork around, last piece of fried potato getting cold while he told me about some new Pratt & Whitney turbojet that could take you to over 1,000mph, when the phone rang. It was Betty.

'Now, listen,' she said. 'Here's the latest. They're taking the king to London on Monday, along the railroad, travelling real slow, so folks can pay their respects. And here's the best bit: it'll be going *right by here*, no more'n a few miles away, and Ed says I can go, just as long as I'm home in time for the girls. So, could you drive down, tell Gayle and Audrey, and I'll call up Lois? I thought I'd throw a coffee tomorrow, so we can plan what we're gonna wear?'

I said, 'Betty, that's easy. Unless there's a sudden change in the climate I'll be wearin Vern's duck field-jacket and his five-buckle snow boots. Heck, I might just see if we still got an Alaska-issue comforter. Get myself sewed up inside it.'

'Peggy Dewey!' she said. 'Shame on you! The queen's gonna be looking right out of that train, and Princess Margaret. We have to do this thing right. I think just a touch of mourning. A little black hat, maybe, or a pair of gloves. Jeepers, we're gonna be seen by royalty.'

Vern thought I was crazy. He was all wrapped round me, after lights out, trying to keep me warm and get what he figured he was owed seeing he was gonna be three nights away, standing the duty.

'What you wanna do that for?' he said. 'Standin' out there, ketchin yer death. Be a bunch a breeds there, too. You seen some of them locals? Bunch a freaks. Now, you gonna get outta that passion-killer so we can mess around a little?'

Messing around was Vern's main interest in life, after his baby, with her static thrust of 3,750lb. And Crystal, of course. He loved throwing her up in the air till she screamed. Arm-wrestling with her, pretending to let her win.

'Did you know kings and queens bunk down in separate quarters?' I got to thinking about that again, after we'd messed around.

'Jeez, Peg,' he said, 'I was just dozing off.' He made himself cosy again, hogging all the covers. 'Who cares?' he said. 'Bunch a throwbacks, sitting round in robes.'

First time I saw Vern he was dancing with a girl, couldn't have been more than four feet ten. She was looking him in the belly-button and he was giving me the eye over her head. He did look cute in his Blues. Still, I should have known better. My sister Connie married the army and that was a five-minute wonder.

Soon as Vern knew I had fallen with Crystal he done the decent thing and my folks were happy to see the back of me, twenty-two and still no sign of any Hollywood screen-test. We were married in August, in the chapel on the base, his folks come down from Costigan, first and last time they ever left Maine, and we had an arch of sabres and shrimp hors-d'oeuvre and the whole nine yards. November he got orders to Ladd Field, Alaska.

Crystal come along in a big hurry, waters busted in the mall at Topperwein and my mom grinding her teeth every time I got a pain, telling me how this was only the start of my troubles. Nine pounds eleven ounces, she weighed, and she was the living image of her daddy, only he didn't get to see her till she was nearly four months old.

We landed at Elmendorf and while I was waiting for the transport up to Ladd, looking for a place to warm the baby's bottle, a girl come up to me, little newborn scrap in her arms and another one at foot, and she says to me, 'Why, Peggy Shea! It *is* you. I'm not usually wrong about a face, but you're carrying a few extra pounds these days.'

Last time I remembered seeing Betty Glick was when Future Home-makers catered a Mother-Daughter Spaghetti Supper for the Class of '42, and she was in charge, in her sweetheart apron, giving her orders, little piggy eyes and a real homely face.

She already knew Ladd. They'd been on the base nearly a year and she'd just been back to Texas for the birth of little Sherry. So we were a marriage made in heaven, me not knowing what in the world I was going to and Betty never happier than when she was showing somebody the ropes.

Four years of marriage and motherhood had left its stamp on her. She'd lost her puppy fat and got herself a permanent too. She seemed real grown up, compared to the way I felt, but then, I think Betty was born grown up. And she was so proud of her Ed. I never thought he was all that. Everything about him was kinda hard and square, even his head. Lois reckoned he was made outta sheet metal.

'I swear,' she used to say, 'Ed Gillis was not born of woman. I think they just punched in a few rivets and rolled him off the line at Boeing.'

Me and Vern were okay, when he was around – which wasn't much. They were putting in long hours, training on the Superfortress, and then when he did get a 96 he liked to go off fishing. Now I think back on it, we didn't hardly know each other.

'Love ya,' he used to say, when he was drifting off to sleep. 'Whoever y'are.'

So I started hanging out with Betty Gillis, née Glick, picking things outta the Sears catalogue and clipping recipes for tuna bake and generally raising hell. Summer nights up there, when it never gets dark, if Vern and Ed were standing the duty, I'd go round to her quarters, tuck Crystal in with Deana and Sherry, and we'd sit out front, drink iced tea and wonder what became of all those other big shots from Topperwein High.

Audrey I met later on, when we rotated through Kirtland. She rang my doorbell, told me there was a coffee klatsch at the Officers' Wives' Club and signed me up for the Blood Drive. Wouldn't take no for an answer on either score.

You could go to some of those wives' clubs not knowing another soul and come away in the same condition, none of the in-crowd being inclined to get off their backsides and welcome a newcomer. But I'll say this for Audrey: she had an open and friendly way about her. She'd stride across any room in her white bucks and make herself known to lonesome strangers.

She was married to Lance Rudman and they made a handsome pair. They were the kind of people knew where they'd come from and where they were going. Lois called them the Class Presidents.

Lo came on the scene while we were stationed at Kirtland too. She was married to Herb Moon. He was kinda dopey-looking, seemed slow on the uptake, except when he climbed into the cockpit of a B-50. Up there, so I heard, he was one cool customer.

'Life's a bitch,' she said, when she found out we'd done a tour in Alaska. 'Herb woulda loved that. All that rugged scenery and weather and stuff. 'Stead of all those cans of Dinty Moore I been feeding him, he coulda bagged himself a whole caribou. But no. He just had to go an' draw Hickam Field, Hawaii. Heaven on earth, girls. You ain't had a rope of Hilo violets hung round your neck, you ain't lived. Papaya juice. Pineapples. Mangoes. I tell you something. Herb may not be no dreamboat, but that man took me to paradise, no mistake.'

'Well, she'll have to trim her cloth a bit different now.' That's what Betty said when Lois fell pregnant with Sandie. But she was wrong. Took more'n a little baby to slow down Lois Moon. They took her straight from the Aztec King Bowling Alley to the General Landers J. Hooverman Mother & Baby Unit and not a minute to spare. I heard language that night I couldn't even begin to spell.

Course, didn't matter what Lois said or did, Herb thought the sun rose and set by her, and seems like nothing since has made him change his mind. They were a pair a love-birds, in a manner a speaking, even though they didn't always fly in formation.

Gayle and Okey were the real pigeon pair, known each other since the day they were born, near enough.

First time I saw Gayle she was hanging around in the laundry room at Drampton, didn't know how to work the driers and too scared to ask. I thought she was somebody's brat, till we got talking. I took her under my wing a little, after that, specially when Okey was away on assignment. There are lonely times when you're married to the military. You gotta hope you can click with a few girls on your post, hang out with them. You gotta get through the days as best you can, waiting around for friend husband to come home from the pad.

Audrey used to pass her some of her story books, but Gayle was no reader, nor much of a homemaker neither, though Betty did try giving her a few lessons. I reckon Gayle lived on potato chips and Dr Pepper, and when Okey was home, they just lived on love. Planned on having a houseful of kids and living happy ever after. On an LT's pay, best of luck was what I thought, but I never said it.

3

Gayle didn't come with us that day. She said she'd sooner stay behind in Lois's nice warm quarters and mind Sandie than wave off some old king, and that suited Lois just fine. 'I'd go and watch for a freight train to go by,' she said. 'Anything to get off this God-forsaken base.'

I wasn't so sure, myself. It was a raw morning, misty too, and there was some creature out in that fen making a unearthly noise. Vern reckoned the whole place belonged under the ocean. He used to say, 'They took this place from the water, and one of these days that water's gonna come and take it right back.'

He left me to answer the tricky questions from Crystal, such as would it come higher'n our house and how could fishes breathe?

Me and Betty took our girls to school, and I don't know who was more excited, Deana and Sherry 'cause they got a extra Milky Bar in their lunch-pail, guilt candy from mommy, or Betty because she was getting out from under.

Then we picked up Lois and Audrey and there were sharp words, on account of Lois wearing a red windbreaker and Betty suggesting she could have showed more respect. I drove and Betty sat up front with me, and she never stopped yammering.

'The Duke of Windsor,' she said, 'he's come sailing in from New York. He's got some nerve, I must say, running off with that home-wrecker, leaving everybody in the lurch. Ask me, he as good as killed his poor brother, and the queen, of course, the old queen, she's not been seen. She's at . . . hold on, here, let me get this right . . .' She'd brought her newspaper clippings with her. 'Marlborough House, that's where she's at. Must be heartbroken . . .'

Audrey, being no slouch, had been following all of this, but she said, 'Whoa, Betty, just back up, would you? You just lost me. I thought the old queen was gonna be on this train we're heading to see?'

'Ah,' she said, 'I see where you're getting confused. Okay. At this time, they have *three* queens. There's Queen Mary. She's the one at Marlborough Castle. Then they have Queen Elizabeth, who was married to the king, just passed away. She's the one we'll be seeing.'

I said, 'What about Queen Mary? Didn't she get a king?'

'Of course she did. He was King . . . something, I'll remember it in a minute. *Then*, there's the new Queen Elizabeth . . .'

Lois said, 'Are we seeing her?'

'No, no. She's gonna be meeting the train when it gets to London. See, she'll have had to stay there, attend to affairs of state an' all. We're gonna see, okay, the old Queen Elizabeth and Princess Margaret. And they are . . . ?' She gave us time, see if we could come up with the right answers. We couldn't. '. . . the mother and the sister of the new queen!'

Betty should have taught grade school. She was a natural.

I said, 'Can you hear that? Like something . . . booming out there?'

Lois lowered her window. 'Yeah,' she said. 'It's the Thing. Herb warned me about it. It hides out in these swamps, and when it smells prime American steak, it starts hollering.'

Audrey said, 'Okay, so we've got the new queen and she's waiting it out in London . . .'

'Yeah, right,' Lois said. 'She's smart enough not to come trailing up here. She's sitting at home, trying on all her jewels, got the royal furnace turned up high as it'll go.'

'. . . so who's gonna be the new king?'

Lois said, 'Now, even I know the answer to that. His name's Prince Philip, and he's a doll.'

I said, 'Lo, close up your window. I don't like that noise.'

'Sure,' she said, 'You worried that the Thing's getting closer?'

'It's a bird.' Audrey leaned forward to tell me. 'I read about it. It's just a big lonely old bird.'

Betty was handing round pictures. 'Now, this is the Duke of Cornwall. He'll be the next king, after his daddy. And this is little Princess Anne. Aren't they cute? I just love these darling coats they wear. Gee, I hope Sherry and Deana are gonna be okay today. Deana looked a little sad when we dropped them off. And Lois . . .' She turned right round in her seat, so Lois'd understand that what she was about to say wasn't to be taken lightly. '. . . do you think little Sandie is in safe hands with Gayle? I mean, I'm not one to sling mud but she does suffer with the nerves and sometimes, well, I'll speak plainly here, she takes comfort in alcoholic drink.'

I took a look at Lois in my rear-view mirror.

'Betty,' she said, 'you're right. You don't sling mud. You just kinda creep up behind a person and smear it. Matter of fact, I think Sandie'll be just fine with her Auntie Gayle. Way I look at things, anybody married to an airman needs a little something to get them through the day. Huh? Bottle a booze, photo album of Princess Margaret, the sound of Frank Sinatra's sweet voice, it don't have to look like a crutch to be one.' And she dropped the pictures of the little Duke of Cornwall right back into Betty's lap.

'Why, Lois!' Audrey said. 'That's almost profound!'

She was sitting forward, peering through the windshield with me, and I was driving like a real old lady, what with the mist and the ice and the fact that over there another vehicle was liable to come at you on the wrong side of the road. One minute they weren't there, next minute they were, about ten or twelve of them, grey as the day itself, stamping their feet, hugging themselves in their poor thin coats, standing right there by the railroad crossing.

Audrey whistled through her teeth. 'Well, look at that,' she said, and they all turned together, like a herd of deer, sniffing for trouble. Like they'd never seen a DeSoto station-wagon in their lives before.

Betty said, 'Okay, girls. Now remember. We are ambassadors for the United States of America, and this is a grieving nation.'

4

Nobody spoke.

Betty said, 'Good morning, everyone! Y'all waiting to see the royal train go by?'

Still nobody spoke. I felt her pressing closer to me.

'Peggy,' she whispered, 'let's hand round some gum or something, show them we're friendly.'

Audrey roared. 'Jeez, Betty,' she said, 'anybody'd think we were in Sioux territory.'

There were people there wearing black armbands, and a woman carrying a Union flag, no stockings on, just zip-front boots, and her hair rolled up in a scarf, and her legs all wind-burned behind her knees. She kept looking our way.

I smiled and nodded and next time I looked she'd moved a bit nearer.

Audrey and Lois smiled and nodded, and she moved nearer still.

It was Lois made the breakthrough. 'Hi,' she said, 'I'm Lois Moon. You care for a stick of Juicy Fruit?'

Close up she was younger than she'd seemed. Thirty, maybe not even that. She just wasn't making the best of herself. Matter of fact, sometimes she still don't. Over the years, I have learned the average Englishwoman has scant interest in good grooming. She's more likely to buy herself a new garden tool than get her nails done. But I'm running ahead of myself. That morning, back in '52, she was plain shabby. And she couldn't take her eyes off Lois in her red jacket. She came and stood right next to her.

Betty found her voice again. She said, 'Do you happen to know the estimated time of arrival?'

She took a while to answer. Or maybe just took a while to understand the question. 'That won't be long now,' she said. 'That's only got to come from Wolverton.'

Betty said, 'The funeral train? But I understood it was coming from Sandring Ham?'

She looked at Betty for the longest time. 'That's right,' she said. 'They're bringing him from the house up to Wolverton, put him aboard the train and that's a fair old step, along that lane. That must be three mile. Jim?' She called across to a man in an armband. Looked like he didn't have a tooth in his head. 'Jim?' she said. 'That must be three mile from Sandringham to the siding?'

He didn't answer. Just blew his nose and turned his back on us. Didn't like her fraternising.

Lois whispered to me, 'How come we're getting the evil eye? I thought we were on the same side as these guys?'

Me too. In fact, my understanding was we were owed a little gratitude.

Betty said, 'Well, we're very sorry for your sad loss.' She said it loud, kinda addressing the assembled throng. 'Your royal family is the envy of the world. And the folks back home are just gonna *die* when they hear about us being here, so close to it all.'

Audrey said, 'Well, I don't know that *die* was the happiest choice of words.'

Lois said, 'You guys see them around much? The King and Queen? They drive around in their carriage, waving and be-knighting people and stuff?'

I heard somebody say, 'Bloody Yanks.'

Then things started to happen. First there was a humming in the rails, and then the ground started to rumble and people were pushing forward, craning and looking left. We could feel that something big was heading our way, bearing down on us, but we couldn't see it.

And then, out of the mist it came, real slow and heavy, a Standard Pacific engine and nine cars, dressed overall in black silk. Someone called out 'God save the King!' and every man there held his cap in his hand and bowed his head.

'And the Queen,' Lois's new friend shouted. 'Don't forget her!'

I didn't bow my head. I didn't intend no disrespect, but we had driven there to see a princess at the very least. I looked long and hard as it passed us, but what with the steam and the mist, I couldn't even pick out which car the casket was in. Audrey nudged me to look at Betty. She was standing to attention, eyes closed, with a kinda ecstatic look on her face. Then the train slid away, back into the mist, and the ground stopped rumbling and the rails stopped humming and Lois said, 'Well, I didn't see a darned thing.'

To her dying day Betty claimed she'd had the best view ever. The Queen, all veiled in black, and the princess, very pale and strained, in a little velour hat and a mink collared coat, who had actually given her a sad wave of thanks.

'You didn't *see* them?' she said, when Lois started bellyaching and any time after that when the subject was raised. 'Why heaven's sakes, girl, what were you doing?'

Our friend turned and gave us a grin. I guess, even with lend-lease food, all that malnutrition must have just ruined their teeth. 'May Gotobed's seen them,' she said. 'She's stood as close to them as I am to you. She's been a backstairs maid, donkey's years, since the old king was alive.'

Betty said, 'Oh boy! A backstairs maid! You hear that, Peggy? Go on! Tell us more!'

'Well,' she said, 'May was on her way up with hot water when they found him. She seen him Tuesday night. He was outside having a smoke. Wednesday, she was carrying water up for a lady of the bedchamber and word come, Dr Ansell been sent for. Nothing he could do, of course. King was long gone. And the Duke of Gloucester, he come over directly in his motor car. That's a cheery shade,' she said, stroking Lois's sleeve.

People were leaving. Just walking away into the mist.

Betty said, 'I just love hearing about all this. I am the biggest fan

[18]

of your royal family. I have so many pictures, especially of your Princess Margaret. She just looks such a sweet girl. Do you know any stories about her?'

The old guy called Jim was still there, hanging back, watching us. 'Time you were getting off home, Kath Pharaoh. Careless talk costs lives.'

'War ended, 1945, Jim,' she said. 'Haven't you heard?'

We offered her a ride, but she came over shy. Looked flustered and said there was no need, she didn't have far to go. Audrey called to the guy. 'How about you?' she said. 'We have room for a small one.'

'Save yer juice,' he said, and both of them disappeared, him in one direction and Kath Pharaoh in the other. And there we stood in the freezing mist, the four of us, feeling about as welcome as a pack of prairie dogs.

Betty gave me one of her pretty-please looks. 'Oh, Peggy, let's go catch up to her, can we? Get her number, at least? I'd love to talk with her some more.'

It was all one to me because I needed to drive on and find a safe turning place, highways in England not being proper highways at all.

Lois said, 'Heaven's sakes, Betty. She's gone. Let's find a bar. Get ourselves a little inner warmth?'

But we soon found her, stepping out at a real brisk pace. It was her flag we saw first, sticking out of the top of her shopping bag. Betty wound her window down. 'Hi again! We seem to be going your way. Are you sure we can't give you a ride home?'

She had a dewdrop hanging from the end of her nose. 'Go on, then,' she said, and she tried to open Lois's door, just tugging on it.

Betty leaped out. 'No, no, you ride in front,' she said, 'then you can tell Peggy which way to go. Lois, move over.'

She got in. I looked at her, waiting for her to tell me which way to go, but she just sat there, so I just kept driving.

'Well now, we should all introduce ourselves.' Betty was bubbling. She was so happy we'd adopted somebody who knew a servant who'd breathed the same air as a real king. 'I'm Betty. This here is Lois, and Audrey. We're from the United States. Our husbands are stationed at the air base.'

Kath nodded. She was tongue-tied.

I said, 'And I'm Peggy. Guess I'm just the driver around here.'

She smiled. 'Do you take Blackdyke Drove,' she said, 'you'd best go steady. That's all frez.'

I didn't know what in tarnation she was talking about, but I soon found out.

'My name's Kath,' she said, 'Kath Pharaoh. Ah. Now you've gone and driv past the turn. That's easy done, when you're moving along so fast.'

Blackdyke Drove was just a track, when we found it again. The ground fell away from it, either side, and disappeared into the mist, and the mud had a frosting of ice that crackled under the wheels. I never got out of second gear, but Kath held on to the dash anyway and once or twice her hand came across towards the steering column, like she wanted to guide me.

'What make of car would this be, then?' she asked me. She'd been peering down into the foot-well. 'So, that's the go-faster pedal and that's the go-slower pedal,' she said. 'I reckon as I could soon git the hang of that. But how does the juice make the wheels go round? That's a mystery to me. And what's this?' She hit the horn. 'Oh, beg your pardon,' she said, laughing, and gave me another good look at her poor English teeth. 'That's enough to waken the dead,' she said. 'That's enough to waken him indoors. STOP!'

I felt the tail slide a little and I heard Audrey's head crack against her window.

'See? You nearly went past,' she said, real accusing. And there it was. Another sway-back house, hunkered down low, just like Gayle and Audrey's billet out at Smeeth.

I said, 'This your place, Kath?'

'Yes,' she said. 'Your friend all right, in the back?'

Audrey said it was no more than a tap and her head was just fine, but Lois thought a little drink would be a good idea. Lois often did.

'You could have delayed shock, Aud,' she said. 'Is there a bar, some place near? One of those thatched taverns?'

'There's the Flying Dutchman,' she said. 'You don't want to go in there, though. That's for men. I could make you a nice cuppa tea.'

Betty loved that idea. 'Then we can keep Audrey under observation,' she said. 'Check she doesn't have a concussion. And I would just *adore* to visit with a real English family.'

Lois said a Norfolk fen was the last place on earth she'd want to be with any kinda medical condition. She said she'd want to be right back where Uncle Sam'd take good care of her, but Betty was out of the car already, and Audrey wasn't far behind.

'Come on!' she said. 'It'll be interesting. See how other people live. And, by the way, I do *not* have a concussion.'

Kath seemed kinda proud to be taking us home, like it was Sandringham Palace itself. Course, in those days she didn't know what lovely homes American people had, and ignorance is bliss.

I've often thought, if that king hadn't died when he did, I don't suppose we'd ever have met Kath or gone driving up that frozen track. We'd just have stayed home and baked cookies, and then a whole lot of things would have turned out different.

5

'John Pharaoh,' she shouted, 'we've got company. Come out here and see this fancy motor.'

We filed in, and Aud had to duck her head. Those ceilings were so low she nearly ended up with a concussion after all. It was dark inside. We pushed through a narrow passageway, old coats hanging on pegs.

'Come on in,' she said. 'You'll have to take us as you find us.'

I could see a wood-range, and a bed, with somebody on it, but my eyes were still getting accustomed to the gloom.

'I seen the train,' she said. 'We give him a good send-off. Jim Jex was down there, said did you want a pup off of his fowling dog, I said no thank you, and these ladies kindly brought me home. They're from Drampton, with the Yankee Air Force, and you should see the big fancy car they got, windows that go up and down and all sorts. Dear God, that smells like a old hoiley in here. John? You awake?'

First impression was, they only had one room. Later on, when I knew them better, I saw the place where he kept his eel traps. Another little room that could have been fixed up, for a bedroom or something, instead of them carrying on the way they did, sleeping in the kitchen.

That's where he was, the first time we saw him, just getting up off the bed. Kath gave him the Juicy Fruit gum. She'd had it in her hand all the time, since Lois gave it to her.

[22]

'Straighten that counterpane,' she said, 'we've got company.'

John Pharaoh was a good-looking devil. He wasn't tall like Lois's Herb or brawny, like Ed Gillis. He was soft-looking for a man, but there was something about him. Black curly hair. And a real winning smile. I guess it was the dimples. One of his eyes wasn't quite right, though, and sometimes it gave him a crafty look, but it had a kinda awful fascination about it, drew you to keep looking at it. Then you felt sorry for staring at a person's affliction.

He slid off the bed and he waved his fingers, like we were invited to sit down, only I couldn't see where, there being just the one easy chair and that was occupied by a old yellow dog, size of a hog.

Kath was running around, still in her coat and her boots. She brought cups from a rack by the sink and extras from a cupboard, with saucers that didn't match.

'You'll like these,' she said to Betty. 'Coronation saucers. King George the Fifth. A course, the cups have all gone west. Pull up a seat.'

There were three wooden chairs around the table, and my God, that room was cold. Either you stood close enough to the range to get scorched, or you froze. Betty gave me a brave little smile, this whole excursion being her idea after all. She was trying to show her appreciation, being a great believer in the importance of politeness, but there was one thing she did care more about than manners, and that was standards of hygiene, and I doubt those cups had ever seen hot water.

Kath made tea in big brown pot and pulled a woolly cover over it, so just the spout and the handle were free. There was no sugar, and the only milk she offered was Carnation, straight from the can.

I declined. Never did take to tea.

Kath said, 'I can do you a Bovril?' but I didn't care for the sound of that neither. It made me realise Audrey was right. Travel gives you the opportunity to understand foreign ways of life. It can make a wiser person of you. And when I seen how those poor English lived, it made me want get down on my knees and give thanks for being born in God's own country.

Kath brought out photos, from a drawer. They were faded and

creased, but Betty loved them. Picture-postcards of some old king and queen, done up in their fancy orbs and sceptres.

Betty said, 'Now, correct me if I'm wrong, Kath, but isn't this Queen Mary?'

'That's right,' Kath said. 'She was Mary of Teck. And she was fixed up to marry one of the princes, but he dropped dead, so they passed her along to his next brother.'

I said, 'That's terrible. I wouldn't have stood for that.'

Kath said, 'Me neither. That's like handing on a dead man's trousers, still got a bit of wear left in them.'

'Well,' Betty said, 'I guess you can't let a princess go to waste.'

Lois was scratching the old dog behind its ears and slurping up that disgusting brew. 'What I don't understand,' she said, 'is why that king had to go outside for a smoke. No wonder he caught his death. What kind of milquetoast was he, didn't just light up any place he chose? All he had to do was pass a edict or something.'

John Pharaoh seemed disposed to find everything Lois said highly amusing. There were some snapshots of poor folk, too. They all seemed to be kin to Kath's friend May Gotobed, or some kinda relations to the Pharaohs themselves, only it was too complicated for me to follow. There was one of them standing with genuine princes, posing in front of a mountain of ducks they just helped shoot, but you had to be in the know to tell which ones were which. When they're not wearing their crowns those princes just look like any ordinary Joe.

Audrey had asked for the bathroom and Kath had taken her, to show her the way, but Aud came back alone, beckoning me from the doorway to come and see something.

Kath was in the car, making believe she was driving. She was sitting at the wheel, window down, arm leaning out, making revving noises like she was barrelling down Route 66, next stop the Rio Grande. She laughed when she saw us watching her.

'I shall soon have the hang of this,' she said. 'You could go anywhere you pleased in a motor like this. You could go to Ely.'

'You should see where I just went,' Audrey whispered to me on our way back into the house. 'It's a seat over a bucket. And get this. There's two of them, side by side. His 'n' hers.'

Kath kept bringing things out to show us. Her best tablecloth, and a badge she got for fen-skating in 1936, and a magazine with pictures of Ava Gardner, and then more tea, though God knows none of us wanted any. She seemed so proud to have us as her guests.

'You must be getting peckish,' she said, when she'd run out of treasures to show us. 'I could find you a bit of something. Slice of bread and butter? We've got a tin of pineapple, sent from Canada, only he's gone and lost the opener. John? Do you look again for that tin-opener these ladies can have a bite to eat.'

But John Pharaoh was more interested in Lois's legs.

Lo was always ready to eat, but I caught her eye, managed to stop her before she took their last crust. I don't believe she ever heard of war rations.

'No, Kath,' Betty said. 'We really have to be making tracks. I'd just have loved to talk with you some more, but we have our girls to pick up from school. But you know, you should come and visit with us some time. I have so many picture albums I'd love to show you. Princess Margaret is my favourite, and I'm just longing for her to find a beau.'

6

Of course, it was my fault. Headlights left on, engine won't turn over, who else you gonna blame but the driver?

'Dead as King George,' Lois said and John Pharaoh laughed. He stood looking under the hood, but I don't think he'd have known a spark plug from a poke in the eye.

Audrey said warming it up might help, so Kath brought the teapot out and stood it on the battery, but I still couldn't get a murmur out of it.

Betty said, 'We have to get the battery inside, connect it up or something. You know what I mean. I've seen Ed do it.'

Ed was always tinkering with their car. First time I noticed she had sump oil the same place as her bruises was the day I realised how things stood between Betty and Ed.

Anyway, all that talk about connecting up batteries, there was a basic fact of life on Blackdyke Drove Betty was overlooking.

Even after Audrey told her, she didn't really get it. 'Heck,' she said, '*everyone* has electricity. Well, we'll just have to call the base. They'll send out a ground-pounder, tow us in.'

Audrey shook her head. 'There's no telephone, Betty,' she said. 'We'll just have to set fire to Lo's windbreaker. Send smoke signals.'

She said, 'Whaddaya mean? This is plum crazy. There *has* to be a telephone. Supposing they were to get a peritonitis or something?'

Her voice was real tight. She wanted to smack somebody, preferably me, I could tell, but Betty never smacked anybody in her life, more's the pity.

'Well, Peggy Dewey,' she said, 'you got us into this fix so I hope you're gonna get us right out of it. I have my girls to pick up at fifteen-twenty and I don't intend on letting them down.'

John Pharaoh said he'd go, fetch help. He had to walk back along the drove, cross the water by the sluice gates, take the highway into Brakey and find someone willing to drive out and rescue us. He set off, real willing and cheerful, and we all went back inside for a long, long wait.

Lois whispered, 'Aud, where'd you say the john was?'

Audrey said, 'It's round the back. There's no lock on the door, and no flush, so just follow your nose. And you probably won't want to make contact with the seat. There's wildlife out there, got heat-seeking equipment.'

Audrey was looking round at the room. There was a postcard thumbtacked to the wall, some place called Cromer, and a broken clock, with no minute-hand.

'Jeez, Peg,' she said, 'did you ever see anything like this?'

'I did,' Lois said. 'Herb's folks' place. I married beneath my station. Now I'm gonna have to take a leak, wildlife or no. Where's Kath?'

She was outside again, standing by the station wagon, just looking at it, so downcast.

'Is it my fault?' she said. 'Did I brek it?'

7

Kath lit the oil lamps and put more fuel on the range.

'There,' she said, 'now we're snug.' But I reckon that yellow dog had the only warm seat in the house.

Audrey said, 'How long have you lived here, Kath?'

'Born here,' she said. 'Born in that bed.'

Lo bounced upright when she heard that. 'Wow!' she said. 'You ever think of moving away?'

'Oh yes,' she said. 'I've told John Pharaoh. We ever come up on the football pools, I should like to move up to Brakey. Be nearer the bus stop.'

Betty was having a little blub about Deana and Sherry, like she was never gonna see them again. I wished she'd stop. I didn't like letting Crystal down neither, and I'm sure Lois was worried about Sandie too, she just never showed it, making herself at home on John and Kath's bed.

'Don't you fret about your young 'uns,' Kath said. 'They'll be right as ninepence. They'll be larrikin about somewhere.'

Which, of course, was the last thing Betty wanted to hear. Whatever larrikin was, it sounded dangerous.

'What time is it?' she kept asking.

'Big hand's still on the five,' Audrey kept answering.

'Kath?' Lo said. 'You go outside to that bathroom in the middle of the night?'

'No,' Kath said. 'I hold on till morning.'

We heard the toot of a horn. John Pharaoh had come back, riding in a General Post Office van, looking real proud of himself. A guy called Dennis Jex was driving, and two others, both Jexes too, had come along to give their advice or eyeball four American chicks, or maybe just to get a ride. One way or another, they seemed happy to be there. They all looked under the hood, but Dennis was the one really knew what he was doing. He jump-started us, while Audrey held the flashlight, and then he offered to escort us back to where the road was metalled, save us running off the track and disappearing into the swamp.

He said he was glad to help. He said there was no doubt in his mind, if it wasn't for America he'd be living under the jackboot.

'When push come to shove, you Yanks done the right thing,' he said. 'Even if you did take your time about it.'

Betty was in the car already, anxious for us to be on our way.

'Now,' he said, 'I'll pull round. I'll take it nice and steady and you can follow my tail lights. And when I put my winker to go left, do you go right you'll be set fair for the base. That's straight on, about seven mile. You can't go wrong.'

John Pharaoh was pacing up and down, eyes shining, like he'd had a real exciting time. Kath looked kinda sad to see us go.

I said, 'Would you like to come out for a drive some time?'

'Oh, I would,' she said, 'I'd like that very much.'

So I promised we'd do that, just as soon as the ice thawed. Then Dennis Jex moved off, and I nosed along right behind him, and Kath and John faded away into the mist.

Audrey said, 'That was the right thing to do, Peggy. We should always try to build cordial relations with the locals.' Audrey had the kinda enthusiasm for good works that could take a girl far at the OWC. If Lance was aiming to be a brass hat, he couldn't have picked a better wife.

I said, 'I didn't do it to be right, Aud. I did it because I wanted to.'

'Never mind,' she said. 'Doing the right thing accidentally is better than doing the wrong thing. Now, I have an idea.'

Betty said, 'Audrey, would you please allow Peggy to concentrate on driving? Charity begins at home, remember?'

Audrey ignored her. 'My idea is,' she said, 'we could take them things. You know, we have so much and they just have *nothing*. They have a can of fruit there and they don't even have an opener. And did anybody notice an icebox?'

I said, 'I believe they're living in it, Aud.'

She said, 'Well, I think a food parcel is called for. Little things that I'm sure would be appreciated. And not just food. I mean, did you see the state of her pot holder? Whaddya say, girls?'

But Lois was in a world of her own, humming a little tune. And Betty wasn't in the mood for talking.

Ed was on the doorstep when we pulled up. Didn't matter Sherry and Deana had been just fine, getting milkshakes with Gayle and playing hospitals and helping Crystal and Sandie to eat all of Lois's cookies. Ed Gillis had just got a mean old mood on him, I could tell. That little dint, side of his jaw, was popping in and out.

'Time you call this?' he said, and Betty hurried right on in, clutching her pictures of the Duke of Cornwall. She didn't even say 'Goodbye'.

8

'Okay, girls. Here's what I got so far.' Audrey was getting ready to air-drop supplies for Kath and John.

'Cheez Whizz, Sugar Pops, Campbell's Soup, two cans of franks, can opener, Oreos, nylons, Chesterfield's . . .'

I said, 'I don't think they use smokes. All that time we were pacing the floor there, I never seen any sign of cigarettes.'

'Well maybe they'd like the chance to start,' she said. 'Jeez, Peg, I'm just trying to help. Then I got cornflakes and Pepsodent, and I thought we could throw in a fifth of Dewar's.'

Gayle said, 'How about cupcakes? Can they get Hostess cupcakes?'

She was real keen for us to take her out there, introduce her to Kath and John, 'cause all she'd heard from us since we got back was about them sleeping in their kitchen and having a open-air privy. Course, Gayle was from Carolina, almost into Tennessee, so she could just have been feeling homesick.

Betty was grounded. The way she told it, it was her own wish to spend more time making their quarters into a real home. She showed me some damnfool thing she'd done with a folding table, General Issue, and a mile of pink cretonne, sent her by her cousin.

'See,' she said, 'I just made it up like a skirt, cover those ugly old legs, then I thumbtacked it down, with this real pretty wrapping paper to cover the top. Now if I can get my hands on a nice piece of bevelled glass, I'll have the darlingest dressing table on the base.'

I said, 'You okay, Betty? Ed's not giving you a hard time?'

'I'm just fine,' she said. 'Now, you give my best regards to Kath and John, and I'd like you to take them a little something from me.' She handed me that bar of Ivory soap like it was a piece of the True Cross.

We drove out one morning, after I dropped Crystal. Betty said she'd have loved to mind Sandie, only Deana and Sherry had caught some terrible skin condition, highly contagious, got it in the school yard, rubbing up close to urchins probably never seen a bath tub in their lives, so they were home, painted with violet-coloured lotion, grizzling and tormenting each other. So Sandie came with us, sitting in the back with her mom and Gayle, begging for more when Lois rolled down the window, pretending she could hear the Thing out there, coming to get us.

9

John Pharaoh was home alone. 'Not here,' he said, pacing up and down. 'She's working at the singling, but do you drive over Brakey way, you'll see her. She's at the Mayday Shed. Hello, tuppence. You want to see what I got?'

Sandie ran off with him and Lois followed her. Gayle helped Audrey carry the food parcels inside, and I just leaned against the trunk of the car and watched some little bird that was hovering and singing about a mile over my head.

'Skylark,' Audrey said, when she came outta the house.

Gayle said, 'Ain't this place something! I mean, my folks don't have much, but they got a TV at least. They got a car. These guys gotta be real poor.'

Aud said, 'And they sleep in their kitchen, I hope you noticed.'

Gayle said 'Oh, folk do that in Boomer. When we were all home there was eleven of us. Girls head to tail in the kitchen bed 'cause girls gotta be up first. Where'd he say she was today?'

She was at Mayday. It was one of the beet farms. That's what she did. Little jobs here and there, whatever was going, according to the season.

I wouldn't have minded some kind of work myself, 'stead of sitting indoors reading my stars in the same old magazines over and over, but when you marry the military you become a Dependent Wife, and

DWs weren't allowed to work. Your job was to stand by your bunk, wait for him to come home from Beer Call and tell you another thousand different ways he'd put his hide on the line up in the big blue yonder. How things have changed.

I found out later, from Kath, that singling beets wasn't no exciting career. You just stood in a shed with a bunch of women, all Jexes or Gotobeds, splitting up the clusters of sugar-beet seeds, chopping them up and getting paid nickels and dimes.

'That's not hard,' she said, 'that's just boring. Then August, I go tater riddling. That's hard and boring.'

I asked her one time, 'How come you're out working and John stays home?'

'He works when he can,' she said. 'But he's not a strong man. He's got bad nerves. He's under Dr Brameld, but he can't do nothing for them though by the seem of it. He catches eels, though, and sells them. When the eels are running, he does well at them. And that's an early start, up at four, emptying the traps. Then he has to get them down to Brandon, in time for the pick-up. He makes traps. Cuts the willow. Strips it. They come from all over to buy his traps. A man come all the way from Welney looking for John to make him a willow grig.'

It seemed like John Pharaoh was a regular little eager beaver. I kinda wished I'd never asked.

Anyways, that was where he'd disappeared to with Lois and Sandie that morning, showing them around his eel-trap empire, making little Sandie squeal with his tray of lugworms. We found them while we were showing Gayle the privy, giving her the full guided tour, like it was the Alamo. Sandie peeping out from behind Lois, daring herself to go and take a close-up look at the worms, and John holding up a basket, shape of a pickle, but six foot high.

'You ever sin one big as this?' he said, giving Lois a knowing smile, and she roared.

'See,' she said, when we were driving home, via Brakey, looking for something that might be a beet shed, 'see, they catch different kinds, depending on the time of year. And sometimes they use nets and traps, and sometimes they use ... like a spear, and just catch them one at a time, and sometimes, on a good night, they might catch twenty pounds of them, just in one of those baskets, and the big traps are called grigs but the little ones are called hoileys, and . . . what else . . . ?'

'Tune in same time next week,' Audrey said, 'for the Wonderful World of Eel Fishing presented by Lois Moon.'

'I understand this right?' Vern said. 'You drove out there, guzzling gas, took half the commissary and a bottle of good liquor too, and she wasn't even home?'

I said, 'Yeah. Must have put fifteen mile on the clock. Jeez, you're starting to sound like Ed Gillis. He's got radar-tracking on Betty.'

'Know what's good for you, you'll stay outta Ed and Betty's business,' he said. 'Know what's good for you, you'll quit running round, fraternising with a bunch of breeds. Hell, Peg, why can't you stay home and make a pie once in a while?'

'Hell is a bad word,' Crystal said. 'Also, jeez. Miss Boyle says.'

'Vern,' I told him, 'I can make pie *and* go visiting.'

I'll say this about Vern. Sometimes pie was all it took.

'Honey,' he said to Crystal, 'you tell Miss Boyle welcome to the free world, thanks to folks like your daddy, and you can say any goddamn words you please.'

'You don't tell Miss Boyle no such thing,' I said to her when I was tucking her in, 'and you know what? Mommy's gonna get you a princess dressing table, all pink and pretty.'

I was thinking I'd get Miss Homemaker of America to give me a hand. Betty always seemed to have a hundred ideas how to turn a prefab cabin into what she called 'a gracious and lovely home'. I figured, if I kept Vern sweet, smartened up the quarters, made the occasional pie, I'd be able get off base once in a while without getting the third degree. Get away from the whine of the jets and the rattling of the windows. Now I'd got the hang of driving on the wrong side of the road, and handling that funny money of theirs, I was starting to enjoy going out there.

Crystal said, 'Mommy? Do I have to have a princess dressing table? Can I get roller skates instead?'

[35]

10

I fell and busted my collar bone, coming outta the PX where the kids had been skidding around, polishing the ice. They strapped me up, till the bone knit, which good as put me in the slammer for a while. Couldn't drive, couldn't hardly pull up my own shorts. Couldn't stop Betty Gillis running in and out performing acts of neighbourly kindness. Vern ate all the soup she brung in. That man was a walking Disposall. I just lived on codeine and Pepsi and prayed next time he got orders it'd be for Ramey, Puerto Rico.

'You rest up now,' Betty said. 'I'll take care of things. You're in the best place. You seen what kinda weather we got today?'

They called it a Fen Blow. Looked like a sandstorm to me. A sandstorm on the far side of the moon.

'Just when you thought it couldn't get worse,' Lois said. 'Here, open nice and wide and I'll steady the gun in your mouth. Hell, no. Let me go first. You can make your own arrangements. I got Herb at home and you'll never guess what he's doing.'

Herb loved chopping wood.

Thirty-six hours they didn't fly a single sortie, because of the Blow, and Vern was like a bear with a boil on his backside, driving out to the facility every five minutes, looking for a patch of clear sky.

I said, 'Why can't you quit prowling around and do something?

Play checkers with Crystal or write your mom. Do you know Lance Rudman writes his folks every week?'

'Yeah?' he said. 'Well that figures. Pushing a pencil's about what Rudman's cut out for.'

Vern didn't have much time for Lance. Okey Jackson was the one Vern rated, even though he looked so wet behind the ears, and there were jocks in the squadron had seen real action in Korea. Whatever it was they got up to up there, and I really didn't care to know, Okey was the one kept showing them he had the moxie.

Soon as I got the strapping off, I shampooed my hair and pin-curled it. I was just going to the closet to get the dryer hood when I heard the siren. Then the crash trucks started up.

First time I ever heard that, back at Kirtland, I ran right outside, looking down the flight-line for smoke and then when I seen it I wished I hadn't, because I didn't know what the hell to do with myself. By the time we got to Drampton, England, I guess I'd learned there was no point. Wait long enough I knew I'd either be getting a visit from the chaplain, standing on my doorstep like the Grim Reaper hisself, giving me my wake-up call, or I'd be hearing from Betty Gillis on the jungle drums.

It took her thirteen minutes.

'Breathe again,' she said. 'It's 366 Squadron. You wanna come up here for coffee?'

So we all rendezvoused at Betty's. She was minding Sandie again, didn't seem to know where Lois was.

I said, 'One of these days that kid's gonna start calling you Mommy.'

'Be fine by me,' she said, 'she's such a little cutie. Way I see it, Peggy, some folks just aren't cut out to be mothers, and if I can lend a helping hand, why, I'm doing Sandie a favour too. You heard the way Lois yells at her sometimes? Tell you the truth, I'd love another little one of my own, only Ed's acting stubborn about it.'

Betty had been putting out feelers, trying to find out the news from 366. See if there were casualties. Pretty soon her telephone started ringing. One of their Invaders had come in on a tight turn and an engine flamed out. The crew had had to eject, and they were all safe home bar one, a sergeant called Benedetto, left one of his legs behind in the wreckage.

We kinda knew his wife. You see girls around, get to recognise their faces. But the Benedettos were quartered on Soapsuds Row, down by the hangars, and besides, we were First Lieuts. We didn't socialise with the enlisted.

Gayle said, 'Is he gonna die?'

Betty said, 'Honey, they can do wonders these days. They'll give him a new leg and a disability pension and everything.'

Audrey said, 'That's right. Air force takes care of its own. Now let's do something to perk ourselves up. How about a Scarf Exchange? And I have a tangerine lipstick somebody might like.'

Gayle said, 'He still could die.'

Betty said, 'We'll have no more of that kinda talk, thank you, young lady. Now, I have a tray of brownies here needs arranging nice and pretty. Care to make yourself useful?'

Gayle dumped the brownies on the plate.

I whispered to her, 'You wanna come out driving, after? Get off the base for five minutes? Celebrate me getting back the use of my shift arm?'

She nodded. Little Sandie was looking at her, so solemn. Even she knew something had happened.

Betty's Best-Ever Brownies

••

2 sticks sweet butter
4 eggs
4 ounces powdered chocolate
2 cups sugar
½ cup sifted flour
1 teaspoon McCormick's vanilla extract

Heat the oven to 350°C. Grease and flour a large baking tray.

Melt butter over a low flame, stir in chocolate and set aside to cool.

Beat eggs and sugar until pale and creamy. Fold in the chocolate mixture and blend carefully. Gently add the flour, pour into pan and bake until just set (20–30 minutes).

Leave in pan until cool. Cut into squares for serving.

••

11

Instead of heading up to Brakey we went over by The Warren, the only little bit of woodland in the neighbourhood, spruce mainly, and came through it on a narrow track, trees pressing in both sides, but I liked it a lot better than having that big Norfolk sky watching every move I made. There was a nice earthy smell in there, too, like spring might be on the move.

Gayle was still quiet, so I just talked to myself.

I said, 'This is like the fairy forest in one of Crystal's bedtime stories. You see any handsome woodcutters? No, well, I guess Herb Moon's still winging his way home with the rest of the boys.'

'How come nobody ever talks about it?' she said. 'Peggy? About crashes and stuff? Like this morning, Benedetto nearly didn't make it, and we just go to coffee at Betty's and sit round, asking her why her brownies taste so good? Can you explain this to me, 'cause I just don't get it? I mean, when you hear there's a plane down, when you hear those trucks going off, don't none of you ever get the shakes, waiting for the holy Joe to come creeping up the path, tell you you're widow of the week? Hell, Peggy, don't none of you get scared?'

I pulled over.

I said, 'Well, course we do, hon, but we're not just any old wives. We're air force. We gotta stay calm and steady for our boys. You know that.'

She said, 'But why can't we talk about it?'

I said, 'Because the boys never do, and if we did, it'd be like jinxing them. Every day they just go out there and do what they gotta do, and you know what? They're the best. Benedetto blew it, is all. Whaddya expect from 366 Squadron?'

I could bullshit for the Lone Star State.

'Peg!' she said. 'I'm not so dumb I'd say anything to Okey. But that don't mean us girls can't talk about it. Picking through Audrey's goddamned scarves and Benedetto's leg's still out there in whatever's left of his plane, sitting there like a piece a baloney.'

She had the shakes.

'Happens to 366, it can happen to 96th, it can happen to the air force Chief of Staff hisself. What about when the flaps jam?' she said. 'What about when the throttle lever seizes? Stuff happens. Ejector seat don't eject. Hell, sometimes these things just . . . they just . . . break. Don't make no difference then if it's a combat ace up there or a blind chimpanzee. I'm scared, Peggy. I'm scared it's gonna happen to my Okey. Then what will I do?'

I just let her cry some, held her in my arms. I caught a whiff of booze on her. She must have downed it as soon as she heard the crash siren.

I said, 'Honey, you gotta get a grip. You carry on this way, you're gonna make yourself ill. Then what's Okey gonna do? Airman without his sweetheart ain't worth a light.'

'Yeah,' she said. She was fixing up her face. 'I know.'

We carried on, looping up behind Pepper Clump and the sugar factory and then starting to drop down towards Drampton, so we could pick up Crystal. And who should we pass, trudging along in her zip-front boots, but the woman herself.

I said, 'There's Kath Pharaoh.'

She ran when she saw me stop for her. She didn't take any coaxing to climb in and get a ride home that time.

'Well, fancy seeing you,' she said.

I said, 'This is Gayle. Now you've met the whole gang.'

'How do you do, very pleased to meet you,' she said. 'You got home all right, then? In all that fog? I've been wondering about you.'

I said, 'But we all came by a few weeks ago. We came visiting but you weren't home. John said you were working.'

'Did he?' she said.

I said, 'Didn't you get the stuff we brought? In a box?'

Kath took her eyes off the road for a minute. 'Biscuits?' she said. 'And strong drink? Was that you?'

I said, 'It was from all of us. Betty. And Lois. The red-head? And Audrey. You remember? The tall one? We wanted you to have a few things.'

'Well,' she said, 'that's no use expecting a man to get a story straight. John Pharaoh said that was the copper-knob brought it. He never mentioned the rest of you. Was that you brought woollens? And good trousers, hardly worn?'

Seemed like Lois had turned into some kinda angel of mercy. Seemed like she'd decided to fly solo.

'Well, I thank you very much,' she said. 'They were grand biscuits. And them funny sausages in a tin. Champion. Fancy him getting his story wrong. You had a airyplane in trouble this morning, then? We heard the siren a-wailing.'

I tried to signal to her not to pursue that line of conversation, but she was intent on watching me drive.

'That's a dangerous thing, flying,' she said. 'That's a mystery to me how a big heavy thing like that stays up in the sky. How they don't come a-tumbling down every time, I shall never know.'

I was quite expecting Gayle to start up again, but she managed a smile instead. 'Yeah,' she said. 'It's a mystery to me too.'

There was no sign of John when we dropped Kath off.

I said, 'I'll come and fetch you out some time, like I promised? You could come and visit with Betty and see her royal scrapbooks? She'd love that. Drives her nuts, she tells us about all the dukes and princesses and none of us can ever remember who they are.'

'Well . . . I could do,' she said. She didn't exactly bite my hand off.

I said, 'Or we could go for a drive some place? Maybe you could take a turn behind the wheel? See how it feels?'

Then you should have seen her smile. It would have lit up the Cotton Bowl.

Gayle said, 'Are you crazy? She puts a dent in your fender, Vern's gonna throw a hissy fit.' I hadn't really thought about that.

I called in on Audrey, when I dropped Gayle. Told her about the little misunderstanding.

I said, 'Far as Kath knew, it was just Lois had took the groceries. And she must have been back since, took clothes for them too. Playing the lady bountiful, and never even said a word to us. I'm gonna see her, right now, find out what her game is.'

Aud said, 'Well, of course, that's Lois. She has no concept of teamwork. Nor of when enough is enough. I just hope she's not going round offending people. You know, Peggy, the Pharaohs may be paupers, but I'm sure they have their pride.'

Sandie was drinking red jello from a cup.

'Don't know what the hell I did wrong,' Lois said. 'Two days in the Frigidaire and it still ain't set.'

I said, 'You've been visiting John Pharaoh, I hear.'

She looked at me. There was just a flicker. At the time, I couldn't have said what it was.

I said, 'You have to tread careful, you know? Audrey was just saying, how you gotta be careful with charity. Give people too much and you might offend them. Or they could just get that they expect more and more.'

'Yeah,' she said, 'I can see the dangers of giving away a couple of Herb's wore-out shirts. Create unrest and discontent among the natives. Next thing you know, you've got an international incident on your hands. There's probably something in Post Regulations about it. Probably something about putting a fist in Audrey Rudman's know-it-all face, too, but I may just go for it anyhow. You know how I do love to live life on the edge.'

One thing about Lois. She never bottled things up.

12

We found a back road with tarmac for Kath's first lesson.

I said, 'Now. Hold the gas pedal right there and listen to the engine. Bring your shift pedal up real slow, and keep listening, till you hear the sound changing, then just hold it there. You feel how it's ready to move? Y'understand what I mean? Okay, let's roll. Gently now. Just give the gas pedal a gentle squeeze.'

I gave her an hour and she was away.

Kath Pharaoh was a natural-born driver. I'd taught a few. My big sister, Connie, didn't know her right from her left; and a girl on the base at Carswell, a New York City girl, never used anything but the subway, suddenly found herself with the whole of Texas outside her door. But I never seen anybody take to it like Kath. I just hoped she wouldn't ask me to teach John too. There was something about that smile of his gave me the creeps. Sometimes when I went to pick her up he'd be round the side, skinning a rabbit or fixing up his traps. He'd smile and smile, like he was real excited to see visitors, specially if Gayle had come along for the ride. She was a pretty little thing and he'd keep sneaking a look at her.

All through the spring of '52 I saw Kath twice a week at least and she'd drive me around. She was so thrilled, specially when any of those Jexes and Gotobeds'd seen her. She'd give them some regal kinda wave, and then she'd turn and give me her new Pepsodent grin.

One time, when it came on to rain, we stopped and picked up a woman trudging along with heavy bags.

'Look at poor old Annie gitting drenched,' Kath said. 'Can we give her a ride?'

It was a proud moment for her, leaning out of her window, shouting, 'Jump in the back, Annie, and I'll drop you near your door.'

She climbed in and perched there, steaming, like a wet dog.

Kath said, 'You all right there, Annie? Soon have you home. Once you can drive a motor, you wonder how you ever went on without it.'

Not that our passenger had asked. She didn't say a word, and when Kath stopped, outside one of those crouched-down houses, she just got out and went. Never a goodbye or a thank-you.

I said, 'Who'd you say she was?'

'Annie,' she said. 'She was Annie Jex, then she married Harold Howgego. Their boy Colin was took prisoner in the last lot; Japs got him. You should have seen him when they sent him home. I've seen more flesh on a sparrow. Now, he married a girl from Lynn, and *her* mother was a Jex, only not the same lot, of course. Annie was one of the Waplode Jexes, and her mother was a Pargeter.'

She killed me, reeling them off. I said, 'I think you just invent these names.'

'Why?' she said. 'Don't your lot have Howgegos? I didn't think there was anything you didn't have.'

'Howgegos!' I said 'What kind of name is that, anyway? I think you lie in bed at night and dream them up.'

She laughed. 'No I don't,' she said. 'But I have thought up what name I'd have if I was to be a film star. I'd be Loretta. Loretta Jayne-with-a-Y Pharaoh.'

Kath always put me in a good mood. Didn't matter how much it blew or rained or if I couldn't make it, after I'd promised we'd go driving, I never heard a word of discontent from her. It was like having a puppy-dog around, always wagging its tail. She was just as happy to come out to play or curl up in her basket and wait.

I said, 'Okay, Loretta Jayne, are you gonna turn this car round nice and neat? Can you do it in three?'

'Piece of cake.'

I said, 'You think you'll ever get your own wheels?'

'When we come up on the Treble Chance,' she said. 'First thing I'd do is get the electric light brought in. If we had the electric light, I could see to do a bit of sewing. Then I'd buy a motor and a new wringer. And I'd pay you back, for all your juice I've been using up. I'd come to America and take you out for a slap-up tea.'

13

None of us had been seeing much of Lois, apart from Betty, who had near enough adopted little Sandie.

'Lois is a restless soul,' Betty said to us one time. 'She's one of those girls derives no pleasure from a shelf of home-made preserves or a stack of nice ironed sheets, so she may as well go out and commune with nature . . .'

Audrey spluttered her coffee all over us. '*Commune* with nature? That's a ten-dollar word for anything Lois might get up to.'

Betty turned pink.

'I don't care what she does,' she said. 'Point I'm making is, she's a girl who can't be cooped up inside four walls. You know what she's like when she gets a mood on her. If I can babysit I'm probably sparing the poor child getting the rough side of her tongue. Heck, Sandie toddles around after me, got her own little duster and pan, just like Deana used to do. She's no trouble at all.'

I walked with Audrey to the PX.

I said, 'You have any idea what Lois is up to? Driving off the base all the time.' She sure seemed to have got over her fear of getting scalped out there.

'Don't ask,' she said. 'Don't tempt me. The germ of gossip may be likened unto a cancer. Gospel according to the CO's wife, Chapter One, Verse One. All I'll say is, I never would have taken Lois Moon for such a *outdoors* kind of girl. Kath ever say anything to you?'

I said, 'Such as?'

''Bout Lois up there visiting all the time?'

Far as I could make out, it was just speculation. I was with the CO's wife all the way on the dangers of idle talk. Made no sense to me, what a girl like Lois'd be doing with a eel-trapper always looked like he'd got a dirty secret, the way he smiled, always fiddling with his fingers and pacing around. I wasn't convinced John Pharaoh was playing with a full deck of cards. Still, I was afraid for Kath. She was such a trusting soul. And I was missing Lois, too. We never hung out any more. Never had any laughs. When friend husband is gone for days on end, you need somebody, help you take up the slack.

Audrey was at the Wives' Club all hours. She loved bridge afternoons and setting up rosters for Red Cross Clothes Closet, and all that stuff. She was always on Gayle's case to get involved. Said if she wanted Okey to get ahead she had to be seen playing her part too. But Gayle hated the Club. The one time she tried it she was taken to one side and told officers wives don't chew gum. She never went back.

There couldn't have been two girls less suited to be neighbours than Audrey and Gayle. And when Benedetto died of his injuries, they had a real ruckus. Gayle said it was plain cruel, the way his widow got three weeks' notice to clear the post.

Audrey said, 'Oh, Gayle, grow up why don't you? You know how many E-5s are waiting to get on base? You can't have the DW of a deceased sitting around, occupying quarters. Hell, she's not even military any more.'

For a whole week they managed not to speak to each other, even though their houses were joined together. Then just when I hoped the Easter Bunny might deliver a little love and forgiveness, Carol Benedetto hanged herself. They found her in her quarters. The place was all scrubbed out and shipshape ready for the final inspection. Just scuff marks on the wall where her feet had scrabbled, at the end. When Gayle heard, she went on a bender. I found her down in her broke-back cottage, still in her robe, and I'd say she'd been drinking all morning.

'I want to go home,' she said. 'I wanna go home, see my kid brothers. Get a little house in Boomer. I want Okey. Can you get Okey for me?'

But Okey was at the pad, and when a man's standing the alert, he can't be reached, don't matter if the sky fell in. I put her to bed and as soon as she was asleep I went round to ask Lois to sit with her, while I put Vern's shirts through the washer. Course, Lois wasn't home. Good old Herb was there, feeding Sandie on grilled cheese.

'Hey, c'mon in,' he said. 'See what I'm making for her birthday.'

He was carving a long piece of wood. 'See?' he said. 'It's a African geeraffe. She always loved them dopey-looking creatures. What'you think?'

I guess when he stood it up it did have a kinda animal shape to it.

I said, 'She'll be thrilled, Herb. You happen to know what time she'll be home?'

'Couldn't say,' he said. 'She likes to drive around some when I'm here to watch Sandie. Get out and about, looking for wishing-wells and newborn lambs and stuff.'

Sandie'd finished her sandwich and was starting on the wood chippings so I left Herb to clean up.

'Peggy,' he called after me. 'Don't forget now. The geeraffe is a secret.'

14

Audrey and Betty were just coming out from the OWC. They'd been helping set up an Easter candy trail for the kids.

'Time for a truce, Aud,' I said. 'This Benedetto business has hit Gayle real hard. I'm afraid she's cracking up.'

Betty said, 'I have a good nourishing soup at home. I'll go fetch some. That girl needs a mother.'

Audrey said, 'Yeah, and I'll come straight down, see Gayle. Maybe I was a little hard on her. You didn't tell anybody else?'

I said, 'Tell anybody else what?'

She lowered her voice. 'Why, that she's drinking, of course. What we have here is a damage-limitation situation. Wife starts to run off the rails, there goes a man's career and Okey's good troop.'

Seemed to me the main thing was to make sure Gayle didn't come to any harm.

'Well,' I said, 'while we're on the subject of problem wives, Lois is out on the loose again. Herb's home playing Mr Mom.'

'Yeah,' she said. 'I've been thinking about that too.'

Gayle was still on the bed, where I'd left her. Audrey climbed in beside her, gave her a hug.

'Baby,' she said, 'I'm sorry I yelled at you. Can we make up? Be friends as well as neighbours?'

Gayle didn't look too good. Far as she was concerned I think the room was still spinning.

'Now listen,' Audrey said. 'I understand how you're feeling. I mean, it's a real tragedy about Carol Benedetto, but you know, maybe she would have done it wherever she was. Or maybe they should have sent her home sooner than three weeks. You ever think of that? Maybe the military has got it right, forcing people to pick theirselves up and get on with the rest of their lives. Hm? And as for us, we're wives of the 96th. Whatever turns up we got to do our bit, keep the military machine humming 'cause those Soviets sure aren't gonna give us any compassionate leave.'

Gayle just lay there listening.

'Now, you take my advice,' Aud said, 'you'll close your eyes and play possum, 'cause Betty just pulled upside with a thermos of that ham-bone soup of hers.'

That raised a groggy smile.

We left Betty coaxing spoonfuls of broth into her.

I said, 'She'll be okay.'

Audrey said, 'She better be. Now. You wanna try and do something about the Lois situation?'

We went in her car.

She said, 'I couldn't give a damn about Lois, you understand? But if Kath Pharaoh finds out, she could make waves. It could get back to the CO, and we don't want that kind of trouble in the squadron.'

I said, 'It's Herb I feel sorry for.'

'Him too,' she said. 'You think you'd be able to keep Kath under control, if it came to it?'

I said, 'Me?'

'Well, she's your friend,' she said. 'You think you could keep her quiet?'

I said, 'Somebody set their cap at your Lance, would you keep quiet?'

'Yes,' she said. 'And so would you. We have our careers to think of.'

First I knew I had a career.

She said, 'You think she meets him at his house? I don't think so. What if Kath came home?'

Just beyond the railroad crossing there was an old piece of hardstand, used to have a gas pump on it. She parked there.

'Let's walk a little,' she said.

So we walked where a path was worn, along a ridge, up above the fields. The sun was shining. There was a warm breeze just riffling through the grass and not a sound except for birds singing.

'There's a lapwing,' she said. 'Hear him? Pee-wit, pee-wit.'

I said, 'Do we have a plan?'

'Well,' she said, 'let's see if we can see her car.'

'And then what?'

'I don't know,' she said. 'I'd just like her to know we've had her in our sights. Give her a jolt. Then maybe she'll come to her senses. Quit running around. I don't see what else we can do, short of getting her seen to by a veterinarian.'

'Okay,' I said, 'and how do we happen to be walking out here ourselves? We sure as hell can't say we're on our way someplace.'

'We're getting a breath of spring air, Peggy,' she said. 'We're *communing* with nature. Oh look. Stop. Don't move. See what I see? In the field? Way over, nearly in the middle?'

They were up on their hind legs, ears pricked, slugging it out like prize-fighters.

I said, 'Jeez, I never seen conies that size before. I didn't think they had anything in this place bigger'n we've got back home.'

'They're not conies,' she said. 'They're jack hares, and they're boxing. That's what they do in the spring. It's a sign the sap is well and truly rising.'

At the end of the ridge we could see across to Blackdyke Drove. No sign of anybody at Kath's. I knew for a fact she was beet-hoeing.

Aud said, 'Let's go as far as the willows over there. They run right down to the water. She could be there. Getting a lesson on eels.'

We carried on along the track. Every step I took, I wished more and more I'd minded my own business. I was feeling like a guilty party myself, sneaking around, trying to catch a person doing wrong.

I never noticed the tyre marks. I think Audrey did though. I seem to remember she suddenly picked up the pace.

We were right past the old tractor shed before I saw the trunk of Lo's old Chevy poking out. Then there was John Pharaoh, staring right at us outta the rear windowshield, but not really seeing us, his being otherwise engaged. Me and Audrey were rooted to the spot. Then he must have said something 'cause the door opened and Lois scrambled out with her nylons round her ankles. Her hair was all mussed up too. She was trying to push it out of her eyes.

I turned and ran. But Audrey stood her ground. Then I heard Lois start up. 'What the hell is your game?' she yelled.

'What's *our* game?' Audrey shouted back. 'Well, that's pretty rich!'

'Can't keep your long nose outta anything, can you, Rudman? Tell you what, you are a sick woman. And *you* . . .' That was me. '. . . I never took you for a snoop. I thought you were my friend.'

I kept running. Audrey walked back in her own good time.

We had to clean the earth off our sneakers before we could get back into the car. I didn't feel too good.

I said, 'Jeez, Aud, now I wish we never had gone.'

'Me too,' she said. 'It's made me feel horny as hell, and Lance is standing the duty the next three nights. Still, mission accomplished. We marked her card. Saved the honour of the squadron.'

15

'Fuck the squadron,' Lois said. Using a word like that in front of her child. I had gone round to see her. Try to explain things, mend a few fences, but she wasn't ready yet.

Saturday I picked Kath up and we drove to Downham. They had a cute little market there, sold eggs and stuff, laid out on tables under canvas canopies. Potatoes covered in dirt and all kinds of rabbit-food greenery. I wouldn't have touched any of it for fear of disease, but it was fun to go look.

Kath said, 'You're quiet, Peg. You all right?'

I said, 'I'm okay. Things on my mind.'

'Have you?' she said.

She was buying something called roe. It comes from a fish. There were seabirds sitting in a line along a roof. 'Look at that,' she said. 'Must be bad weather coming in. You sure you don't want any roe? That's smashing on a bit of buttered toast.'

We walked on.

I said, 'Friend of mine has been playing around. You know what I mean? Married woman. And I don't want to see her go ruin her life.'

'Well,' she said, 'I don't see what you can do. I think I'll get a bit of celery while I'm here.'

I said, 'Her husband ever finds out, or the other wife, I don't like to think. If I had that done to me, Vern ever played away, I'd kill him.'

'But that's different with men,' she said. 'That's in their nature. They can't hardly stop theirselves, what I've seen of it. That's like trying to keep a tomcat from straying.'

I said, 'Like hell it's different. A man stands up and makes his vows, he oughta keep to them.'

My heart was pounding.

She said, 'I agree. But how do you get them to do it? That's the question. You can't be watching them every minute.'

I was lost for words.

'I tell you what,' she said. 'I always say to John Pharaoh, "Be good, and if you can't be good, be careful. You bring trouble to my door, I shall get you spayded. Then you'll be sorry." Oh, there's May Gotobed. Can we give her a ride home?'

I reported to Audrey, soon as I could.

I said, 'I am in shock. I'm sure Kath don't know what's been going on, but then, I'm not sure how much she'd care, if she found out. She has some highly unusual ideas about husbands, I must say.'

'Mm,' Audrey said. 'So we keep Lois under surveillance. And when she's had time to cool down, I think I'll make a gesture of reconciliation. I think I'll invite her to join the Reading Circle I'm starting up. First book we're gonna read is *The Good Earth*.

I said, 'Yeah. I'm sure Lois wouldn't miss that for the world.'

16

A letter come from Mom Dewey. Crystal'd had her picture took at school, looked real cute, so of course I'd sent one to his folks and one to mine.

'Dear Vern', she wrote,

I put Crystal on the ledge in the front kitchen, pride of place, and everybody that has seen her has remarked what a angelic face she has, spitting image of yourself aged five. We have had our troubles, your father brought in some grade ewes and some wethers, Romneys and Blue Faces, five got loose, got pasture bloat so bad they were goners, another one swallowed a French letter, excuse my language, and I'd sure like to know how one of them things got on Bolster Graze. If there's a way to die young, you can depend on a sheep to find it. Good money thrown after bad. I had my way we'd sell up, open a yarn store in Skowhegan. Norton Beebe, you'll remember Norton, pumped gas down in Palmyra, had a sister with a withered leg, he got killed out in Korea, he was in the infantry, National Guard, darned if I understand what this war is all about. I just give thanks that you're not out there, risking your neck. Best regards to your wife. Your loving mother, Clementine Dewey.

Vern screwed it into a ball and sent it spinning across the room. 'You read that?' he said. '*Not risking your neck?* She ever hear about the Soviet Union? She ever hear a nucular capability? What's she think? I'm sitting here on my finger, flying a desk?'

I said, 'I dunno, Vern. How's she supposed to know what you're doing? I sure as hell don't.'

'Norton Beebe,' he said. 'Guess he's some kinda hero now. Tell you, the trouble with Maine, folks there don't see the big picture. They're so busy thinking 'bout some yellowskin shot Norton, they don't even know there's a big Russian grizzly after their asses. I guess you gotta look at the world from 42,000 feet to understand.'

He was doing his sit-ups.

'You seen anything of Lois?'

I wondered where he might be coming from with a question like that. 'Yeah,' I said. 'I think I did. Why d'you ask?'

'She say anything 'bout her birthday?'

'No.'

'Only, Herb's fixing a surprise for her and he's worried she might have gotten wind of it.'

'She never said.'

'He brung it down to Beer Call tonight,' he said, 'show us what he'd done so far. He's carving her a roebuck. Amazing what that man can do with a knife. He's got a real knack.'

I said, 'You sure it's a roebuck?'

'Yup,' he said.

I said, 'You sure it's not a giraffe?'

'Nope,' he said. 'Legs were too short.'

17

I kept a low profile, stayed outta Lois's path for a day or two, but in the end she come to my door.

'Guess we better clear the air?' she said.

She came in and I made coffee. It was hard, though, trying to talk normal with her, after what I had seen.

'Peg,' she said, 'I know it didn't look good . . .'

I said, 'I didn't want to get involved, Lo.'

'No,' she said. 'Well, I figured it would have been Audrey's idea, snooping around, checking up on me. Thing is, you know, some-times things happen that shouldn't . . . but it was the only time. I swear.'

I said, 'I don't wanna talk about it.'

'Me neither,' she said. 'So that's that.'

'Yup,' I said.

She said, 'You do believe me?'

'Of course,' I said. I lied.

'So we're friends again. Clean slate?'

'Sure,' I said. 'Clean slate.'

'Great!' she said. 'So you coming to Betty's tomorrow night? We're gonna have a pyjama party for my birthday. Booze, records, every-thing. Crystal can sleep over.'

Vern and Ed and Herb were starting three weeks of night missions.

Okey was on assignment, Norway or some place we weren't meant to know about.

I said, 'How about Audrey?'

'Yeah. She's up for it,' she said. 'We declared a ceasefire. She's bringing potato chips.'

18

I said to Audrey, 'Betty's twittering around making party favours and popping corn and I feel like I'm going to a party in a minefield.'

'Panic over,' she said. 'I think we've put a stop to that little adventure. And no casualties!'

I took along beer and a card, but I didn't wear my pyjamas. I kinda forgot, but it could just have been my way of holding out on Lois. I still had a certain something on my mind, until I seen some genuine sign of her shaping up.

I said to Crystal, 'You gonna play nicely with Sherry and Deana?'

'Only if I don't have to be the baby or the patience,' she said. Mommies and Hospitals were about the only games the Gillis girls knew. And sure enough, when we got there they were hauling Sandie around like a sack of grain, telling her she had to get a Band-Aid on her head.

Crystal sat in the corner, going through Betty's albums. She never minded entertaining herself. I could hear her making up names for all the people in the photos. 'Princess Nancy and Princess Jennifer and Princess Crystal Margaret Dewey, and they live in a palace and they are allowed a dog of their very own.'

By the time the kids crashed it was ten o'clock and I was the only one left sober.

'I'd like to toast a drink,' Betty said, up-ending a Schlitz all over the rug. 'To our birthday girl, Lois. And to my Ed, 'cause Friday it'll be our ninth anniversary.'

'Nine years!' Lois said. 'D'you get a emerald or something for that?'

'Gosh, no. Nine is . . . Audrey, help me out here, is nine years cardboard or tin?'

'Well, whatever you get, you've earned it.' Lois was on the floor, sharing cushions and a bowl of potato chips with Gayle. 'Nine years with Ed Gillis. You deserve a Purple Heart. Where'd you find that man, anyway?'

'In Warsaw, Indiana,' Betty said. 'I was visiting with Glick cousins and Ed was the boy next door. It was love at first sight. How 'bout you, girls? Audrey? How about you and Lance. Was it love at first sight?'

Underneath that rosebud nightdress Betty had a heart of pure mush.

'Kind of,' Audrey said. 'I liked his freckles first. I took my time deciding about the rest of him.'

Betty said, 'And what brought you together?'

'Naked ambition,' Lois said. 'Audrey's the only one of us gonna make Mrs Full-Bird Colonel, and you heard it here first.'

Audrey smiled. Seemed like the peace was gonna hold.

'Actually,' she said, 'I suppose it was Route 94 brought us together, 'cause I was in Chicago, and Lance was in Great Lakes, Illinois. I wouldn't mind a buck for every time I drove that highway.'

Lois had it about right, though, Lance being Lance T. Rudman II, son of the late Commodore Lance T. Rudman, US Navy, Annapolis Academy, white gloves and all and Audrey having such a cut-glass style about her.

Anyway, I told them about me and Vern, and Gayle told us how she couldn't ever remember a time when she didn't know Okey. They used to swing on the same old truck tire and go to the same Baptist church. In 1946, he enlisted in the Army Air Corps, told her he'd be back for her and everybody said, 'Hell'll freeze over before any Jackson boy keeps his word.' First thing he did after he made the Officer Candidate School was write her 'You coming, then?'

'A real romantic proposal, huh?' Lois poured herself another shot.

'Well, my turn now. I was a Roller Derby queen, with the Corona Park Demonettes, and I was just gri-i-i-nding my skates one time when this Bluesuiter come up to me, says, "You don't mind my saying, miss, you got the prettiest hair I ever seen." That was Herbert P. Moon, come up to the big city from McGuire on a weekend pass. I don't know where he learned his manners, but he was a gentleman. He kept writing me, after he went back, and I never was much of a penpal. Next thing I knew, he got orders to Hawaii, wanted to know would I make him a happy man? That was a tough call. Never thought I'd end up marrying a woodchuck, though . . .' She squealed. 'Speaking of woodchucks, I haven't showed you what I got for my birthday. I've been waiting till Sandie's little ears had stopped flapping for the night.'

She crawled across the floor, behind Betty's couch, looking for her bag, sent the popcorn flying. 'Hold on there, girls,' she said. She had her hand inside the bag. 'Now . . .' she said. 'I want you to bear in mind, this is a hand-crafted item. It was lovingly fashioned by my dear husband, using his own fair hands, and I think I can say, without fear of contradiction, you'll never have seen the like of it before. Girls, are you bored with those dreary gifts of Parisian scent? Do you dread unwrapping yet another pair of silky drawers trimmed with Chantilly lace and having to fake delight? Then why not drop a hint to the man in your life? You too could be the proud owner of a Herb Moon original . . .' she brung it out with a flourish, 'carved . . . dachshund-type animal!'

I daresay that's the way it goes if you're a wood-carver. You hit a knot in the wood, you just got to go where it takes you and make the best of things. I guess there's a lesson there for all of us. I could still see a hint of giraffe about that dachshund's head, though.

We laughed till we thought we'd die. Woke Sherry up with all that screaming, holding our aching guts and begging for mercy.

'Mommy,' she said, standing there with her little eyes all scrunched up. 'Mommy? Did Daddy shout at you again?'

19

Vern was busy mixing up a mess of his Real Mean Barbecue Sauce.

Vern Dewey's Real Mean Barbecue Sauce

*Mix 1 cup oil, 2 yellow onions (minced), 2 bell peppers
(minced) and 2 red chillis (minced) with 2 cans of tomato
pulp, 3 big spoons of sugar, 3 spoons of vinegar, a good
pinch of salt and a dash of liquid hickory-smoke. The
longer you leave the ribs in this, the better they'll be.*

!WARNING!
*You better scrub your fingers real good afterwards. You
get chilli juice on your privates you'll be sorry.*

He said, 'I suppose you gotta drive out there, running a limousine
service for the breeds?' He was mad at me for inviting Kath and John
Pharaoh for the Fourth of July. 'Don't you know your history, Peg?'
he said. 'It's a day of mourning for them. Day they lost the greatest
nation on earth.'

I'd just invited them for ribs and hamburger, was all.

I said, 'How about a little Christian kindness and hospitality? You
seen the meat rations they been getting out there?'

I had. I'd seen things on sale, I swear, bodily parts never intended to see the light of day, never mind the inside of a skillet. Brains. And tripe.

'That's not so bad,' Kath used to say, 'if you can get an onion or two to put with it, cook it nice and slow – that's quite tasty.' How the years can change a person.

We were using the Gillises' front yard, so Ed was in charge of ops. Audrey brought potato salad, Betty made brownies and Johnny Applesauce cake, Gayle and Lo were in charge of some evil brew they swore was Bloody Mary, and I made fried chicken. Vern and Okey were meant to be assisting Ed; Lance too, when he turned up. Recipe for war if ever I heard one, four jocks gathered around one barbecue pit.

Wasn't long, though, till Okey and Vern lost interest in the secret of the perfect hamburger. Vern fetched a ball and they went across the road to Deek Kurlich's quarters, shoot a few hoops with him and his boy. Crystal followed, of course, getting under their feet, determined to be one of the gang.

Herb was away on assignment. Just as well. First thing I seen when I pulled up outside Kath's house was John Pharaoh wearing one of Herb's old shirts. Lime green Ban-Lon, with a blue stripe. I'd have recognised it anywhere. He was carrying a raggedy old pillowcase, with something inside it. Gave me that sly smile and I blushed scarlet thinking of what he was at, the last time I seen him.

'I got a surprise for you,' he said. 'For your party.'

I really didn't want any more surprises from him. And if I had known what it was, I'd never have allowed him in my car with it.

When Kath walked out the door, I hardly knew her. She'd had her hair curled up all night, touch of tangerine lipstick given her by Audrey, and a polka-dot ballerina skirt, Lois's one and only try at dressmaking, far as I knew. I'd wondered what had become of it. God knows she made us all suffer while she was working on it. Said the dots made her eyes hurt. Gave us earache, more to the point. Still, it had finally gone to a good home. Kath looked so pretty in it.

By the time we got back to the base, Ed was cooking up a storm. It smelled so good. Deana run across and told Vern our company had arrived and food was near enough ready.

I said, 'Vern, this here's John. Why don't you get him a cold beer?'

'Right,' he said. Then, real quiet, to me, 'Why? He lost the use a his legs?'

Okey heard it. He said, 'I'll get it, Vern. You ready for another?'

So Okey passed John a beer and then he hung around the pit watching the Maple Short Ribs turn mahogany-brown. He didn't seem bothered Vern had turned his back on him. He just stood there, sucking on his beer and holding his pillowcase.

Kath said, 'You go steady with that ale, John Pharaoh.'

I seen Ed sneering.

'Easy to see who's wearing the pants there,' he said. Priceless remark from a man that was wearing PT shorts and a plastic apron, but Vern sniggered anyway.

I was so mad at him. He knew better than behaving like that, even if Ed didn't, but that's jocks for you. Put more than two of them together and you have a bunch of show-off kids.

John had been studying the barbecue. He said, 'You ever cook a barley eel on a griddle like that?'

'No, my friend,' Ed said, 'I don't believe I did.'

It was Okey looked inside the pillowcase. 'Christamighty, Vern,' he said, 'you should see the size a this sucker.'

Then John brought it outta the bag. It must have been four feet long, still had its head on, but no skin. Betty screamed. I think I did too. I heard Vern whistle. Get him on to fishing and all that talk about breeds and knuckle-grazers was soon forgot.

'Jeez!' he said. 'You catch that hereabouts?'

John said, 'Yes. That's a green barley. They just started running.' He looked so proud. 'He's a big un, this one,' he said. 'When I seen him in the grig this morning, I thought to save him, bring him along. I know how you Colonials like your grub. Kath'll tell you how to cook him.'

Kath Pharaoh's Way with Eels

The young ones are the best, before they've turned yellow.
Put them in a pillowcase with a handful of salt and swish
that around in a tub of water till the sliminess is gone.
Fry them in bacon fat. They're soon done. If you can't
get elvers, then get an old boy, eight or nine years old.
After you've skinned him, cut him into two-inch pieces
and bake him on a grid. That needs a good hot flame.
Nice with piccalilli.

Vern and Okey were inspecting the beast.

'Stun it with a mallet?'

'Had to,' he said. 'Generally I pierce them through the spine with a skewer. Couldn't hold this old boy, though. I had to give him a clout with my hammer.'

'Skin come off easy?'

'Not too bad. Do you put a slip-loop round him, hang him from a good strong hook, then cut round him, just aback of his head – Stanley knife does it nice and clean – then grab holt of the skin here, use a pair of pliers and just give that a good old pull, that comes off, like peeling off a glove. He might still jerk around a bit, but you just pay no heed. Do you cut his head off, he'll soon calm down.'

I heard something behind me. Turned just in time to see Lois, running to the bathroom. Ed fetched a good knife and they carved that evil-looking creature into steaks and made space for them on the hot grid.

Lance made a big entrance. He'd been at the Officers' Club helping to set up the fireworks. He strode in, said a few kind words to everybody, shook John and Kath by the hand like he was some visiting dignitary, asked them had they come far and all that. Then he called us to order and we all looked to the flag.

Little Gayle stood on a kitchen chair in her gingham pedal-pushers and sang us the Star Spangl'd Banner, fine voice she had. I had to wipe a tear, I felt so far from home. Wherever that might be. I didn't miss my mom nor my sister, and me and Vern had moved around so much I didn't really belong anyplace any more. Maybe it was the fumes from the Kurlichs' charcoal briquettes made my eyes water. Maybe it was the eel.

Vern said, 'There goes 366 Squadron, generating more smoke than heat, as usual.' Just a little light enmity between aircrews. We were playing them at softball after eats and we had plans to whup their hides.

Kath was acting shy, with the guys around, I guess, till she saw Okey start giving the girls pony-rides on his back. Then she joined in, down on her hands and knees with little Sandie clinging round her neck, shouting giddyup.

She didn't eat much, pecking at her food. John was eating enough for the two of them, though. He kept going back for more – chicken, cake, hamburger, ice cream, eel. He just piled it high, pacing up and down, with that funny little smile of his. He never went near Lois, though, never even looked her way. I know because I was keeping my eye on her. And all she had was crackers and booze, crackers and more booze.

I said, 'Lois, what's your problem?' after she told me she didn't feel up to playing softball. 'That leaves us a man short.'

'Come inside a minute,' she said.

We went into Betty's kitchen.

'You keep a secret?' she said. 'I'm expecting. Only don't you say a word t'anybody else.'

She didn't look good. Kinda blotchy. I hugged her.

I said, 'In that case, I forgive you. First three months with Crystal, I couldn't even keep water down. Herb pleased?'

'That's what I mean, Peg,' she said. 'Me and Herb haven't had time to sit down and talk about it. You know? So keep it to yourself.'

Dorothy Kurlich was waving us it was time to go down to the diamond.

'Take my advice, Lo,' I said, 'you've got a migraine. Go home, lie down, get your face outta here, before the interrogation starts. Leave Sandie. She'll be fine.'

20

Betty said, 'Migraine, my eye. That girl's in the family way. But don't you worry, I won't tell a soul. Well, I hope that means the game's off. I never wanted to play anyhow. Swinging at a silly ball.'

Lance was our captain. He had to be. He was the tallest and the blondest and he had 'Leader' written all over him. He said how about recruiting John, take Lois's place, but Kath heard that. She said, 'No. He won't manage that. He can't hit a ball. If you're short, though, I'll have a go.'

Ed muttered something to Vern about too many women. Something about why didn't we just let them run for president and be done with it. But Lance put Kath in to bat 9, and he asked Betty to help her along till she got the hang of the game. Which was like asking Mr Magoo to lead the blind.

366's line-up was Ax Bergstrom, captain, and his wife, Ruby; Dorothy and Deek Kurlich; Pat and Yvette Franklin; Ginger Bass and Lorene; and Tom Hannegan. His wife was home to Nebraska, dropping their firstborn any day.

First inning, Okey homered in to centre field, Lance popped up to third and then Ed put us up 2–0 with a home run to left, Betty squealing, 'Oh Ed, oh Ed!' Then Vern popped up to Ruby Bergstrom at short and then I done the very same thing myself.

Me and Vern Dewey had a long-running disagreement regarding the ability of the female of the species to hurl a ball and, this being the military, the fact that I pitched for Topperwein High, 1939 to 1941, helped them on their way to a team-low ERA of 3.09 in the Guadalupe County Senior Girls' League, counted for nothing with our captain. I guess he felt he'd done enough for womankind that day. So it was friend husband who stepped up to the mound, pitched so wild he gave away three walks, then Deek Kurlich hit a home run. Nice work, Vern.

Hannegan fouled out to first base and Ruby B and Dorothy both grounded out.

Lance walked alongside me as we changed sides. I said, 'Is that a change of pitcher I hear clanking through the cog-wheels of your mind?'

'I guess,' he said. 'I hate to cause strife between husband and wife, though.'

'Woman's game.' That was the unkindest cut Vern could come up with when he heard I was taking his place.

Ax Bergstrom pitched to Gayle and she singled down the left field-line. Audrey walked, Betty struck out, never got the bat off her shoulder and then there stood Kath, with her sleeves rolled up and that polka-dot skirt tucked up in her drawers. Next thing Bergstrom knew, the ball was well on its way to Norwich. Trouble was, Kath didn't know she was meant to drop the bat and Captain James Maggs, who was umpiring, was the type of unbending bastard does everything by the book. Still, Kath had showed us what she was made of.

'Well, just look at that,' Okey said. 'We gone and adopted ourselves a left-handed power-hitter.' He was so excited he lined out to short.

Lorene Bass faced my first pitch. I had her and First Lieutenants Franklin and Bass struck out, all three.

Third inning, Lance and Ed singled, then Vern hit to second and by the time he moved his ass, Deek Kurlich had stepped on to the bag and whipped the ball across to first. I was so mad at him, I lost my head and popped up to third.

I pitched well after that, kept 366's finest pretty much pinned down.

Fourth inning we got there, slow but steady, put us 6–4 up. Then fifth inning if Vern didn't go and make the same foolish error again. I walked, but then Gayle grounded out to first base.

I said to Lance, 'Please tell me you're not allowing Mr Double-Play Dewey near a bat again.'

'Hey,' he said, 'whatever happened to wifely devotion?'

'He gets that in buckets,' I said. 'Now, why don't you use the brain God gave you and let little Deana pinch hit for Vern? She can't do worse.'

He said he'd think it over.

Sixth inning the question didn't arise, but Kath homered to right field and Lorene Bass never even saw it go.

I gave up two runs when I should have held them scoreless, but Ruby Bergstrom had a good eye – and Yvette Franklin too, when she put her mind to it. I'd have had the both of them on my team if I'd had to name USAF Drampton's Best.

Final inning Lance said to Vern, 'Why don't you rest up that shoulder? Young Deana here's itching to take a swing.'

'All the same to me,' Vern said. And it was, too. He just wanted to get back to the beer and talk lugworms some more with John Pharaoh.

We were ahead 7–6. They put Hannegan in to pitch, instead of Ax Bergstrom, ask me that just smelled of desperation. First pitch, Lance popped up to short. Ed singled to left. Deana walked. Only eight years old and that linthead Hannegan couldn't get the better of her. I got a walk too. Then Gayle stroked a double to the left. She could have walked into second. Audrey hit a slow grounder but beat it out to first. Bases loaded. Betty, of course, struck out, called strikes being something of a speciality with her, same as her chicken pot-pie. Kath was up and darned if she didn't hit a rope to right, scoring two more. 11–6.

I held them scoreless. It wasn't hard. Once they'd seen what I could do to Pat Franklin, they kinda lost the will to fight.

'You enjoy that?' I said to Kath, when we were headed back for more eats. I knew she'd enjoyed it.

'That was all right,' she said. 'That's like rounders, only with daft rules. Can we stop for the fireworks, if that's not too much trouble?'

21

I was in Kath's kitchen, giving her a home-permanent. We had the door open, on account of the fumes, even though it was raining out there fit to drown a duck, and I could hear John Pharaoh the other side a the wall, moving his traps about, getting up to whatever it was he did in there.

I said, 'We could have done this at my place, shone a bit more light on the subject. Way I'm groping around in this gloom, you're gonna end up with some kinda hairstyle. You know I never mind fetching you over.'

'I know,' she said. 'Now, don't take this the wrong way, but that gives me the creeps, the place you live. Barbed wire. Men with guns looking in your motor every time you drive in. That puts me on edge.'

I said, 'I didn't know that. I thought you liked coming to the base? You like the electric light.'

She did, too. Every time she came she flicked it on, make sure it was still working.

I said, 'You like the commissary.'

She loved the commissary. Seeing all those products stacked high. Stuff she had never heard of. Miracle Whip. Niblet corn. My-T-Fine Chocolate Pudding. We always bought something for her to take home and try.

'Yes,' she said, 'I do like some of it. I like seeing you, and little Crystal, and your pals. But it's all the rules and regulations I don't like. You haven't hardly got a mind to call your own. Can't go down near the airyplanes. Can't get yourself a little job, put a bit of jingle in your pocket. You can't even pin a nice picture on your wall for fear you'll get in trouble with the bosses. I couldn't be doing with that, Peg. I mean to say, I know we haven't got the electric in yet, but at least I can please myself. I can go anywhere I choose.'

I said, 'And where would you go? If you could choose anywhere?'

Her eyes shot across to that old postcard she had pinned up. 'Cromer?' she said.

I said, 'Not London, then?'

'No,' she said. 'That's a terrible place. Hundreds of streets. I'd get lost in a minute. I've been to Norwich, though. That's another big place. We went for a Sunday School outing. Superintendant got a charabanc up. We had a crate of fizzy lemonade on the back seat, started exploding. Must have been all the jolting.'

I said, 'You got any photos? I've never seen any pictures of you when you were a kid.'

'We did have,' she said, 'but they're long gone. When Mam was poorly, near the end, she got some funny ideas. One day she emptied the drawer. Photos, certificates, she firebacked the lot, thought they harboured disease. And you can't replace them. She couldn't help it. She didn't know what she was doing.'

I said, 'You got on well with your mom?'

'Oh yes,' she said. 'I do miss her.'

John appeared in the doorway. He laughed when he saw Kath's head sprouting curlers.

'Never mind laughing,' she said. 'When Peg's done this I shan't have to bother putting it up in pipecleaners every night. You going now?'

'Yes,' he said. 'I just paunched a few rabbits.' *Foo*, was how he said it. 'I thought I'd take 'em down to Brakey. See what I can get for them.'

'All right,' she said. 'But don't bring strawberries. I'm sick of them.'

She had brought some to the base one day. Real live strawberries with their leaves on and a smell of fruit and everything.

John started to go.

'And do you see Jim Jex, don't end up leaning on a bar with him . . .' she said.

He left.

'. . . come home reeking of ale,' she shouted after him. 'Talking a load of twaddle.' She looked up at me. 'It's for his own good,' she said. 'He's easy led. You still got your mam alive, Peggy?'

I did, for what it was worth. Thing about Mom was, she was always more interested where the next man was coming from than how her kids were doing. Whoever my daddy was, I didn't remember him. Just a long line of new daddies breezing through, making Mom laugh behind closed doors, then yelling some and disappearing in a cloud of dust. Some of them were okay. Most of them didn't stay long enough for me to find out. One took his belt to me and my sister Connie bit him on the leg. Only act of sisterly solidarity she ever showed me. Mom liked Connie better because she would usually oblige the latest daddy with a winning smile. Also, she had pretty blue eyes.

I said, 'Yeah, my mom's in San Antonio, Texas. But you marry a aviator you're always on the move. Makes life easier if you're not all the time looking back over your shoulder, hankering for family.'

'Yes,' she said. 'I can see that. You've got a nice bunch of pals, though.'

There was something I had to tell her, made me feel nervous.

I said, 'Yeah. And did you hear, Lois is having a baby?'

'Is she?' she said, and her face lit up. Then I knew, whatever she was thinking, it wasn't the terrible thought I'd been having from the moment Lois told me she was pregnant.

'Oh, how lovely!' she said. 'What a lovely bit of news. I shall have to knit her something. I'll do something in blue. They'll be hoping for a boy this time, I expect. Or lemon. Either sort can wear lemon. When'll that be, then?'

'Christmas,' I said. 'Now, shall we plan a trip? You really want to go to Cromer?'

'Oh, yes please,' she said. 'That's a proper seaside there.'

Kath had never been to the beach.

'All that water,' she said. 'Do you think you can see to the other side?'

I said, 'Well, I never was at Cromer, but I believe it's some kinda ocean there, so I guess not.'

She said, 'I know the water comes in and goes out again 'cause that's called the tide and Harold Jex was at Cromer, sent us a picture-postcard, and he seen this tide business with his own eyes. But the thing that mystifies me is, how does it know when to come in and go out? What if it forgot to go and just kept coming?'

I said, 'Kath, that's two questions more'n I have answers for. Now, let's have a glass of soda while your curls are cooking.'

22

Lois went from never being home to never being any place else. I went round to see her all the time. Her quarters were messy, unless Herb had been home and had a field day, and she just grouched around, watching *The Roy Rodgers Show* and feeding Sandie on cookies.

I said, 'You still feeling rough?'

'I could sleep round the clock,' she said. 'Was I like this with Sandie?'

I said, 'I don't recall. But I think your temper was a little sweeter.'

She said, 'You and Vern gonna have any more?'

I said, 'Nope.'

She said 'You seem very sure.'

I said, 'I am. I have my Dutch cap. House catches fire, after Crystal it'll be the first thing I grab.'

'I can't stand those things,' she said. 'By the time you've remembered where you left it. Then it has life of its own. Springs outta your fingers, goes flying across the bathroom and it always lands in that skronk behind the WC. I'd sooner take my chances.'

I said, 'Well, there y'are then. And now you have one of those little chances on the way.' I said, 'You could always clean up the skronk behind the john. You could always wear your Dutch cap every night.'

'Hm,' she said. 'How come you're so damned smart?' She just sat there, stains down her sweatshirt.

I said, 'You just tired?'

'Sick and,' she said.

'Nothing else wrong?' I said.

She looked at me. 'No,' she said, 'nothing else. Why? Ain't that enough?'

I couldn't read her.

I said, 'Kath's knitting for you. You have a preference for lemon or blue?'

'Couldn't care less,' she said. 'How about *grey*?'

I still couldn't read her.

'Well, you're good fun,' I said. 'You wanna come on a trip, next week? To the beach? The girls are all coming. Two cars.'

'I dunno,' she said. 'What beach? Does it have surf and everything?'

I said, 'All I know is, it's called Cromer and it probably beats staying home.'

She said she'd think about it.

I said, 'You do that. If you'd rather sit here, sniffing jet fuel, we'll understand.'

By the time I walked through my door, she was on the phone.

'I'll come,' she said. 'On one condition. Can Sandie ride in a different car than me? I can't stand her climbing all over my belly.'

I said, 'Fair enough. Course, you might be trading for Deana or Sherry.'

'No problem,' she said. 'One look from me and those Gillis girls turn to stone. Is there a funfair at Cromer?'

23

So the deal was, I'd take Betty and Kath and Lois, and Audrey'd bring Gayle and all the kids.

Gayle said, 'I'm getting in practice for next year, Peggy. Soon as this tour's done, me and Okey are gonna have a little baby.'

Of course, the minute it seemed like we were all set, Betty started changing everything around.

'I'll have to take my own car,' she said. 'Ed don't like the girls riding with other drivers.'

Then she was worried about Cromer. 'We don't know a thing about the place,' she said to me. 'What if we break down and they don't even have telephones out there?'

Tuesday was dry and bright. We said we'd try for Wednesday, and Tuesday night there was such a sunset, that great big sky was all pink and orange and then it turned green and mauve. Crystal had her lunch-pail packed and ready. Snickers, potato chips, and her rabbit-fur mittens sent by Mom Dewey.

I said, 'Precious, you're gonna lose them and then you'll be sad. Why don't you just leave them safe at home?'

Her lip started to tremble.

Vern pitched in. 'Don't you start snivelling,' he said to her. Fastest way to get the tears flowing, of course. Amazing how a man can know so much about aerodynamics and so little about psychology, but I guess the brain only has space for so much.

Then he turned on me. 'You only don't like her treasuring her mitts on account they come from the Deweys. What she ever get from your side of the family? What did your mom ever send her?'

Crystal was now going full throttle. Then Betty phoned. 'Ed wants to know what time we'll be home,' she said.

Me and Vern picked up where we'd left off. He was right about Crystal's Gramma Shea, but I wasn't gonna give him the satisfaction.

I said, 'I could care less who sent what. It's high summer, high as it gets in this two-bit island you brung us to, and I ain't having my day in the sunshine ruined when she loses her fur mittens. Which I guarantee she will do.'

'Yeah,' he said, 'you're having a real hard time of it here, Peg, I can see. Hanging out with the girls, uh-oh, Pepsi Hour again – my, how the time does fly! Driving around, taking in the sights. Running a beauty parlour for breeds.'

I just had to laugh in his silly face when he called Kath's kitchen a *beauty parlour*. He raised his hand to me. I said, 'Don't even think about it,' and the phone rang again.

She said, 'Ed wants to know . . .'

I said, 'Betty, what is wrong with your husband? Does he wanna come along with us, ride shotgun?'

'Well!' she said. 'There's no call to take that attitude. Ed just wants to know . . .'

I said, 'He think you're going on this trip to meet men? Put him on. I'll tell him he's right.'

By the time I was through with her, Vern had got a smile back on Crystal's face, pulling one of his tickle-fight stunts, and he was on his way out the door, going eel-netting with John Pharaoh.

Goddarned mitts. Probably full of bugs and all sorts. But that's Maine folk for you.

24

We had such a day. Never got to Cromer 'cause Ed had decided that would have took us too deep into Indian country. He said Betty was allowed to go to Hunstanton, so that's where we went. I had lost the will to argue. Same stretch of water, far as I could make out. Audrey was navigating.

I asked Kath if she minded about Cromer. She said she didn't, and she sure didn't look like a disappointed woman. Got her head tied up in a scarf Lois gave her, to cover where the permanent had gone a little wild, and she was wearing a pair a peep-toe sandals, bought with her beet-hoeing money.

We got buckets and spades soon as we arrived, and Crystal ran on to the sands, started right in digging. She said she was building an air base for Sandie.

It was a wide, wide shore. Kath asked a man selling newspapers where was the water and he said the tide was out, gave her a withering look. So we spread our blankets up against the sea wall and waited.

Crystal was getting unwanted help from Sandie, trampling across the nice runways she had made.

I said, 'I thought you said it was *for* her?'

'No,' she said. 'She's too young for an air base. She'll just wreck it.'

So Gayle tried to distract Sandie and get the Gillis girls playing in the sand too, helping her to build Fort Jackson, but they were too busy torturing their dollies and calling them bad names. Deana banged Sherry's doll against the wall in a blind fury. Then she bit its face and threw it back at Sherry.

Betty was a little way off from us, laying out the picnic, all nice and dainty. 'Play gentle, now,' she kept calling.

Kath was watching them. She said to me, 'I suppose they play so nasty 'cause of what they've seen at home. They'll have seen her getting a few weltings.'

In some respects, Kath was ahead of her time.

We had cold chicken and meatloaf sandwiches. Welch's Grape Juice to help it down and Lois and Gayle never travelled far without some hard liquor. There was some kinda puppet show just along the sands, and Audrey and Kath and Gayle took the girls along there, give us five minutes' peace. We could hear Crystal and Sandie squealing at the puppets from where we sat. Betty was tidying away the picnic. Lois was stretched out alongside of me.

I said, 'How're you doing there, red-haired momma? You glad you come along?'

'Yeah,' she said. She still sounded kinda weary. 'Sooner I drop this brat, the sooner I'll be my sweet old self.'

I said, 'I can't hardly wait.' I looked her in the eye. I said, 'Herb happy? About the baby?'

'Herb's always happy,' she said, making herself a pillow out of sweaters.

I said, 'Then you're a lucky woman.'

She missed a beat. Then she propped herself up on her elbow. 'Meaning?' she said.

I hadn't realised till then how a thought, once you have thought it, can never be laid to rest. It may lay low, but any time it can pop right up again, put certain words in your mouth. 'Meaning nothing,' I said, but I was blushing at what I had remembered, and she saw.

'Right,' she said. 'Anyway, four weeks and I'm outta here.' She was going back to Astoria, Queens, staying with her cousin Irene till her time come. 'Back to the world, Peg!' she said. 'Root-beer floats, yellow cabs, the Coney Island Steeple Chase . . .'

I said, 'You are going on a *ride* in your condition?'

'Well . . . no,' she said.

I said, 'And I thought Irene had roaches?'

'Okay, roaches,' she said. 'But what about egg creams? I bid vanilla egg creams against roaches.'

I said, 'I guess there's no point mentioning crime, vermin and high humidity?'

'No,' she said. ''Cause I'll just come right back at you with hot corned beef and Radio City Music Hall.'

I said, 'It must be real hard to drag yourself away from us.'

She was quiet. I could see the gang coming back from the puppet show.

Kath and Gayle were showing off, seeing who could walk on their hands the longest time. That was something I never could get the hang of.

'Well, I'm gonna miss you, Lo,' I said, after a time.

She turned away from me, but she grabbed my hand and took it with her. 'Gonna miss you too,' she said. If I didn't know better, I'd have said Lois Moon had a tear in her eye.

Somebody sighted the sea about two in the afternoon. It was just a strip of silver, far across the sands, but we set off to get a closer look at it. Betty stayed behind with her knitting and Lois was asleep. Kath carried Sandie on her shoulders.

'Lois'll have her work cut out,' she said, 'after that little baby comes along. I could give her a hand. When I'm not at the singling, I could push that little baby out in its pram, sit this one on the top. Give her five minutes.'

I said, 'She won't be here, Kath. She's going back Stateside to have her baby. Then the boys'll get orders, some time in the fall, and we'll be gone too.' I heard my words fall, ruining her plans.

'Oh yes,' she said, 'that's right. I remember that, now.'

Audrey was first to the water's edge.

'Excuse me,' she said, 'I was looking for the rocky shore that beats back the envious siege of watery Neptune? Is that anywhere hereabouts?' Miss Scholastic Quiz Kid.

[81]

That North Sea Ocean or whatever it was called was just creeping across the sand like it could hardly be bothered.

'Is that it, then?' Kath said. 'That's nothing much, is it? The way Harold Jex spoke, I thought that'd be something worth seeing.'

The lagoon at Matagorda was the only thing I had to measure it by, but Audrey said it was a real apology for a shoreline. Still, I liked the smell of it. I liked the cool wet sand under my feet. Crystal was fascinated with some little squiggly lines she found. Audrey said they were worm-casts. Then Gayle showed Sherry how to walk on her hands, so Crystal had to have a go at that too. Kath held her legs in the air, till she found her balance, then she was off, her and Sherry giggling at what we looked like upside down.

Kath said to Deana, 'You want a try?'

Deana said, 'No. We're not allowed. And if Sherry gets sick, then there'll be trouble.'

There was a band playing on the promenade and a little carousel we all rode on, and a stand selling crab claws. We just had so much fun. Looking back, years later, I realised that day was the last time ever we were together, all six of us.

Lois had been improved by her nap. One side of her nose was sunburned, but she was smiling again, walking arm in arm with me and Kath. 'Find me some cotton candy,' she said, 'and I'll make believe I'm at Coney Island.' She started singing 'On the Good Ship Lollipop', and some old bubba sitting on a bench took exception to it.

The English don't care for high levels of noise. One of the first things I learned about them was, they never speak out loud and clear, and they don't like it if others do neither.

'Why don't you stop your caterwauling and git back where you belong?' he said.

'Any day now,' Lois shouted back to him. 'Soon as our brave boys have blown those Russkies outta your back yard. And I wonder how long it'll be till you need us the next time?'

'Ruddy Yanks,' he shouted. He was waving his stick at her. 'Clear off where you come from!'

'Our pleasure, y'old tight-ass.' Lois loved a fight. 'Think we *like* being in this mouseshit country of yours?'

Betty was trying to get the kids into the cars, Deana and Sherry playing up because they didn't want to ride with her, Crystal snivelling because Sandie had gotten taffy on her rabbit mitts.

Lois had to have the last word, of course. 'And another thing,' she shouted. 'You call that an *ocean*?'

I offered to drive in front, knowing what a old lady Betty could be when she got behind a wheel, dithering at every turn she come to, but she insisted she wanted to lead the way. And when I seen her taking that right turn when she should have kept straight ahead, I did my best to stop her. Flashed my beams, got Audrey to lean out and wave her arms around, but she wouldn't be stopped and, even when she knew she'd gone wrong, she still kept going, thought she could cut across country and make good instead of turning back, till we ended up in a barnyard.

She blamed me, of course. Said I'd flustered her, signalling an' all. She also blamed Lois for upsetting everybody with that ugly scene and Audrey for looking smug, like she never took a wrong turn in her life.

'Hey,' Lois said. 'How about Gayle? You ain't blamed her for anything yet. And Kath here. This some kinda discrimination? And you ain't even mentioned General MacArthur.'

'Meanwhile,' Audrey said, under her breath, 'back at USAF Drampton, First Lieutenant Ed Gillis paces the floor . . .'

Soon as we were back on the highway I kept my foot on the gas. Kept checking my mirror, making sure I could still see Betty's worried little face peering out at me. Personally I was in no big hurry to get home. But I did it for Betty, 'cause I kinda knew what she was in for.

Six grown women, travelling in broad daylight, with plenty of good American steel between us and the Cherokee, but we were scurrying home like a bunch of scared kids. Hell, in the end we were only twenty minutes late. Half an hour, max.

25

It was so hot the tarmac was melting. I took back every word I'd said about the English climate. I was over at Lois's with Audrey and Gayle, helping clean out the quarters before she flew home. Herb was going off-base for the remainder of his tour.

When friend husband gets orders and the time comes to clear the post, you better make a good job of it. Quartermaster sergeant comes around, he better not find a speck of grime or your life won't be worth living. That's why we had organised a clean-up party for Lo. Her ankles were all swelled and anyway, she never had much idea about housekeeping.

Crystal was playing out front with the Kurlich kid, gotta a little table Dorothy Kurlich had carried out for them and they were selling Kool-Aid, five cents a cup, strawberry flavour and green.

All of a sudden we heard a woman screaming. I was first out of the door, and there was Betty, standing in the middle of the road, got Sherry in her arms. 'Somebody help me!' she was crying. 'Somebody help me!'

Sherry had a towel wrapped round her foot and it was turning bright red as I looked at it.

'Oh Peggy!' she said, when she saw me. 'She's cut herself so bad. Can you drive me to the dispensary?'

Deana was watching from the door. Crystal come running to the scene, eyes goggling at the gore dripping from Sherry's foot. She said, 'Does she have to be put to sleep? I'm coming to watch.'

I said, 'You're to stay right here with Aunty Gayle and Aunty Lois. You too, Deana.'

Deana shook her head at me, sullen child. She went inside.

Audrey's car was the nearest. She fetched a plaid blanket outta the trunk, spread it across the seat, save it getting stained.

Betty said, 'Oh please hurry! She's losing so much blood.'

Aud said, 'Trust me.'

Like the medic said, a cut toe can look a lot worse than it is. Still, he said he'd put a suture in and give her a tetanus shot, so I took Betty outside, away from the action, and Audrey stayed with Sherry, singing her 'I Know an Old Lady That Swallowed a Fly'.

Betty was kinda grey and shaking.

I said, 'There, now. She's gonna be fine. And when they're through stitching her, y'all can come to my place, get an iced tea. You look like you're in shock.'

She said, 'He took the car keys, Peggy.' She was whispering. 'Ed took the keys, 'cause we were late back from the beach. I couldn't stop her foot bleeding and I couldn't even drive her 'cause he took the keys.' Ed was on assignment. He was gone for five days, same as Vern. She said, 'I know I should have been home when I promised, but I'm in a real fix without the car.'

I said, 'How're you getting your shopping? You walking to the commissary in this heat?'

'No,' she said. 'I have my store cupboard. I always keep a store cupboard.'

They did that at Future Homemakers. Being Prepared for Hurricanes, Twisters and Enemy Invasion.

I said, 'You idiot. Why didn't you get a ride with me? You wanna go later, when Sherry's fixed up? There must be stuff you need.'

She looked down at her feet. 'He took my ID,' she said, real quiet.

DW don't have ID, she can't go anyplace. She may as well not exist. I said, 'Betty, I never heard anything like it. How much more of this are you gonna take?'

'He can't help it,' she said. 'It's just the way he is. He worries

[85]

about his little family. You know? He's doing a tough job out there, and when he gets home he doesn't need more pressure. He needs to know where we are and what we're doing, otherwise he gets in a spin. That's all.'

I said, 'That's *all*?'

Sherry come out in a wheelchair, looking all pleased with herself, foot bound up and a candy bar from the medic for being so brave.

Betty said, 'He's a good man really, Peg.'

Betty wheeled Sherry to the parking lot. I hung back a little, then me and Aud walked behind.

I said, 'Sonofabitch only grounded her. Left her with no car while he's gone. And no ID. It's her punishment for getting home late from the beach. She reckons a jock like Ed, he's under so much pressure when he's flying he can't help turning a little cranky when he gets home.'

'Mm,' Audrey said. 'Course, there's some truth in that.'

I was thinking, it was a pity Betty had spent so much time learning about store cupboards. It was a pity Future Homemakers didn't teach Being Prepared for Bristle-Headed Bullying Husbands.

Then I thought out loud. I said, 'Pity she didn't learn how to swing a bat and hit a moving target.'

'My word!' Audrey said. 'Aren't you the avenging angel? I hope you don't have any ideas about reporting this? It wouldn't look good, you know. It wouldn't look good at all.'

[86]

26

It was Lois's last day. She was all packed and ready for the transport, couldn't wait to get back to the city, even though it'd be like a hothouse. I was meant to be going over to Kath's, let her drive to Smeeth.

Betty said, 'Lois, honey, why don't you go along for the ride? Let me have a last little time with Sandie, I'm gonna miss her so.'

I said, 'Betty, this girl's got a long enough trip ahead of her. Why'd she want to come out driving with me?'

But it was too late. Lo had already decided she liked the idea.

When we got to Kath's, she got outta the car, rubbing her back, saying she couldn't get comfortable, didn't matter which way she sat.

'I'll stay here, Peg,' she said. 'I'll wait here, till you and Kath get back. Maybe take a walk down to the eel reach. I think I just need a little exercise.'

I didn't care to think what kinda exercise she might have in mind. I just said, 'Lois!' Tried to give it a warning tone. I couldn't say more in front of Kath.

'Yes, Peggy?' she said, so insolent.

What was I supposed to do? She was a grown woman. I wasn't her keeper. Anyway, there was no sign of John Pharaoh anywhere about.

I said, 'Well, stay here. Bring a chair out in the sunshine. And don't go wandering off near that water. You fall in, I'll have Herb to answer to.'

'Yes, Mommy,' she said, in a stupid baby voice.

Kath said, 'Help yourself to a glass of pop, Lois, if you get dry. Make yourself at home.'

Kath wanted to go to Dr Lowe's surgery.

I said, 'You feeling okay?'

'Yes, thank you,' she said.

We got to Smeeth, she pulled up outside a public house there, called the Flying Dutchman.

I said, 'Where's the doctor's office?'

'In the snug,' she said. That was the deal in Smeeth. The doctor came once a week and hung his shingle outside the pub.

I was planning on staying in the car, reading my murder mystery.

'No, you'll have to come in with me,' she said. 'I'm not sitting in an ale house on my own.'

There were three waiting ahead of Kath, two Jexes and a Gotobed, sitting in a little bar with the smell of that dark English beer. The doctor was just the other side of a partition, asking somebody to hold their breath and then let it out slow. We could hear every word that was said.

Kath said, 'That's Thad Chaplin in there now. His mother had nine girls. Just kept on going till she got Thad. Can't think why. He's always had a bad chest.'

I kept my head in my book. I figured that was my best hope of Kath falling silent.

'What you here for, Lilian?' she said. But Lilian didn't seem like she wanted to tell.

'Makes no difference,' Kath whispered to me. 'We shall hear soon enough.'

'Kath,' I said, 'I'll be right outside when you're done.'

27

She was happy, driving home with all the windows down. The doctor had given her muscle rub for where she claimed she had a stiff neck.

'We've got the National Health now, you know,' she said. 'We don't have to pay. We can be poorly as often as we like now.'

I said, 'The doctor give you anything reduce the size of your ears?'

She laughed. 'Why,' she said, 'that's a good morning out. Nice little drive. Get a bit of gossip. Lilian's got trouble with her waterworks. Hilda's got ulcerated veins. I tell you what, when you go back home to Yankeeland, I shall have to walk down there.'

The door to the house was open. It usually was.

'This heat,' she said. 'I don't know about you, but I'm parched. Come on in. I've got a bottle of dandelion-and-burdock fizzy pop or Tizer.'

Something was wrong. The oilcloth was pulled halfway off the table and the teapot and a cup lay smashed on the floor. There was no sign of Lois.

'Now what?' she said. 'John Pharaoh! Now what have you gone and done? Look at my teapot. That's in pieces. Look at it, Peg. That's in smithereens. I'll have his hide.'

She must have heard something outside because she turned on her heel and pushed past me. I followed her, round the other side of the house, where he kept his traps, and there they were. Lois, with that

[89]

high colour she got so easy. He had her pinned up against the back wall, looked like some kinda spear he had in his hands, evil-looking prongs on the end, pressing right up against her belly.

His head was jerking around, spittle flying outta his mouth, and Lois had her eyes closed. I believe she was preparing to meet her maker.

Kath grabbed John from behind, pulled him off balance. Then she pushed him away from Lois with the shaft of the spear.

'Drop that now, John Pharaoh,' she said. 'Drop it or I'll give you what for.' She had gotten herself between him and Lois. 'Get her out of here,' she said to me. 'Now leave go of this glave, John. Leave go of it. You don't behave yourself, you'll have to be took away and locked up.'

Lois ran for the car. 'That's right,' Kath called after her. 'You clear off out of here. You must have done something, get him all worked up like this.'

He'd allowed her to take the spear outta his hands, but he still had a wild-eyed look about him. I didn't want to leave her there alone with him, but I sure didn't want to stay neither.

I said, 'Kath?'

'Just get her out of my sight,' she said. 'Go on. Clear off, the both of you.'

Last thing I saw as I looked back was Kath pushing John into the house. She had the eel-glave in her hand. She looked like she was in charge. His head was down and he had a kinda defeated look about him. Except for his hands. I could see them, twitching, twitching.

I drove back to Drampton. Lois didn't speak. Neither did I. I felt sick to my heart. I didn't even look at her till we were parked outside Betty's.

'Pair of throwbacks,' she said. 'My God, what a pair!' She was pretending to laugh it off, but she was shaken, I could tell.

I said, 'You should never have gone there. You knew he might show up.'

Crystal come running out with Deana Gillis. 'We made a Farewell for you,' she said to Lo. 'We made cake and everything.'

Then they ran back in, to tell Betty the guest of honour had arrived.

I said, 'You sure do like to make the big exit, don't you. You afraid folks might forget you, if you just go nice and quiet? What happened? You ask him for one last roll in the hay?'

'Peggy,' she said, 'I swear, I couldn't have rode in that car another minute, and I was just minding my own business, sitting out on the grass in the sunshine, when he come along and started in on me. He's some kinda crazy.'

I said, 'Well, it's a pity you didn't work that out sooner. I mean, if me and Kath hadn't turned up when we did, I reckon you'd have been skewered, you and that poor child you're carrying. You ever think of that? You ever think of poor Herb? You ever consider Kath?'

She started getting outta the car. 'Hell, Peggy,' she said, 'how's it feel to be so goddarned perfect?'

Betty was at the door in her sweetheart apron. She was carrying Sandie on her hip, smiling and waving. Little did she know what Lois was hissing at me under her breath.

'You and the Pie-Crust Queen there, and Mrs Audrey "when we get to be Captains" Rudman. The whole lotta you just drive me nuts.'

She slammed her door. I slammed mine. Then we went into Betty's and sat around drinking coffee, like nothing had happened. I kept thinking of Kath, though, on her own out there with that madman. It was all right for Lois. She was gonna climb aboard that transport and leave all her troubles behind.

There were gifts for the baby. Cute little things Gayle had knitted and a kinda rag doll Betty had made for Sandie. Real neat. Betty was so clever with her hands.

Lo was fooling around. She sang 'I'll Be Seeing You', close harmony with Gayle, and we drank her good health in Canadian Club. Wished her a happy landing and a baby with a small head.

Everyone was sad to see her go. Even me. Darned if I could say why.

28

Four weeks passed by and I didn't see Kath. I wanted to go up there, straighten things out between us, but I was scared he'd be there, waiting to skewer any callers. The eels were finished for the year, so Vern had stopped going too – and I never dared tell him what had happened that day. He ever found out, Herb'd have heard about it. Hell, there could have been a lynching.

Month of September, Vern was flying night sorties so I hardly seen him. Suited me. We didn't talk much any more. He was doing things he couldn't tell me, top secret, he reckoned, and even when he wasn't, I hated all that jock stuff, talking like bad things could never happen to him up there, like he was untouchable, or if they did, that he had what it took to get himself outta trouble. I guess that's the kinda arrogance it took to climb into one of those death traps every day. Didn't make good pillow talk, though.

And me, I just didn't have anything much to say. Never went anywhere. Hardly did anything. Lorene Bass's cosmetics party. Bake Sale at the OWC. That was my action-packed life. With Lois gone, there weren't too many laughs neither.

Then one day I smelled that sickly old sugar-beet smell and I knew the harvest had started. Only time of the year John Pharaoh was in paid employment, far as I knew, so I figured there was a good chance I could see Kath without running into him.

There'd been a hard frost, first one of the fall. But I could see her, as I come along the drove, sitting outside the door in that red windbreaker Lois gave her, working at something. Soon as she heard the car, she jumped to her feet.

'I thought you'd gone,' she said.

I said, 'I wouldn't have gone without saying goodbye.'

'No ... well ...' she said, 'I spoke very harsh to you last time ... when we had the upset ...'

I said, 'Hey! It's forgotten.'

'No, but I shouldn't have done it,' she said, 'after all your kindness. It was copper-knob I was mad at. Not you.'

I said, 'Let's just forget it ever happened.'

'I'll make a brew,' she said. 'Only I'm sitting out here, 'cause I'm peeling these onions. I'm making piccalilli, go with the eels. But do you get that smell in the counterpane you can't shift it anyhow.'

I said, 'How're things with you?'

She knew what I meant. 'Yes,' she said, 'right as ninepence.'

Then she said, 'Copper-knob had that little baby yet?'

'No,' I said. 'Not till Christmas-time. And now we've got another one on the way. Betty's expecting.'

She thought about that for a minute. 'You'd have thought she'd have been more careful,' she said.

But Betty was thrilled. She'd been on at Ed about it, ever since Sherry was born. Kidded him she'd found out a sure way of getting a boy next time, douching with baking powder or somesuch.

'I swear,' Lois had said, when Betty was trying to explain how it worked, 'she's a one-off. She's the only woman I ever met found a way of combining sex and baking. Keep your eye on her, Peg. She sounds like Vern's dream woman.'

Kath finished putting the pickles in brine and we went out driving, just like old times. She took a turn behind the wheel and we went all around, Smeeth, Beck Warren, Brakey, so she could give all the peasants her royal wave, show them she couldn't only drive, she could do it one-handed.

She slowed right down when we got to May Gotobed's. There was laundry hanging on a line, must have been out all night, sheets and skivvies frozen like boards.

Kath laughed. 'Look at her drawers, all frez,' she said. 'They look like they're made out of wood.' There was no sign of May. She said, 'She only hangs them out to show them off. She thinks owning a pair of bloomers makes her a cut above.'

We drove on. 'I don't know why she bothers,' she said. 'That only makes for extra washing and I know for a fact she never had none till she went into service.'

I said, 'Are you telling me there are women round here don't wear undies?'

'Too stifling,' she said.

We passed one of the little trains hauling beets up to the factory. 'John working?' I said.

'Yes,' she said. 'He's on the unloading at Mayday. He had a bit of a setback, you know, after that business with the glave. I thought he might not be straight in time for the campaign, then we'd have been in a fix. We'd have missed that money. But he's pulled through. I made him stay on the bed, nice and quiet, and he's pulled through.

'Peggy,' she said, 'I hope you won't take this amiss . . .' She hesitated. 'Do you think,' she said, 'there could have been a bit of carrying on, with copper-knob and John Pharaoh?'

You can think a thing over many times and still have no idea how you'll answer the question, if ever it's asked. I said, 'Do you think so?'

'I asked first,' she said. 'Do I turn along Hiss Drove, we can come up along the back, go and call on Audrey and little Gayle?'

They called it Hiss Drove on account there was river otters along there, cute little things, and if you were real careful and quiet you could see them playing in the mud. Audrey had showed me one time. But if they caught wind of you, they'd start hissing and whistling – like sounding the alarm, I suppose.

Eventually I said, 'I don't know, Kath. Lois is a law unto herself. As for John, well . . . you'd know better than anyone.'

She nodded.

I said, 'Whatever, she's gone. She won't be back.'

She parked nice and tidy, outside Audrey and Gayle's place.

Gayle come bouncing out. 'You hear?' she said 'We're going home! Okey's got orders. Wichita, Kansas. November fifteenth. Vern heard anything yet? Lance didn't.'

There was more to that than met the eye.

29

They all got orders, excepting Lance. He made Captain, so him and Audrey moved into quarters on base, some ways down from us, or up from us, in a manner of speaking, farther away from the whine of the jets.

'Farther away from the scraping of cheap flatware,' as Lois wrote me. 'Six weeks to go and I'm about the size of King Kong. Irene reckons they'll have to knock down a wall to get me out of here. I told her not to worry. My waters go, like they did with Sandie, they'll take the whole building with them.'

Betty was blooming, making lists and advising me on the correct way to clear a billet.

'Start at the top and work down,' she said. 'You'd be amazed how dust does settle on drapes.'

Vern and the rest of them had drawn Temporary Duty to Smoky Hill, through April, then on to Wichita, training on the B-47s. It was all the same to me. Killing time till he come in off assignment. Killing time till he went back. Waiting for my life to start happening. I looked at it this way: at least I'd be waiting on the right side of the Atlantic Ocean.

Most days me and Gayle'd meet for a Pepsi, and sometimes Betty'd come along too.

'My, we're like the ten little nigger boys,' she said. 'And then there were three.'

She was down at the laundry all hours, freshening up her baby clothes and diapers even though she had months and months to go.

'Peggy,' she said to me one time. 'Why don't you and Vern have another one? Be company for Crystal. I always think it must be a tragic thing to be a lonely only.'

There was nothing tragic about Crystal. She was out roller-skating in all weathers. Then she'd come in, all red-faced from the cold, and eat everything I put in front of her. She was like her daddy in that respect. He'd have ate skunk, as long as it was under a pie crust.

Come bedtime, she'd say her prayers like she'd learned in school and she'd settle down, her rabbit-fur mitts on the pillow next to her, and her skates where she could see them. She never gave me a speck a trouble, even when Vern was away. Not like the Gillis girls, always having nightmares and climbing in with Betty the minute Ed was gone.

I said, 'No, Betty. I'm done with babies. Some day I'd like to do something with my life, instead of mopping the same patch of floor day after day. I have another brat now, that'll set me back six years.'

'But you *are* doing something,' she said. 'You're caring for a highly skilled aviator. You don't take care of him, he can't do his job and next thing you know, those Russians'll be ruling the world.'

Funny enough, I'd been giving some thought to Vern not being able to do his job. Not the way Betty meant. Him losing his edge 'cause he wasn't getting enough pie. Augering in because I couldn't get rid of the ring around the tub. I wasn't buying that. But his sinuses were causing him trouble. Change of altitude and he was in agony some days. He had swore me to secrecy, of course. Any doubts like that about a man, he can wave goodbye to promotion. So it'd started me wondering, if it really came to it, that he couldn't be of further use to the United States Air Force, how we'd get by.

'Know what I do?' Betty said. 'Every morning when I look in the mirror to fix my hair, I say to myself, Betty Gillis, just think of that young Queen Elizabeth of England. She's pledged to put duty first, the rest of her life. Now you do the same.'

Two days before we were due out on the transports, I took Kath driving one last time. We saw swans flying in, low, come all the way

[97]

from Russia, according to Audrey, to get away from the Russian weather. It was a sobering thought that there were worse places to spend November than Drampton. If you were a swan.

I said to Kath, 'Do you know, all the places we've been posted, I never made a friend before. Somebody from outside, like you.'

She said, 'What I've seen of that base you're on, you don't hardly need to venture outside the fence. You could live inside there and never bother with what's outside.'

I said, 'I'm glad I did, though.'

'Yes,' she said. 'I'm glad you did too. And I hope we'll still be pals. Send Christmas cards.'

I said, 'And who knows, maybe some day you'll come and visit? See how we do things.'

'What?' she said 'In America?'

I said, 'Sure. You'd love it.'

'That's across the sea,' she said. 'I can't see that coming off. Not unless we come up on the Pools.'

I said, 'You know Audrey's staying on? You might see her.'

'Well,' she said, 'she knows where to find me.'

I said, 'Anything you'd care for from the commissary? Last chance for Almond Joys.'

'No, thank you,' she said, 'but that was nice while it lasted. And I hope I didn't speak out of turn, about copper-knob. I mean to say, I liked her really. She had a bit of spark about her, didn't she? That's the thing, though. It's the sparky ones you got to keep an eye on. And you can't watch a man twenty-four hours a day.'

I said, 'Kath, don't give it another thought.'

'I won't,' she said.

And that was how we parted. I would have liked to tell her how much I was gonna miss her, but you have to watch your step with the English, that you don't overstep the mark.

I kissed her goodbye.

'Cheerio, then,' she said. 'And all the best. I hope you go on all right.'

30

Me and Crystal were back in Converse, Texas, for Thanksgiving of '52, in the bosom of my loving family. I wish I could say it was a happy occasion, but my sister Connie was there, always got some hard-luck story, and there wasn't no killing of the fatted turkey on my account. Matter of fact, it was Swanson's TV Dinners all round, and Crystal, being cussed, had to start with dessert, burned her mouth on the apple pie.

She was having a tough time of it anyhow from her Gramma Shea. My mother, who had never showed a ounce of interest in her only granddaughter, said she couldn't understand a word the child said since she'd been away among foreigners. I don't think Mom or Connie had the first idea where we'd been. If it was east of Texarkana, they just shook their heads.

I stayed down there through Christmas. It wasn't what I wanted, but there was no quarters ready for us up in Kansas and the Sheraton penthouse suite was already took. Vern blew in on a four-day pass, looking for a little action, seeing as we'd been apart so long. It didn't deter him I was on the couch and Crystal was right there, in two easy-chairs pushed together.

'Tell your Mom we gotta have the other bedroom,' he said. But we couldn't. Connie had to have that, for her bad back. Ask me, the only problem she had with her back was getting it up off the mattress.

It felt like we were sleeping in Santa's Grotto, all the glittering stuff my mom liked to deck the place with. Anything that didn't move got tinsel. Connie sat around so much I wouldn't have been surprised to come in and find her covered with twinkling lights.

Christmas Eve, I said to Vern, 'I wonder how Lois is doing. She's due any day now.'

'Oh yeah,' he said. 'Meant to tell you. It's a boy.'

I'd have loved to call her up, but of course friend husband didn't know where she'd be. If she was back at her cousin Irene's, that was no help, 'cause I didn't have an address or even Irene's name. And if they'd gone up to Herb's folks, I doubt they even had the telephone there.

I said, 'Everything go all right?'

'I guess,' he said.

I asked how much he weighed and Vern said how the heck would he know. I asked did he have a name yet.

'Yup,' he said. '. . . It'll come to me.'

I said, 'Herb happy?'

'Like the cat that got the canary,' he said. 'You wanna mess around?'

After Christmas Vern was back at Smoky Hill on instrument training. We were promised quarters at Wichita within the month.

I said to him, 'I don't know I can stand another night on this couch. I might see if I can get a rental.'

'You stay where you are,' he said. 'You think we got money to burn? What's wrong with you anyhow? Wives like going home to see their mom.'

So most days me and Crystal roamed the mall. There wasn't anything we needed and there wasn't much we could afford, but it beat sitting indoors listening to sister Connie's catalogue of woes.

She used to say, 'Everything always went your way, Peggy. I'm the one had all the bad luck in this family. Only way I can look at it, though, if my failing health hadn't brung me back here, Mom'd be all on her own.'

Meanwhile Mom was working on the loose-meat counter in Avery's, setting her cap at anything in trousers that showed signs of life.

I ran into Arlene Wilday one time. We were getting malted milks, Crystal perched on a stool seeing how much racket she could make drinking through a straw, when I heard someone say, 'Peggy Shea? Is it you?'

I used to hang out with Arlene sometimes when we were in elementary school, but by the time we got to eighth grade we had come to the parting of the ways, she being a keen member of Sewing Club and me having sporting ambitions.

She said, 'This your little girl? My, she's cute!'

Crystal never left off making gurgling sounds with her straw.

Arlene had married Ted Pickett. I remembered the name, but I couldn't picture the face. She said he was in hardware now.

'You remember Junior Chorus, Peggy?' she said. 'You remember standing next to me?'

I didn't remember that. She sang a little of 'Burro Bells in the Moonlight' and then it kinda came back to me.

She told me Jim Sparks never came home from Korea, which I didn't know, and the Siro twins were both still single, living at home with Mrs Siro, which didn't surprise me.

I said, 'You keep up with Betty Glick?'

Arlene and Betty had been leading lights of Future Homemakers. Used to do food sales, Saturday mornings outside the Glad Tidings church. She was thrilled to hear all about Betty's exciting life. Gave me her address and made me promise faithfully to pass it along.

She said, 'You tell her, I expect pictures of her little family.'

Arlene and Ted had had a boy. Lost him with poliomyelitis in the summer of 1950. I didn't rightly know what to say, after she told me that.

January fifteenth, me and Crystal were on a transport out of Randolph AFB up to Wichita. Betty was there ahead of me, got quarters right across the road from us. Ed had driven her down from his folks' place in Indiana. Eight hundred miles with Deana and Sherry getting sick and Betty needing the bathroom and Ed holding a bad opinion of every other driver on the road. Took more than that to get Betty Gillis down though. By the time I hit town, she was waddling around, size of a house already, putting up nice fresh drapes.

Wichita was just another cinderblock row, but life was sweeter, being back in the world. We had a base school and a brand-new laundromat and a great commissary, and if there was something else we wanted, drug store, movies, all we had to do was drive into town. Made me realise what a wearing thing it had been, getting posted to a backward country. Audrey was welcome to stay on at Drampton. Heck, Kansas wasn't much, but at least folk there smiled and stood tall.

Gayle arrived the day after me and got quarters next door. She was so thrilled to have good dry American closets and wipeable counter-tops. I'd never seen her looking so happy. I don't believe she was drinking at all. There was a letter waiting for me from Lois.

'We decided on Kirk,' she wrote.

Kirk Herbert. I was only in labour two hours, but then I got after-pains and milk fever, so I've paid my dues. My child-bearing days are through. We're on a transport February third, so start getting the tickertape parade ready. Been in Hoosick since December, so I'll be the one wearing the strait-jacket, in case you forgot what I look like. Also, Herb's mom believes in two weeks' lying-in and a stack of maple syrup pancakes three times a day to make up for iron-loss, so I have SPREAD. You could land a B-36 on my rear. Then she had me churched. That's another story.

31

Betty insisted on organising the Hail 'n' Welcome for Lois.

I said, 'Just a coffee'll do. Lois won't expect home-baking.'

But she was already under way, flour in her hair. It would have been like trying to stop a Cunard liner. She sent me round to see if Herb needed a hand. Their boxes had come and he was meant to be turning a house into a home.

'If Herb's anything like Ed, all he's done is rigged up the TV and filled the icebox with Schlitz,' she said.

Of course, Herb Moon wasn't anything like Ed.

He'd made a rocking crib for Kirk and a little rocking horse for Sandie. I helped him unpack a few pieces. Plates and stuff. Lauhala mats from the time they were at Hickam Field. A hula doll. The carved giraffe-type dachshund.

'Can't wait to get my little family all together again,' he said. 'Where I know they're safe. You hear about Drampton?'

I hadn't heard anything. I'd been in Betty Gillis's kitchen watching her make refrigerator cake.

'Floods twenty foot deep,' he said. 'Ten dead. Ax Bergstrom's missing.'

Lo was looking great in spite of her incarceration with the in-laws. She come round to Betty's as soon as she'd fed the baby, Sandie clinging on to her leg, peeping round at us, like she'd never seen us before.

'My, how she has grown!' Betty said. 'That country living has done her good.'

'Yeah,' Lois said. 'She's learned the difference between an elk and a moose. And her Uncle Ivan's taught her to *hawk* real good . . .'

I said, 'Anybody heard about the sea flooding in at Drampton?'

Lo said, 'Yeah, Herb told me. Hundreds dead.'

Gayle said, 'Not Americans, though.'

I said, 'Herb told me Bergstrom was missing.'

'Now, now,' Betty said, 'we don't want to spoil the party. Nothing we can do. And I'm sure the CO will have everything under control there.'

Lois said, '. . . And when I've unpacked my bags, remind me to let you have Herb's mom's recipe for fried squirrel.'

I said, 'What about Audrey and Lance, and 366? What about Kath and John Pharaoh? You guys sure have short memories.'

Betty said, 'Peggy! Well, what do you expect us to do? If there's news, I'm sure we'll hear it. Now, clear a space on the table, because those pigs-in-blankets are ready to eat.'

'You found a good bowling alley yet?' Lois had kinda hit the tarmac running, baby or no baby.

Betty said, 'You should be resting. Childbirth and travelling and setting up home again. You don't get some rest, you'll regret it.'

Lois said, 'If I rest any more, I'll take root. Besides, I'm worried if I stand still, Herb'll put me on carved rockers.'

I held Kirk in my arms a while, smelled his milky, soapy little head. Watched his little fingers weaving dreams.

'Well?' she said. 'Who'd you think he looks like?'

Darned if I knew.

Herb's Mom's Fried Squirrel, As Told to Lois

••

*Clean out the squirrel and rub it with salt. Cut it in
pieces. Roll it in flour and pepper. Fry it in a skillet till
it's brown. If the squirrel is long in the tooth, make a
brown gravy with the drippings, return the squirrel meat
to the pan and smother until done.*

So sweet it will bring tears to your eyes.

••

32

Vern said it was the ocean had come flooding in, just like he always said it would. Then I couldn't sleep.

'Chrissakes, Peg!' he said. 'Will you quit tossing and turning.'

There were airmen missing from the base at Walsh. Bergstrom had turned up safe, didn't realise there was a search party out looking for him. But it was Kath I wondered about, in her tumbledown house.

I wrote Audrey soon as I heard, asked her for news. Our letters crossed.

'We'd had two days of rain,' she wrote,

and high winds, and Tuesday night there were men up on the canal banks with oil lamps, watching for any sign of flooding. Still, when it came, it came so fast it caught us out. Twelve missing from the base at Walsh, no bodies recovered so far but they've given up on finding any of them alive. Bergstrom was reported missing from Drampton, but he's accounted for. There's a story going round he was in Fairford, in bed with a war widow, but you didn't hear that from me.

Kath and John are safe, but they lost their house. Lance was out on one of the search parties Wednesday morning and he said beyond Smeeth it was just like a lake. He made enquiries and the Pharaohs were evacuated to Walsh. Good job you taught Kath to speak American! I'll try to get over there some time, see if there's anything they need.

There were twelve enlisted washed away near Hunstanton. I never would have believed that trickle of water we paddled in could have turned so powerful. Those Wherry cabins by the school were smashed to matchwood.

Seems like things were even worse further down the coast. Five hundred missing near London and they've been finding bodies in trees. One report said an eight-foot wall of water had swept in at high tide. It just doesn't seem like the kind of thing that should happen in England. It's been kind of exciting for those of us that didn't lose any loved ones, but probably not as exciting as Wichita once Lois Moon arrives in town. Anyway, Holland has had it much worse. They have water forty feet deep in some places. Tell Betty, Queen Juliana of the Netherlands is going around in rubber boots, visiting the afflicted.

Pregnancy had kinda taken Betty's mind off royalty. Once she'd brung out all those layettes, packed away since she had Sherry, and crocheted a new shawl, the bloom seemed to go off her. Her fingers swelled up so bad she had to get her wedding band cut off. Then she got acid indigestion and varicose veins, but she would struggle on, ironing and starching all those frills she dressed her girls in, and fixing chicken-fried steak for Ed whatever hour of the day he showed up.

She hardly ever minded Sandie any more, just when Lois could really have used some help. Kirk was a grizzling child, always hungry, and Sandie had taken a disliking to him. The minute Lois was busy, changing his diaper or bathing him, Sandie'd start up, peppering the floor with baby powder or climbing up on the counter-top, helping herself to cookies or rat poison or something. Then Lo'd start hollering.

It was usually Gayle stepped into the breach. Sometimes she'd take Sandie, push her on a swing for a while. Sometimes she'd take both of them. Drive them around till Kirk fell asleep.

'I'll do it while I can,' she used to say. 'Once we get our own little baby, I won't have the time.'

She hadn't fallen yet, but God knows they were trying. I never met a pair spent so much time in the sack. And she'd started collecting a few things, little bassinet covers and shawls and stuff. She even got a second-hand stroller from a girl who was clearing the post, husband going back into civvies.

'Well, why ever'd you let her do that?' Betty said. She seemed to think, just because she had to rest up with swollen ankles, I was supposed to take over supervising everybody's lives.

'Why, Peggy,' she said, 'bringing items like that into the house before the baby's born and safe in your arms, before it's even on the way, that's just inviting bad luck. Any fool knows that.'

I liked having Gayle next door. She didn't mind how many times Crystal hit her ball over the fence. She'd just hit it back. Ask her if she wanted a popsicle.

Okey put a basket hoop in their back yard, so Vern was round there every chance he got. Sometimes Okey'd come calling for him to go out and play. Twenty-two, going on thirteen. He'd stand in the doorway, shy about stepping inside, and he'd bounce the ball, kerdunk, kerdunk, kerdunk, till Vern had gobbled down his food. They'd fool around till it was too dark to see the hoop and then they'd just sit out there, and Gayle'd sit with them, Okey's gangling arms wrapped around her, listening to all that talk about combat ceilings and take-off ground-runs.

There was a Combat Crew Training Wing rotating through Wichita, first six months we were there. That was where I met Pearl Petie and Ida Batten. I was glad to see some new faces. Some days I felt like I'd spent my whole life drinking Cola with Betty Gillis, watching her clip coupons.

Once a week Lois'd leave Kirk and Sandie with Gayle and we'd drive into Wichita with Pearl and Ida, see a movie. Far as Ida and Pearl were concerned, me and Lois were some kinda heroines, having been posted to England and lived to tell the tale. Sometimes, under that big Kansas sky, I could almost have been back in Norfolk. Then I'd look around me, see all those sparkling American smiles, and I'd remember.

'Yup,' Lois said. 'You had to be the pioneering type, no two ways. Outside of that perimeter fence, it was a wilderness. We nearly got ambushed one time, remember, Peg?' She winked at me. 'We took the brats to the sea shore, just quietly minding our own business, and we got this bunch of natives surrounded us. If you and Betty hadn't drove away fast, they'd have overturned the cars.'

Pearl and Ida were lapping it up.

'Envy,' Lo said. 'You ever have the misfortune to get sent there, you'll find envy is a big problem. See, they know we got the best of everything. Over there everything is nickels and dimes. And old. Whole darned place needs pulling down and starting over. They got roads been there since the Romans, must be a hundred years old. Two hundred.'

We had been at the Cowtown Drive-In to see *Creature from the Black Lagoon*. Reminded me of Vern climbing outta the shower. When I got home, there was the letter I had been hoping for, from Norfolk, England.

'Well, as you heard,' she wrote, 'we have had a bit of excitement.' Typical Kath.

We had terrible floods, hundreds of people drowned, some of them your lot. I told John Pharaoh we should have to get out but he didn't want to leave his traps. Then of course there was the dog. But the water kept on coming and that was blowing a gale. I said to him if that kept up we should have to clamber up on the roof, and we did have to. We were up there hours and I nearly fell in. I nearly fell asleep and dropped off that roof. My knees were all scraped. And when it got light, all you could see was water.

I thought we were goners, Peg. I said a prayer or two. Any road, then along come a row boat, with Nev Jex and two nice Yankee boys. They fetched us down and took us to Walsh. We had a lovely time there even though they had troubles of their own. They put us up in folding beds in the Officers' Club, gave us stockings and aspirins and anything we needed, and we had fizzy drinks and hot meat dinners. It was a proper holiday, I can tell you.

Annie Howgego was in the bed next to me, worriting about her house, how she'd ever get it dried out, everything ruined, but I couldn't have cared less. I said to John Pharaoh when we were up on that roof, main thing was, not to get swept away. As long as you've got breath in your body, you can always make another eel grig. And if indoors got ruined, we'd just have to get our names down for a council house. If I'd had my way we'd have had our names down anyway, because that can take years. When the waters went down we hadn't got a house to go back to anyway. Dog was gone as well, of course, but she was thirteen so she'd had a good innings. She never did like water.

Audrey come out looking for us while we were at Walsh. She gave me money. She said that was from you and her which brought a tear to my eye, to think what kind friends you've been. I was going to put it in the Savings Bank because that'll come in handy when we get a place of our own again, but then I thought better of it, everybody in the Post Office knowing your business, so I've kept it tucked inside my brassiere. That'll be as safe as the Bank of England in there.

We're in huts at Adderley, used to be a POW camp, till the housing people find us somewhere and we've got all lovely new things, blankets and frying pans, sent in by people. Toys for the ones with kiddies, and nice warm coats. You should see the good stuff they give away. They say the Queen might be coming to see us, tell Betty. And one of your boys is getting the George Medal for rescuing trapped people. Anyone says a bad word about the Yanks, they'll soon get the rough edge of my tongue.

Well, I hope this letter finds you in good health. I expect you're glad to be back with your own kind. I expect Kansas must be a bigger place than Brakey. Anyhow, I wish you all the best. I should like to hear how you're all going on.

Yours faithfully, your friend Kath Pharaoh.

P.S. John Pharaoh had a bad turn, must have been brought on by clinging to that roof waiting to get drowned. The man from the council said he might get disabled money, if he's not fit for work. He's getting us the forms.

I said to Lois, 'You know Kath and John lost everything they had? Sea came in and took it all away.'

'That so?' she said. 'Well that'll be a tough one for the loss-adjuster.'

Then she heard Gayle and Betty were knitting blanket squares to send, so she slipped me a few bucks.

She said, 'We're a bit short, but if you're sending stuff to Kath . . .'

33

Vern and the boys were training on a plane called the Stratojet. Could top 600mph and carry 20,000 pounds of bombs, with rocket-assisted take-off capability if extra thrust was required. This was the kinda talk we had at our dinner table.

Funny thing, I never was interested in aviation and I hardly knew a Thunderjet from a horsefly, but there was something pretty about the B-47. I guess Vern thought so too, amount of time he spent down at the hangars. She had thin wings, real delicate-looking and swept back. He told me he'd seen them bend and quiver, when they hit a jet stream at high altitude one time.

Also, of course, she could be refuelled in flight, and she was capable of delivering death and destruction to a whole bunch of Reds. All in all, he thought she was a real babe.

She had a tendency to roll on take-off, but hell, those jocks loved that. I believe they probably prayed for strong cross-winds on days they were going up, so they could show they had what it took to keep that little lady under control.

'Takes an extra helping of standard male insanity to make an aviator.' That was Pearl Petie's theory. She was one of the few willing to discuss the facts of air force life. Betty would just change the subject. Lo'd turn up the radio. Gayle seemed like she had got the jitters under control, but Lois said she knew different. She reckoned when Okey was flying, Gayle was drinking.

She said, 'She just holds it better than she used to. She ever gets this baby we keep hearing about, he's not gonna want formula. He's gonna be looking for pints of Jack Daniel's.'

Like Pearl said, it might be a good thing for the free world, our boys being willing to risk their necks, but it sure was hard on family life. 'Thing is, Peg,' she said, 'if they didn't convince themselves they're indestructible, they'd never fly another mission. Things they get up to in those tin cans, they have to believe they're gods. It's no wonder they have a hard time of it when they come home, have to mix with mortals. Get asked to drag out the garbage once in a while. You ever been around when one of them buys the farm? You ever listened to them? We were at Castle, California, and one of Walt's squadron didn't make it, had a loose connector on his oxygen hose or something, nose-dived into the desert. You shoulda heard them. This guy, used to be their big buddy, one of the indestructibles. All of a sudden he's some kinda idiot, didn't check his hose-connector. You know? Aviator doesn't stay on the ball, doesn't notice he's getting a little light-headed 'cause his oxygen's leaking, he has it coming. I tell you. They think they're too darned superior to just luck out and get sent home in a box. I'm just resigned to it. Every time Walt flies a sortie and comes home safe, I count it as a bonus.'

That was pretty much my outlook on life. I was kinda hanging on in there, thinking Vern might quit. His sinus trouble was getting worse, on account of the B-47s doing real steep climbs. And though we weren't exactly love's young dream, still, I didn't want to be left a widow. What he'd do if he quit, though, that was the big question. Unless he could find somebody to pay him to go fishing.

It was our day for the movies. Gayle was minding Sandie and Kirk, taking them out to a petting zoo near Watson Park so Sandie could feed the ducks. Me, Ida, Pearl and Lois drove into town, but *African Queen* was showing again and I was in a minority of one willing to watch it a third time. So we got burgers and root beer and just moseyed around the stores. Lo wanted a sweater, like the one she'd seen Marilyn Monroe wearing on the front of *Moviegoer* magazine, but the way the old biddy looked at us in Drew's Drapers, I got the impression the real tight-fitting look hadn't arrived yet in Wichita.

Pearl said, 'Lo, why don't you just hot-wash one you already have? Never fails.'

We seen the smoke as we crossed the Gypsum River. Nobody said anything, but Ida drove a little faster. By the time we got to the base we could smell burned rubber, and fuel and other things too. Everything was quiet though. The crash trucks had already gone down, and military don't gather in the street, waiting on bad news. They stay home, stand by their telephone.

Ours had been ringing out. It stopped just as I come through the door. I tried Betty. Her line was busy. I tried Gayle, she wasn't home yet. It was nearly time to pick up Crystal from school, but I wasn't really thinking of that. I wasn't thinking anything much. All I knew was, I wanted to keep on the move. If there was bad news on the way, I didn't want to be an easy target.

I was nearly out the door when the phone went again. It was Betty. She sounded real tense.

'Where were you?'

'In town. You heard anything?'

'Nothing. I don't like it. Why don't you call the squadron office?'

Wives did not call the squadron office.

I said, 'Betty, you want that call made, you do it.'

'I'm not allowed,' she said. 'I ever called around, checking up on him, Ed'd kill me.'

I said, 'Tell you what. Why don't we both get off the line? Give Ed and Vern the chance to call home personally and put us out of our misery?'

I paced around some, then I ignored my own advice and called Pearl.

'You hear anything yet?'

She missed a beat. 'Well . . .' she said, 'the word down here is, it's a crew from 96th. But, honey, don't take my word.'

I sat down.

'Peg?' she said. 'Want me to pick up Crystal? I have to get Ritchie anyhow. Peg?'

I didn't wanna stay indoors. If somebody said they *thought* it was 96th, then it *was* 96th. The odds against Vern Dewey coming home safe had shortened. That's when I started trying to cut a deal with God.

Betty had heard the same rumour. She was mopping her floors when I got over there. She stopped to pour iced tea, but neither of us touched it. We didn't even talk. I was just going over things in my mind, see if there had been any omens. Trying to remember the last thing Vern had said to me. And Betty kept mopping, mopping. When her phone rang, we both jumped a mile. Then Betty just froze.

'You get it,' she said.

I got it.

Lois said, 'Peg? Is that you? I could have swore I dialled Betty's number.'

Lo had been out looking for Gayle and failed to find her, but she'd seen Dewitt Haas, meant to be on a rest day but he was on his way down to the pad, and he'd heard it was a B-47, no survivors. That meant three men.

He'd also heard, not confirmed, it was a major, a first LT and a non-com. It was tight inside a Stratojet, I knew. Just the pilot and co-pilot, one behind the other, and the navigator in the nose section.

'I'm coming over,' Lois said. 'Might as well go out of our minds together.'

I went out on to the front yard to wait for her, and Betty come as far as the doorstep, and then there was Lo, striding across the street, and Gayle cruising along in her old Ford, waving and tooting, not even realising an incident had occurred, and coming the other way, two faces nobody ever wanted to see. Chaplain Major Lawrence Conyers. And Mrs Lieutenant Colonel Shelby Munt, Friend of Widows and Orphans.

34

Landing a B-47 was a finely judged thing. This was a well-known fact. The undercarriage was dropped, to act like a air brake, so the plane would lose altitude fast, but the flaps weren't lowered until the final approach. First problem was keeping its speed down somewhere in between stalling and running outta tarmac and that depended on how light she was, coming in from a sortie, low on fuel. Then, once you had her down, there was the problem of keeping her down. The main wheels were mounted in tandem and if they didn't touch down together, she'd bounce right back up off the runway. If that happened, main thing was to avoid trying for a go-around, because you probably didn't have the acceleration to succeed. She was fitted with a extra drogue, so they could maintain power and still come to a halt, kinda having your cake and eating it, but even so. That day the senior officer was bringing her in, not so used to handling her skittish ways as his co-pilot. He deployed the drag chute, bounced her, one wing dipped, he used too much rudder and over she went, 6,000 gallons of fuel inside her and three good men.

Captain John Deacon. First Lieutenant Carl 'Okey' Jackson. Warrant Officer Lyle Clark.

3 5

We took turns sitting with her. When you held her in your arms, she felt like a little bird. I got home from one of my sessions, Vern had bust the bathroom mirror with his fist.

I said, 'You all right?'

'I am now,' he said.

I never seen him cry, but there was plenty going on inside.

Ida loaned Gayle a black coat. I went to Drew's Drapers for black chiffon scarves. Okey's dad come up from Boomer, but his mom couldn't face it. She was prone to sinking spells. All Gayle's mom had said, when she heard, was, 'I'm sorry for your loss, but don't think you can just come back here. Your bed's took.'

Vern and Ed and Herb were honorary pall-bearers. I sat up front with Gayle, Lo the other side of her, then Betty. Her hands were froze, even though it was a sunny day. The chapel door was open so we heard the escort being called to attention. Then the band started 'Rock of Ages' and I didn't know if I could hold myself together, sitting up there where everybody could see me. I wished Audrey was there in my place. She'd was good at that kinda thing.

Then they carried him in, and our boys were all chewing up the inside of their cheeks, screwing up their eyes, taking it like men.

The chaplain said it was a humbling thing, to honour the patriotic sacrifice of Carl Jackson and bring the message of hope to his young widow that God so loved the world he gave his beloved Son, Jesus Christ, to die for our sins and give us life everlasting.

They fixed the casket back on the caisson while the band played 'Eternal Father, Strong to Save', and then we got in the first car, Gayle, Mr Jackson, Lois and me.

Gayle smelled of liquor, but I ain't criticising. The escort was brought to order.

She said, 'They never let me see him.'

Her voice was like a little bird squeak.

There was a fly-over, of course, in formation, one position empty. That was when Vern nearly lost it. I was watching him. Okey was like a kid brother to him. When he first joined 96th, Vern used to play jokes on him, send him for a gallon of propwash, or a dozen skyhooks. But he soon stopped, when he saw what kind of aviator Okey was.

The body-bearers brought the casket to the grave while the escort presented arms and then they lifted the flag over him and held it there while the padre said his piece, earth to earth and all that. Then the firing squad fired three volleys and the bugler sounded Taps.

Fades the light, and afar goeth day.
Cometh night.
And a star leadeth all to their rest.

Me and Lo were just about holding her up by then. Darned if I know who was holding us up.

The CO presented Gayle with the flag, but she gave it to Mr Jackson.

'I always knew this'd happen,' she said. 'I knew right from the start.'

Later on, Betty said, 'Best thing now would be if she found out she was in the family way after all.'

'No, Betty,' Lois said. 'Best thing'd be if you kept those kinda dumb ideas to yourself.'

36

'See,' Vern said, 'Okey would have handled it. Used the flaps and been sparing with the rudder. He'd have brought her in all right. He was a natural.'

Vern was already rearranging the facts, blaming events on the pilot, a man he never did rate, nothing but a chairborne-ranger, etcetera, lost his nerve and took two good men with him.

I didn't argue with him. I could see, if Vern was gonna get outta bed next day and do what he had to do, we better not start on all the ways that underpowered top-heavy bitch of a B-47 could find to kill you, even if you were a natural-born aviator.

Crystal said, 'What house'll Auntie Gayle live in now?'

We'd been over there, helping her to pack. She'd gotten three weeks to quit.

I said, 'She's going back to North Carolina, see her mommy.'

Crystal was sitting on Vern, squashing his face up with her little hands. 'But why didn't she just stay with her mommy and daddy anyway? That's what I'm going to do,' she said. 'I'm never going away. I'm gonna stay here for ever and ever, amen. Daddy? Uncle Okey got all burned up. Sherry and Deana told me. Why did he?'

'Because he was defending us from the threat and cancer of

Communism, and I want you to remember that. What was he defending us from?'

'From the threat,' she said. 'Can I go play out with Ritchie?'

Gayle took the Greyhound back to where she'd come from. There was a rollaway bed and a job packing cigarettes waiting for her in Winston-Salem, thanks to Okey's sister.

I drove her to the bus. Lois and Betty come along too.

'Well,' she said, 'I guess this is goodbye.'

I don't know what kinda fairweather friends she took us for.

'That poor child,' Betty said, after we'd waved her out of sight. 'I don't care to think what lies ahead of her.'

'Put it like that,' Lois said, 'I don't care to think what lies ahead for any of us. Tell you what. Gayle's young. She ain't got brats to feed. And she's still got her looks. All up, I'd say her chances were pretty good.'

'Well *I* wouldn't trade places with her,' Betty said. 'I'm so glad I have my Ed.'

'Sure,' Lo said, 'we're all glad too. Keeps him off the streets. If *you* didn't have him, there's no telling.'

THE CROWNING OF QUEEN ELIZABETH II

The impressive scene in the Abbey as the Archbishop of Canterbury holds aloft St. Edward's Crown before placing it upon the head of Queen Elizabeth II. Her Majesty, seated in King Edward's Chair, has received the Orb, the Ring, the Sceptre with the Cross, and the Rod with the Dove. On the extreme right is the Duke of Edinburgh, and on the left the Archbishop of York. In front of the Royal Gallery are the Mistress of the Robes, the Dowager Duchess of Devonshire, and the Maids of Honour.

The Queen seated in her Chair of Estate in the Abbey. In the Royal Gallery (left to right) are: Princess Alexandra, the Duchess of Kent, the Princess Royal, Queen Elizabeth the Queen Mother, Princess Margaret, and the Duchess of Gloucester with her two sons.

The Duke of Edinburgh kneeling on the steps of the Throne to do homage to Queen Elizabeth II. "I, Philip, Duke of Edinburgh, become your liege man of life and limb, and of earthly worship . . ."

37

On May thirty-first, 1953, Betty washed all her drapes, made a double quantity of Five-Can Casserole and pressed Ed's blues before she gave in and admitted she had had a few pains. At 6 p.m. on June second she produced another 10lb girl, just as Queen Elizabeth the Second was arriving at Westminster Abbey to get crowned. Betty wanted to name her Elizabeth Regina in honour of the coincidence, but Ed said it had to be Carla, in memory of Okey Jackson.

Audrey wrote me from England. She was expecting herself by this time.

'Well,' she wrote, 'Another girl! I guess it's back to the laboratory with the baking-powder theory. I hope Ed's taking it on the chin.'

'It'll be Betty taking it on the chin, if Carla starts robbing Ed of his beauty-sleep. You heard it here.' Lois was reading over my shoulder.

I'm sending Yardley's lavender water for the new mom. I figure baby Carla already has coatees in every shade of pink.

The Coronation was so beautiful. Crown jewels, velvet robes, marching bands. This is some country. Betty would have adored it. Tell her I'm sending pictures from the magazines. We watched it on TV at the Officers' Club. It rained, naturally, but there were people had slept out all night, including Kath, to see the Queen go by in the gold carriage. I invited Kath and John to come and watch with us, but Kath had already arranged to go with her friend May. I get the feeling that flood washed away more than Kath's poor old house. She's not such a shrinking violet any more, specially now she has electricity and all the latest appliances, but John is in quite a bad way with his nerves so I guess she's just had to take over.

I wrote Gayle at the address you sent me but I didn't hear anything. Sometimes it's better to let these things go, you know? Once a girl's out of the military, you don't have anything in common any more. I've seen it happen.

Love to the gang,

Aud

38

Next I heard, Kath had gotten herself a regular job.

'I wish you could see us,' she wrote. They had been housed in a kind of duplex. It was called a maisonette.

I've decorated all through, nice bit of wallpaper and gloss paint, and I'm buying a green settee on weekly terms. If I ever can get John Pharaoh to shift his carcass I could stretch right out on it. Give me a box of soft-centres and I shall be like Lady Docker. I've gone part-time at the laundry, eight till one, and they're a smashing crowd. We do have a laugh and that's a lovely smell, suds and nice clean sheets. Better than them old eel traps any day. Better than them beet sheds.

Time hangs a bit heavy for John without the fishing, and he can't manage the traps any more. He can't sit at it like he used to, with his nerves. But when we get the telly, he'll be right as rain.

Audrey is in the family way; I suppose you know. She runs round, always got some affair coming off at the base. She's always got flowers to arrange or her hair to get pinned up. But she never forgets me. She drives out here sometimes on a Sunday, and she always brings John a bar of chocolate.

Annie Howgego passed over. You didn't really know her, but I haven't got that much news. That place of hers never dried out properly, but she wouldn't leave. She could have had a flatlet, but she wouldn't even go and have a look at it. You've got to move with the times, that's what I say.

I sent a sympathy card to little Gayle, but Audrey says she probably never got it. She'll be moving around, trying to pick up the pieces. I shall always think of him, at your lovely party, looking at that barley eel John had brought. I told John about what happened, but I don't know if he remembered who Okey was. All the best to your hubby and your Crystal. I don't suppose I'd know her now, they grow so fast.

Yours sincerely,

Kath

Audrey was back Stateside by the fall of '53, but we didn't have the pleasure of her company on base for a while. She was in Chicago giving birth to twin boys, Lance Jnr and Mikey. Then they had a big affair up there for the christening. Six godparents for each boy, including a rear admiral and a congressman.

When Lois saw Audrey's letter she said, 'Uh-oh. Brigadier general the best they could come up with from the army? This list of godparents seem a little lightweight to you, Peggy?'

Still, we all agreed, twins were neat. A whole family in one go.

They got bigger quarters than us, on Delaware Row, and Audrey kept everything so neat and nice I wondered how she managed it, with two peevish brats to see to as well. Then when Herb Moon made captain and him and Lois moved up, just opposite the Rudmans, I found out the secret of Audrey's success. She had some enlisted DW going in, three mornings a week, mopping her floors and folding her laundry.

This freed Aud to become a serious brass-polisher, what with Lance bucking for major and everything. When Herb got his promotion I warned Lois she'd have Audrey on her case, trying to get her involved at the Wives' Club.

I said, 'You'll soon forget your humble roots.'

'Don't worry, Peg,' she said. 'I get a free moment from all that bridge-playing and volunteering, I'll come down here and see you. You know how I do love to *slum*.'

None of us ever heard from Gayle. I wrote her every week, for a while, then there didn't seem much point. Only subjects I had were air force and kids, probably the last two things on earth she wanted reminding about.

The day of Okey's anniversary, me and Betty took flowers out to the cemetery. When we got back there was a card from Gayle. Just said, 'Please remember Okey on the fifth. Still packing smokes. Missing you.'

Next promotion board, Vern and Ed both got passed over. They were reassigned to transports. Betty said Ed was of a mind to quit anyway, but that was just brave talk. Three growing girls to feed, they had to be struggling.

Vern took it real bad. I mean, I could see the board's point of view and I could see Vern's too. Anybody could get sinus trouble. There's no shame in it. But when a man's been a real aviator and he gets sidelined, he feels like a waste of space all of a sudden. He doesn't want to hang out with the jocks any more 'cause they're going higher and faster, and he's going nowhere. So that was when the chip on his shoulder started growing. Ended up it was all chip and no Vern.

Crystal started hanging out with Sherry Gillis about this time.

I said 'How come? You never liked her before.'

She said, 'We both got grouchy dads. Plus, she hates Deana and Carla's just a kid, and I don't even have a sister.'

Nineteen fifty-four was a bad year for me. I could see where me and Vern were headed, but I didn't have anybody I could tell. Ida and Pearl were gone, back to Castle, and it wasn't like it used to be with the old gang. Kirk and Carla and Audrey's boys were all at that troublesome stage. Getting into everything, falling over every two steps they took. When you have a smart eight-year-old who can tell you how frogs get babies and where flies go in winter, you don't have patience with the diaper stage any more.

I did a few turns at the base thrift-shop, but my time for that had passed too. What I needed was a job. Heck, even Kath Pharaoh had a job.

'The laundry offered me full-time,' she wrote me. 'But for one thing, I fancy a change. I'd like to get out and about. Meet different people. I went after something at R&D Modes. That's a dress shop. I didn't get it, though. I don't think I was smart enough dressed. Then the other thing is, John Pharaoh. He's going downhill, so I can't be gone all day.'

Every time I wrote and asked, she just wrote back, 'It's a nervous thing.'

Couple of times in town I saw places were hiring and I made enquiries, but soon as they seen my address they tore up the forms.

'No military,' they'd say. 'You just get a girl trained up, then she's gone.'

The only one halfway understood what was bugging me was Lois, and sometimes I didn't think even she did. Sometimes I thought she'd caved in, started shinning up that greasy pole at the OWC. Going to coffees. Painting her nails Peach Pastelle instead of Red for Danger.

Then the squadron got a Temporary Duty to McDill, Florida, and Lo was pissed as a nest of hornets 'cause the wives didn't get to go.

'I am so bored,' she said. 'Let's go someplace. Remember that time we all went to the beach?'

Wichita, Kansas, was a long way from any beach, but Labor Day weekend there was a Wild West show over in Butler County, so we fixed to all get together and take the kids. Even Audrey said she'd come along, for old times' sake.

Lois said, 'Long as I don't have to have that Gillis girl riding in my car.' Deana always got car-sick. It seemed to me Betty brought it on. You have your mommy asking you every five minutes, 'Y'all right, precious? You feeling ill yet?' of course it'll happen. Crystal never was sick in her life. We never asked her if she wanted to be.

So I had Deana ride up front with me. I told her to read me out all the signs along the way, take her mind off her stomach. Audrey sat behind with her boys and Kirk.

I could have spent hours watching Kirk. He was like a little old man sitting there. Funny beaky little nose. He wasn't much of a talker yet. He just looked out the window and pointed at things. I noticed Audrey was studying him too. I caught her eye in my mirror.

I said, 'Cute kid, isn't he?'

Deana was reading out road signs, like I'd told her. 'Pure Oil. Ice. Pumkin Pie Diner. Nothing Refreshes . . . like Seven-Up.' She was the dead spit of Betty. Big for ten too.

Audrey said, 'Yes, he is cute.'

Deana said, 'My mom says that baby is from the Devil. Thrifty

Maid Tomatoes. 400 East. Snap Beans Serve Yourself.' She hardly broke rhythm. 'Pickrell Feed and Harness. Dogie Gulch Wild West Show first left!'

Audrey was still looking at me next time I checked the mirror. Raised her eyebrows.

I said, 'Well, motherhood seems like it suits you, Aud. You think you'll have any more?'

'Oh no,' she said. 'I've done my duty by the Rudmans. Given them an heir and a spare. Once they're in school, then I'll have time to do some of the things I want to do.'

I said, 'Would you ever get a job?'

She looked shocked. 'I have a *job*, Peggy,' she said. 'I run Captain Lance Rudman, Inc. But I'd really adore to do something artistic. You know? Paint pictures or something?'

We'd all took blankets, excepting Audrey. She'd brung lawn chairs. I helped her get them outta the trunk.

I said, 'You believe what that brat said about Kirk?'

She said, 'She's only repeating what she's heard. Betty ever discuss it with you?'

I had never heard Betty say a word about Kirk, except her usual head-shaking over the slapdash way he was being raised.

Audrey said, 'Maybe one of us should have a word to her? Deana goes round saying things like that, I don't care to think . . .'

I said, 'Maybe. But not now. I don't want the day ruined.'

It was the first time the four of us had been out on a spree since England. We had a great time. There was steer-roping and bull-riding, and stick-horse races for the kids. There was burgers and hot dogs at the Chuck Wagon, all you could eat for a buck, and a bank robbery at three o'clock.

Lo was yee-hawin' all over the place, flirting with some good-looking boy in fancy high-heeled boots and leather chaps, his hair grown just like a girl, meant to be Buffalo Bill or somesuch. He sounded East Coast to me. If he was a cowboy, I was the Yellow Rose of Texas.

'Is it true, what I heard?' Lois said. 'Cowboy gets undressed, last thing he takes off is his hat?

'Yes, ma'am,' he said. 'And in the morning it's the other way around. First thing I do is reach for my hat. Third thing I do is roll me a cigarette.'

39

When we got home, friend husband was prowling around, waiting for his dinner to jump outta the Frigidaire and fry itself.

'Where you think you've been?' he said, even though I'd told him a hundred times where we were going, and Crystal had her Sitting Bull totem-pole souvenir balloon an inch in front of his nose.

He had turned morose since he stopped flying bombers, and he was getting a little paunchy too. Time was, he was as religious about doing his squat thrusts and his sit-ups as he was about Beer Call. Then it got, it was just Beer Call. Final stage was he just stayed home, sat in front of the TV with a cold one.

I sat with him, watched him shovelling in the corned beef. Crystal was trying to rope the cat.

I said, 'Betty's having a Tupperware. You get a free gift, or something.' I thought I'd keep the conversation light, till the storm-clouds passed.

'I'm thinking of quitting,' he said.

'Okay,' I said. 'Nobody stays in the military for ever.'

Times I'd longed for him to be out of it. Then when he said it, I felt like a big hole opened under me. We'd always been a threesome, me, Vern and the US Air Force.

'Go back to Maine,' he said. 'Give Mom a hand.'

I said, 'You got three sisters up there to give her a hand. She's got your pop. Besides, she don't want a hand. She wants a yarn store. That what you gonna do? Sell knitting patterns?'

It was a fool thing to say.

He was up on his feet, chair went over one way, table went the other, fried eggs, ketchup, beer bottle splintered into a thousand pieces. Crystal shot into her room and the cat went with her.

He never said a word. Just banged the door on his way out. Lois said she never heard a thing, but Nancy Windler, who was the other side in Gayle's old quarters, asked me next day if I'd heard a sonic boom. She said it had made her wedding group fall off the wall.

So I braced myself for hard times with Vern, but one upturned table was as bad as it got. He got his discharge leave the same week Pop Dewey electrocuted himself saving money on getting a repair man in, so he'd have had to go to Maine anyway for the burying. I cleared the post. Audrey didn't make it to my Farewell, she had some Luncheon Club committee, but Lois dropped by. Betty was crying, said she didn't know what she'd do without me.

Lois said, 'Will you quit dabbing your eyes, Gillis? What kind of a send-off is this? Don't you realise Peg's *escaping*? We should be drinking some of that French champagne.'

I said, 'You think I'll ever see any of your ugly faces again?'

'You never know your luck,' she said.

You get used to a whole lot of goodbyes when you're with the military. There are faces I remember, without names. Some are names without faces. Just the gang from Drampton who've stayed kinda true over the years. That's adversity for you.

So I took Crystal back to San Antonio and stayed at my mom's. Had a bedroom to ourselves 'cause sister Connie had moved on. She was in Lubbock, living in sin.

I said to Mom, 'We won't be under your feet long.'

'Good,' she said.

It took me a month to get a job stacking shelves at the Piggly Wiggly and two rooms to rent, and I guess by that time, I knew Vern wasn't coming back. We just kinda fizzled out. We never even bothered getting divorced till he met Martine and hell, that was years after.

40

Lance Rudman made major in '56. Herb Moon didn't, but according to Lo he had already decided to quit, had his fill of all that schmoozing you got to do, if you want to reach the heights. They went back to the East Coast and he got a job as foreman in a lumber yard, somewhere up the Hudson.

'Herb's happy as a pig in a toilet bowl. I'm slowly going nuts,' Lois wrote. 'So no change there. Good news is, we get twenty per cent off rafters and planking.'

Me and Betty seemed fated to go through life together. Nineteen fifty-eight she came back to Converse after Ed flipped one night, busted her jaw and was declared unfit for duty. There were some people thought the neighbours had been over-hasty, calling out the MPs when they heard the kids screaming, getting Ed thrown in the glasshouse, and once her swollen face went down it wasn't long before Betty started agreeing with them.

'I blame myself,' she said.

I was working in layaway at Woolworth's and I told her they were hiring. She got a start as a part-time checker while Ed was coming to terms with civilian life.

I said, 'Betty, I never heard such a load of hogwash. What did you do? Walk into his fist?'

'I didn't handle him right,' she said. 'You can't make a trained killer of a man, then expect him to just turn it off when he comes home. I should have took the girls and gone for a drive. Leave him alone, he soon calms down.'

'Trained killer my ass,' Lois said when I wrote her about it. 'Thank God Ed Gillis never took Bayoneting 101.'

But Betty was still hanging on in there, working her shift at Woolworth's, then going home to the ironing and the cooking and the picking up. Ed got driving jobs, but he never lasted long. Didn't matter which outfit he went to work for, there was always some fool there he couldn't get along with.

'Ed's a good man,' she used to say. 'He just has to learn to master that temper of his.'

I knew she was getting food stamps, but she didn't know I knew. Crystal and Sherry were both in eighth grade at Kirby Junior High, so sometimes I found things out without even trying.

One time she came home from school, she said, 'We had to write about what we wished for and Sherry wrote she wished her dad'd drop dead and Miss Hopko saw her after school and asked if she wanted to talk about it or anything and now she's scared her mom'll find out. Do you think Miss Hopko would tell her mom?'

I said, 'What did you wish for?'

'Trainer bra,' she said. 'And a pet ferret. And to see my dad sometimes.'

41

It was a hard thing, raising a child on your own back then. Course, everybody does it now. Vern'd send money. I can't fault him there. But he was shackled to that damned Dewey place up in Maine and Crystal did pine for him, I know.

I guess I wasn't much fun. Work, come home, fall asleep. That was my life. I got offers sometimes, but most of them I wouldn't care to repeat.

I had the idea to learn typing and shorthand, try and improve my prospects, but all I seemed to do was watch the *Lawrence Welk Show* and then wake up with a crick in my neck. I wasn't feeling too proud of myself at that period of my life. Even Kath Pharaoh was taking classes.

'I'm doing night school,' she wrote.

Book-keeping. So far I've come top in all the tests. And you meet all sorts. I'd never realised how many different kinds of people there are. Some of them go for a pint afterwards, but I have to get back for John. Dennis Jex comes and sits with him. Or, if he can't, May does it, or the couple from next door. They're all good pals to me. I don't know how I'd manage without them. The doctor says I should think of putting him in a home, but I'm not having that. I've promised him I won't send him away. He understands. He's all seized up now, can't hardly move. But he understands.

I loved Kath's letters. There was always something new she was up to, in spite of her troubles with John. It was like she was waking up to life.

Audrey kept the letters coming too, always full of the brilliant achievements of the Rudman family. Lois preferred the phone. And all I ever got from Gayle was new addresses:. c/o The Coffee Can, Wallace; c/o Reba's Dinette, Haw's Run; c/o The Stay A While, Delco.

Nineteen fifty-nine Lance Rudman made lieutenant colonel and he got orders to Oxfordshire, England. Audrey was thrilled.

Lois said, 'Well, that silver creamer of theirs never did look right in Wichita. They'll probably get a castle or something now.'

I wrote Audrey, asked her if Oxfordshire was near enough to visit Kath, find out just how bad things were with John. But we were too late. He died on January first, 1960.

All Kath wrote was:

I had him cremated. I do miss him. That's a lonely place to come back to when I finish work. I leave the telly on now, so the place sounds a bit cheerier when I come in. There was a bit of money left from the insurance so I've had the phone put in. First time it went off I jumped a mile high. I'm putting the rest in Premium Bonds.

She answered that telephone like she thought it might bite her. Then she screamed when she realised it was me.

'What!' she said. 'All the way from America? What ever is that costing you?'

I said, 'Never mind how much. Ain't this a miracle, that we can talk?'

'That is,' she said. 'Miracle's about right.' It was good to hear her funny old way of speaking.

I said, 'I was so sorry to hear about John. You bearing up?'

'Not too bad,' she said. 'I forget sometimes. I'm busy at work, I don't have time to think. It's when I come home it hits me. But life goes on. I shall be all right.'

I said, 'I guess it just takes time, Kath. How long were you two together?'

'How d'you mean?' she said.

I said, 'Married.'

It was a weird conversation. I could hear a kinda echo of my own voice, and then I had to wait while her answer came back. I pictured my words going down a long tube on the bottom of the Atlantic Ocean. Her answer took even longer coming back that time.

I said, 'You still there?'

'Yes,' she said. 'I thought for a minute you asked me how long we'd been married. Must have been a crackle on the line.'

I called Betty after. I said, 'Do you think maybe Kath and John Pharaoh weren't married?'

'Well,' she said, 'I never saw her wedding album. Did you?'

I phoned Lois. Herb picked up. 'Hey, Peggy!' he said. 'When are you gonna come up here and visit? You should come in the fall, see the leaves turn.'

He put Lois on.

I said, 'John Pharaoh died. I don't suppose you heard?'

'Who?' she said. 'Oh . . . yeah . . . I think I remember . . .'

I said, 'Don't go through that charade for *my* benefit. I just thought you should know. You might drop Kath a line.'

'Sure,' she said. 'What happened?'

I said, 'Pneumonia. But he had all that other business. Nerves and everything. Still, he was only thirty-eight, Lo. Makes you think, don't it?'

'Yeah,' she said. 'Kath okay?'

I said, 'She's a wonder.'

We talked about the kids and stuff. Sandie was in her school band, learning to play the cornet, and Kirk had been sent home – disruptive behaviour.

Lois said, 'He's boisterous, that's all. It's natural in a boy. But his teacher is such a 'fraidycat, so he gets sent home.'

I said, 'Lo, you know John and Kath?'

'Yeah?' she said, kinda weary.

I said, 'Did it ever cross your mind they weren't married?'

'No,' she said, 'and who the hell cares?'

42

Christmas of 1960 I got two neat surprises: a card from Gayle, actually had more than a change of address in it; and a telephone call from Norfolk, England. Kath Pharaoh herself, gone international.

'Peggy?' she was shouting so loud she probably didn't need the phone line.

'Peggy? My Premium Bond's come up. I'm in the money.'

She had won hundreds of pounds.

'You know what this means?' she said. 'I shall be coming to see you.'

I said, 'When?'

'I don't know,' she said. 'I shall have to see when I can get the time off.'

So I told her about Gayle's news. I said, 'Little Gayle's getting married again. Why don't you wait till she names the day? Come for the wedding?'

Gayle wrote she had met a marine, Ray Flagg out of Camp Lejeune. He'd come into the diner and she'd given him extra pie. Love at first sight.

'I love him to pieces,' she wrote. 'We're getting married, soon as he's back from this extended float, and I want all you guys to be here.'

That was the trouble with a marine. If you didn't catch him before he got deployed, you could have an awful long wait. In the end it was a close-run thing between Gayle and Deana Gillis. First boy to say a kind word to her got more'n he bargained for. A shotgun wedding and a child bride. Deana was sixteen. Dwayne was nineteen, a first-termer from Lackland AFB.

It was a quiet affair at City Hall, then back to Betty and Ed's for a home-cooked spread. Betty was passing the photos around at work like it was an occasion to be proud of. Deana looked like beaver with bangs. Dwayne looked like he was in shock.

I said to Betty, 'You'd have hoped these kids had learned something from us. Finish school; get themselves a life before they start saddling themselves with brats. And I'd have thought Deana never wanted to smell jet fuel again as long as she lived.'

She gave me one of her old-fashioned looks. 'There's nothing wrong with marrying a airman and having babies,' she said. 'Deana's always been a homemaker. It's what she's cut out for. And if Dwayne gets an unaccompanied tour, she can just homestead here. It'll be great having a baby in the house again. Maybe we'll get a boy this time.'

I wanted to make sure the lesson wasn't lost on Crystal. She was starting to show some interest in boys herself. Just hanging round the jukebox Saturday afternoons at Grunder's Soda Fountain. Nothing serious. Plus, she hadn't filled out much yet, and she still kept lizards in her bedroom and gave them names. But, better safe than sorry.

I said, 'Well, there goes Deana's life.'

'Mom,' she said, 'Deana is such a dope. You know what Sherry told me? Deana stayed home, pretended she had cramps, so she wouldn't have to take the class about how you get babies. She said she kinda knew already, but I guess she didn't.'

I said, 'They teach you all that in school?'

'Sure,' she said. 'In freshman year. I already know, though, so don't worry. I read it in *Complete Home Encyclopaedia of Health*. And I told Sherry, but it's a secret. She says if her mom found out she knew about all that stuff, she'd die of shame.'

I said, 'Well, reading it in a book is one thing. Remembering what you read when you're wrestling in the back seat of a car is something else.'

'Mom!' she said, come over all bashful.

'Now,' I said, 'you remember Aunty Gayle?'

'Kind of,' she said. 'Why, she pregnant too?'

I said, 'You wanna come to her wedding?'

'Do I have to wear something dumb?' she said.

She wanted to know how we were getting to North Carolina. 'On the bus?' she said. 'With Deana's mom and that brat? No way. I'll bet she gets sick.'

It was true, Betty had done a thorough job of training Deana and Sherry to throw up in moving vehicles, and there was no reason to think Carla would be any different.

'Is Aunty Gayle the one makes you laugh?' she said.

'No,' I said. 'That's Lois.'

43

Kath asked for three weeks' vacation from the office she was working in, so they fired her.

'I didn't ask them to pay me for all of it,' she said. 'I know I'm not entitled to that. They said just because I could afford fancy holidays to America, I needn't think I could lord it over everybody at Harrison's. I've never tried to lord it over anybody, Peggy. I tell you, I've come up against a lot of ugly feelings since I had my win. But I'm not going to let it stop me enjoying myself. Blow Harrison's. I'll find something to do when I get back. I've always found work. I've never been a slacker.'

She was flying into Idlewild and then on to Fort Worth. She was so excited, I was getting wardrobe updates in my mailbox every day. 'I've bought a new roll-on and I'm breaking it in at night, while I watch telly'; May Gotobed says I should get a pair of slacks for travelling, but I don't know as that's the done thing'; 'Will two cardigans be enough, do you think?'

I was excited too, only Crystal was raining on my parade. She had gone to bed one night a normal kid and woke up the next morning with a disrespectful attitude. Her skin had broke out, too.

All I was asking was for her to give up her room for one week. All she had to do was sleep on the couch till we went to Gayle's wedding.

'She's your friend,' she kept saying. 'You sleep on the couch.'

I said, 'Or you can double up with me. Was a time you loved climbing in beside me.'

'Oh *please*!' she said.

Once she had turned fourteen, it was hard to get a civil word out of her, and any time I said anything she'd threaten to run away to Maine and live with her daddy. I bit my tongue a few times over that.

By the time Kath landed she had been travelling more than thirty-six hours. First thing she wanted was to get out of her corset. Second thing she wanted was a cup of strong, hot tea, but she settled for iced.

She had loved the flight. 'I was frit when it started up,' she said. 'It was going faster and faster and I thought that'd never get off the ground, but once you're up there, you can't hardly feel you're moving. And they come through, give you dinner and everything. It was like the Ritz.'

She'd brought an airline spoon to show me.

Crystal was meant to be rolling out the welcome wagon, not messing up my kitchen counters. I wanted everything to look nice for Kath. I'd gotten new covers for the bed and matching drapes, all drip-dry, and scented soap for the shower cabin.

Midnight, Crystal was still up, popping corn. She seemed like she was hanging around, waiting for something. Wasn't till morning I found out what.

I left Kath till ten, figured she needed her sleep. When I tapped on her door she called out, 'I'm all right, Peg, but do you come in, you better open the door slow.'

She was propped up against the pillows, curlers in her hair, and halfway up the comforter was one of Crystal's goddamned lizards. Kath was looking at the lizard and it was looking right back at her.

'Come in gentle,' she said. 'I'm worried that might turn nasty if you startle it.'

It was Crystal I intended startling, when she got home from school. She had promised me to get all livestock outta her room and into the carport.

'Elvis!' she said, when I told her what Kath had woken up to. 'You better not have hurt him.'

Kath said she didn't like putting anybody out of their quarters, not even a lizard, but that was only after she realised Elvis wouldn't bite. She said, 'Let him stop. He's quite a character now I'm getting used to him.'

So Crystal brought in another lizard, called Presley, too. Give that child an inch. I could see she was relenting a little, though, over Kath sleeping in her room.

Betty drove over next evening, to welcome Kath to Converse and have a powwow about travelling to Gayle's wedding. Soon as all the squealing and hugging was done she said, 'Peggy, we have a crisis. Ed says it ain't safe to go.'

There was a story about a bunch of black kids riding in white seats on a Greyhound out of Washington DC.

I said, 'We're not going anywhere near Washington.'

'Maybe so,' she said, 'but Ed says this kinda thing could spread.'

I said, 'So what are you gonna do? Drive all the way to North Carolina?' Old heap of junk Betty drove, never would have made it.

Kath said, 'I don't understand. What's happened?'

Then Crystal pipes up. 'I can tell you. Blacks don't want to be treated different any more,' she said. 'They are rising up.'

'See,' Betty said. 'Even Crystal knows about it.'

Kath said, 'Are they tret different, then?'

I said, 'Course they are. They got their own schools. Got their own neighbourhoods.'

Betty said, 'And got their own place on the bus. Always did. I don't see why folks have to meddle with what don't need fixing.'

Kath said, 'Well, I don't know about it. They've got them in London now, working on the buses, but I don't know what happens if they just want to ride. And we haven't got any in Lynn.'

I said, 'Please yourself, Betty. Me and Kath are going on the Greyhound.'

Crystal said, 'And me.'

I said, 'You told me you weren't coming. I've fixed for Mrs Kaiser to keep an eye on you.'

'I changed my mind,' she said. 'I want to see an uprising.'

44

Betty dithered the rest of the week. Ed told her if she went she could expect to come home murdered. On the other hand, she had made herself a blue rayon sheath-dress and a pillbox hat out of a Sugar Smacks carton and the remains of the rayon. In the end fashion won the day. Her and Carla turned up at the bus terminal five minutes before departure time.

'I've labelled Ed's dinners,' she said. 'All Sherry has to do is heat them through when he gets home.'

He had gotten a job at last, selling leaf-blowers.

I reckon that trip aged me ten years. The way I'd planned it, we'd take three days getting there. Stop off at Shreveport and Birmingham and find ourselves bed and breakfast. But Betty was worried about money and I didn't want to get her into any more trouble with Ed. We stayed on the bus that first night and she kept folding and re-folding the Woolworth's bags she'd brung for Carla to be sick in, only Carla wasn't getting sick.

We bought water-melon slices at Jackson, Mississippi. Kath had never had it before. She had never seen so many black faces neither.

She said, 'So they can't sit where we sit. And we can't sit where they sit.'

Betty said, 'Oh yes, we can. But of course, we wouldn't want to.'

Kath said, 'I still don't understand it.'

Crystal was sitting next to her. She said, 'You scared of an uprising, Aunty Kath? I'm not.' All of a sudden it was 'Aunty Kath'.

By the time we got to Atlanta I was so crazy for lack of sleep, I was ready to lay my head anyplace, and I did. We got a three-bed family room at the Chattahoochee Club Motel and, even though the sheets smelled a little sour, I went out like a light. Next morning at the terminal there was something going on. Newspaper men running around, with cameras.

Betty said, 'Somebody famous must be expected. Keep your eyes open, now, girls.'

But it wasn't anything like that. We had just took our seats when they towed in a Greyhound, all burned out. Our driver said it had been took over by blacks in Gainesville, called themselves Freedom Riders, and when they were asked to sit in their intended seats or get off, they had set the bus alight.

He said, 'Any nigras try to take over my vehicle, they'll get more'n they bargain for.'

I saw Betty's knuckles whiten. 'I hope you're satisfied,' she hissed to me. 'I knew we shouldn't have come. Putting ourselves in mortal danger. Now Carla's gonna be terrified.'

Carla said, 'I ain't terrified, Mom.'

Betty said, 'Well, you should be.'

Crystal winked at Carla. Gave her a stick of Hubba Bubba. It was a kinda solidarity thing, I guess.

All the way to Wilmington, Betty was braced for Freedom Riders to climb aboard and set us on fire. Kath was just drinking in the passing sights. Couple of times we passed through bad areas she said, 'Look at that. I thought everywhere'd be spick and span over here. I thought I'd be seeing film stars everywhere.'

I said, 'You disappointed in America?'

'Oh no,' she said. 'I like it. Everybody gives you the time of day over here, even the darkies.'

I could hear Carla and Crystal talking about the wedding.

Carla said, 'You allowed to wear your dungarees to the marrying?'

Crystal said, 'No. I have to wear a dumb dress.'

'Me too,' Carla said. 'It's white organdy. Mom made it.'

Crystal said, 'I'm never getting married.'

Carla said, 'Oh, you have to. When you've finished high school, that's what happens next.'

Crystal said, 'No it isn't, you noodle. Who told you that? Millions of people don't get married. Zillions. Aunty Kath didn't get married, did you?'

I looked to see if Betty was listening. She was.

'No,' Kath said. 'I never married.' And Betty gave me a knowing smile.

Carla said, 'Weren't you pretty enough?'

Kath laughed. 'I don't think I was that bad,' she said. 'But I had my brother to look after. First I had my mam, when she got poorly. Then I had my brother, John Pharaoh.'

I opened my mouth and something came out, more a mew than a squeak. I coughed some, to cover it up. My head was spinning. He was her brother. She'd just said so. John Pharaoh was her brother. And Kath had shared a bed with him.

Carla said, 'And then what?'

'And then he died,' Kath said.

I turned and looked outta the window. I didn't want to see Betty's face. I needed time to think, and we were eating up the miles to Wilmington.

Soon as we stepped down off the Greyhound, I was watching for my opportunity. I wanted to take Betty to one side and say, 'Now, I know what you're thinking, but you're not to make a scene in front of these kids. I'm as stunned as you are, but we have to look at it this way. They were different times. Different country, different customs.'

But I never got to say my piece. Kath was never outta earshot. Betty insisting we even went to the restroom together in case of riot and mayhem. She gave us all a fistful of Kleenex, too.

'You never know,' she said, 'what kinda *element* has been in contact with these seats.'

I looked her right in the eye. Allowed her the opportunity to give me her famous scandalised look. Nothing there. She hadn't even heard what I had heard. Kath had dropped a little bombshell, and nobody even realised. I was on my own with the information. I had time to turn it over in my mind and decide who I was going to share it with first.

45

Camp Lejeune was the biggest facility I ever seen. It stretched along fourteen miles of sand bars and beach, all set up for combat training. There wasn't a thing they didn't have there. Bowling alley. Movie theatre. They even had black marines.

Gayle and Ray came down to the main gate to escort us to the hostess house. She broke into a little run, when she spotted us. Ray come loping along behind. He had a look of Okey about him, gave me a moment of sadness. I think it was the way his ears stuck out.

She still felt like a little bird in my arms. Still had her wispy hair in a pony-tail. 'Oh, Peggy,' she said, 'I'm so happy, I could scream.'

I seen a roughness about her I didn't remember from before. Hard times and heartbreak, I guess.

Crystal was tongue-tied.

Gayle said, 'Don't I get a kiss, Crystal Dewey? Number of popsicles I stood you!'

Kath had a little speech prepared. She said, 'I should like to thank you for inviting me. That was a very kind thought.'

Gayle said, 'Hey, you're the guest of honour. We don't know anybody ever had a English to their wedding. That right, Ray?'

'Yes, ma'am,' he said. That was about all I ever heard him say, excepting his marriage vows.

I said, 'Lois here yet?'

[145]

Gayle said, 'She's late. Her dress wasn't ready.'

Me and Lois had talked dresses. I'd called her up, see what she was gonna wear. 'Something that has not yet seen the light of Benny Gold's machine room,' she said. 'My cousin Irene can get it at cost. I'm thinking of a matador-cape collar. How about you?'

I said, 'I don't know. I'm outta touch.'

'I know what you mean,' she said. 'You live up here long enough, you start wearing men's socks. Next thing is, you think they look okay.'

It was something to be back inside a perimeter fence, hearing men marching in those heavy boots, and the Big Voice barking out.

We were in issue bunks. Ray Flagg was only a E-4 corporal, so we didn't get any fancy accommodations. Crystal and Carla took a top bunk together, Crystal having decided Carla wasn't so bad for seven, nor for a Gillis brat. Betty and Kath took a pair together. Started shaking out their wedding outfits and making themselves at home. Looked like I was left with Lois. I slung my stuff on the top half. I didn't want her tossing and turning all night two feet above my head.

Five o'clock, a bugle sounded Retreat.

Betty said, 'Oh, Peg! Don't that take you back? Happy days.'

I said, 'Happy? Are you nuts?'

'They *were* happy,' she said. 'Least, we had the air force looking after us. Least, we didn't have to punch in every morning or lose the roof over our heads. I'd go back. Give me the chance, I'd go back in a heartbeat.'

We had just given up on Lois and decided to take the girls into Jacksonville for hamburgers when we heard her car horn. Five years since I'd seen her, but it was like yesterday. Her hair was still big and red, and her mouth too. She was wearing white pants and a harlequin shirt, tucked in, and ballerina shoes.

'Okay,' she said. 'Let the fun begin. Where's the bar?'

She picked Gayle up off her feet and swung her round. 'You happy, kid?' she said. Betty was hailing her outta the dormitory window. 'That you up there, Gillis?' she yelled. 'Get your junk on your bunk. Gear inspection in five minutes!'

I was watching to see how she was with Kath. Last time they'd met, Lo had had a eel spear digging into her belly.

'Kirk,' she said, 'you get out of that car. Come and meet a real English lady.'

Kirk was still small for his age. Carla towered over him. He was screwing up his face about having to meet a bunch of people, hanging back, pulling on Lo's shirt.

'Quit that!' she said. 'Now, offer Kath your hand and say howdy-doo. She's come all the way from England to take a look at you.'

Kath and Kirk shook hands. 'Nice to meet you,' Kath said. 'I see you've got another copper-knob in the family, then, Lois?'

Lois said, 'How are you, Kath? I'm real glad to see you again.' She said it nice, like she meant it.

We took her dress in to hang it, keep the big cape collar in shape. It was kinda aquamarine.

I said, 'Kirk's a little gentleman.'

'Ha!' she said. 'He's still full of Dramamine. You wait.'

I knew he'd been in a couple of different schools. He had been asked to leave because he got unruly.

Lois said, 'I couldn't come without him. He's too much of a handful for Herb's mom, and Herb couldn't get time off. I've threatened him, though. He better behave. I haven't come all this way to have to drag him outta the chapel, miss Gayle's big moment. You met the bride-groom yet?'

I said, 'Yes. He's young; he's in shape.'

'Sounds good to me,' she said.

So we spent Gayle's wedding eve at Snead's Ferry, drinking Dr Pepper and eating Krystalburgers.

I said to Gayle, 'How about your friends from the camp? They coming along?'

'I didn't really make any yet,' she said. 'I guess it's because I'm older.'

Betty said, 'And, honey, they probably heard you were an officer's wife. You know what enlisted can be like.'

'Nothing wrong with enlisted,' Gayle said. 'Matter of fact, they're my kind. I'd sooner be with them than the types you get at the OWC. Arranging their flowers. Looking down their noses at you.'

Lois said, 'And how is dear Audrey?'

Audrey was at Truxton Ferrers in Oxfordshire, England, Lance now flying a big desk for Strategic Air Command. They had sent Gayle and Ray a beautiful Wedgwood-blue Jasperware table lighter. Real elegant.

Gayle said, 'I didn't mean Audrey.'

Lois gave her a quizzical look. She said, 'Well, that's funny, 'cause you just described her to a "t".'

Kath said, 'Well, I speak as I find. Audrey was the soul of kindness to us, after we got flooded out.'

Lois said, 'Sure. Well, that's Audrey's kinda thing. Good works.'

Kath flashed right back, 'Better than making mischief.'

Lois turned away.

Betty said, 'Girls, let's all tell what we're gonna wear tomorrow. Lois, why don't you start?'

Sometimes Lois wouldn't be saved from herself.

'Just my usual horns and a tail,' she said. 'Hell, do we have to drink this kiddie stuff all night? Can't we get something a little stronger?'

'Lois,' Gayle said, 'I'm off the drink and I'm staying off.'

'Okay,' Lo said. 'Did you take the pledge for me too?'

I kicked her under the table.

'Ray a Baptist, by any chance?' she said.

'Yes, he is,' Gayle said. 'And y'all are gonna be drinking peach nectar at the wedding breakfast.'

46

There was trouble when we got back to the hostess house. Kirk erupted when he found out Crystal and Carla already got the top bunk. I guess the Dramamine was wearing off.

He climbed up, tried to drag Carla off the bed. Betty and Crystal were fighting him off but he kept coming back for more, pinching and trying to bite. It took Lois to stop him. She grabbed him by his hair and the seat of his pants and shook him till he stopped thrashing.

'I warned you,' she was yelling, 'you ruin this trip you'll go home in pieces. I'm in no mood.'

She threw him on his bunk and he just lay there, turned in on himself, picking at the comforter, wiping his eyes with the back of his hand.

Everybody was quiet, acting busy putting on their face cream and curling up their hair. It was Kath went to him eventually.

'You know what?' she said. 'You could make yourself a little hideyhole here. Look. We can hang this blanket down from the other bed. That'll be like a curtain. That'll be like your own little tent. Then you'll be the lucky one.'

He let her fix up the blanket. Just lay there, watching her.

She said, 'How's that?'

We couldn't see him any more. I heard him say, 'This is my tent. No one is allowed.'

'That's right,' she said. 'Now you can get in your pyjamas and be all private. All right?'

He grunted.

'You get some shut-eye in your special tent,' she said. 'And in the morning we'll see what we can find in my bag.'

47

Gayle was intending to carry a white prayer book instead of a bouquet but I didn't see why she shouldn't have both, so, first thing, me and Lo went out to buy flowers. Kirk promised to behave. He was busy with a colouring book Kath had given him. There was one for Carla, too, and crayons. Kath's bag was like Santa's sack.

She had brought Scenes of London table-mats for Gayle and Ray, and scarves for all us girls, except for Betty. She had lugged a book of royal photos for her, but Betty had kinda lost interest after Princess Margaret didn't marry her Group Captain.

She said, 'Kath, you're such a darling. But you know, we practically got royalty ourselves these days. We have Jacqueline Bouvier Kennedy.'

Me and Lo were on our way out the door.

I said to Lois, 'I hate Jackie Kennedy. She makes me feel so washed up and wore out. I'm sick of her perfect cheekbones and her French outfits.'

'Yeah,' she said. 'Me too. Why the hell can't she wear a hat that says "Blumms Auto Parts"? Ask me, it's time we had a First Lady knows how to make duck calls with her armpit.'

We got in the car.

I said, 'Lo, I have to talk to you about something.'

'Uh-oh,' she said, 'what did I do now?'

Pretty Polly Nylons
Exquisite stockings
that cost no more

NEWS CHRONICLE

No. 34,110   **   TUESDAY, NOVEMBER 1, 1955   PRICE 2d.

NAVY MINTS
THE SWEET WITH THE HOLE
AT TWOPENCE A ROLL

'Mindful of the church's teaching... and conscious of my duty to the Commonwealth...'

PRINCESS DECIDES 'NO'

'Strengthened by devotion of Group-Captain Townsend'

PRINCESS MARGARET ISSUED THE FOLLOWING PERSONAL MESSAGE FROM HER HOME, CLARENCE HOUSE, LAST NIGHT:

I would like it to be known that I have decided not to marry Group-Captain Peter Townsend.

I have been aware that, subject to my renouncing my rights of succession, it might have been possible for me to contract a civil marriage.

But, mindful of the Church's teaching that Christian marriage is indissoluble, and conscious of my duty to the Commonwealth, I have resolved to put these considerations before any others.

I have reached this decision entirely alone, and in doing so I have been strengthened by the unfailing support and devotion of Group-Captain Townsend.

I am deeply grateful for the concern of all those who have constantly prayed for my happiness.

The message was dated Monday, Oct. 31 and was signed "Margaret."

THE announcement came shortly after Group-Captain Peter Townsend had called at Clarence House at teatime to see the Queen Mother and the Princess.

He stayed there nearly two hours, then drove back to Uckfield (Sussex), where he and Princess Margaret had been house-party guests.

It is stated that "according to present plans" he will be returning to Brussels to resume his duties as Air Attaché next Monday.

The Church and the Princess

BY OUR OWN REPORTER

... her statement announcing her intention to marry Group-Capt. Townsend, Princess Margaret said last night that she accepted the Church's teaching that Christian marriage is indissoluble.

This is the doctrine of the orthodox following in the Church of England.

It has been stated lately ... said firmly by the Archbishop of Canterbury in his evidence before the Royal Commission on Marriage and Divorce and in a paragraph which he published last February.

Princess Margaret concurred, Dr. Fisher, The Archbishop

...point last Thursday. She was with him for more than half an hour.

There can be no doubt of the statement he gave her, and that he confirms that teaching with tact and sympathy. He is remembering that, the world has relied on, that the State has legislated for divorce and puts the bar upon the divorced remarrying.

'Abundantly blessed'

The Archbishop views approve of some of these marriages, though he refuses to permit them to be solemnised in church.

"Let me say quite frankly," he wrote in his pamphlet, "that in some cases where a first marriage has ended in tragedy, a second marriage has, to every test of the State Spirit that we are able to recognise, been abundantly blessed.

"For this very reason I do not find myself able to forbid good people to come to me for advice to embark on a second marriage ... The decision is in their conscience."

Lifelong

The Commission of Canterbury and York—the Church of England's definite-to Parliament—declared 12 years ago that "in the physical union of man and wife, which is of the essence of marriage, two become one flesh; and it is inherent in every marriage entered between Christians and to see the Marriage Service, in the Marriage Service, the Church should and that service in the case of people who have declared their life-long...

That was but is a standing ... a Couple Lord, as it has present ... that the Partite ...

There was an article of account Anglican view that had the Church's teaching: cheap for the marriage of divorced should be done before...

The two obstacles

IAN TRETHOWAN WRITES:

The story can now be reconstructed. When the Group-Captain returned on leave from Brussels on Oct. 12 and the couple met again after a two-year separation—they have, in fact, met 11 times since then—they wanted to marry.

In private talks during the following days the Princess began to piece together in earnest the dilemma which had been hovering just below the horizon during the two years of waiting.

As is now clear from last night's statement two obstacles had to be put in her way:

● *Her having had to insist that she must renounce her right of succession to the Throne ; and* ·

● *Her church had to insist that she ought not to be married in a religious ceremony.*

The need for her renouncing succession was inescapable. If she had become Queen while married to the Group-Captain she would have breached her a Church which did not approve of her marriage in view of the fact that she referred only to the possibility of a CIVIL marriage. This would suggest she had herself ruled out the possibility of being married by a minister of the Church of Scotland.

Inevitably the question will be asked : Was the decisive voice that of the Archbishop of Canterbury? If it was, then it can be said that the views spoke in humane service.

The Princess saw the Archbishop last Thursday at Lambeth Palace. Otherwise she seems to have relied on the counsels of her family and friends.

The decisive voice

How deeply she was affected by the Church's teaching emerges from her statement—not only in the reasons for her decision, but also in the fact that she referred only to the possibility of a CIVIL marriage. This would suggest she had herself ruled out the possibility of being married by a minister of the Church of Scotland.

Inevitably the question will be asked : Was the decisive voice that of the Archbishop of Canterbury? If it was, then it can be said that the views spoke in humane service.

The Princess saw the Archbishop last Thursday at Lambeth Palace. Otherwise she seems to have relied on the counsels of her family and friends.

While the world waited...

RUMOURS of the romance between the Princess and Group - Captain Townsend first began in earnest two years ago when he was posted to Brussels as Air Attaché in June 1953.

For most several short visits to Britain from Brussels mostly on official business.

Then, early in October this year, he announced that he would be going on leave to Belgium for about a month, adding that he could be present at ... as he could as Air Attaché in the meantime. He flew over on Oct. 12.

Next day he called at ... Clarence House and saw the Princess, who had arrived that morning from Scotland. He stayed for several hours.

He stayed for nearly two hours on the Monday, Oct. 17, when they again dined together. On the 14 he went to Allenby, near Wokingham (Berks), to spend the weekend with Major and Mrs. John Wills. Princess Margaret arrived five hours later.

Their host meeting was took at London on Monday, Oct. 17, where they were guests at a dinner party given by Mr. and Mrs. Bretham Clarke at Mansfield-court, Kensington.

On Oct. 18 there was another ... meeting at Clarence House, followed two days later by a fifth at Kisserton - street, Knightsbridge, where the couple were guests at an informal dinner party given by Major and Mrs. John Wills.

Their last meeting of the week was on Oct. 21, when they dined with Mr. and Mrs. Marquad Heard at Mr. Leonard's-house, Cuckoo.

Princess Margaret and the couple were at a week-end as a guest of Lord and Lady Rupert Nevill at their home, Uckfield House, Sussex. Group-Capt. Townsend was also a guest.

Cut-together please : Page Two

Princess Margaret arrives back at Clarence House after a week-end visit to Uckfield House, Sussex.

Group-Capt. Peter Townsend in London-square, where he is staying, just before the announcement was made. He had returned from a visit to Clarence House.

SHUT DOWN OUT-OF-DATE MILLS

"Way to soften cotton blow"—Sir Alfred Roberts

NEWS CHRONICLE REPORTER

SIR ALFRED ROBERTS, general secretary of cotton's biggest spinning union, yesterday called for Operation Streamline to save the cotton industry.

Out-of-date mills, he declared, should now be shut down with the co-operation of the Government, employers and unions to "soften the blow" to the workers.

He told the conference of the Lancashire T.U.C. of the substantial redundancy in the industry.

Most mills were running at 80 per cent. or less of their working capacity and 37,000 workers were on short time.

The selection of mills, for closure should be on the grounds of age and out-of-date machinery. There would be human and social problems.

"We cannot wait until the forces of attrition close the mills down," said Sir Alfred, an experienced member of the T.U.C.

The cotton industry was to be put on a competitive basis it would now have to see how far it could go towards a redundancy scheme which would save the most efficient mills to stave off decline.

There are 1,888 spinning and weaving mills in Lancashire. So far this year it is estimated 50 mills have shut down.

6d. more for a bag of coal

FROM today the householder will have to pay an extra 6d. for a bag of coal.

The coal trade's winter season starts today, and the summer "rebate"—to encourage people to stock up in the winter—is being withdrawn.

Grade IV coal which, with Grade III, is usually delivered for household use, goes up from 6s. 0½d. to 6s. 6½d. in the Manchester area, and from 6s. 2d. to 6s. 8d. in the Blackburn district.

The 6d. increase will be made in most parts of the North of England and Scotland.

Life ban on drivers

Italian motorists will lose their driving licences for life after 11 convictions under a new law being studied by the Government.

Top jobs switch in B.E.A.

SIR ARNOLD OVERTON, a part-time member of British European Airways Board, is to be its full-time deputy chairman for the time being because of the illness of Sir John Keeling, the deputy chairman, and the resignation of the chief executive, Mr. Peter Masefield, to join the Bristol Aeroplane Company.

Lord Douglas of Kirtleside, the chairman, will act in addition as chief executive.

ISRAELIS SPURN RUSSIAN ARMS

GENEVA, Monday.

ISRAEL will not seek from Russia any defence guarantee such as she wants from the West, nor will she accept Communist arms if they are offered.

This was disclosed authoritatively in Geneva tonight just as Israel's Premier, Mr. Moshe Sharett, was arriving at the Soviet villa for his long-awaited interview with Mr. Molotov.

Mr. Sharett is reported to have told the Soviet Foreign Minister that the Russian manoeuvre in Middle East power has imperilled the life of the seven-year-old Jewish State.

He asked for a halt to the supply of Communist arms to the Arab States in fear of halting that could engulf Europe in the world. It also prompted Israel's matter of non-alignment, which Russia appeared in other parts of the world.

Earlier today Mr. Molotov placed before the Western Foreign Ministers a new European security plan calling for a 36-nation pact, based on an indissolubly divided Germany.

Buffer zone

It proposed a buffer zone made up of both halves of divided Germany and 47 of some neighbouring States.

The plan drops the previous Soviet demand that the Atlantic Pact and the Communist counterpart should be replaced by a new one. In the past three years, the eventual abolition of the two groupings is still provided for, but no time limit is set.

Mr. Harold Macmillan, for the West, said that he would make a careful study of the new Soviet plan. At first sight, some points held out the hope of advance.—Reuter.

RSPCA in talks about National

AFTER discussions between the R.S.P.C.A. and Aintree racecourse owners about the Grand National, Mr. Richard Clitheroe, the society's Liverpool secretary, said yesterday he had been invited to watch this year's race.

The society's chief officers have pressed for a number of safety regulations, but they could be carried out.

If no satisfactory conclusion is reached, the R.S.P.C.A. will ask its members to bring pressure to bear through the Ministry.

R.A.F. owed 9d...

EX-NATIONAL SERVICE man G. Donald Laws, of Rochester, demanded on Oct. 1 received a money order for 9d. back pay yesterday.

It met the R.A.F. 1s. 9d. to send him a final repayment enclosing another 9d.

NEW RAFT TO SAVE LIVES IS TESTED

By VERNON BRANDS

RAFTS are being seriously tried out by the Ministry of Transport into the use of inflatable rubber rafts as part of a merchant ship's normal equipment for saving life at sea.

During the Ministry Inquiry into the loss of the P and O cargo-ship Trentino at the coast of Ireland last November it was revealed that such craft were among have been of service.

Now the Inquiry concluded yesterday Captain Edward Lewis, having realised the vapour of the Ministry, said rubber rafts could contribute to safety, and the Ministry had associated itself with private tests and organised tests itself.

Best chance

Such rafts did not come under the international sea safety regulations, but they could be carried to ships in addition to the standard equipment.

"I feel myself," said Capt. Lewis, "that in the case of the Trentino, rubber dinghies would have stood the best chance."

When the Trentino sank in a gale the ship and taken a list and it was difficult to get lifeboats away. Inflatable rubber rafts, or dinghies, could have kept them near the side without difficulty.

Bleriot taught him to fly

MR. Gerald Higginbottom, the first man to take pilotless flights, died today in a nursing home at Buxton, aged 80.

He was the builder of a Bleriot Trade flying fleece taught in England, first man to take pilotless training.

In 1911 he carried the first air mail in the North.

Eden to meet TUC on Budget

By DOUGLAS BROWN

THE Prime Minister the Chancellor the Exchequer, and the Minister of Labour will meet leaders of the T.U.C. this afternoon.

This meeting, to discuss the threat of a spate of wage claims as a result the Budget was announced by Mr. Butler in the Commons yesterday.

In a debate on an Opposition motion censuring the Government's decision to be defeated by 324 to 261—he only becomes quiet and liberals.

Throwing aside his mace said : "I think the effect of Budget on the wage-earning population has been very much exaggerated."

Mr. Gaitskell interrupted to seriously suggesting a wrong to claim there was when he has deliberately put the cost of living by an increase in purchase tax and in producing it up still further when go up?

Mr. Butler : "It seems to a pernicious doctrine—the Conservatives will repeat it if ever—

LATE NEWS

Manchester Blackfriars
London—Float-at.

return to power—that in event of taxes being reduced there has to be a rise in wages.

An appealed for a united front from the House to country—not that, facing the to get full employment and standard of living" which we inherited from the loss—(laughter).

At those final words Mr. B suddenly shook his head.

CENSURE DEBATE
Page Two

Property abroad
Property and equipment allover the world in the face Bowes Bowerman is valued £4,335,089,000.

TODAY'S WEATHER — RATHER cloudy ; some bright intervals, over normal temperatures. Sun rises 7.04, sets 4.36. Lighting-up: 5.06. High-water (Liverpool) : 11.33, 11.54.

I said, 'It's about John Pharaoh.'

I heard her sigh. 'Chrissakes, Peggy,' she said, 'can't you let a thing rest?'

I said, 'Just listen, will you? I found out something and it's the darndest thing. I don't have anybody else I can tell, if I don't tell you. Did you know they weren't married? Kath and John?'

She didn't know. I could tell. I said, 'And here's the thing. Reason they weren't married was, they couldn't be. They were brother and sister.'

She pulled the car over and stopped. Then she sat there, looking at me.

I said, 'So you didn't know either? I wondered if it was just me.'

'Say it again,' she said.

So I told her exactly what I'd heard Kath say on the Greyhound.

'Brother and sister,' she said. And she started to laugh. 'You're kidding me.'

But she knew from my face, I wasn't. She laughed and laughed.

Eventually she said, 'I guess that means I wasn't as bad as everybody painted me.'

I said, 'Well . . . if we leave Herb out of the reckoning.'

'Herb's my business,' she said. She'd stopped laughing. She said 'Are you gonna ask Kath? About their sleeping arrangements?'

I said, 'Any suggestions how that conversation might go?'

We bought enough carnations and maidenhair fern to make boutonnières all round, plus rice for throwing. All the while Lois kept saying, 'My God! Brother and sister!'

I said, 'You won't say anything to Kath? You won't get a drink inside you and say anything?'

'At a Baptist wedding?' she said. 'No. Anyway, I don't want to start up with Kath. I like her. And she's looking great. She looks younger now than when we met her. She got a man? Now her . . . *brother* ain't around?'

I said, 'No. She's just got a decent place to live. And dentures.'

Lois said, 'How about you? You dating?'

I didn't have any inclination for dating. Figured I'd spent years enough fitting in with a man. Besides, I knew Crystal was still hoping me and Vern'd get back together some day. I could imagine the kinda welcome she'd give any man came calling for me.

I said, 'You and Herb still going strong?'

'Rubbing along,' she said. 'Herb's happy. Sandie's happy. Any day now, Kirk'll get happy. If I had my way, we'd move back to New York, or Albany at least. Then I could get a job. Have a few bucks to call my own.'

I said, 'What could you do?'

'I dunno,' she said. 'I could be a secretary.'

I said, 'Do you know how to type and do shorthand and everything?'

'I can *look* like I know how,' she said.

I said, 'I wish I could do something.'

'What's stopping you?' she said. 'Hell, Peg, it's not like you're out in the wilderness, like me. Right now, nearest place of employment for me is Puffer's Guns and Ammo. And don't think I haven't considered it. Get myself a staff discount, go home and blow my brains out. You could be a secretary. Answer the phone. Send out for the tuna subs. Keep your nails nice. How hard can it be?'

When we got back, Carla and Kirk were both still crayoning-in like demons.

Betty whispered to me, 'Have you noticed? How messy he colours? I don't believe he even tries to stay inside the lines.'

48

Gayle looked so pretty. She was in ivory, with a crinoline skirt, knee-length, and a lace shrug and spike heels. Ray and his best man were in their Dress Charlies: khaki shirts and ties, blue trousers with the red stripe, and white caps.

The marrying was at the Hubert First Baptist Church and refreshments were served at the Legion Hall. Peanuts, devilled eggs, moon pies and fruit cake.

Apart from us, it was mainly folk that knew Gayle from the cafeteria. There was one old boy, said he'd been set on Gayle hisself only he didn't want to stand in the way of a younger man. He seemed to have gotten over his disappointment, though, because he was very attentive to Kath. Only the language barrier and his habit of talking whilst chewing on a plug of Levi Garrett stopped things running out of control.

Ray's folks sent a telegram from West Virginia and Audrey and Lance sent one from England. Gayle's folks sent nothing.

'You're my family,' she said to me and Lois.

Lo said, 'Heaven help you, my child.'

Gayle said, 'I mean it. And when we get our baby, I want y'all back here for the christening.'

We all knew that might take a while. Ray and Gayle were having three days at Cape Hatteras, fishing for white marlin, then he was getting deployed to the Indian Ocean or someplace and she'd be on her own again.

'I'll be fine,' she said. 'I've got the Silver Moon. I can work as many shifts as I choose and there's always somebody to talk to. It's not like with Okey. Sitting home waiting for him to . . .'

We waved them off, cleared the hostess's house, and then headed out to Surf City for one last night together. Seven of us in Lois's old Nash. It was the kind of heat that makes people quarrelsome. First Carla started up, claimed Kirk kept pinching her – and I wouldn't have been surprised. Then Carla complained about the type of music we had on the radio, and Kirk got balled out by Lois for getting chewing gum on his wedding pants.

Betty said, 'Just put it in the icebox when you get home, and it'll pick off easy as anything.'

Lois said, 'Where the hell did you learn a thing like that?'

'Future Homemakers,' Betty said. 'Didn't you ever have Make-Good Week at Future Homemakers?'

I guess they had different things in Astoria.

Betty said, 'Make-Good Week. Hobo Days. Bake Sales. Remember, Peggy?'

Lois said, 'Not you too, Peg? Y'all wear special aprons and everything?'

I said 'Not me. I was Softball, One, Two, Three and Four.'

Betty said, 'Well, there you are. I don't believe you've pitched a ball since we were at Drampton, but Future Homemakers is still doing me proud.' She started reciting. '. . . for we are the builders of homes. Homes for America's future . . .'

Lois said, 'Sounds like Levitt Town.'

'. . . Homes where living will be the expression of everything that is good and fair. Homes where truth and love and security and faith will be realities, not dreams . . .'

'And gum on your pants will be fixed in no time . . .' Lois was laughing. And the more offended Betty got, the more Lois teased her. I was glad when we checked into the Topsail Beach Motel and went right out again for boiled shrimp and beer.

Betty said, 'Lois, I don't want to quarrel with you. I love you really.'

Lo said, 'I love you too.'

The cold beer was having an improving effect.

Betty said, 'I just don't always get your jokes.'

Lois said, 'Hey, I open my mouth, don't care who I upset. Herb threatens to get me fitted with a muzzle.'

Betty said, 'No, no! You make people laugh. Everybody says so. I just don't have a sense of humour.'

Lo said, 'Well, at least you have humility.'

'That's true,' Betty said.

Peace reigned while we peeled shrimp.

Kath said, 'You do have lovely grub in America. And all different kinds. Like these shrimp. They're so tasty, but I've never seen anything like that in Lynn. Chops. That's what I get at home. Chops, everlasting chops. If I stopped here long I should get to be such a size.'

We talked about little Gayle, and her new-found happiness. We talked about the day Okey augered in. First time we'd felt able to really let rip about it, now we were all outta danger. First time we'd owned up to each other about the nightmares and the shakes and jumping a mile high when the phone rang. If Crystal hadn't been there, listening in, I could have added never really losing your heart to friend husband, in case he don't come home some day.

Betty said, 'I'd always do a terrible thing. Any time anything happened ... I'd tell God I'd do *anything*, long as it was somebody else's husband they were bringing back in a casket.' One beer and Betty could get pretty mournful. But then she stopped. She said, 'Oh Kath, I'm sorry. Talking that way, after your sad loss.'

Kath said, 'That's all right. Everybody loses somebody. Far as I know, nobody lives for ever.'

Betty said, 'Well, no, but ... here I am talking about losing Ed, but I still have him. You're the one has lost your ... husband.'

I could hear the blood pounding in my ears. I knew what was coming next, and I couldn't stop it. I asked the kids if they wanted more Cola.

Crystal said, 'I thought you never got married, Aunty Kath?'

'I didn't,' she said.

Carla said, 'Are we talking about people dying?'

Betty said, 'No, we are not. Why don't I give you a nickel, and you and Crystal can go and pick out something on the jukebox?'

Carla took the nickel. She said, 'Aunty Kath's brother died and now she's all alone.'

Kath looked at Betty, Betty looked at me, Lois was studying the bottom of her glass.

I said, 'Kath, you want to hear something crazy?' I could feel my face was flushed.

49

Kath said, 'I think I know what you're going to say.'

I said, 'When we met you, went back to your place . . .'

'That's right,' she said, 'you took me home and there was John Pharaoh and you thought he was my husband. I never even thought. I mean, everybody in Smeeth and Brakey and all around, they've known us since we were nippers. That never occurred to me. And then after he passed over, one or two things that were said . . .'

She laughed. 'That's funny, really. If I'd gone in for a husband, I'd have picked somebody better than my John. I'd have picked somebody that weren't so sickly.'

I said, 'Well, it was a kinda embarrassing mistake for us.'

Betty was sober all of a sudden. She said, 'You knew about this, Peggy?'

I said, 'I've been realising, slowly.'

'Carla,' she said, real sharp, 'go play that jukebox right now!'

She waited till Carla had gone. Then she turned to Lois. 'Did you know?' she said. Lois took a swallow of beer.

'Kind of,' she said. 'Why are you getting all shrill about it, Betty? It's just a stupid mix-up.'

'That's right,' Kath said. 'And I tell you what, that's probably a lot funnier for me than it is for you. Wait till I get back and tell May. She'll see the funny side of it. Me and May used to push John round in a potato box, when he was a toddler, pretend it was a dolly's pram.'

Betty was quiet a moment. 'But . . .' That was all she said.

Kath said, 'Well, that was how we muddled along in the bad old days. We only had one room, same as a lot of people.'

Betty whispered to me, 'It's contrary to nature, Peggy. Contrary to nature and contrary to scripture.'

Lois said, 'Crying out loud, Betty. Anybody's think you just found out the moon was made of cheese. Didn't you ever drive through West Virginia?'

Carla come running back with the information that a guy making his selection at the jukebox had told her to get lost.

'Time we were going anyway,' Betty said. 'Before I hear any more bad surprises.'

Kirk was hanging on to Kath on the way to the parking lot. I couldn't take to the kid myself, but he didn't act so cheeky around her.

He said, 'I'm gonna be a Marine like Ray.'

'Are you?' she said. 'I reckon you'd be good at that.'

He said, 'I'm a brave fighter.'

'I can see that,' she said. 'But they won't have you if you can't add up. So you've got to settle down at school. Pass all the tests.'

'Yeah,' he said. 'I can do all that.' And he threw himself down and wriggled along on his belly and his elbows, Marine-style, till Lois bawled him out for ruining his wedding clothes.

I got a few questions from Crystal when were back in our motel room.

'What does "contrary to nature" mean?' she said. 'And how come a black can be a Marine but he can't ride on any bus seat he chooses?'

Seemed to me, fourteens were a deal more forward than in my day.

Lois and Kirk waved us off at the bus terminal next morning. Lo tried to kiss Kath goodbye but they bashed noses, the English not being accustomed to kissing on the cheek.

Lois said, 'Next time, Kath, you come to New York, and I'll show you a different side to things.'

I said, 'You really think you're gonna get Herb down there?'

'Yes. Just watch me,' she said.

I cried when the bus pulled out. I cried all the way to Fayetteville, embarrassing my poor child.

Betty said, 'You got the blues, honey? You're probably over-tired. Have one of my happy pills.'

First I knew Betty Gillis was taking anything stronger than BiSoDol.

Kath said, 'That gets you thinking, when you haven't seen people in a long time. How the years do fly.'

She was exactly right. I was feeling so old. Nearly thirty-eight and I hadn't done a damn thing except hang drapes in a dozen different Wherry cabins, try to give Crystal a home.

I said, 'Lois is gonna be a secretary.'

Betty said, 'That's just talk. She better stay home, straighten out that boy, or she'll be sorry. Secretary!'

I said, 'I wouldn't mind being a secretary myself. I could go to classes. Kath did, didn't you?'

'I did,' she said. 'I went for book-keeping, and I soon picked it up. But that's boring, Peggy. I can't see that being up your alley. You know what I'm thinking of? Get myself a little motor and teach people to drive, like you taught me. I might just teach ladies. The way I see it, the motor'd soon pay for itself. And I'd be out and about all day. I'd call it Kath's School of Motoring. Have it painted on the side.'

I said, 'See, Betty? Everybody's planning something. What are you gonna do when your girls are all grown up and gone?'

'Mind their babies,' she said.

I said, 'But what if they never have any, or they move away?'

'Peggy!' she said. 'No wonder you have the blues! Well, first, of *course* they'll have babies. And second, even if Carla and Sherry don't, I'll always have Deana's to mind. And anybody else who needs me. The world will always need babysitters.'

I looked at Crystal, sitting there in her dungarees, playing Go Fish with Carla. Still hoping to see a revolution, I daresay. We were barrelling along the Interstate 20 and I was forming a plan. Write to Vern. Put it to him, we could try again. Crystal'd have her daddy.

There'd be two of us to meet the payments every month. And I'd learn typing. Take a leaf outta Lois Moon's book. First time for everything. Hell, I was even willing to relocate.

Turned out, same time I'd been thinking of Vern he'd been thinking of me. The day I took Kath to catch her plane, I got his letter. Crystal was hopping around, dying for me to come home and open it.

'Dad sent for me?' she said. 'He send bus money?'

'Dear Peg,' he wrote. 'Hoping this finds you well. Mom has a hiatus hernia, has to sleep sitting up else she gets acid indigestion. Heather had to have a mole took off, all the way to Portland. Otherwise can't complain.' Heather was one of his sisters.

Reason for my putting pen to paper, I have met somebody, and hoping to make a go of it. Her name is Martine, very nice, I think you'd like her. She has a boy, Eugene, same age as Crystal – same month, too; it's a small world. Anyways, we have found a place, looking to start up a bait farm. Always was my dream to have a fishing store, as you know, but it's a risky business, tying up all your money in rods and stuff. Bait farm has lower start-up costs. We're going in for leather worms. Grow a quality worm, have it available all through the season, it has to beat nightcrawlers for reliability and freshness. Eugene has read up on it and we think this could be a sure thing. I'd say the sky is the limit.

So if you and me could do the necessary I'd be obliged. Be nice for us if we could get wed in the winter before business gets going. You let me know what you spend and I'll send you a check for my half. Love to Crystal. She's getting to be quite the young lady.

I said, 'You're getting a step-brother. His name's Eugene and he's a expert on worms.'

She said, 'I guess that's a "No" on the bus money?'

I said, 'Don't you want to hear about your step-mom?'

'No,' she said. 'Why can't we be a normal family, like Carla's or Kirk's?'

I was filling up again, feeling so sad for my kid, so sad for myself. Then I seen her cheeky smile.

'Carla,' she said. She had Betty's voice exactly. 'Here's your sick-bag, now, honey. Hurl into it nicely for Mommy.'

I said, 'Crystal, what am I gonna do when you're gone?'

'Darned if I know,' she said. 'Answer my fan-mail?'

50

First thing Kath did when she got back to England was spend the rest of her winnings on a car. Then she took her friend May Gotobed out in it and taught her everything she knew. That was the start of Kath's School of Motoring.

Vern and Martine were married in December, and Crystal marked the occasion by burning his picture. She was just mad about not being there, I guess.

Vern had said, 'Put her on the bus. I'll meet her.'

I said, 'Out of the question. I guarantee you, somewhere between here and Maine she'd take up with a bunch of black revolutionaries and we'd never see her again.'

He said, 'Sounds like you need to take a firmer line with her.'

I said, 'I'll bear it in mind.'

Men have no idea.

October of '62, Deana gave birth to Dawn, a baby sister for Delta and a second grandchild for Betty and Ed, and Fidel Castro and the Russians pushed their luck a step too far. Betty laid in an extra store of canned corned beef in case of atomic war. I didn't bother. Crystal had become something called a vegetarian.

When Audrey wrote, at Christmas, she described it as an exciting time, although that wasn't my recollection of it.

'We were sealed off here,' she wrote. 'We were in a state of combat-readiness and the perimeter was secured with armed patrols. But, as the president said, we faced the Soviets eyeball to eyeball, and they blinked.'

Lois, said 'Can't you just imagine Audrey ready for combat? Standing alert with her sugar tongs. We'll probably be seeing the inside of the Rudman bunker in *Better Homes and Gardens*. How about Gayle, though? Ain't she the lucky one?'

Ray Flagg had got an accompanied tour to Honolulu, but Gayle wasn't happy. She had left behind all her friends at the Silver Moon Luncheonette and, being a *haole*, she didn't have a snowball in hell's chance of getting work.

I said, 'She's lonely. Lying on a beach ain't everything.'

Lo said, 'I'll trade with her. She can come to Kurpenkill and listen to Herb holding forth on the termite resistance of the Douglas Fir.'

EXTRA | REPRINT BROUGHT TO YOU BY N-C ASSOCIATES | **EXTRA**

The Evening Star
WITH SUNDAY MORNING EDITION

111th Year.   No. 326.   Phone LI. 3-5000   XX   WASHINGTON, D. C., FRIDAY, NOVEMBER 22, 1963—76 PAGES   Home Delivered: Daily and Sunday, per month, 2.25   10 Cents

SNIPER KILLS KENNEDY
JOHNSON IS PRESIDENT

JOHN F. KENNEDY

LYNDON B. JOHNSON

DALLAS, Tex., Nov. 22 (AP).— President John F. Kennedy, 36th President of the United States, was shot to death today by a hidden assassin armed with a high-powered rifle.

Mr. Kennedy, 46, lived about 30 minutes after a sniper cut him down as his limousine left downtown Dallas. Reporters said the shot that hit him was fired about 12:30 p.m. (CST). A hospital announcement said he died at approximately 1 p.m. of a bullet wound in the head.

Automatically, the mantle of the presidency fell to Vice President Lyndon B. Johnson, a native Texan who had been riding two cars behind the Chief Executive.

In Washington, Air Force officers said Mr. Kennedy's body would arrive at Andrews Air Force Base in Maryland at 6:05 p.m. Washington time, with the new President and Mrs. Kennedy.

Assistant Presidential Press Secretary Malcolm Kilduff said Mr. Johnson was not hurt. The new President previously had been wounded. Mr. Kennedy died at Parkland hospital, where his bullet-pierced body had been taken in a frantic but futile effort to save his life.

Lying wounded and in serious condition in the same hospital was Gov. John Connally of Texas, who was cut down by the same fusillade that ended the life of the youngest man ever elected to the presidency.

Gov. Connally and his wife had been riding with the President and Mrs. Kennedy.

The First Lady cradled her dying husband's blood-smeared head in her arms as the presidential limousine raced to the hospital.

"Oh, no," she kept crying. She was not hurt.

Slumped Beside President

Gov. Connally slumped in his seat beside the President.

Police ordered an immediate dragnet of the city, hunting for the assassin.

They believed the fatal shots were fired a white man about 35, slender of build, weighing about 165 pounds, and standing 5 feet 10 inches tall.

The murder weapon reportedly was a .30-30 rifle.

Shortly before Mr. Kennedy's death became known, he was administered the last rites of the Roman Catholic Church. He had been the first Roman Catholic President in American history.

Even as two clergymen hovered over the dying President in the hospital emergency room, doctors and nurses administered blood transfusions.

Mr. Kennedy died of a gunshot wound in the brain at approximately 1 p.m. (CST) according to an announcement by Mr. Kilduff.

The new President, Lyndon Johnson, and wife left the hospital a half hour later. Reporters had no opportunity to question them.

The horror of the assassination broke in full upon a somewhat unbelieving city in an eyewitness account by Senator Ralph Yarborough, Democrat of Texas, who had ridden three cars behind Mr. Kennedy.

"You could tell something awful and tragic had happened," the Senator told reporters before Mr. Kennedy's death became known. His voice was breaking and his eyes red-rimmed, Senator Yarborough said:

"I could see a Secret Service man in the President's car leaning on the car with his hands in anger, anguish and despair. I knew then something tragic had happened."

Counted Three Rifle Shots

Senator Yarborough had counted three rifle shots as the presidential limousine left downtown Dallas through a triple underpass. The shots were fired from above—possibly from one of the bridges or from a nearby building.

One witness, television reporter Mal Couch said he saw a gun emerge from an upper story of a warehouse commanding an unobstructed view of the presidential car.

Mr. Kennedy was the first President to be assassinated since...

See SHOOTING, Page A-

Biography of President Kennedy.   Page A-

Johnson Takes Oath on Plane

DALLAS, Nov. 22 (AP).— Lyndon B. Johnson was sworn in as President of the United States at 3:39 p.m. (CST) today.

The oath was administered by United States District Judge Sarah T. Hughes.

Mr. Johnson took the oath aboard the presidential plane at Dallas' Love Field, then took off to fly to Washington to take over the Government.

"I do solemnly swear that I will faithfully execute the office of President of the United States, and will to the best of my ability, preserve, protect and defend the Constitution of the United States."

Details Not Available

Further details of the swearing in were not immediately available.

Present at the swearing-in were Mrs. Kennedy and Mrs. Johnson, several staff members and several Congressmen.

Mr. Johnson asked as many of the White House people as possible to crowd into the executive area of the plane to witness the ceremony.

Judge Hughes wept as she administered the presidential oath.

The presidential plane took off with Mr. Johnson, Mrs. Kennedy and wide House aides aboard.

Mr. Johnson married Claudia Taylor in 1934, but now know to everyone as

Lady Bird, a name given her in infancy by a nurse.

Their first child was named Lynda Bird Johnson, and their second, Lucy Baines Johnson.

During the 1930s, Mr. Johnson became associated with President Roosevelt through his connection with the New Deal.

Get Key Committee Post

The President's influence and him appointed to the important House Naval Affairs Committee in 1937, a singular honor for a freshman Congressman.

His political career continued mostly upward from then on, although he lost a runoff election for the Senate in 1941 to Gov. W. Lee O'Daniel.

He was the first member of the House in an active military duty after Pearl Harbor. He became a Lieutenant Commander in the Navy. He had been in the Reserve for several years.

While stationed in New Zealand and Australia he won

bombing missions in the South Pacific and won the Silver Star. He was decorated personally by Gen. Douglas MacArthur.

After serving for eight months he returned to Congress, the Democrats were in the saddle and Mr. Johnson became the Senate Majority Leader, the most powerful job on Capitol Hill.

In 1960, Mr. Johnson, backed by many Southern delegations, made a determined effort to win the Democratic presidential nomination. But he was frustrated by the young Senator from Massachusetts.

Bid for Presidency in '60

Mr. Kennedy received the votes on the first ballot, and Mr. Johnson, 480. The number required for nomination was 761.

Offered Second Spot

To offer the country a balanced ticket, Mr. Kennedy asked Mr. Johnson to accept the second spot on the ticket. He said, "Lyndon Johnson has demonstrated on many occasions his brilliant qualifica-

tions for the leadership we require today."

Although it meant giving up considerable political power to assume the vice presidency Mr. Johnson accepted. His support was considered a major factor in the Kennedy victory.

Mr. Johnson, a Southern Protestant, balanced the Yankee Catholicism of Mr. Kennedy.

Mr. Johnson started his career with a civil political heritage on both sides. Both his father and maternal grandfather, a Confederate veteran, served in the Texas House of Representatives.

On his maternal side, he was descended from Baptist preachers and educators.

Mr. Johnson worked his way through Southwest Texas Teachers College at San Marcos near his birthplace and hometown, Johnson City. He, after graduation in 1930, he taught school before coming to Washington in 1931 with Texas Congressman Richard Kleberg as secretary.

In 1935 he returned to Texas as State administrator for the National Youth Administration.

Early in 1937 the 10th Congressman, James P. Buchanan, chairman of the

See JOHNSON, Page A-4

Ted Kennedy Gets News in Senate Chair

A shocked Senate abandoned all business and adjourned today when it heard the tragic news of the assassination of President Kennedy.

The Senate had adjourned while doctors were still trying to save the President's life, but they had joined their chaplain, Rev. Dr. Frederick Brown Harris, in offering a prayer that God save his life if it be His Will.

The Senate was considering a routine bill to expand Federal aid to public libraries, with Senator Edward Kennedy, the President's youngest brother, sitting as presiding officer.

Richard Riddell, the press liaison officer of the Senate, had heard the early bulletins from Texas and whispered to Senator Kennedy that his brother had been shot.

Holland Takes Over

The Senator hurriedly gathered up his papers and left the chamber as Senator Spessard L. Holland, Democrat of Florida, offered to take over as presiding officer.

No public announcement of the assassination was made to the Senate galleries, but Senator Mike Mansfield, Democrat of Montana, leader of the pending bill remarked that "this is a time to pray."

The Senate then recessed briefly while Senators gathered around two news service tickers, their heads bowed, to read the developments in the cloakroom to scan the latest bulletins.

Mansfield Weeps

After a few moments Democratic Leader Mansfield and Republican Leader Dirksen descended to reconvene the Senate and have the Chaplain offer a prayer. The Senate then adjourned until Monday and will go on hold an hour in tribute to President Kennedy. The suspect was captured a telephone call from Texas confirming the news that the President had died.

There were tears in Senator Mansfield's eyes when he said, "This is a deep and personal loss. The President gave so much to the world and should

See COMMENT, Page A-3

Robert Kennedy Hears News During Lunch in McLean

Attorney General Robert F. Kennedy learned of the assassination of his brother at a luncheon conference at his estate with a New York district attorney in the Robert Kennedy home at McLean, Va.

A Justice Department aide said word came to the attorney General shortly after the meeting is a luncheon call from J. Edgar Hoover, director of the Federal Bureau of Investigation.

Mr. Kennedy was eating lunch with District Attorney Robert Morgenthau of the Southern Federal District Court in Manhattan, and one of the prosecutor's assistants.

A short time later, Joan McCone, director of the Central Intelligence Agency, which has its headquarters in nearby Langley, Va., hurried to the Attorney General's side.

Mrs. Ethel Kennedy, the rosy-cheeked wife, went away from their side at 4700 Old Chain Bridge road, where some of the grieving family.

About 3 p.m. a short drive in a white station wagon with one of the Robert Kennedy children, 7-year old David. They emerged from the car silently. The man handed little boy his lunch pail and the two strode into the house without a word to newsmen and others standing outside.

The Kennedy comp.

About 1:10 p.m., the Attorney General was informed in his office that were notified their wait.

Nearby two large black dogs romped beside them.

At 2:30 p.m. a break from a nearby Catholic church hurried to the home of the grieving family.

Mr. Kennedy was expected to see if he had any connection with the slaying of the President. The suspect was said to have been under questioning arrest earlier from the Texas Theater where he fled following the slaying of a Dallas policeman.

He was also being interrogated to see if he had any connection with the slaying of the President. The suspect was earlier today in connection with the slaying of a Dallas policeman shortly after President Kennedy was assassinated.

Dallas Policeman Slain, Suspect Being Questioned

DALLAS, Tex., Nov. 22 (AP). —The Dallas Police Department today arrested Lee H. Oswald, 24, in connection with the slaying of a Dallas policeman shortly after President Kennedy was assassinated.

He was also being interrogated to see if he had any connection with the slaying of the President. The suspect was arrested earlier today in the Oak Cliff section of Dallas.

The Secret Service denied an earlier report that one of the agents had been slain in Dallas.

CAROLINE, JOHN TAKING NO NOT TOLD AT ONCE OF DEATH

Caroline and John F. Kennedy Jr., the children of the slain President, were taking their afternoon nap when word reached the White House that their father was dead at the hands of an assassin.

The 5-year-old daughter and the 3-year-old son were at the White House with their governess, Maude Shaw, when the news came.

The children were not immediately told what happened.

Miss Shaw took the children to their play period soon as the tots too, when the Kennedy always said, John-John, was awake.

51

November twenty-first, 1963 was my fortieth birthday. It was over-looked by everybody except Kath Pharaoh, who sent me a card all the way from Norfolk, England, and my daughter Crystal, who made me a dinner of rice and beans.

At 12.30 p.m. on Friday November twenty-second, 1963, President John F. Kennedy and his wife Jackie were riding in a open-top limousine through downtown Dallas when a sniper opened fire. Two rifle bullets struck the president at the base of his neck and in his head. He was dead on arrival at Parkland Memorial Hospital.

At 11.30 a.m. on Monday November twenty-fifth, the presidential cortège arrived at the White House from Capitol Plaza. The Naval Academy Catholic Choir sang 'Dona Nobis Pacem' and Ed Gillis hurled his family's TV set from the window of their second-floor apartment on Gibb Street South.

First I knew of it, Betty was hammering on my door and when I asked her why she wasn't home, didn't she know the requiem mass had already started, she near enough fainted in my arms. Crystal helped me get her inside and we wrapped her in a blanket, put her between us on the couch so we didn't have to miss any of the funeral. Wasn't long before she was watching with us. We got through a whole box of Kleenex that day.

All she kept saying was, 'I'm so ashamed. I'm so ashamed a thing like this could have happened in Texas.'

I made potato-chip sandwiches and coffee while they were taking him to Arlington Cemetery. I heard Crystal say, 'Everything okay at home, Aunty Betty? Sherry and Carla okay?'

'Well,' she said, 'Sherry is watching with the Lopezes. She's seeing Freddy Lopez, you know? And Carla's out to the base, helping Deana with her babies. I don't know that everything's all right at home, though. I'm not sure if I still have a home.'

Then she told us about Ed and the TV. 'He was in one of his jealous fits,' she said, ''cause I've been so upset about the president. Not paying him attention, I suppose. But he's gone too far this time, Peggy. I've had as much as I can take.'

Mrs Kennedy looked beautiful. I was really sorry for all the bad things I'd said about her.

Betty said, 'She's a inspiration, to stand tall in adversity. I only just finished paying for that TV, and now it's lying in pieces on Gibb, advertising the fact Ed Gillis flew into one of his rages again.'

I said, 'What'll you do?'

'Well,' she said, 'I'll have to go round there. I ran out without my pills or anything. I'll go after they box the flag. I oughta make sure Ed didn't hurt himself neither.'

I said, 'We'll come with you. Get Perry to come with us, in case there's trouble.' Crystal was kinda seeing Perry Kaiser.

I said, 'You think you should stay here a while? You can do.'

'You're a good friend, Peg,' she said. 'If Carla could have your couch and I could manage with pillows on the floor, and maybe Sherry could stay with the Lopezes for a day or two.'

Crystal said, 'You don't want Sherry staying in the same house as that sidewinder. Next thing she'll be pregnant and then she'll never finish school. You and Carla can have my bed, Aunty Betty. I got a double. Me and Sherry can bunk down in here. It'll be fun. We can talk in the night.'

Everything was quiet on Gibb. Betty's downstairs neighbour had cleared away the remains of the television, but I got the impression she had done it in the interests of neighbourhood standards, stop the place looking like a slum, not as a act of kindness. She had a face on her would have stopped an eight-day clock.

Betty ran round, gathering up her bits and pieces, twittering to herself whether to take this or leave that, kinda gay, like she was going on vacation. I guess in a way she was.

I was taping brown paper where the window was broke, looking over my shoulder all the time. I figured he had to be somewhere in the neighbourhood and I didn't want him walking in on us.

I said to Betty, 'Has Ed got a gun?'

She looked at me. 'Well, of course he does,' she said. 'But he wouldn't shoot family.'

I made Crystal wait outside in the street. Perry Kaiser had declined when we asked him to accompany us, said he wasn't allowed out on a day of national mourning.

'He's history,' Crystal said.

Betty was nearly done when I heard Crystal whistle. She could do it with two fingers, so piercing they probably could hear her in Laredo. Vern taught her the trick of it when she was seven years old. Didn't matter how hard I tried, I never could do it.

Ed must have bounded up those stairs.

I said, 'Let's go, Betty.'

He was a sight. Had a two-day beard and a real sloppy shirt. When I think how sharp those boys were turned out when they were in the military. Their belt buckle wasn't in line with their fly, somebody'd want to know why. But those days were long gone for Ed.

He sat down and put his head in his hands, started weeping. I braced myself for Betty to put her bag down, take off her coat. Start some big forgiveness scene. What I knew of her, she wasn't gonna walk out on a broken man. But she just said, 'Ed, I'm leaving. There's only so much a person can take.'

He dropped down on his knees and sobbed and sobbed. Great big Ed Gillis, built like a meat-locker.

And I have to hand it to her. She never looked back. When it came to it, if there was anybody liable to go back in there, try to offer him a word of comfort, it was me. I did so hate to see a man cry.

52

'I don't intend imposing on you,' she said. It was a week since they moved in, but I wasn't chafing to get rid of them. Betty worked eight till four at the Jitney Jungle, brought in all kinds of goods they had on sale, had to be eaten or dumped. And by the time I got home, she always had dinner fixed. Made me realise what a thing it must be to have a wife. She didn't just serve up stew or pie. We had fresh-baked stickies and fudge and a great thing she made with black cherry jello and shredded pineapple.

I had just started as junior bridal consultant at Clancey Reed and it was hard work. I had so much to learn. All the silver patterns and the porcelain and the linen. Last thing I wanted to do was come home and start folding laundry and frying food, and with Betty staying I didn't have to lift a finger.

Crystal was getting on okay with Sherry, too.

'How come I never got a brother or a sister?' she said to me one time.

'So you could be raised in the lap of luxury,' I said, 'like a regular little princess.'

'Right,' she said. 'And when did that idea start to go horribly wrong?'

53

Betty had made one of my favourites: spaghetti with canned turkey-chunks and Velveeta cheese. Even Crystal ate it. Under the influence of Sherry Gillis she had quit being a strict vegetarian and become a strict atheist instead, which was a deal easier on the cook.

'It's our last night,' Betty said. 'Ed's gone back to Indiana, try to straighten himself out, so we'll go home tomorrow. Leave you kind folks in peace.'

I said, 'How are you gonna manage?'

'We'll get by,' she said. 'I've put my name down for extra hours at the JJ, Friday nights. And when I'm not working, I'll find plenty to do. Dressmaking. Babysitting Delta and Dawn.'

I said, 'Well, if you're sure. But I'm gonna miss your company.'

'Likewise,' she said. 'Now, Crystal, whatever is that you're studying?'

'Chambers of the heart,' Crystal said. She was tracing a picture out of her science book. 'We cut up real hearts today, from lambs.'

My kid had a good head on her shoulders. Planning to go to college and then be a nurse to a veterinarian. The word squeamish meant nothing to that child. She'd pulled a thorn outta Mrs Kaiser's dog's foot one time and she couldn't have been more than thirteen.

Betty shuddered. 'Honey, why don't you study something nice?'

she said. 'You're handy. You could make lampshades, or be a fashion designer. Sherry too. You're both kinda artistic.'

I said, 'What's with you and Ed? You divorcing him?'

'No,' she said. 'I'm giving him his chance.'

I said, 'He won't change. In twenty years what did he do? He got worse. Next twenty years what'll he do? He'll get worse still.'

'I guess,' she said.

She was clipping pictures of the president's funeral for her album, sighing over the ones of Mrs Kennedy in her black veil. 'Me and Jackie,' she said. 'Both alone, starting out in our new lives.'

54

In '64, Lois and Herb moved to Albany. They had finally run out out of schools for Kirk in Rensselaer County so they were trying some special place, had new theories about child development.

'The method is,' Lo said, 'let him do as he pleases. His teacher says there's no such thing as a problem child. Only problem adults too uptight to allow him to express himself.'

I said, 'How much are you paying this person to insult you?'

'I'd pay double,' she said, 'because it's working. He's quietened down. Learned to read. Never thought I'd see the day. And you should see some of the fishing flies he's tied. Real works of art. His teacher says a lot of the kids she gets are geniuses almost.'

Herb was selling furniture. She said, 'His heart's not in it, of course. Riles him to see what folk are willing to spend on rubbish. All I hear is *veneer, veneer, veneer.* He sells a person a veneer sideboard, he feels bad about it. Like he'd robbed them at gunpoint. He's gonna stick at it, though. Kirk's settled. Sandie's doing great in school. And he knows better than to upset things for me now.'

Lois was working as secretary to a realtor. She still didn't know shorthand, but she'd talked her way in somehow.

'Nothing to it,' she said. 'I swear, they could train a monkey to do what I do.'

I said, 'How many fingers are you using to type?'

'Why, what's it to you?' she said. 'Well, okay, two, but I do my letters while Mr Holladay is out showing properties. He comes back, letters are done, coffee's on, and I'm wriggling my ass round his office, watering his cheese plant and generally making him feel like God Almighty. Besides, I improve his letters. When it comes to stringing words together, he don't know shit from Shinola. Anyway, what's new with you? You got yourself any dates yet?'

I said, 'I never see any men I want to date.'

'That's because you're looking in the wrong places,' she said. 'Let's go on a trip some time. I'll find you a hundred men. Let's go to Chesapeake Beach Resort. There're dance floors and casinos and everything. Guys looking for a little fun.'

I said, 'You are a forty-year-old married woman. When are you gonna stop this?'

'When they certify me dead,' she said.

I said, 'I would love to see you, Lo. Forget looking for men. I'd love us all to get together again, like we did for Gayle's wedding.'

'Well,' she said. 'I wouldn't mind Gayle. But not Betty, please!'

Betty said, 'Gayle, yes. Lois, no. She wears me out. And if that child of hers is a genius, I'm the Fiesta Queen.'

Gayle said maybe. But only if Ray was deployed, because she hated to be apart from him any more than she had to. And only if it didn't cost big bucks. And only if she could get time off from the Silver Moon. As soon as Ray's tour in paradise was through, she had hurried back to her old life in Jacksonville.

Lance and Audrey were on the move again.

'We're heading east,' she wrote.

US presence at Truxton is being reduced, and Lance got orders to Halby, Norfolk, so we'll be back on familiar territory. Lance informs me we're getting a sail-boat for weekends. Could be the greatest fun if the boys ever find their sea-legs.

We have Mikey and Lance Jnr in a very good school near here, so they are going to stay on and board. It's what you have to do if you want your child to get a decent education and mix with the right people. Also, it teaches them independence. It will take a lot of pressure off me, too. I am so busy with Red Cross and the Air Force Aid Society and a hundred other things, sometimes all I have time to do is come home from my lunch appointment, change for cocktails and run out again.

As soon as we're settled at Halby I intend having Kath over for coffee. Did I tell you I'm getting tennis lessons?

Audrey was as good as her word. By the time I phoned Kath to wish her a happy birthday, she had been honoured with afternoon tea at the Lieutenant Colonel Rudmans.

'Very fancy,' she said. 'Great big place they've got and that's only the two of them. Those boys are hardly there. Beautiful wood floors, and curtains right down to the ground. They've spent some money.'

I said, 'How's Audrey looking?'

'Lovely,' she said. 'She wears her hair pinned up now. She's got a French pleat. And you should see the carry on for a cup of tea. All different kinds, she was offering, didn't mean a thing to me. I told her, "Do you come to see my bungalow, you'll get a Co-Op teabag." She laughed. But that was all silver. The tray and the teapot and so forth. Nice china slop-bowl. Slices of lemon with a little fork. Talk about creating washing-up. But of course, she has a woman to do all that.'

I said, 'She's left us far behind, Kath.'

'Well,' she said, 'she's still nice to me. And I tell you what, Peggy. Who'd swap places with her? I wouldn't. Making fancy dinners for people she don't even know. And she never sees her boys. They're away at some school. Imagine that? Having kiddies then paying strangers to see their smiling faces of a morning?'

Kath's School of Motoring was going well. 'I'm getting known,' she said. 'Ladies a speciality.'

I said, 'You making enough to think of taking another trip over here?'

'No,' she said. 'Not yet a while. Everything I make, I have to put back in. And if I go on holiday, that's not just what I'm spending. I'm not earning neither. But you could come here, you know? You could have my zed-bed and I could borrow May's Lilo for Crystal.'

I said, 'Can't do it, Kath. Crystal's in her senior year, and I have my brides to consider.'

Afternoon Tea – Guidelines for Young Officers' Wives

BY AUDREY J. RUDMAN

••

Guests should wear their nicest afternoon dress, a gay hat and white gloves. It is polite to stay for at least half an hour, but do not linger beyond three-quarters. On leaving, the convention is to say, 'I must be going. Thank you so much.'

It is quite acceptable for a junior officer's wife to repay her luncheon and dinner obligations with lighter repasts, in keeping with her budget. Use your loveliest tablecloth. Have fresh flowers on the table. In winter, candles may be lit. Coloured candles are sometimes seen, but white are in better taste.

Offer small fancy cakes, plain cookies, and tiny sand-wiches, with a choice of fillings. Meat paste or cucumber are always acceptable. The service of tea is presided over by the ranking officer's wife. This courtesy should be extended to the CO's wife, if she cares to pour.

••

55

If you asked me to pick out a silver pattern for myself, I think I'd have chosen Buttercup. Or maybe Chantilly. But when I had a bride come into the registry, I couldn't allow my own tastes to intrude.

You could tell things about a girl from her pattern. Whether she was the retiring type or more outgoing. After a while I got so I could spot a Chrysanthemum girl soon as she walked through the door. Many of my San Antonio girls had Repoussé because that was what their great-gramma had had. But in Dallas I met a different attitude. Girls there just wanted the best. Silver, crystal, china, linen. They went for the big price-tags, and I was happy to help.

I moved there after Crystal enrolled for the diploma of veterinary nursing.

I said, 'Would it bug you? Me moving to Dallas too?'

'It's a big city,' she said. 'Just as long as you don't have me tailed.'

Betty said she didn't know how I could bear to live in such a blood-stained place, but I loved it and I loved my work. I never missed a day. Never got sick. And in the morning I was always first in, checking the cleaners hadn't left scuffs on the carpet or fingerprints on my beautiful silver.

The only thing would have made me even happier was if my own flesh and blood had shown the least interest in choosing a pattern. I could have started collecting pieces for her, with my employee discount, and there were some new patterns coming in, from Copenhagen, Denmark, I thought she'd have loved, having such modern tastes, but she turned her nose up at the whole bridal thing. The only kinda knives Crystal was interested in was scalpel knives.

'Tell her to take the Face-Lift course,' Lois said. 'And remind her of all the kindness I showed her when she was a child. I don't know about you, Peg, but I'm about ready to start calling in some of the gratitude we're owed. We still on for Chesapeake Beach?'

We were. Me, Lois, Gayle and no brats. Betty didn't want to come anyhow. She was busy with her Avon cosmetics, bringing fragrance and beauty to the homemakers of Converse.

But our weekend never happened, because President Lyndon Johnson bombed North Vietnam, and Ray Flagg went MIA when his battalion landed at a place called Da Nang.

Gayle phoned me. She said, 'He's dead, Peggy. I know it.'

In my heart I knew it too, or at least I thought better for her to be prepared for it. But of course what I said was, 'Maybe not, honey. He might turn up.'

Fool thing to say.

It was October before they found him. Identified him by his dog-tag.

Gayle had already left Camp Lejeune. Couldn't bear the sight of all those Marines getting ready to ship out. She was back in Greensboro, slinging hash. Wondering what to do with the rest of her life.

I talked her into coming south for Thanksgiving. I guess I had my own motives, it being my first holiday without Crystal, but Gayle needed a place to go. She had Flagg in-laws and Jackson in-laws, and a thousand kin of her own, but there didn't sound to be a charitable human being among them.

I sent her a ticket into Dallas-Fort Worth and then we drove on down to San Antonio with a baked ham and a Sara Lee All-Butter Pecan Coffee Cake. We were invited to Betty's.

First thing Gayle said when she got in my car was, 'Peg. I'm drinking.'

I said, 'Okay. I like a drink myself.'

'No,' she said. 'I mean I'm really drinking.'

I didn't know what to say.

She said, 'I don't get drunk or anything. I won't do anything to scandalise Betty. But I have liquor in my bag, and I just wanted you to know, I'll be drinking it. It helps me sleep.'

I said, 'Well, Betty takes pills. Pills to make her sleep and pills to make her happy, and she dishes them out like candy, so just promise me you won't mix any of Betty's little helpers with the stuff in your bottle.'

'I promise,' she said.

I said, 'And maybe some day you'll get by without it. Give yourself a chance. My God, honey, it's a miracle to me you're still standing.'

'Two fine husbands,' she said, 'and I never did get to have a little baby. It just wasn't meant to be.'

I said, 'It might happen yet. You still have time.'

She was only thirty-five. She was still a pretty woman, considering what she had been through.

'No,' she said, 'I'm resigned. Tell you the truth, Peg, I don't think my insides are working right. Little procedure I had when I was fourteen, I think it maybe threw a wrench in the works.'

I said, 'It don't seem fair. You were always so nice with Crystal and Sandie.'

'Yeah, well,' she said. 'Being nice to other folk's kids ain't hard.'

That was before she had eaten dinner in the company of Betty's three grandbabies, Dawn and Delta and Danni.

56

Betty had done up the duplex. She had created a dinette, with a table in wood-effect Formica and bench seats and a big new TV on a swivel stand, so you could eat dinner and not miss your favourite shows. She had made changes in her bedroom too. Crocheted covers for the bed and the cushions and the lamps in a pale shade of pink.

Gayle said, 'Wow! You got yourself a real boudoir here!'

Betty come over all modest. She said, 'I just like to keep it nice and dainty.'

I noticed she still kept a photo of Ed on her night table. Ed in his Blues, long ago and far away.

There was no sign of Sherry. She was spending the day with her boyfriend's family, out near the Kelly air base.

I said, 'Not another of your girls gonna marry air force?'

'They're civilians,' she said, 'but what if she did find an airman? I'd be proud.'

Carla said, 'Why didn't Crystal come?'

I said, 'Well, she's all grown up and pleasing herself these days. She's gone to Maine to visit with her daddy. She's a college girl now.'

Carla said, 'I'm gonna go to college.'

Then Deana arrived with her brats. Delta was four, Dawn was going on three, and Danni was one year old. Dwayne was away on exercises.

Gayle said, 'I wouldn't have known you, Deana.'

I should think not. She was remembering Deana the brat. Gayle had kinda stood still in time, in spite of the liquor and the widowings. But Deana had grown up and out and messy. She was barely twenty-one, but she looked ten years older. Only thing I'll say is, her kids were turned out clean. Nice little dresses, all matching. I guess that was Betty's handiwork.

Deana said, 'You hear about Perry Kaiser, Mom?'

Perry was that boy Crystal had hung out with. News was, he was on his way home from Vietnam, blown up by a mine, not expected to walk again.

Betty said, 'Deana! Not in front of Gayle! She's had her own sorrows.'

Gayle said, 'Don't mind me. I don't have anything left the military can take. They cleaned me out. But y'all better get used to it. There'll be a whole buncha Perry Kaisers coming home.'

Betty said, 'Well, anyway . . . dinner's ready. So let's all wash our hands, and then we can give thanks. Peggy? Would you like to do that for us?'

I don't know what her game was, dropping a thing like that on a person. I didn't know any prayers. Far as I knew neither did Betty. This seemed to be some new thing she'd gotten up for the benefit of Deana's girls. Gayle picked up on my difficulty.

She said, 'Can I do that, Betty? If Peggy don't mind, I'd just love to do that.'

And she stood up and said some real praying words, about feasting in paradise. Little Gayle from Boomer, North Carolina. All the years I'd known her, I'd felt like a kinda mother to her. Guess it was my turn to feel like the child.

Betty had prepared us a feast, I must say. Turkey, cornbread dressing, baked sweet potato, fried squash, Niblet corn, marshmallow and fruit-cocktail salad and, of course, her Three-Color Refrigerator Cake. We were as full as ticks.

Delta had been eating candy all morning, so she had to have every mouthful coaxed into her, Betty cutting it all up small and playing games to get her to swallow another bite. There was no need. Delta looked like she could have gone a week without eating.

She said to Gayle, 'Where's your daddy?'

'In heaven,' Gayle said.

Delta said, 'Why ain't you crying, then?'

Betty said, 'Delta! Would you like to see the princess gown Gramma's making for your dolly?'

'Already seen it,' she said. She still had her beady eyes on Gayle, waiting on an answer.

Gayle said, 'Because you don't cry at parties. You wanna play a game? You know how to play Simple Simon?'

I helped Betty clear away while Gayle played with Delta and Deana changed two diapers.

I said, 'If you don't mind, I'll drive round to San Jacinto Street. Say hello to my mom.'

'Of course,' she said. 'You must be missing Crystal.'

I was.

Connie and Mom were watching the *Loretta Young Show*. They had had Thanksgiving dinner on trays.

I said, 'Didn't know you were back, Connie.'

'How could you?' she said. 'You're the one walked out on us.'

I said, 'Three hundred miles. And you have my number.'

She said, 'You ever call Mom?'

I said, 'She's never home.' It was a feeble excuse. We both knew I didn't call because all I'd hear was another hard-luck story, and never an enquiry about me or Crystal.

Mom said, 'You're wearing your hair different. You making good money up there?'

I noticed she still had the walrus-tusk Bambi I'd brung her when me and Vern come back from Alaska.

I said, 'I'm working hard. Helping Crystal through school. She sends her love.'

Mom said, 'She courting?'

I said, 'No. She's studying.'

'Ha!' she said. 'Then she'll be gone. You'll see.'

I said, 'You living here again, Connie, or just visiting?'

'I'm getting back on my feet,' she said. Connie was always getting knocked off them by lying, cheating men. Every one she took up with was the one who was gonna be different, but sooner or later he'd turn out to be exactly the same.

Me and Gayle shared Carla's room that night.

After we'd closed the door, Gayle said, 'Okay, Peggy. I'm gonna spend a little time with my friend Jack Daniel's and if you want to creep out and fetch yourself a glass, you're welcome to join us.'

I said, 'I can't touch that stuff. But you go ahead.'

I wished she wouldn't. All the drive down, all through dinner, she had been so bright and brave. But it was clear she was just papering over the cracks. Seemed to me she probably needed to dress in black and do a little weeping and wailing. She read my mind.

'I'll cry tomorrow, Peggy,' she said.

Crystal come back from Maine in an ugly mood. She called her step-brother Eugene 'the missing link'.

I said, 'What does that mean?'

'It's evolution,' she said. 'It means he's what you'd expect for a bait farmer.'

I said, 'How about Martine? She treat you nice?'

'Yeah,' she said. 'She makes pie.'

I said, 'So your daddy's happy?'

'I guess,' she said.

I told her the news about Perry Kaiser. She stood gazing outta the kitchen window for a while, drinking a can of soda. Then she crumpled the can with her bare hands and hurled at the wall.

I said, 'There's no call to act so tragic. It's not like he got killed. Think of poor Gayle, and her Ray.'

She looked at me.

I said, 'Anyway, you weren't that keen on him.'

She said, 'I didn't have to be *keen* on him. What kind of a fool attitude is that? He could have been my worst enemy, I still wouldn't have wished that on him. He's nineteen.'

Get on to the subject of Vietnam was the surest way to ruffle her feathers. Also, she had started using the F-word.

Betty Gillis's Three-Color Refrigerator Cake

••

*Make up a box each of lime, orange and strawberry jello
and put in a cool place. Cover the bottom of the cake tin
with Graham crackers.*

*Cream together half a cup of fine sugar with one egg
yolk and a tablespoon of Crisco. Add a can of crushed
pineapple and one cup Angel Flake coconut. Beat egg
white till stiff and fold in. Pour over the Graham crackers
and refrigerate. When set, cover with layers of colored
jello. For a lighter cake, break up the set jello with a
fork before spreading. For a fancy finish, if you have
company, cover the top with Cool Whip and silver candy-
balls.*

••

57

I was under a person called Marguerite, at the Dallas Bridal Registry. Marguerite was always threatening to retire to Florida and I was waiting to step into her shoes, but the day never seemed to come. She was given to changing moods. Sometimes she was friendly. She'd bring me in romance stories she had finished with and back issues of *Vogue*. But the next day she was just as likely to give me the cold shoulder. You never knew where you stood with her. Looking back, it was probably the time of life she was going through.

Anyways, during that period I had troubles of my own, namely Crystal. Whatever I said, Crystal would argue the opposite. We were seeing terrible things on the TV every night. Rioting and buildings set alight and coloured folk marching, which she was all in favour of, and then our boys coming home from Vietnam, shot up or worse, which she said was their own fault for going. Seemed to me, everything in her mind had turned topsy-turvy. Also, she had quit wearing nylons, and she didn't keep her hair nice any more neither. It just hung there, getting longer and longer, till you could hardly see her face.

One thing about it that bugged me was, everybody else's kids seemed to be turning out nice. Audrey's boys were learning to talk French. Kirk and Sandie Moon were giving Lois a smooth ride. And Sherry Gillis, who was never all that, had gotten strawberry-blonde highlights and the chance of a career in movies. She was still waiting tables at the Alamo International House of Pancakes, but she had met a man said he definitely could get her into something in Hollywood, so she was just biding her time, waiting for the contract to come through.

Betty said, 'I told her, she has my blessing, just as long as she keeps her clothes on.'

Betty was having a few problems in that direction herself. She had Slick Bonney trying to coax her out of her undies. He had run into her when he was in K-Mart buying his spring wardrobe. Slick had never married, never crossed the state line. Never shown any interest in Betty, neither, when we were in high school, but the minute he heard she had split up from Ed, he set his sights on her. He said he'd never forgot her running round in her apron, when Future Home-makers catered a Father-Son Banquet for the Topperwein chapter of Future Farmers of America. He had been very keen on tractors in those days. Still was.

Betty said, 'I've given him no encouragement, Peggy. Far as I'm concerned, I'm still a married woman.'

But that didn't stop Slick going round with his flashlight when she thought she could hear critters in her roof space. It didn't stop him buying her a heart-shaped box of candies.

Lois called me up one night. Woke me up. I had come home from the Registry, ate my fried-egg sandwich over the sink, and fallen asleep in front of another race riot. That was my life.

She said, 'Sandie's coming to Fort Worth. Her band's in some kinda contest.'

I said, 'She need a place to sleep?'

'No,' she said, 'they got places in a hostel. But you could take her for a soda. You anywhere near the Irving Center? You wanna try and meet up with her?'

I said, 'Sure. How come of child of yours has musical talent?'

'Whaddya mean?' she said. 'I played triangle in second grade.'

I hadn't seen Sandie since Vern quit the service and we left Wichita, or McConnell as they call it nowadays. She had only been knee-high to a cricket then, always got a smile on her face. I picked her out, though, with her hair, real carroty red.

I said, 'Well, you remember me?'

'Course I do,' she said. 'Mom has your picture. She has one from that wedding, and a real old one, from when we went to the beach? In England? The beach where there wasn't any ocean.'

She was such a cute kid, bright and cheerful and full of good plans. Reminded me of Crystal before she started trying to overthrow governments.

I said, 'You've got your mom's beautiful hair.'

'No,' she said. 'This is all my very own.'

I said, 'Tell me something. Does she dye hers? When we went for Gayle's wedding she was the only one of us didn't have a trace of grey.'

'Well,' she said, 'you'd have to apply to the Pentagon for that kinda information.'

I asked after Herb. 'He doesn't dye his hair,' she said. 'He doesn't have too much left to do anything with. He just kinda *arranges* it.'

She showed me all the stuff they were playing in the contest, real advanced, full of tricky little notes. The cornet was her instrument.

I said, 'How's Kirk?'

'He's a pain,' she said. 'Gets his own way all the time.'

I said, 'I suppose he's growing up. Once he's grown up you'll like him better.'

'If you say so,' she said.

I said, 'I hope you win your contest.'

'I think we might,' she said. 'We're good enough. You wanna come and listen?'

So I went to the Irving and listened to 'The Liberty Bell' being played a hundred times over. Sandie's band won bronze and it couldn't have happened to a nicer kid.

I had taken the afternoon off to meet Sandie, something I'd never done before, even when I had a toothache. I was real conscientious in my work so I resented it when Marguerite blamed my absence for her making a mistake with the Preston wedding list, two sets of grapefruit spoons getting despatched instead of one set of spoons and one of lobster forks.

To tell the truth, I had had it with Marguerite anyway. Only two weeks before, she had blamed me unjustly for a mix-up over Susie Henry's stemware, and it was plain to me Florida was just something she talked about. She had no intention of retiring, and I'd never get any further ahead while she reigned.

I was starting to think about setting up something on my own. Kath had done it. Vern had done it. I was lying awake nights, wondering what I could do. It would have been a consolation to me if I could have talked it over with Crystal, but she had no respect for bridal affairs. She said she couldn't think why anybody'd be picking out candelabra when they could have been trying to stop a war we had no business fighting. She'd started going on marches too. Skipping classes, going up to Washington with a bunch of reprobates. I just hoped she didn't get her picture in the paper. Her daddy ever knew she was hanging out with a crowd of draft-card-burners, it'd have broke his heart.

Peggy Dewey's Kitchen-Sink Supper

••

Fry an egg, sunny side up, sprinkle with salt and slap between two slices of Wonderbread, spread thick with mayo.

Eat it over the sink.

••

58

I always phoned Kath on her birthday. It was her forty-fifth.

I said, 'You don't sound too happy.'

'I've got a bit of trouble, Peg,' she said. 'They reckon I'm not properly licensed. Somebody must have got on to them – you know how it is. Some folk can't bear to see you doing all right for yourself. So I had an inspector come round. I told him, I can drive with my eyes shut.'

I said, 'So what happens now?'

'I shall have to take their silly test,' she said.

She promised to let me know how it went. But the next call I got was from Betty. I hadn't heard from her in so many weeks, I'd begun to think Slick Bonney had had his wicked way with her and she was avoiding me.

She was all a-flutter. 'Peggy,' she said, 'I'm so excited, if I don't tell somebody I'll just burst!'

Sherry had gotten her big break in California, starring in a TV advertisement for ketchup. 'A lot of stars started out in commercials,' she said. 'It can lead on to other things.'

I said, 'You be sure to let me know when they start showing it.'

'I will,' she said 'But it'll be a while yet. There's more to making a film than meets the eye.'

I said, 'So those big Hollywood bucks won't be rolling in just yet?

You're gonna have to wait a little longer for that pool in your back yard.'

'I'm doing just fine,' she said. 'I'm doing so well with my cosmetics I might even get my own area. Course, Deana could always use a little help.'

Deana was expecting brat number four, and Dwayne had got orders for Tinker, Oklahoma, so Betty was dreaming up ways of making their miserable lives sweeter. She had even offered to have Delta stay with her a while.

I said, 'Why would you take on a child again, your time of life? How're you gonna get out at night, deliver your Avon?'

'Carla can mind her,' she said, 'or Delta can come with me. She's so cute she'd be an asset. She can model the new eye colours.'

I said, 'And what about your love-life? What's Slick have to say about it?'

'Peggy Dewey!' she said. 'I do *not* have a love-life.'

All I could say was, Slick Bonney wouldn't have kept bringing bottles of Newts D'Amour scent if he wasn't expecting to hit pay dirt. I said, 'Well, whatever you call it. Just stop and think before you start raising Deana's family for her. Put Slick's nose outta joint. You may need him some day.' Slick owned Bonney's Farm Vehicles. Had done real well for himself.

Lois agreed with me.

'Yup,' she said. 'A girl never knows when she might need a good price on a grab-loader. Course, get to our age, what we really need is men with Lincoln dealerships. Or mink warehouses. Dentists are good too. If ever I trade in Herb it's gonna be for someone who does bridge-work.'

I said, 'Sandie's cute.'

'Yeah,' she said, 'she liked you too. Listen, Peg. You remember Dorothy Kurlich and Deek? When 366 were at Drampton? You remember their kid's name?'

I thought it might have been Joe.

'Me too,' she said. 'It was something began with J. Well, I saw in the paper there was a Joseph Kurlich, listed KIA. Makes you think. This keeps going a few more years, Kirk could get drafted.'

What I had heard about the draft board, they were pretty particular. They'd turned down Vern's step-son Eugene and all he had was fallen arches.

'Course,' she said, 'Kirk could be the weapon that wins the war. Those gooks ever see him throwing one of his rages, they'll all come running outta the jungle with their hands held high. Maybe I should call up the White House, offer his services? You think they'd accept a collect call?'

Kath sent a clipping from the *West Norfolk Herald* with her letter. FLYING COLOURS FOR KATH, it said. DRIVING-SCHOOL WOMAN BEATS BAN. And there was a picture of her, holding up a Learner Badge ripped in two.

'What a carry-on,' she wrote.

I passed with full marks, of course, but they still fined me, so there goes my new twin-tub. It's been in the papers about me, and I got a lot of people writing in, giving me testimonials, so that was nice.

I seen Jim Jex in the market, before I'd took the test. He said to me, 'There goes all your winnings, down the drain,' such a nasty smile on his face. He always was a spiteful bugger. That did cost me a fair bit, though, not being allowed to work. There was ladies already booked, I had to let down. And the inspector who come round, he said, 'Well, you can always draw the unemployment.' I told him I work for my money. This country's going to the dogs. And there's girls walking round Lynn in skirts not much wider than my hand. Do we get a Fen Blow they'll have windburn in places I won't mention.

59

Nineteen sixty-seven I started doing a little moonlighting. Here is how it come about. The Baker-Crawford wedding list was registered with us, Phoebe Baker marrying Hunter P. Crawford, and Mrs Baker come in one day, nearly fainting away with exhaustion. I brought her an iced tea and she said, 'Well, people are invited for Thursday to view the gifts, but I don't see how I'm going to be ready.'

Marguerite wasn't around, listening in and interfering, so I jumped right in and offered my services to set up the sip 'n' see, make sure everything looked nice. I didn't even think about getting paid. I just thought it'd be fun to do. Wednesday evening I drove up there, and everything was still in boxes. Gifts from the kitchen-shower, gadgets and pots and pans all mixed up with the good stuff. I could understand they were run off their feet, though. Phoebe was having ten brides-maids, five flower-girls and two pageboys to carry the ring cushion, all got to have last-minute fittings and rehearsals. I just rolled up my sleeves and set to.

I spread a damask cloth on a table and laid out the Rose Point silver and the Royal Doulton and the Waterford crystal like for a real dinner. I wished I had brought along ribbons in old gold or terracotta, which were the wedding colours, but that's how you learn in business. I soon got that I never went anywhere without a full range of ribbons.

Then I had a brainwave, right there in front of Mrs Baker herself, probably turned around my whole life. I suggested I make up a bed with the lovely Porthault sheets, maybe lay out one of Phoebe's honeymoon negligées on top. She said, 'Peggy, what an adorable idea!' and a great many people who came to that sip 'n' see wrote down my name and number.

What I had in mind was, some day I'd be offering the complete service. Peggy Dewey Weddings. I started making it my business to know suppliers of the best of everything, which was why I recognised the quality of Audrey's new headed writing-paper, a good glazed paper, with the address engraved.

They were back in the US, in Yuba City, California. Lance had made 0-6 Colonel, just like Lois always predicted.

'Well, here we are,' Audrey wrote.

Lance drew Beale AFB. We managed a long-promised trip to Europe before we left for the States. Paris, Rome and Florence. I could hardly tear myself away. Lance got a bug, unfortunately, so we had to do the Uffizi Gallery and the Pitti Palace without him. The boys were lost for words when they saw all that wonderful art. As I reminded them, Europe was civilised when America was just a place where the buffalo roamed.

Lance says next vacation we are going to see some of the wonders of the United States, so I guess we're talking Grand Canyon. Also, we're handy here for the Sierras, so we're planning to do some hiking on weekends, and maybe some river-rafting too. Quality time with our boys. I feel I hardly know them.

I didn't want to hear about quality time. Me and Crystal had had the biggest falling out. She had quit school, said there was no point in anything any more because we were all gonna get vaporised in World War III.

She slammed outta my apartment one day, and I didn't see her again for more than a year. I phoned Vern.

I said, 'If you happen to hear from her, you'll let me know?'

'Sure,' he said. 'But I warned you not to allow her so much rope. Can't say I'm surprised.' He had no idea how my heart was breaking.

I said to Lois, 'Way Vern talks, I'm to blame for Crystal and the way Crystal talks, I'm to blame for everything else. Black slavery. Annihilation of the Indian. Nucular radiation . . .'

'Yes,' she said, 'I heard you had a hand in that. Don't worry, doll. She's flexing her muscles a little, that's all. She'll be back.'

I said, 'You getting grief from Sandie?'

'No,' she said. 'All she does is practise on her cornet. But you never know. There's still time. And what I saw of Crystal, you've done a great job raising her. Hell, Peg, she coulda turned out like Deana Gillis.'

Deana had split up from her husband, Dwayne, and gone back home to Converse with Dawn, Danni and baby Dixie. Delta was already there getting spoiled by her gramma Betty. I don't know what Carla had to say about it, having to give up her room when she had school and studying and her Saturday job at Donut Heaven. As I said to Lois, seemed to me Carla had more need of a decent night's sleep than Deana, sitting on her butt all day, trimming her split ends and watching TV.

Lo said, 'I guess she stays glued to the set, watching out for the film star of the family.'

Sherry's ketchup commercial had been on. She had played the role of a tomato. After that she'd tried out to be the hands in a handcream ad, but we hadn't heard any more about it. Hands weren't exactly Sherry's star feature.

Lo said, 'Deana getting support from the husband?'

I said, 'Well, he's quit the service. According to Betty he's promised to pay regular once he's had better luck with his metal detector.'

'Right,' she said. 'He sounds like a guy with a firm grip on reality. So who's paying the bills? Poor old Betty digging deep again?'

Didn't matter what happened, I never heard Betty complain. Lois thought she must get some kind of weird satisfaction out of picking up the pieces. 'Makes her feel like some kinda heroine,' she said. 'Either that, or she's just plain dumb.'

I said, 'I don't know any of us'd do different. You telling me if you had grandbabies, you'd see them go hungry?'

'Go hungry?' she said. 'Are you crazy? All they need is breakfast at Bob's Big Boy and they could live off the calories for a week. Anyway, you know what I'm getting at. There's something about Betty, like she's a great big empty space waiting to suck in trouble. There'll always be a story with Betty, I guarantee you. There'll always be some reason why Deana can't pull her weight and Dumbo or whatever his name is can't get off the stick and feed his kids, and then there'll be some tragic reason Sherry needs a hand-out. One of these days Betty's gonna get up and find a line of starving Africans outside her door. You can depend on it. And what's up with Gayle? Last number I had for her, there's never anybody home. It just rings out. You know what I think? I think she's fell of the wagon.'

I feared Lois might be right. I had even called the Over Easy in Greensboro and they said Gayle was long gone.

60

I tiptoed around for a while, keeping my day job. I helped out a couple of Mrs Baker's friends, just organising gift displays, writing out place-cards, that kinda thing, but I knew if Marguerite ever found out what I was doing I'd be road meat, so I planned to stay one step ahead of her. October I gave notice I was leaving the Registry, and her face was something to behold.

'I wish you luck,' she said, like she really wished me poison ivy. 'You'll need it,' she said. 'There's a lot more to the wedding business than you know.'

She underestimated me. I wasn't just talking about seating plans. I had contacts in ice-carving. I knew the best people for the dyeing of satin shoes. I even had some ideas on exclusively created punches, alcoholic and non-alcoholic, to co-ordinate with wedding colours.

I always think of '68 as the year of weddings. First, Peggy Dewey Weddings went into business. Then Jackie Kennedy married that Greek. Boy, was Betty bitter about that.

'I'm finished with that woman,' she said. 'I feel so let down.'

Lois roared when I told her. 'Tell her I had my radar locked on him myself. Jackie Kennedy didn't snap him up, I was gonna dump Herb Moon, force myself to go and live on that floating palace.'

I said, 'I thought you got seasick?'

'There's pills,' she said.

Then there was Gayle. She called me up just before Christmas, finally broke the silence.

'Peggy,' she said, 'A wonderful thing has happened. I have said "Yes" to Jesus. And Jesus has brought me another chance of happiness. I'm marrying Lemarr Passy, and I want you to be there.

61

Lemarr Passy was a older man, but had kept his looks and a fine head of silver hair. He had known tragedy himself, lost his first wife to a cancer of the blood aged only forty-one.

'Good to have you on the team,' he said, first time I met him, but I didn't plan on joining any team of Bible-bashers. I was just there to help Gayle with her wedding arrangements.

'We are entering the last days of time,' he said to me. He always held on to your hand when he was talking to you, so it wasn't easy to make a getaway. 'The Four Horsemen of the Apocalypse are riding out and it's time to put our hope and faith in the Lord.'

Still, endtimes or no, he wasn't stinting Gayle on her big day. She was having lilac and dark green for her colours and a fruit cup made with black grapes. As a contrasting touch, I had white violets scattered on the cake and on the lawn too. They made their vows before a pastor friend of Lemarr's, wore a shiny suit and had his front hair in a pompadour.

I was the only one from the old crowd could be there. Betty sent an Avon gift-casket. Kath sent pillowcases. Audrey sent a five-section hors-d'oeuvre tray in stainless steel.

Lois just said, 'Uh-oh. If the end of the world is at hand, I think I should stay home with my loved ones. Give her a hug from me. Give her a smack if you think she's making a big mistake.'

I couldn't say I did think that. He was so nice with her and she was a picture of happiness.

Gayle said, 'You know what we're gonna do, Peg? We are gonna get a truck with a side that lets down and we're going out on the road, taking the Lord to the people.'

I said, 'Honey, I didn't even know you believed in the Lord.'

'Sometimes I did, sometimes I didn't,' she said. 'But turns out he's believed in me all along.'

She wanted me for her maid of honour, but I didn't see how I could, if I was already her wedding-organiser. Besides, she had two of her sisters coming, and her mom. First time I'd ever seen their faces, all the years I'd known Gayle. I think they smelled money. In the end, she had all three of us, sister Pattie, sister Kaye and me, all in a darker shade of lilac, with elbow-length gloves and velveteen bows in our hair.

Betty said, 'I got Gayle's wedding pictures. He looks a fine figure of a man.'

I said, 'You see what she made me wear? I felt like mutton dressed up as lamb.'

She never contradicted me. She just said, 'Well, you put duty first, and that's what matters. And what church is it, where he's pastor?'

I wasn't exactly sure of that myself. It was the Lemarr Passy Sidewalk Ministry, but he didn't have a actual church. 'Wherever the Lord is needed,' he'd said. 'Wherever the devil has pitched his tent, we pitch right next door.'

I said, 'I don't know, Betty, but ask anybody in Whiteville and they've heard of him. He's even probably getting his own radio show.'

She said, 'He do healing?'

I said, 'I wouldn't be surprised, the way he looks into a person's eyes.'

The news from Converse was, Carla had graduated Third-Ranking Honor Student, Deana's dizzy turns had gotten so bad Ace Hardware had had to let her go after her first week, and Delta had won her heat of the Eastern Texas Junior Beauty Pageant.

I said, 'Jeez, Betty, leave you alone for five minutes! What's new with Slick? And Sherry?'

'Enough about me,' she said. 'You heard from Crystal?'

I hadn't. Every night I prayed she'd come back. Trouble with my praying was, I didn't really believe anybody was listening.

Wisconsin 🏛 State Journal

WEATHER: Fair Today. High Near 80. Warmer Tuesday.

GOOD MORNING   Vol. 212, No. 110   129th Year   MADISON, MONDAY MORNING, JULY 21, 1969   ★ ★   MORNING FINA

ON THE MOON!

And It's 'One Giant Leap for Mankind

In Practice Session at Manned Space Center. Astronauts Aldrin, Right, and Armstrong Practice Lunar Surface Activities —AP Color Photo

Americans First to Walk on Dead Lunar Surface

By JOHN BARBOUR

SPACE CENTER, Houston (AP) — Two Ame
landed and walked on the Moon Sunday, the fir
man beings on its alien soil.

They planted their nation's flag and talked t
President on Earth by radio-telephone.

MILLIONS ON THEIR HOME planet 240,000
away watched on television as they saluted the fir
scouted the lunar surface.

The first to step on the Moon was Neil Arm
38. He stepped into the dusty surface at 9:56 p.m
His first words were "That's one small step for m
giant leap for mankind."

Twenty minutes later, his companion, Edw
(Buzz) Aldrin Jr., 39, stepped to the surface. His
were.. "Beautiful, beautiful, beautiful. A mag
They had landed on the Moon nearly six ho
destalion."
fore, at 3:18 p.m.

The Eagle module was scheduled to leave the
for a rendezvous with the Apollo command a
12:55 p.m. today.

PRESIDENT NIXON'S VOICE came to the
the astronauts on the Moon from the Oval Room
White House.

"This has to be the most historic telepho
ever made," he said. "I just can't tell you how
am. Because of what you have done, the heaven
became part of man's world. As you talk to us fr
Sea of Tranquillity, it inspires us to redouble
forts to bring peace and tranquillity to man.

"All the people on Earth are surely one in t
pride of what you have done, and one in their
that you will return safely."

Aldrin replied, "Thank you, Mr. President
"The surface is fine and powdered, like po
almost shuffled.

ARMSTRONG'S STEPS WERE cautious at
charcoal in the soles of the foot," he said. "I can
footprints of my boots in the fine sandy partic
Armstrong read from the plaque on the
Eagle, the spacecraft that had brought them
surface. In a steady voice, he said, "Here man
foot on the Moon, July, 1969. We came in peace
mankind."

In the moments he walked alone, Armstron
was all that was heard from the lunar surface

HE APPEARED PHOSPHORESCENT in th
sunlight. The so-called kangaroo-hop
the Moon, only one-sixth as strong as on Eart
he tried with gazelle-like leaps.

Aldrin tried a kind of kangaroo-hop but
unsatisfactory. "The so-called kangaroo h
seem to work as well as the more convention
he said. "It would get rather tiring after awh
dred."

In the lesser gravity of the Moon, each of
165-pounders on Earth, weighed something
pounds on the Moon.

Armstrong began the rock picking on
surface. Aldrin joined him using a small scoo
lunar soil in a plastic bag.

ABOVE THEM, INVISIBLE and nearly
was Air Force Lt. Col. Michael Collins, 38, k
lonely patrol around the Moon for the mom
his companions blast-off and return to him for
back home. Collins said he saw a small wh

Turn to Page 2, Col. 1

'Houston...Tranquillity Base Here'

By SAUL PETT
(Associated Press Writer)

SPACE CENTER, Houston —
Why, oh why, did we tire and
age them before their appointed
time?

Why did we waste them on
elections and no-hitters, on bull
markets and murders, on TV
shows and circuses?

WHY DIDN'T WE pull out of
the language long ago and save

Meanwhile, Back on Earth, It's Nice

Although attention is turned
on the Moon, weather continues
on the Earth, and for the Madison area it is generally pleasant,
partly cloudy weather. There is
Sunday was fair and sunny
with a high of 84 at 5 p.m. and

for this special moment in the
story of man such words as historic and momentous, dramatic
and breathtaking, fantastic and
incredible?

What are we left with now except to feel a silent feeling, a
wordless awe, a still reverence,
perhaps for the fact that mortal
men from Earth, our part of
Earth, at that, have landed on
the Moon?

Today should continue pleasant with a forecast of fair and
partly cloudy weather. There is
only a 10 per cent chance of
rain. The high should be near 86

ALL ALONG, it turns out, the
astronauts had to work, the
simple right words. the noun
pitted its soil, and scurried up
toward home.

"Eagle, you are go for pow-
ered descent." Go, Eagle, go.
Go true. go safe.

They indulged themselves in
only one metaphor. It couldn't
have come at a better moment.

"The Eagle has wings," they
said, and didn't it and didn't
we? The lunar lander was sep-
arating from the mother ship
and taking life of its own.

"SEE YOU LATER," chirpy
Columbia says to departing
Eagle. Later would be 30 long
hours later in history after they

(Compiled From Wire Services)

America and the world held
its breath Sunday and then let
out a sigh of pride and relief.

Crowds screamed joyously in
London's Trafalgar Square, people danced in Chile, and a Russian shouted "Hooray." Almost
everyone on Earth was touched
somehow by man's arrival on
the Moon.

PRESIDENT Nixon and a half
billion other people watched the
Moon show on television, ex-
perts estimated.

Another billion couldn't see it
because it was not shown in the
Soviet Union or Red China. The
remaining 2 billion earthlings
had no sets.

There were prayers for the astronauts in churches throughout
the United States and elsewhere

IN THE U.S., a network official estimated the TV audience

had landed and walked on the
Moon, photographed and sam-
pled its soil, and scurried up
toward home.

"FOURTEEN hundred feet.
Eagle, Eagle, oh, gently.

"Five hundred and forty feet."
Eagle. Eagle, oh, gently.

"Four hundred feet . . . Face
forward and hatch down . . .
. Coming down nicely . .
Lovely. Eagle. Lovely.

"One hundred feet . . .

"SEVENTY-FIVE feet . . .
Oh, Eagle!

"Lights on . . Forward.
Forward. Good. Forty feet . . .

"OUR POSITION indicated
shows us to be a little long,"
says Eagle, 40,000 feet over the
Moon. Steady, Eagle. Slow,
Eagle.

"Fourteen thousand feet, and
coming down beautifully."

"Two thousand feet."

"picking up some dust . . .
Paint shadow . . . Drifting
the right a little." Careful, Eagle, careful.

"Contact light. Okay engine
stop . . . Engine arm off."

HOUSTON: "We copy you
down, Eagle."

"Houston — Tranquillity
Base Here. The Eagle has
landed." Eag.. tells Houston
and the world and eternity.

Columbia: "Fantastic."

Fantastic, Eagle, fantastic.
The word was made for you.

... and the World Watches and Marv

for the Moon walk might be 150
million, 95 per cent of total audience.

AS THE long, historic afternoon wore on, Americans went
about their usual Sunday ways
with the world of space always
within ear shot, sometimes before their eyes — the calm, stac-
cato voices of Astronauts Neil
Armstrong and Edwin Aldrin Jr.
and their ground controllers the
fliers maneuvered their way to
the floor of the Moon.

The voices from space and
their televised images followed
Americans to the beaches, the
golf courses, the ball parks, the
camping sites, all the places
where they could still see or
spend a summer afternoon away
from work.

On Sunday night, there were
parties and gatherings of many
of their sets for the duration of

be pretty sure the Moon would
understanding.

be the great adventure.

PRESIDENT Nixon sat rapt,
before his television set during
the epochal Apollo 11 Moon landing and called it the greatest
moment of our time."

The president sat alone in his
hideaway office in the Executive
Office Building adjacent to the
White House to view the landing
on a portable color television
set.

He told his press secretary,
Ronald Ziegler, the last 20 minutes of the descent "were the
longest I have ever lived
through."

"WE'VE PROVED that we're
No. 1," said Les Vigil, 51, of Albuquerque, N.M. said. Vigil's
wards were echoed by most
Americans.

"The Moon landing is the
most fantastic thing that ever
happened," said Cecil T.

Morris of Leawood,.
landing comes to pa
it means to my Ap
pride in accomplish

There were thou
doesn't do any good,"
Rosen, 76, of New
said about the landin
Earth there are no o
who are unhappy, bu
here."

PERCY SIMPSON,
cago, said, "I don't
should be fooling
sky. I feel the
now the Moon, he'd s
here."

Kings and Preside
premiers and prelate
gratulatory cables t
astronauts, to o
Space Center at Hou
President Nixon.

"It is an achievem

Turn to Page 2

More on Apollo ...

● Moon Land Quite a Thrill
for Knowles, Page 2.

● Next Step Up to Man's
Mind, Page 2.

● Astronaut White's Widow
Rejoices With Armstrong.
Page 4

● Full Page of Pictures of
U.S. Space Milestones, Page 5.

● Three Generations Watch
Historic Moment, Page 8.

● New Look at Earth. Say
Leaders, Page 9.

Aldrin Asks World to Give Thanks

SPACE CENTER, Houston
(AP) — Edwin E. Aldrin Jr.
Sunday asked everyone in the
world to pause and give thanks
for the lunar landing.

The astronaut, speaking in a
calm voice from the lunar module (LM) Eagle said:

"This is the LM pilot. I'd like
to take this opportunity to ask
every person listening in,
whoever and wherever they
may be, to pause for a moment
and contemplate the events of
the past few hours and to give
thanks to his or her own way."

Immediately afterwards, Aldrin resumed his discussion of
technical matters with the
ground control station.

apollo
SOUVENIR
EDITION
Wisconsin
State Journal

62

Kath used to write me every month. She always claimed she had nothing to tell me.

'15 August 1968. Same old boring things,' she wrote.

I've got a lady going up for her test, six times she's failed. It's the reversing flummoxes her. She just can't seem to get the hang of it. If she doesn't pass this time, I shan't take any more money from her. Some people are safer kept off the roads. It's a pity because she's a nice person. Her sister married a GI, lives in Pike, Pennsylvania, so I don't suppose you'd know her.

Me and May Gotobed have started drinking in public houses. We only drink shandy, but we get our Sunday dinner. No slaving over a hot stove and all the washing-up afterwards and having to eat it cold on Monday. You can have a roast with all the trimmings, or a cheese-and-pickle plough-man's, or scampi in a basket with tartare sauce. Do you remember the Flying Dutchman, used to be the doctor's surgery? You wouldn't know it now. They've ripped it all out and done it up. Fitted carpets. Course, the old boys don't like it, now the women have started going.

Well, now, what about this man on the moon? Isn't that a marvellous thing? I've been following it on the telly, then I go outside and look up, see if I can see anything.

I know it must be a worry to you, your Crystal acting up, but I don't think you should fret. What I seen of her, she's a champion girl and you've raised her right. She's probably just got swept along with all this hippy-hippy-shake business. It's the same over here. They're all wearing white lipstick and having sit-ins. It's just a fad.

They had the Mersey Blue Jeans come to Norwich and Dennis Jex had to go for a steward. He's with the St John Ambulance. He reckoned they had girls fainting and screaming till they made theirselves sick, some of them only fourteen. So it's not you, Peg. It's the whole world gone mad. Makes me glad I'm just a poor old maid.

Christmas Eve I got a collect call from California. It was Crystal. She said, 'I just thought of you. You okay?'

I said, 'Are you coming home?' My hopes soared, but not very high.

'No,' she said 'I'm travelling.'

I said, 'Give me your number. Give me your address.'

'I told you,' she said, 'I'm travelling. Don't lay this family scene on me.'

'I said, 'Will you call me again?'

'Sure,' she said. 'Stay cool.' Then she was gone.

I went to my bed and cried till I fell asleep.

63

Nineteen sixty-nine, things really took off for me. I was doing weddings with all the trimmings: showers, bridesmaids' luncheons, rehearsal dinners – and everything themed. I loved it, but the way things were shaping up in the fall I knew I'd be needing an extra pair of hands, and in March 1970 Grice Terry came to work for me. It was a unusual line of work for a boy but, soon as I met him, I knew he was the one to hire, he was so darling and polite. I knew he'd have all those brides' mothers eating outta his hand. Also, he had a very good feel for colour.

'Mrs Tate,' he'd say, 'those harvest hues are lovely, but they can be hard on a girl's complexion. Can I just ask you to reconsider blush pink?'

We worked so hard. Easter through Labor Day we didn't take a weekend off.

'My brides,' he called them. And nothing was too much trouble.

We were just finishing up one night, been checking things off for the Carlyle-Colquhoun bridesmaids' luncheon, when the door opened a crack and somebody threw in a crochet hat, flowers stitched all over it. Then Crystal peeped round.

'Hi,' she said, 'This the Prodigal Child Department?'

She allowed me to give her a kiss. She always was given to squirming somewhat. But she whispered in my ear, 'Sorry, Mom,' and that ache lifted from my heart, first time in more than two years.

We all went to Duke's Surf 'n' Turf to celebrate. Grice was for leaving the pair of us to it, but I wanted him along. Tell the truth, I felt kinda awkward around her, it'd been so long.

She wouldn't have ribs. Looked like she hadn't ate red meat in a long time, she was so washed out. 'It's okay, Mom,' she said. 'You can have them kill the fatted shrimp instead.'

Grice went to the bathroom. Crystal said, 'He's cute.'

I said, 'I interviewed twenty girls and not one of them had the right touch. Then Grice come along.'

'Cool,' she said. 'Well, I have some news for you. I have good news and I have bad news. Which do you want first?'

First bombshell she dropped was, she got married. His name was Trent Weaver. I'd met him one time when she first started associating with beatniks and Communists. He had a long thin neck and a big beaky nose, looked more like a game bird than a human being.

'Then there's the good news,' she said. 'We're divorced.'

I said, 'Whatever were you thinking of?'

'Search me,' she said. 'I guess we must have been stoned.'

My child, raised to know right from wrong, had been smoking herbal cigarettes.

I ordered more drinks. I said, 'Your father know about this?'

'He's my next call,' she said. 'Him and Trent wouldn't have hit it off, Dad being a capitalist an' all. You realise I'm probably near enough a worm heiress these days?'

Grice looked at me. I said, 'My ex-husband. I don't talk about it. And Crystal, would you kindly keep your voice down? I have a certain image in this town.'

She said, 'I'm sorry. I didn't mean to yell it out so loud about Daddy being a *worm* farmer.'

'Enjoying the shrimp?' Grice said.

I said, 'Now, what about your education?'

'Well,' she said, 'I guess I still have it, somewhere in the back of my mind.'

She was commencing to look for work, something in the veterinary line.

She said, 'You look great, Mom. I've been missing you. Wondering if I dared show my face.'

I said, 'You idiot girl. I missed you so much.'

Grice had to wipe a tear.

I said, 'You need a place to stay?'

'Hey,' she said, 'I didn't say I was missing you *that* much.'

We shared a plate of Floating Islands Dessert, between three.

'Oh yeah,' she said. 'One more thing I ought to confess. When we got married . . . I didn't like to come to Bloomie's with our gift list, let you see the kind of low-rent stuff we were hoping for, so . . . me and Trent . . . we registered at Wal-Mart.'

64

'Never suspected a thing,' Vern said. 'First I knew it was all over, same as you. You ever meet him?'

I said, 'I believe I did. He was a long streak of nothing, hair he could nearly sit on. I never figured on getting him as a son-in-law. I thought we'd raised her to have more sense.'

'Well,' he said, 'I guess we had a lucky escape. She coulda turned up married to a coloured. She coulda turned up with a child and no husband.'

I said, 'Vern. You better quit talking like that and catch up. The world's changing.'

'Not here it ain't,' he said. 'How're you?'

I told him about the business. Course, Vern didn't really want to hear about bridal matters. He was just being polite till it was his turn.

'Yup,' he said, 'we're doing great. We just launched our Weekender Bait Bucket. You get a one-gallon bucket, with a hundred worms and a pack of worm feed. Comes with a illustrated instruction sheet and, provided you don't park it next to the furnace, you've got a shelf-life of six to eight weeks. Makes a nice gift for a fisherman.'

I said, 'I'll make a note.'

'We're thinking of branching out, as well,' he said. 'Breeding redworms for people want to aerate their garden, or make their own compost. Redworm consumes half his own body weight in garbage every twenty-four hours.'

Sounded like Deana Gillis.

'And they're breed real good, too.'

Sounded even more like Deana.

'Yup,' he said. 'It'll be a nice little sideline for Martine. Leave me and Eugene to carry on with the bait side of the business.' He said Martine was well, and Mom Dewey was doing good too, for seventy, and Martine's boy, Eugene, was dating a girl, but by correspondence. It was some kinda pen-pal arrangement.

Crystal said, 'I hope he's not using any of that Bait Farm scented writing paper.'

She had got a job in Fort Worth at a beauty parlour for dogs.

I said, 'I thought you wanted to cure the sick? All those insides you used to study up on?'

'Mm,' she said, 'I could still do that. But right now I'm studying the *owners*. I mean, I could understand a person spending big bucks to save the life of their pet, stop it suffering. Pet is like a child to some people. But you should see what they spend just to stop a dog smelling like a dog. We get poodles booked every week. Shampoo and clip.'

Mondays she'd usually come over and we'd go someplace for dinner. Grice too, if he was free. They had really hit it off right from the start and it was nice they could entertain each other. Sometimes, after a big wedding, I was so tired I hardly could talk. The only thing was, if Grice and Crystal were to get more than friendly, if they were to start dating or something, I didn't want pleasure to interfere with business. Grice was such an asset to me, I didn't want any complications.

One Monday when he had to visit his friend Tucker and couldn't join us, I took the opportunity to say something about it.

I said, 'I don't know what I'd do without Grice. I'd sure hate to lose him.'

'Why?' she said. 'Somebody trying to lure him away?'

I said, 'No. But when you have staff, you can't take things for granted.'

She said, 'From where I'm looking, you've got Grice for life.'

I said, 'Well, circumstances can change. A person might move away. They get their heart broken. Feel they have to start over. Or he might meet somebody, from out of state. He's still young. He could decide to up sticks and go. My only hope is, I don't think Grice is the marrying kind.'

'No shit, Sherlock,' she said. That was the kinda language she had picked up being married to Trent Weaver for five minutes.

'Well,' she said, changing the subject, 'I found Sherry.'

She had been trying to track down Sherry Gillis, the two of them having been so close at one time, keeping the whole house awake with their giggling while she was staying with us. Betty had given her a number in Culver City, LA, but Sherry never seemed to be home.

I said, 'And? She still in show business?'

'Kind of,' she said. 'She was just up in Fresno at the Home Show. She was demonstrating a gadget cuts up potatoes and stuff into fancy shapes.'

I said, 'She tell you she was on TV, as a tomato? She got a thing about vegetables?'

She was laughing. 'More'n you know,' she said. 'Matter of fact, I think she's moved in with one. His name's Justin and he drinks his own urine.'

She swore that was what Sherry had told her. Said it keeps you eternally young. I tried it out on Lois next time we spoke.

'Yeah,' she said, 'I think I heard of that. I think I read it in a magazine. He take it on the rocks? Twist of orange and a little grenadine, maybe? Tell you what, get Betty to try it out. If it works for her, I'll cancel getting my neck ironed. Hey, you get the Rudman Team Photo?'

As usual, Audrey's Christmas card had a family photo on the front and a newsletter inside, covering the past year.

Lo said, 'Talk about their royal majesties. I'm predicting next year's card, they'll be sitting on thrones.'

I said, 'Well, Audrey always was destined for great things.'

'And what about those boys?' she said. 'You ever hear of a thing called body language? I got a book you should read. It's for if you're in business and you want to know if somebody's jerking you around.'

I said, 'Lo, I deal with people in a very happy situation. They don't jerk me around.'

'Okay,' she said. 'But in *my* business we have a saying: buyers are liars.'

Lois had taken the tests, got her real estate salesman's licence. Soon as Kirk was through with school she wanted to move to New York and take the broker's test.

'I tell you,' she said, 'I'm gonna go far. Anyway, you could still read this book. Then you'd understand, those Rudman boys are standing there, dressed up like a pair of crown princes, but what their body language is saying is GET ME THE FUCK OUTTA HERE.'

They just looked to me like nice clean-cut boys. According to Audrey's update, Mikey was all set for the Air Force Academy, Colorado Springs, and Lance Jnr was aiming for the Brigade of Midshipmen at Annapolis, following in his grampa's footsteps.

'Another hectic year,' she wrote.

The OWC has kept me busy most days with fund-raisers and my volunteer hours at the thrift shop on base. Also, I must admit I'm now hooked on mah-jongg and try to play two or three times a week. We vacationed in Yosemite National Park this year, a great adventure for all. Saw bluebirds, chipmunk, black bear. As usual, I took along my paints but never got around to using them. One of these days! Unfortunately Lance put his back out unfurling the awning on the camper so he wasn't able to join us on all of our hikes. He's now recovered, thanks to an excellent chiropractor, so we're planning a romantic trip to Hawaii for our up-coming twentieth anniversary.

'That's just Christmas-card talk,' Lois said. 'Those boys are ready to eee-rupt. The Big One! Coming soon to a perfect family of your acquaintance. You heard it here.'

I thought that was pretty rich coming from Lois Moon. I thought she had some nerve. Last I had heard, she wasn't even allowed in to change Kirk's sheets. What Sandie had told me that time, Kirk's room hadn't been picked up in years.

65

'We're going to Spain,' Kath wrote, 'me and May. It's called a package tour. £20 all-in, and they reckon it gets so hot you can't walk on the sands in your bare feet.'

I called her.

I said, 'I was hoping you'd be coming out here again.'

She said, 'I'd love to, Peg, I really would. But see, that's a question of the time. I can take a week off, go to Spain and come back with a bit of a suntan. But I can't come to you for a week. By the time I got there it'd be time to turn round and come back.'

That was the hole we were all digging for ourselves. For years we had time and no money. Now we had money and no time.

She said, 'Then Audrey invited me as well, said they had plenty of room. So that'd be another week. I looked on the map, see where California is. I tell you, Peggy, that's such a big country. You could take a lifetime and never see half of it. I mean, I haven't hardly seen what we've got here, but I don't even know if I want to any more. I went to Great Yarmouth with May, on her Women's Fellowship outing, and that did nothing but blow and rain. Sitting in a wet mac all day, keep looking at your watch, hoping it's time to go home. I said to May, I can stop in Lynn and get rained on. Least I wouldn't get thrown all over place by a loopy charabanc-driver. The way he kept stamping on his brakes, that was terrible. So then May fetched the brochure about Spain, and that's where we're off to. You should see the pictures. Beautiful blue skies, smart hotels. Flamingo dancing. I don't know how they do it for the money. Hilda Jex says you wouldn't catch her going. All that oily food, and getting the runs. Course, Hilda always was a worry-guts. She'd get the runs sitting looking at her own four walls. Anyway, Peg, how're you?'

I could remember a time when it was hard to get a word out of Kath Pharaoh.

66

Summer evenings Grice'd make me a mint julep and we'd sit a while, wind up the day.

Grice's Guaranteed Mint Julep
Generous for two. Sufficient for three.

Fill the glasses with crushed ice until they are frosted. Strip the leaves from ten good sprigs of fresh mint. Using a pestle, crush them in a bowl with a large spoon of fine sugar and a jigger of club soda. Add six jiggers of bourbon and leave to stand for no more than five minutes. Strain into the glasses of ice, stir, garnish with extra mint.

Wear chiffon and sip through a straw.

We were in the early stages of the Jenneau-Carson wedding, and we already realised Mrs Jenneau was gonna be one of those make-or-break clients. For a start, there were twenty bridesmaids plus ten flower-girls and ten pageboys who had been matched for height; but they were flying in from all over so rehearsing them was gonna be a nightmare if not downright impossible. Then there were the butterflies. Rose Jenneau wanted a cloud of them, all the same shade, preferably pastel-lemon, released at the moment she and Robert E. Carson started making their vows.

Grice had his doubts it could be done. He said we should persuade her to go for doves, but I didn't like to think Peggy Dewey Weddings should be so easily beat.

He said, 'Even if we can get them, I don't know that a butterfly can be made to perform. They're only a form of insect life, after all. Mood takes them, they might just fold their wings and stay put for hours. You can rely on a dove.'

The phone rang. 'Or, how about this,' he said, '*silk* butterflies, on wands, waggled about by the junior attendants. Peggy Dewey Weddings, Grice speaking, how may I help you?'

He put his hand over the mouthpiece. 'Marie Hollick?' he whispered. 'Calling from California?' He fluttered his hand over his heart. 'I think we may be about to go inter-state!'

'Hello,' she said. She had a slow, dopey way of speaking, like she was pacifying a child. 'Am I speaking with Mrs Peggy Dewey?'

She said, 'I am calling on behalf of the Rudman family. I have been asked to let you know that the funeral service for Colonel Rudman has now been fixed for Friday next at 3 p.m.'

I could hear Grice, busy with something behind me, humming a little tune.

I said, 'Excuse me? Are we talking about Lance Rudman?'

'Colonel Lance Rudman,' she said. 'Is this Mrs Peggy Dewey?'

I said, 'It is. Are you telling me about funeral arrangements? I didn't even know he had died.'

I heard her gasp. 'Oh my!' she said. 'I am so sorry. We are working in teams here, to help out Audrey at this sad time, there being so many people to call, and I was given to understand you had already received the news of his passing. I can only apologise. I guess your name was checked off by mistake.'

All she'd say was, it had been sudden, which I had worked out for myself. All she wanted to tell me was the arrangements for parking, and that Audrey was not taking calls. 'Messages can be left with the Adjutant's Office at any time,' she said. 'May I help you in any other way?'

I said, 'Yes. Tell me who else you got checked off on your list.'

I knew if Betty had heard, or even Lo, they'd have called me for a pow-wow. But Marie Hollick, being military, was real cagey. Name, rank, number. That's all, folks!

I said, 'Well, it's hardly classified information, is it? But okay, let *me* tell *you*, I don't believe Lois Moon or Betty Gillis has been informed either, because if they'd have heard, I've have heard. Probably neither has Gayle Jackson Flagg Passy. But I intend calling every one of them as soon as I'm through talking with you.'

'Well, I'm obliged to you,' she said, 'And I'll certainly make a note of that. And may I know whether you'll be attending?'

I said, 'I'm thinking about it.' I was staring at my schedule, trying to remember Lance's freckled face. 'Yes,' I said, 'I'll be there.'

Grice had made a butterfly shape out of Kleenex and Scotch-taped it to the end of a coat-hanger. He flitted round in front of me and flapped it a little. 'Or,' he said, 'here's another idea. We issue the guests with bubble pipes and little tubs of liquid soap. The bride and groom make their vows, the guests start blowing and *voilà*, hundreds of pretty bubbles float up into the sunshine. Well? What's up? Are we going to San Francisco?'

I called Vern first. He said, 'He must have been near retirement. What'd he get? Coronary arrest?'

I said, 'Don't know. I don't suppose you'll cross the country for his funeral?'

'You kidding?' he said. 'Like Rudman would have come to mine?'

Lois didn't think Herb would either. She said, 'Jeez, Peg. Folks have their lives to get on with. Herb's place has a big dining-set event on, stock clearance. I doubt he could get away, and anyway, him and Lance were never close.'

I said, 'How about you? Audrey'd appreciate it.'

'Hey, kid,' she said, 'don't make me feel bad about this. I can't just drop everything, fly out there. Audrey'll understand. People go their ways, you know? It's not like it's family.'

A foreign person answered the phone at Gayle's. Said Pastor Passy and Mrs Passy were at the radio station. She gave me the number, but the secretary was as far as I got. She said Gayle and Lemarr had appointments all day, but that she would be sure to pass on the sad news. She did call me back later, too. 'Gayle asks me to tell you Colonel Rudman and his family were remembered in her prayers today, and will be again on Friday, 6 p.m. Standard Time.'

I said, 'She won't be coming then, to the funeral?'

She said, 'Lemarr and Gayle have preaching commitments in Charlotte and Hickory, Friday through Sunday.'

I knew it was one of Betty's late days at K-Mart. Still, I thought it was worth a try. I was dying to talk to her. Course, Deana picked up. I said, 'Tell your mom, Lance Rudman died. Tell her, call me the minute she gets home. How're you doing these days?'

'Yeah, pretty good,' she said. 'Delta won two pageants.'

I said, 'I'm surprised you're home, this time of day. You still not working?'

'I do crochet,' she said. 'Pillow covers and stuff. I got somebody might be interested in selling them.'

Betty called me that evening. 'It had to have been his heart,' she said. 'Or an aneurysm. That's like a tyre blowout, only inside your body. You can walk around, never know you have got one till it blows. Carla was telling me.' Carla was doing her nurse training at State. Looked like she was gonna be the only one of Betty's brood to lead a normal life and pay taxes.

Betty said, 'Audrey must be in shock. They tell you how she was?'

I said, 'They told me nothing. You know the score. You'd think it was NASA launch, not some little old funeral. I think we just have to go there, see for ourselves.'

'Well, I can't go, Peggy,' she said. 'They're laying people off here. I go missing for a day or two, I'll be one of them.'

I said, 'Can't you use vacation time?'

'No, I cannot,' she said. 'I have to conserve that, so I can take Delta to her pageants.'

67

They had a service for Lance in the base chapel at Beale, but I just flew in for the burying, Golden Gate National Cemetery being situated just along the freeway from the airport. I took flowers, from me and Kath.

Mikey Rudman was greeting people as they arrived. Last time I had really seen him, he was still in diapers. There had been the photos every year, of course, but it was still weird to see him standing there in a dark overcoat, six foot tall, just like his daddy.

Lance Jnr was taking care of his mom. He had his daddy's features but not his build. In fact, he was quite a delicate-looking bloom for somebody that had been white-water rafting and all those manly things expected of a Rudman boy.

I didn't get to speak to Audrey till the buffet lunch afterwards, at the Geary.

'You came all this way? she said. 'How kind. People are so kind.' She seemed a little hazy. I guess they'd given her something, help her through the day.

'The whole gang wanted to be here, Aud,' I said, barefaced liar that I was, 'but we're so scattered now. It's hard for people to get away at short notice.'

'Peggy,' she said, 'there's something I want to say to you.' She was wearing a beautiful two-piece, black slub linen, and a big brimmed hat. She kinda took me to one side. 'There are some people,' she said, 'they're not coming right out and saying it, but it's obvious they're thinking it – some people feel that this was all brought on by Lance Jnr. But I won't have it, Peg. I won't have him blaming himself.'

I just nodded. Tried to look understanding. It didn't seem decent to come right out and ask the burning question. I thought I'd work my way round to it. I said, 'Will you go back east?'

She still had family in Chicago. She said, 'I don't have any money worries.'

I said, 'Well, that's something. But what do you think you'll do?'

'My brother's here,' she said. 'You ever meet my brother?'

That's how it went. Whatever you asked her, she answered about something else. Then somebody came along, wanted to condole with her, so that was the end of our conversation.

There was a face I knew, waiting on line for coffee. I couldn't put a name to it, but she had me picked out anyway. 'Peggy?' she said. 'Remember me? Yvette Franklin, 366 Squadron.'

She had gone platinum. 'I was grey by the time I was forty,' she said, 'so I figured I'd find out if it's true what they say about blondes.'

I said, 'And?'

'Jury's still out,' she said. 'Course, I'm still married to Pat, so fun has to come a way to find me. Well this is a terrible day. I don't think Audrey's taken it in yet.'

I said, 'Do you know what happened? I still don't know what happened.'

'Sure,' she said.

She steered me outside. 'They were all having dinner, you know how Lance insisted on that. No running in, grabbing a sandwich, in his command. There was a fight. They'd been having a few of those lately, with the boys. You know the kinda thing. You thought they'd go to law school and they join a rock group instead. Been there, seen that movie. Anyway, there was a shouting match and Lance got a piece of steak caught in his throat. They tried whacking him on the back because he couldn't get his breath. All those first-aid classes Audrey musta been to, whiling away the hours. Anyway, by the time they got a medic out to him he was gone. Asphyxiated.'

I said, 'You get this from Audrey?'

'No,' she said, 'I know somebody from the OWC at Beale.'

I said, 'Audrey's worried people are blaming Lance Jnr. You know anything about that?'

She said, 'Well, Lance Jnr told me he doesn't want people blaming Mikey. They are weird boys, Peggy. And I'll tell you something else: I haven't seen either of them shed a tear. Not even when they sounded Taps. You show me any right-feeling person stays dry-eyed through that.'

Yvette and Pat had settled in Sacramento after he quit the force. He was teaching flying, little planes for people with big money. She was teaching high school.

'I've had to start at the bottom,' she said. 'And that's a hard place to be when you're nearly fifty. Comes of spending the best years of your life being a camp-follower.'

She told me Ruby Bergstrom was back in Minnesota, breeding pug-nosed dogs, and Ax had married an Oriental girl young enough to be his daughter. Lorene Bass she didn't know about.

I said, 'There was a Kurlich, J., killed in action. Was that Dorothy's kid?'

'Yeah,' she said. 'Joey. I read that too. I lost touch with them, but that was him, for sure. Last few years, I've been glad we never had a boy.'

I called Grice from the airport. I said, 'Well, how was your day?'

'Okay,' he said. 'Apart from the building burning down, the dawn raid by IRS investigators, and Mrs Jenneau finding out I served time in Sing-Sing. How were the obsequies?'

I said, 'Do you want to pick me up from the airport. Get a late dinner?'

He hesitated. 'Would you be very offended?' he said. I guess he had a date. Grice always kept those kinda cards close to his chest.

68

Lois got her broker's licence beginning of '72.

I said, 'Congratulations. Now you'll never get a day off.'

She said, 'I've had enough days off.'

I said, 'And you'll lie awake nights worrying.'

She said, 'Done plenty of that already. Worrying I was gonna spend the rest of my life making fifty per cent of four per cent. Anyway, what's your beef? You're doing it.'

I was, and I did love it. There were times, when we'd solved some big headache – like finding a replacement harpist at two hours' notice or the time we had to work out a seating plan for the Linwood-Friend rehearsal dinner with two ex-Mrs Linwoods, the second one insisting on bringing along somebody she called her *same-gender partner* – times I really felt satisfied with my work. And when folks really loved something we suggested, like Grice and his soap bubbles. After Rose Jenneau's wedding, everybody wanted soap bubbles.

It was neat, getting paid to make people happy. But most days all I did was work and sleep. Mondays me and Grice'd see Crystal for dinner, Fridays I'd get my hair done and my nails. That was it. At least when Betty punched out she had the energy to deliver her Avon orders or go to a movie with Slick. She even made Delta's dresses for her contests. 'She's such a darling,' she always said. 'Her waist's so tiny I can almost get my hands around it. She does fire-baton and

[221]

tap dancing and she's getting singing lessons too. She's set fair to follow in her Aunty Sherry's footsteps.'

What I heard, through Crystal, Sherry's footsteps led mainly to the Home Shows. She demonstrated things. Electric carving knives, trouser presses. She had done a car show too, had to wear a G-string, but I don't think Betty had heard about that and I wasn't going to be the one to tell her.

Apparently Sherry had split up from the guy who drank his own water. Crystal said, 'She's in another relationship now.' That's what people were starting to have, instead of getting married: relationships.

She said, 'He's half Comanche.'

Grice said, 'Wow! Does he live in a teepee?'

She said, 'I don't think so. He cleans pools.'

I said, 'Well, I just hope she doesn't go in for one of those mixed marriages. Betty's got troubles enough.'

She said, 'Mom, that is *such* a disgusting thing to say. Don't you know everybody's equal now. The colour of a person's skin don't matter.'

I said, 'All I know is, it leads to talk and the children suffer. They don't know whether to act white or act coloured.'

'There you go again,' she said. 'You're such a throwback. Act coloured! What century you living in?'

I said, 'Heaven's sakes – all I asked was, is Sherry gonna marry this breed?'

I don't know what Grice Terry found so amusing about that, nearly falling off his chair. I'd have expected a little more respect from him.

Crystal said, 'Nobody in their right mind gets married any more. And don't bring up the subject of Trent Weaver; that was a temporary aberration. Soon as I realised what a fool thing I had done, I undone it. Marriage is finished and weddings suck.'

Well, that may have been the case in California. But in Texas business had never been better. And little Sandie had just gotten engaged. Lois had told me she'd begged her to reconsider, but she was set on it.

I said, 'Well, she is young, I suppose.'

Lo said, 'I'd feel the same way if she was thirty. Bright girl, got the world at her feet. Why'd she want to go and tie herself down with a man?'

Sandie had met Gerry Carroll at a brass-band contest. He played tuba and he was taking the tests, hoped to get into the fire department.

I said, 'He sounds nice and steady. Maybe she's picked a good one, like you picked Herb.'

'Yeah,' she said. 'But did you ever hear a man learning a new tuba melody? At least Herb has a hobby he can take outta earshot. He goes down into the cellar, I can hardly hear him *whittling*.'

I said, 'I know what it is. You're worried Sandie's gonna start giving you grandbabies.'

'Peg,' she said, 'Whenever I'm feeling low, I know I can always depend on you to push me over the edge. You're as bad as Herb. He can't wait. He's planning a whole *ark* full of carved animals.'

I told Crystal. I said, 'Sandie Moon's a bright girl. Working in New York City. Got a modern outlook on life. But she's getting married.'

Crystal said, 'Who the hell is Sandie Moon?'

69

None of us heard from Audrey. She had cleared out of quarters, of course. I wrote her, care of the OWC, and so did Kath, but there was no word. I even called up Yvette Franklin, but she'd heard nothing either.

'That's how it is,' she said. 'Always was the same story. The military's your whole darned existence. Then you just disappear. Nobody knows where you come from or where you go to.'

I said, 'She told me she was okay for money.'

Yvette said, 'I'm sure she is. Now she has to find something to do with it. If I hear anything, I'll let you know.'

Lois said, 'Peg, what are you doing, worrying about Audrey Rudman? I'll bet she's lying on a beach in Grand Bahama. I'll bet she's on a cruise, playing deck quoits with some old millionaire.'

Lo was full of her own troubles. She was eager to move down to the city, but Herb was dragging his feet. He had kinda said he'd do it when the kids were off their hands. Now Sandie was married and Kirk starting at the Institute of Meat, gonna stay with Sandie and Gerry in their walk-up, in the Bronx, but Herb was backtracking. He said New York was full of danger.

'Yeah,' Lois said, 'Danger Number 1: I'll double my income.'

The months went by. We did a beautiful Camelot theme at Benbrook Lake, bride and groom made their vows out on the dock. We had such trouble finding waiters willing to wear tights and all that Merrie England stuff, but that was the kind of problem Grice was good at solving. I never did find out where he got those boys from, and their silver service was a little rough around the edges. But I will say, they did have good legs. He also got us a great deal on period feasting-ware.

Then we did the Skelton twins, double ceremony, every last thing had to be in exact duplicate. They even had two pastors, one of the bridegrooms being some kind of lapsed Catholic. Those Skelton girls got so many gifts the sip 'n' see ran to three rooms. They even each had a set of olive-spoons.

Six months after Lance, I got a call from Kath.

I said, 'What's up? You don't sound right.'

'No,' she said, 'I'm all right, but I've got to be quick, in case she comes back – and if she does, I'll pretend you just happened to phone me. I've got Audrey staying.'

She had turned up on Kath's doorstep. Kath said, 'I told her, when I wrote, if ever she needed a little holiday she was always welcome. Well, I nipped home between a four o'clock lesson and a six o'clock and there she was, sitting outside in a hire car. She had to have bacon and eggs because I don't keep much in these days.'

I said, 'How long is she staying?'

She said, 'That's the thing, Peg. I don't know. She's been here two weeks now. Don't get me wrong. She can stay as long as she likes. She's no trouble. She's the first one slept on my spare divan and she says that's comfy. Only thing is, I don't know what she's got in mind. Whether she's got other people to go and stay with or when she's booked to go home or anything, and I don't like to ask her. I don't want her thinking she's not welcome. I hear her crying sometimes, in the night. That's a terrible thing to hear.'

I said, 'She paying her way?'

She said, 'She's offered, but that's not about the money. She don't cost a lot to keep. Drop of soup and she plays with that till it's gone cold. She hasn't half lost some weight, Peg. Anyway, the money don't matter. I'm not hard up. Thing is, though, me and May have booked up to go to Benidorm again. I mean, she could stop here on her own, I suppose, but I don't know as that'd be good for her. She'd be better off somewhere with company. Anyway, what I wondered was, if you could ring me up, pretending you don't know she's here, and then I can put her on and you can ask her, casual like, how long she's planning on staying. What do you think?'

I said, 'What's she do all day?'

'Walks,' she said. 'Walks, walks, walks. That's where she is now.'

'And she hasn't said anything? About her plans?'

'No. The only thing she said was, she always loved it here. You know what I wonder? Where are those boys when she needs them? She never mentions them. All the things she did for them, fancy trips, piano lessons and all that kind of carry-on. I bet they don't even know where she is.'

I left it a day then I called back, acted all surprised when Audrey answered.

'It's a long story,' she said, 'but Kath's been my port in a storm.'

She said Norfolk, England, was the only place that made any kind a sense to her. 'I counted up,' she said. 'I went with Lance on fifteen different postings. And now he's gone, I don't belong anywhere.'

I said, 'You could have come to me. Why didn't you come to me?'

'I needed to do some walking, Peggy,' she said. 'Listen to the birds singing. Tire myself out so I have half a chance of getting to sleep at night. I know you'd have made me welcome, but Dallas doesn't do good birdsong, you must admit.'

I said, 'When do you plan on moving on?'

She missed a beat. 'Well . . . soon, I guess. I suppose Kath needs to know.'

I said, 'How are the boys?'

She said, 'I have a mind to rent a little cottage. Somewhere by the water.'

I said, 'And will you please come and see me? When you've had your fill of birdsong?'

She said, 'Peg, when you and Vern, you know, when you split up? Did you sometimes wake up in the night and think he was still there?'

First little while after me and Vern split, I had Crystal climbing in beside me every night, rucking up the sheet, making me hot as hell.

Aud said, 'I wake up with a start and I think I can hear him breathing. It happens nearly every night. I see him in the street, too. I saw him in Sacramento and Chicago and I've seen him a dozen times in King's Lynn.'

70

I was so thrilled when Crystal told me she had in mind to go back to school. She was a bright kid and it bugged me to think of her trimming poodle hair all day long. Seemed to me, if Carla Gillis could be getting herself a proper profession, my Crystal definitely should. Besides, she wasn't getting any younger.

I said, 'I'd been wondering whatever happened to that brain of yours. Well, glory hallelujah. And if I can help out, you know I will.'

Then she told me what she intended doing. She hoped to take a eight-week course at the Deschutes School of Taxidermy in Bend, Oregon.

I said, 'Cancel that offer of financial assistance. Are you outta your mind?'

'Here we go,' she said. 'What'd you think? I was going to Harvard Law School?'

I said, 'Taxidermy is antlers on walls, right?'

'Correct,' she said. 'But that's not the half of it.'

'Okay,' I said, 'I was just checking I hadn't heard wrong and you were actually gonna do something useful with your life like be a tax attorney. So we are talking about prize fishes in glass cases? And men who chew tobacco?'

'Mom,' she said 'I never saw a good ole boy actually stuffed and mounted, but you may be on to something there.'

I said, 'If you want to ruin your life, why don't you just cut to the chase, move up to Maine and go into partnership with your daddy? He can sell the worms, you can stuff whatever they catch with them.'

'Okay, enough,' she said. 'Now, listen to what I have in mind. I want my own business, Mom. There are people out there with so much money they don't know what to spend it on next and I want to help them. There's women come into our place, buy real gold chains for their dogs. They pay people to walk them. They get their portraits painted, for Chrissakes. So here's my idea: pet eternalisation. The loved one barks his last, I go to work on his little doggy carcass, mount him in some lifelike pose and there he'll be, like he's returned from the dead. I might do cats too, if I can get the hang of them. I think there's real money to be made. Soon as I graduate, I'm gonna hire some work space and set up. I'll need a work bench. And somewhere with ventilation. And anybody you know got a pet of advanced years, you might want to mention to them to keep me in mind. I haven't set on a name yet. I thought maybe Perpetual Pets?'

Grice suggested Friends Forever.

I said, 'How definite are you about doing this?' Seemed to me, if she was willing to go back to vet school and settle down to her books there was a lot more money to be made keeping pets alive than by stuffing them.

'Definite enough I've bought myself a skinning knife,' she said.

I said to Grice, 'You can wipe that smile off your face. Some day you'll have kids breaking your heart.'

'Oh, I don't think so,' he said. 'How about Memorial Mutts?'

She said if everything went according to plan she'd be enrolling for September. 'It's intensive,' she said. 'I have to mount five fish, or four and a fibreglass repro. I have to do waterfowl and game birds, flying and standing, number depends on whether one of them is a turkey 'cause they take longer. Then there's game heads, small mammals, horn-preparation for antler mounts, and two rugs, one flat, one open mouth.'

Never having had a lick of encouragement from my own mother, I hated to be so negative about Crystal's idea. But all I could foresee was her ruining her hands, in and out of chemicals all day long, not to mention the kinda animal odours she'd be getting into her hair and clothing. It was a line of business that could say the wrong thing about a woman. I guess I was still hoping some day I'd get to organise a wedding for family.

I said, 'And then? Do I have to come up there for your graduation?'

'You don't have to come anywhere or do anything,' she said. 'When I've finished my training I'm gonna come right back, get myself a work room with running water, and open my order book.'

Lois screamed when I told her. 'Dear God, Peg,' she said. 'Didn't we get anything right with these kids? This is gonna be a real asset to you. When you're schmoozing with those Junior League dames. They find out you're related to a pooch-stuffer *and* a worm-farmer, hell, they're *never* gonna forget your name! Well, backwoods blood will out, that's what I always say. Must be a proud moment for Vern. She could be on to something, though, you know? Fools and their money? I'm all for it. Empty those suckers' pockets. Specially dog-owning suckers. I tell you we got a spaniel? It was just another way Herb thought he'd stop us getting to New York. He said it was for Kirk. Reckoned dogs are soothing, but seeing my rugs ruined sure don't soothe me. Meanwhile, of course, Kirk's gone and we're left with the rug-stainer.'

I said, 'Why did Kirk need soothing?'

'Oh, you know,' she said, 'he always was a irritable type of kid and I guess all those guy hormones made him worse.' She said he had girls throwing theirselves at him, he was so good-looking.

'That's half the trouble,' she said. 'He doesn't have to do a thing except smile and they come running. He'd have two or three on a string all the same time, then one of them'd phone up want to know where he was. Herb didn't always know what to say for the best. There was one turned up on the doorstep, sobbing and begging him to stop two-timing her, and he just went wild, Peg, screaming and shouting, broke the screen door. That was when we got the creature. Anyway, it'll do him good, staying at Sandie's. Gerry won't stand for any upset. He guards Sandie like she's made of glass.'

Sandie had suffered a miscarriage. 'I don't know what was the big hurry anyway,' Lois said. 'I told her. Time enough for babies. She reminds me of Gayle sometimes. You know how she always had that doomy feeling about the boys when they were flying? Always waiting for the worst to happen to Okey? Well, Gerry's in the fire department now, Westchester County, and that's how Sandie is. Whenever he's on watch, specially nights, she's waiting for that knock at the door. I told her, she has to relax. He's a nice kid too, for an Irish. I like him. I told her she could wait ten years and still have plenty of time to raise a family. Know what she said? "Ten years time, Mom, there may be other things I have to do." Maybe she thinks she'll be pushing me around in a bathchair. Maybe she thinks I'm going senile. I don't think I am. Brain's working fine. It's the rest of me has started to slide south. Top of your arms turned to jello yet, Peg?'

So Crystal quit the poodle parlour and headed out to Oregon to learn caping and fleshing and a lot of other things I didn't care to know about, and the wedding season wound down, except for an all-gold fiftieth-anniversary party we did for Mrs and Mrs Achilles Ruskin III. Grice went to Key West for a week, helping a friend with his aged mother, and I sat around the office playing with this idea he had for branching out.

'Why stop at weddings?' he kept saying. 'We could be party-planners for the whole cavalcade of life. I wasn't so sure. Christenings I knew we could handle. Rose Jenneau had been so pleased with her wedding, she called me, the moment she knew baby Rose was on the way, asked me to take charge of the christening lunch and the gift display. But I feared the taint of funeral teas might affect the happier aspects of our work. And as for that big party Tootie Gunzhauser had hosted after her divorce, French champagne and a firework display, I thought that was in the worst possible taste. Still, I was feeling stale. I'd have gone on a cruise myself, if I'd had anybody to go with.

I was just thinking of closing up early, going home and tidying a few drawers, when the phone rang. It was Betty.

'Peggy!' she said. 'You'll never guess who's coming to town.'

71

'Gayle and Lemarr,' she said, 'are on a world-wide tour of Texas!'

She read out to me from her newspaper. '"Friday next, at the Assembly of God, Converse, Pastors Lemarr and Gayle Passy bring their ministry of prayer and healing to San Antonio. Dr Passy . . ." Peggy?' she said. 'I didn't know Gayle had married a *doctor*. "Dr Passy and his wife Gayle, who is also a licenced minister" – did you know about this? ". . . and his wife Gayle, who is also a licenced minister, hail from Fayetteville, North Carolina. Lemarr describes his early years, selling life insurance, as *a time of rebellion against the call of God. It took a herniated disc and the loss of my livelihood to open my heart and mind to His Purpose for me. With my late first wife, Eveline, I accepted the call to ministry and we began taking the Good News to the streets of Wilmington and Jacksonville, places where many fine young men, serving in the military, had lost their spiritual way in life. I too lost my way, as I watched my wife suffer with a cancer of the blood. I left my Bible unread and took comfort in strong drink, which is no comfort at all. Then, on March tenth in 1967, the Lord came to me. Lying on my bed in a motel, suddenly the room was filled with a wondrous light and I heard the voice of God telling me to return to Fayetteville where I would find a helpmeet to resume my ministry. I was so exhausted, fighting the Truth, I obeyed and in Fayetteville I found Gayle, whose own life had been a Vale of Tears. Soon after our marriage we began*

broadcasting on JCIL-FM and our prayer programmes ran daily until last year, when the baton was taken up by Pastor Ronnie White. This has enabled us to take to the road with Gayle's awesome ministry of healing."
It says here Gayle is a graduate of the Rocky Mount Bible College. Did you know that? My, that girl's a dark horse! There's a whole list of places they're appearing. Bethel Church, Jasper; Christian Fellowship, Cloverleaf; Living Waters Tabernacle, Edna; Pentecostal Church, Beeville. Friday they're at the Assembly of God, Converse, then they're up to Abilene, Unity Praise Center, Perrytown Assembly of God and then to Oklahoma. Peggy, you just have to come down here and see her. There's a picture of her in the paper looking so pretty.'

Well, wild horses wouldn't have kept me away. I was more a believer in the power of positive thinking than any of those old epistles to the Trojans, but Gayle was the only person I ever knowed got her own radio show and I wasn't gonna miss seeing her perform.

I said, 'I'll get a hotel.' I couldn't face staying at Betty's little place, all those brats of Deana's under my feet.

'You will not!' she said. 'Deana and the girls got a place of their own. When Carla's working I'm rattling around here, don't know what to do with all this space.'

I travelled down Thursday, stopped off just after Austin for a salad platter and got into town about four. Drove around the old neighbourhood, saw a few faces I thought I knew. Then I realised the kids I was looking at couldn't have been older than thirty. I always do that, forget to allow for the passing years. Then I turned on to San Jacinto.

I hadn't called ahead, tell my mom I'd be in town. I hadn't even finished weighing up whether I was gonna pay her a visit. I drove past anyway. The place was looking run down, but there was a light on inside. I kept going. Decided to sleep on it.

Betty didn't finish till six but Carla was home, getting ready to work a night-shift. She looked so smart in her nursing whites.

I said, 'Look at you!'

'I'm on Renal,' she said, real proud of herself, and rightly so.

I said, 'So Deana moved out at long last. Where'd she go?'

She rolled her eyes. 'Trailer park,' she said, 'other side of Salado River.'

I said, 'She working?'

She said, 'Depends what you call work. She's moved in with a guy called Bulldog. They get stuff out of dumpsters, try to fix it up and then sell it. Trouble is, most of the stuff in dumpsters is there for a very good reason.'

I said, 'Well, has to be better than sitting on your mom's couch all day watching TV.'

'I guess,' she said. 'Long as I don't have to come home and listen to her bellyaching, I could care less what she does. I don't like Bulldog, though. If Dwayne knew about it, I don't think he'd like a guy like that round his girls.'

I said, 'He beating up on them?'

'Oh no,' she said. 'He's not like that. He brings them stuff home and everything, makes a real fuss of them. He gives me the creeps. Ask me, he makes too much fuss of Delta. Ask me, it's not natural.'

I'd have thought she'd be glad Deana's kids had a new daddy being kind to them, but I guess it was hard on Carla having a junior-pageant queen in the family and her being so homely herself.

I said, 'Delta's the pretty one, right?'

Carla said, 'Yeah, she's pretty. And she knows it. She's had Mom telling her every day of her life.'

I said, 'Honey, you're pretty too.'

She laughed. 'Aunty Peggy,' she said. 'You think I'm jealous? Of Delta? I mean, she has Deana for a mom, and now she has Bulldog slobbering all over her, plus she doesn't appear to have much going on between her ears. Far as I'm concerned, that pretty face is the only thing ever went right for her. It's just she's just too knowing about it. You understand what I mean? I've seen her around Bulldog, and she's more knowing than's good for her. Heck, she's only eleven.'

She said things hadn't worked out between Sherry and the Comanche. 'She makes earrings now,' she said. 'Silver and amber and stuff. They're okay. She sent some for Christmas for me and Deana's girls. Moves around a lot, though. She stays with people and then moves on. I've filled up the whole 'S'-page in my address book with

Sherry's wanderings. What d'you think about Gayle getting religion?'

I said, 'I don't know till I see her. Do you remember her? Remember going on the bus, when she married Ray?'

'I sure do,' she said. 'We went to the beach afterwards and had boiled shrimp and Aunty Kath was there, and Crystal, and that kid who kept pinching me when nobody was looking.'

'Kirk,' I said. 'By all accounts he's turned into a big handsome heartthrob.'

'That right?' she said. She was lacing up her big rubber-soled shoes. 'Well, who'd have thought it?'

Slick Bonney came with us to the Assembly of God. Whatever Betty wanted to do was what Slick wanted. We could tell from two blocks away there was gonna be a big crowd. Everybody in town seemed to be heading the same way. By the time we parked and pushed our way through, all we could get was seats right at the back.

'I knew I should have got off work early,' Betty said. 'Now Gayle'll never see us, right back here.'

'Tell you what I'll do, precious,' Slick said. 'You write her a note and I'll give it to one of the ushers. Give him a dollar, get it passed up to her.'

Betty turned scarlet, me hearing Slick call her 'precious'.

It got there was standing-room only and still they were packing people in. There was an electric organ playing. Then a pastor stepped out up front and asked us to be silent and prayerful. He had a kinda Mexican look about him but everybody was respectful to him. Nearly everybody. Slick was coaxing wax outta his ear and when the little brown pastor asked us to bow our heads, I heard him say, 'Bow my head when I'm good and ready, beaner.' He said it real quiet, though.

We sang 'No Other Name' and then he brought on Lemarr and Gayle and the whole place erupted. It was like a show at Cesar's Palace. Lemarr was in a beautiful suit, dark grey, white cotton shirt fresh outta Bloomies. He looked like a senator or something. Gayle was in electric-blue, peplum jacket, pencil skirt, and a single row of pearls.

'St-a-a-and up for Jesus!' she cried. And there wasn't a body in that church didn't get to their feet. 'I was down and out,' she said, 'and the Lord lifted me up. I drank hard liquor and spoke profanities.

My soul dwelled in a dark corner because I believed Lord Jesus had abandoned me. But friends, it was me had abandoned Him. "Come to Me, all you who labour and are heavy laden," He said, "and I will give you rest," Matthew, 11:28. But the only place I was interested in going was the liquor store. "If anyone has ears to hear, let him hear," Mark, 4:23, but the only sound I enjoyed was the glugging of my next drink. "Blessed are the pure in heart, for they shall see God," Matthew, 5:8, but I was looking at life through the bottom of a glass. Friends, the Lord sent Lemarr Passy looking for me. The good pastor found me, frying eggs and pouring coffee for truckers. He saw through the hardness of my heart. He endured the coarseness of my tongue and the darkness of my unbelief. He persevered with me to bring me to the love of our Lord. He promised me I'd be lifted up outta my despair. And I was lifted up. I was . . . lifted up . . .'

She sang 'Lift Me Up, Lord'. That was when I really believed it was Gayle. That high sweet voice of hers, just the same as when she used to sing 'Hushabye Baby' to Sandie.

By the time she got to the end she was kinda overcome with emotion so Lemarr took up the story, about how they had battled with the waywardness of Gayle's heart and prayed on it and how it had come to them that she was called to the ministry of healing. Gayle was holding his hand. Betty was holding my hand. She kept saying to the woman in the next seat, 'This is our friend,' but the woman was listening to Lemarr.

He preached about the healing of two blind men and a man possessed of a demon and just as he was finishing up with a prayer, Gayle called out, 'There's somebody here tonight with terrible pain in their knee and the Lord is ready to heal them.'

A woman right there at the front got up and shouted, 'It's me! It's me!'

Slick said, 'That's woman's nothing but a shill. They planted her, get gullible folks believing.' And I must say, she did leap to her feet pretty nimble for a person supposed to be in pain.

Gayle said, 'The Lord is healing you now. You have a shard of cartilage floating around, causing your suffering, but believe and the Lord will heal you.'

Slick said, 'Now she'll say she can feel something at work. I know anything, it'll be tingling.'

Betty hushed him.

The woman with the knee had started calling out, 'I feel something happening. It's like electric tingling. I believe! I believe!'

Slick sucked his teeth.

There were other people trying to get up front too, all got pain in their knees, I guess. But Gayle was calling out somebody with a spondylitis of the spine that the Lord wanted to heal and a woman who was suffering secretly with a prolapse of the womb.

'Well, I am *scandalised*,' Betty said. 'Healing a thing like that in mixed company.'

There was healed folk dancing around by the altar, people down on their knees with their arms held up high, the organ was playing 'Amazing Grace' with Gayle leading the singing and the ushers were passing among us with buckets, so we could honour the Lord with our free-will offerings of cash or cheques.

Me and Betty both tried waving to Gayle, try and catch her eye, but she was deep in prayer and anyway, the whole darned place was full of waving arms. I doubt she even got Betty's note. Everybody was asked to remain seated until Pastors Gayle and Lemarr had left the building and started their onward journey to Abilene.

'Well!' Betty said. 'Least she could have done was come back for an iced tea.'

Slick said, 'Don't you give her another thought, darlin'. She ain't worth a light. Fame goes to a person's head, you might as well forget them because they'll forget you.'

I said, 'Betty, I don't think she even knew we were here. Long list of places they've been preaching, different place every night, she probably don't even know for sure what town she's in.'

Still, I did feel kinda flat. Everybody was just pulling on their jackets, like it was the end of a movie.

Betty said, 'What about the ones that got healed? I'd sure like to speak with them. Find out what it felt like.'

Slick said, 'Well, tell me now, do you see any of them?'

The man with the frozen neck had been wearing a mustard-yellow pullover. That much I did remember. But we couldn't see him anywhere.

I said, 'They must have all left.'

'Darned right, they did,' he said. 'They gotta drive to Abilene. Get healed again tomorrow night.'

'Now, Slick,' Betty said, 'you don't know Gayle like we do. She's a good, gentle girl, seen more suffering in her life than the three of us put together. I'm not saying I hold with folks dancing around, taking off their shirts in a house of God, but I have to believe what I seen tonight. She has the power of healing and there's only one place it could have come from.'

'Okay, honey,' he said. He was helping her on with her wrap. 'I believe! I believe!' He winked at me.

But he didn't know Gayle. I couldn't believe she'd be scamming people for money. But then, I didn't much like the other idea neither. If she was really performing miracles, she wasn't our little Gayle any more.

Slick drove us home, but he didn't come in. 'Guess you girls'll be up half the night jawing,' he said.

He was right too. Betty made Velveeta scrambled eggs with sliced banana and hot drop-biscuits and we talked till it nearly was daylight.

She said, 'What do you think, Peggy? Have we seen the Lord at work tonight?'

I said, 'Don't know what I think. Probably 'cause we've known her so long. But you thought it was for real.'

'Yes,' she said. 'But I can't get over her coming to San Antonio and snubbing me. She was glad enough to come here after Ray was killed. She'd have been all on her own for Thanksgiving, if you and me hadn't looked after her.'

I said, 'Well, seems like she's in show business now, and that can change a person.'

'It's true,' she said. 'Look what's happened to Elvis Presley. And you know, healing may be a gift from God an' all, but I wouldn't want it. People bringing their sickness and sorrows to you. People getting their hopes up.'

I agreed with her. If I'd have been Gayle, I'd sooner have stayed wiping down that coffee counter hundred times a day than have strangers bringing me their prolapses. I said, 'Slick didn't believe.'

She said, 'He will. I won't have him calling Gayle a fraud. Even if she did snub us.'

I said, 'You ever gonna marry him?'

'Oh, don't start on that,' she said. 'Deana's always on, I could move in with Slick. He's got a nice split-level out Randolph way, then her and Bulldog could get this place.'

Might have known Deana'd be putting her mom's happiness first. I said, 'This Bulldog treating your grandbabies okay?'

'Yeah,' she said. 'He's great, for a man never had any of his own. He idolises them.'

I said, 'Well, I can't say I blame you, not giving up your home. Get to our age, a woman has to look out for herself. Slick does treat you nice, though. I get the impression he'd just about do anything for you.'

'I know,' she said. 'Tell you the truth, though, Peggy, I never did care much for the married side of life.'

72

When Carla came home from her night-shift, I was trying to find my way round Betty's kitchen, make some coffee. We'd only had a couple of hours' sleep.

Carla said, 'Well?'

I said, 'It was amazing. Gayle was standing up there, singing hymns all on her own. Healing floating cartilages. And when they passed the buckets round, you should have seen the bills people were dropping in.'

Betty put her head round the door, looking the worse for wear, wondering whether she dared to call in sick. She always was a woman who needed her sleep.

Carla said, 'Gayle do raisings from the dead? Looks like we could do with her here this morning.'

She sat with me while Betty showered.

I said, 'You ever hear from your daddy?'

'Only in a roundabout way,' she said. 'Mom has Glick cousins up there and anything happens in Warsaw, they get to hear about it.'

'He working?'

'He was,' she said. 'He was driving a truck. Transporting hogs up to Chicago. Then he got mad at some traffic lights, said they were slower'n shit so he fixed them with his shotgun. He got in the papers. I don't know what he's doing right now. Mainly we just get the bad news about him. How long are you staying?'

Betty wasn't the only one dithering about the day ahead. I still hadn't made up my mind if I was gonna knock on my mom's door before I headed home. It seemed like a terrible thing to pass her by when I was so near, specially after all that hymn-singing and praying. But, as I explained to Carla, I knew if I did pay her a visit I'd come away with murder in my heart, specially if sister Connie was around, and that wasn't a Christian way to think neither.

I said, 'I've oftentimes wondered if they didn't mix up the babies at the nursing home.'

'Yeah,' she said. 'I expect it's a common fantasy.'

Betty had decided to do the right thing. 'If I call in, play sick, I know what'll happen,' she said. 'Next thing I really will get sick. God watches.'

I said, 'Okay, you do your duty and I'll do mine.'

I hugged her goodbye. The older I got, the better I liked her.

I drove past Mom's place and parked three houses down. There was nobody about. As I remembered it, when we moved in there was kids in every house in the street. Then there was older folk, with kids grown up and gone. Middle-aged, I guess, but to me they seemed like old-timers. Then they got to be real old. After that, I guess the whole thing starts over. New families coming in.

I could hear a dog barking, out the back. I could smell fried food. Big fat guy, put me in mind of a sea lion, come waddling out.

I said, 'Mrs Shea home?'

He just looked at me. There was something about the vacant look in his eyes, and the fact he was wearing a belt-buckle the size of a hubcap, made me connect him with my sister.

I said, 'How about Connie?'

'Connie!' he yelled. 'It's the Avon woman.'

She took her time coming to the door. She always was a slow mover.

'Well,' she said, 'just look what the cat left on the step.'

If there was one thing my sister Connie had a gift for it was turning a house into a health-hazard. I may not have much good to say about my mom, but at least she'd wipe out her skillet once in a while. At least when she unwrapped a pack of smokes she didn't let the cellophane just drop wherever she was standing.

There was still the same rug on the floor, autumn leaves motif, Mom's pride and joy when she got it. There was a new couch and chairs, though, and a big TV. Connie offered me a soda and Bobby Earl went back to watching *Scooby Doo*. I gathered his name was Bobby Earl 'cause that's what he had scorched out on the back of his belt. Actually, it said BOBBY EAR. He had made the letters so big I guess he'd run outta space for the L.

I said, 'Where's Mom?'

'On the old-age ward at State,' she said.

I said, 'Since when? She real sick?'

'She was a danger to herself,' she said. 'I did the best I could. And you've got some ginger, blowing in like this, asking questions.'

Mom had been in the hospital about seven months. She'd started wandering off, getting up in the middle of the night insisting she had to be somewhere urgent, putting on three or four pairs of underwear and nothing on her top half.

I said, 'She getting better?'

She laughed. 'They don't get better. They get worse, then they die.'

Connie had ceased visiting her some while before. 'She didn't know me from Davy Crockett,' she said, 'so what's the point, dragging all the way out there, using up gas?'

I said, 'Why didn't you call me? I'd have come.'

'What for?' she said. 'You never called us. Anyway, she never asked for you. Matter of fact, I think she wrote you off for dead.'

I said, 'I'm in Dallas, Connie, not the Arctic Circle. And the last time I came visiting she didn't even turn off the TV.'

The little walrus-tusk Bambi was still on the shelf.

I said, 'She got everything she needs?'

She said, 'Why don't you go and see for yourself. Could be your last chance.'

I said, 'Don't give me a hard time here, Connie. I'm sorry I haven't been around; but all those years I was here, I swear I couldn't do right for doing wrong. She didn't like me marrying Vern. Then she didn't like me splitting up from him. She didn't like me living in foreign parts. She didn't like me turning up here, treating the place like a hotel, as she used to say. Some hotel! And I'll tell you what, all the years Crystal was growing up, Mom never spent a cent on her. Vern's folks'd send stuff, didn't matter where we were in the world, they never missed her birthday. Not Mom, though.'

Bobby Ear turned round, gave me an ugly look. I guess I was ruining his enjoyment of the Tootsie Roll commercial. Person gets distracted for a few seconds, he could lose the plot easy.

Connie said, 'She's on Vicksburgh, if you're going.'

I could feel the soles of my shoes kinda sticking to the rug as I left.

'She starts up about folk stealing her money,' Connie said, 'pay no attention. The doctor up there told me, it's a very common thing that a old person believes they've been robbed. They hear it all the time.'

Bobby Ear got to his feet when Connie was showing me to the door. 'This furniture is all mine,' he said. 'And the TV.'

'You look like you're doing okay,' Connie said.

It crossed my mind to leave her a few bucks, conscience money. Then it crossed my mind that it wouldn't be wise to give her and the sea lion expectations.

I drove along by Topperwein High on my way to State, made myself feel real melancholy thinking of how the years fly by. Thinking of Jim Sparks, cut down in Korea, and Slick, still going home every night to a lonely bed and his tractor catalogues, and me, that used to be the star of the softball team, got stiff ankles and hot flashes and a daughter learning to stuff muskrats.

73

The nurse said, 'Mrs Shea? Yeah, she'll be in the day room.'

I said, 'I've been out of town.'

She said, 'Well, she won't know that. She don't know what day it is. You family?'

I started trying to explain how come my mom had been there seven months and I only just found out. Blaming Connie. Blaming pressure of work. Trying to explain to this nurse, young enough to be my own daughter. Like she could care.

She said what happens is, bit by bit the brain closes down and eventually it stops altogether. She said they did what they could with them, isometrics twice a week and bingo and Spot That Tune.

I walked down to the day room, just followed my nose. Mainly they were in wheelchairs. Mainly they were asleep.

I went around and looked at all the old ladies that were about the right size. Mom was five ten, in her prime. Then, allowing that shrinkage does occur with the passing years, I went around again. She was wearing day clothes. A caramel-colour dress. It seemed like they kept her nice.

She was kinda dozing, facing towards the TV, but not watching. I said, 'Mom? It's Peggy.'

She didn't even look at me.

I said, 'I'm sorry I didn't come before.' I *was* sorry, too.

She had a pocketbook she kept opening and shutting, didn't seem to have anything in it. I touched her hand and it felt like paper.

I said, 'I didn't know. I come in from Dallas to see you and I didn't even know. Connie should have called me. I'd have come.'

Her face was lined so deep. Creased with all those years of frowning and complaining.

I said, 'Crystal sends her love. You remember Crystal? She's grown up so beautiful.' I took a photo out of my bill-fold, but she just looked in the empty pocketbook some more.

I said, 'Mom? Is there anything you'd like?' But she had closed her eyes again. I just sat for a while, feeling awkward. Watching *The Flintstones Comedy Hour* in a room full of the living dead.

I said, 'If you think of anything, you just ask the nurse to give me a call? And I'll come again. I'll come again soon.' Then I tiptoed away.

I left my card with the nurses' station. As I explained to them, I had a long drive ahead of me. And as I explained to myself, on that long drive, my mom didn't know me any more. All my life I'd been waiting for her to take an interest, waiting for her to mellow, but she was holding out on me to the very end. I couldn't ever remember being with her when there wasn't a stupid TV show playing.

74

I started sending flowers and soft-centre candy. Once in a while I'd phone State and get told there was no change in her condition. I'd promise myself to visit her, next weekend, next month, but I always found some welcome reason not to do it, and the only person I owned up to was my darling Grice.

I said, 'I always complained about my mother's stony heart. Turns out I'm built just the same.'

'Go ahead,' he said. 'Beat yourself up a little.'

I said, 'You never talk about your mom.'

'No,' he said. 'I just hatched out of a giant white egg.'

We were looking through candle catalogues, trying to find something unusual for the Fisk-Melly wedding. Carrie-Ann Fisk wanted everything to look real ancient and holy.

Grice said, 'Tell me something good about your mom.'

It took a while. I said, 'She used to smell of Blue Fern dusting powder.'

'That's nice,' he said. 'Let's hold on to that thought.'

I said, 'I lie awake. I think about when I get old and Crystal leaves me parked in some old-age rest home. Never comes to visit. It'll be my punishment. My mom always said, "What goes around, comes around."'

'So did mine!' he said. 'Don't you hate that?'

He said he didn't think Crystal would abandon me. 'Not Crystal,' he said 'She'll stick around. She'll be looking to mount you on a polished walnut plinth.'

She was gone a month before she called me. I was starting to think the whole School of Taxidermy thing was a front and she'd been kidnapped. Sold into a life of prostitution.

I said, 'I suppose they don't have telephones yet in Bend, Oregon.'

'That's right,' she said. 'Matter of fact, they haven't caught on to the wheel yet neither. They just pile their stuff on to sleds and *drag* it home from the mall.'

I said, 'Well, a girl takes off into the wilderness and doesn't call home in four weeks, what's her mother supposed to do? I was this close to calling the FBI. Are you the only female taking these classes?'

'I believe so,' she said. 'But there's a couple of guys here have got bosoms bigger'n mine.'

So far she had done a ground-squirrel, two duck, an antler mount and an elk foot – might be suitable, she said, as a novelty base for a reading lamp.

I said, 'Give me time. I may get used to the idea.'

She had also got a commendation for her fish. 'I've done a two-pound yellow perch, and a seven-pound walleye,' she said. 'You have to be real careful with the fins. You have to ease them out, spread them out wet on to balsa wood and just let them dry naturally.'

I said, 'Why are you doing fish? I thought you were intending to stuff poodle dogs?'

'I am,' she said. 'But fish can be a taxidermist's bread and butter. Fish, and game heads. Anyway, you sign up for a course, you can't arrive and start picking and choosing.' The kind of money she was paying, I'd have thought that was exactly what you could do.

She said, 'I'm here to learn technique, Mom. If you have good technique, you can mount anything. I'm just starting on a cougar. Female, so she's not very big, kinda pale buff with black tips to her ears. Cute little thing. Could you call Dad?'

I said, 'Excuse me?'

'Dad,' she said, 'I think he'd appreciate a call. I gotta go, that was my last quarter. Bye.'

Grice was writing out cheques for me to sign. 'Well?' he said. 'Tell me how she is, but I don't want to hear anything about eyeballs or entrails.'

I said, 'She sounds happy. God alone knows why. She asked me to tell you, did you know the best thing for getting skunk-scent off your clothes is tomato juice.'

'Well, I'm obliged to her for that,' he said. 'Peggy? You don't think she's going to come home with a snuff habit or anything, do you?'

I didn't call Vern right away. We'd stayed pretty civil, over the years, but we weren't given to casual phone calls. Way I looked at it, if he wanted to talk to me, he knew my number. The only thing I could think was, he needed money. Only thing I could think was, the bottom had fallen out of worms. But I couldn't imagine he'd come running to me.

A week went by, then I got a postcard from Crystal. Picture of the Cascades, and all she had written was 'You called Dad?'

He picked up. 'Vern's Vermiculture.'

I said, 'You must be a proud man. You hear about your daughter getting a gold star for mounting fish?'

'I did,' he said. 'She told me they have a twenty-five-pound chinook salmon in the ice chest they might let her loose on. Well, if you've spoken to her, I guess you've heard about our troubles?'

Martine was in Bangor, awaiting surgery. She had found a lump. I said, 'They can do wonders these days.'

'Yup,' he said.

'They catch these things early, they can really root it out. Give a person a clean bill of health.'

'Yup,' he said.

'And there's different causes,' I said. 'Woman finds a lump, don't mean to say it's cancer.'

'Yup,' he said. 'But it is. So she's in there, getting it all took away some time this week. Probably be Thursday. I'm going over there. Old man Beebe's coming over, give Eugene a hand with the worms. Martine's gonna be laid up a while, won't be able to drive, or even brush her hair . . . Then we just have to wait and see . . .'

He was near to crying, I could tell. 'She's only fifty-one, Peg,' he said.

I told him I'd send flowers. Didn't see what else I could do. They had Mom Dewey living with them, never was afraid of hard work, and from what I heard she had had a new lease of life, after Pop Dewey electrocuted himself. And they had neighbours would rally around and help. When I was married to him, I heard often enough about the neighbourliness of Maine folk.

'Peggy,' he said. He just caught me before I put the phone down. 'Tell me to mind my own business, but I hope you know about all that checking women are supposed to do. You know what I mean? They told Martine she should have been checking herself all along, but she didn't know that. Nobody ever told her.'

All the years I was married to Vern Dewey he never showed me that kind of consideration. When I was carrying Crystal, he didn't want to know any of the details and neither did any other man I ever met. Now they even see their babies getting born, which as far as I'm concerned is not a good idea. A man sees a woman in that kind of disarray, it could change the way he feels about her. But it's all the fashion. Men learning about labour pains and women standing in bars, cussing like rednecks. Everything turned topsy-turvy, men acting like women and women acting like men, and, to prove it, I had a daughter up in Oregon hadn't worn a skirt in years.

I was touched, though, him mentioning such a thing. He must have been dying of embarrassment.

I said, 'Sure, Vern. And you take care of yourself too, you hear?'

'Well,' he said, 'course, it's a woman's thing Martine has got. But thanks for the thought.'

75

Crystal was back by late November. I was afraid they'd get some kind of weather up in Oregon and she'd be there for the duration, but she showed up on my birthday with a picture portfolio of her achievements, the head of a mule-deer buck mounted on a plaque and a black bearskin rug lined with plaid Scottish-style material.

I said, 'You really shouldn't have.' Turned out she really hadn't. She never was good at remembering birthdays.

Grice was taking me to the Blue Bayou Cocktail Lounge so Crystal come along too. I never did care for strong liquor. The waiter picked me out something real nice, looked like pale-blue milk, tasted fruity, but the younger generation were trying to drink each other under the table with Texas Twisters. We had a reservation at the Gardenia for eight o'clock and darn it if we didn't nearly lose it they made us so late with their messing around.

I said to her, 'You seem happy to be back.'

She said she hadn't had too many laughs in Bend, there being just nine males and herself and them being the kind of guys to keep a respectful distance from a girl unless she had her picture in *Rustler* magazine.

She said, 'Are you okay? You're so quiet. Am I butting in, ruining your evening?'

It wasn't that. I loved having her there. Although of course, when you're the only one who's stone-cold sober words like 'Wickiup' and 'duck-plucking' and 'mail-order tongues' don't seem so humorous. I guess I just wasn't in the mood to have a birthday.

I said, 'Gramma Shea is in hospital, doesn't know who anybody is. If I ever get like that, you're to put a pillow over my face.'

'What?' she said. 'And go to jail?'

I said, 'I'll put it in my will that you had my permission.'

'Don't bother,' she said. 'I still won't do it. It's hard enough chloroforming a pigeon.'

It was just the two of us for Christmas. Grice was away to his good friend Tucker's for a few days.

I said, 'The hell with cooking.'

She said, 'I'm with you, all the way.'

We ate corn chips, watched *Jaws* and *The Omega Man*, then we moved on to Pet Cherry Ice Sandwich and *Love Story*. In between I called England.

Kath said, 'I've got May here. We've just had a beautiful piece of fruit cake, shop bought, and now we're putting a dent in a bottle of Double Century. First of January we're cutting down, though. We're both going on diet biscuits, otherwise they'll never let us on that airyplane to Spain. They'll be charging us excess baggage.'

I said, 'You get a card from Audrey? She's in Chicago.'

'Yes,' she said, 'I did. But she says she can't settle, bless her. She'll be turning up at my door again, I shouldn't wonder.'

Crystal had a word, told her about Oregon, then she put me back on.

Kath said, 'See? I told you she'd turn out lovely. How you moithered about her, and now you've got her there. You're a lucky woman, Peggy.'

On the twenty-sixth we drove out to the Palace of Wax and the Grand Prairie Craft Village. There was a car broken down, had caused several other cars to shunt into one another, and traffic backing up on the freeway.

'Oregon's real beautiful, Mom,' she said. 'You get on a back road up through Deschutes Forest, drive for an hour and never see another vehicle.'

I said, 'You're not thinking of going back there by any chance?'

'No,' she said. 'I was just saying.'

Before she had gone away to train for her new profession she had as good as had her first customer promised to her. A lady with a elderly shih-tzu dog, regular customer at the grooming parlour. Unfortunately for Crystal it was not to be. The animal upped and died the week after she left for Oregon, and the bereaved owner got tempted away by the new Pet Cemetery that had opened in Cedar Hill. What I had read, the prime sites, with lake views, were getting bought up fast.

After Christmas she started placing advertisements and ordering supplies. Moulding plaster, borax powder, gasoline, wire, shredded wood, resin for making glass eyes. It looked like the devil's kitchen. Perpetual Pets, she was calling herself. She set up in an old studio, used to be occupied by a person, called herself a chronicler of urban life, who had moved to New York because people there were willing to pay big money for works of art made out of old car bumpers.

Her first job was a canary, which was hardly gonna pay the rent, and her second job was a garter snake for some joker who never came back to collect it, nor to pay what he owed.

I said to Grice, 'At least in our business the customers know how to behave.'

I spoke too soon.

We had been asked to handle the Dekker-Prowers wedding. Courtenay Dekker was marrying Scott Prowers in a poolside ceremony at her parents' lovely ranch home and we had been given a blank cheque to ensure everything was perfect, the Dekkers being millionaires practically.

The wedding colours were soft primrose and pastel-green and the bridesmaids and flower-girls were having tiny spring blooms woven into their hair, as was the bride's horse, which was invited to the ceremony like it was a human being. We had arranged for voice coaching and then a recording of the bride's mother singing 'Hawaiian Wedding Song', plus a string orchestra to play some Vivaldi tunes, and Grice had designed the pre-dance 'n' dinner buffet, which included a seafood mélange, served on giant half-shells instead of plates, and French champagne.

Relatively speaking, Randy Dekker was a new name in town. Grice reckoned he was all hat and no cattle. He didn't hold his drink well neither. By the time our team of meat chefs were ready to start cooking the steaks, Randy was so tight he just had to take one of those bridesmaid's into the saddle room, show her the size of his bank roll. Which is where I found him when I went to check on the powdered ice we were planning to sprinkle on the table-flowers, help them keep that dew-fresh sparkle.

The bridesmaid saw her chance and nearly knocked me off my feet, making her getaway. Randy Dekker, meanwhile, was on the floor, with his pants round his ankles and his face an alarming shade of purple. He looked like he might be having some kind of cardiac emergency, and I was bending over him, trying to loosen his collar when in walked Mrs Dekker herself, and misread the situation. Made no difference what I said.

'Trash!' she yelled. 'You are fired. And I'll see you never work again in this town again. And *you*,' she yelled at him, 'you stay outta my sight.'

That old goat wasn't sick at all. He was getting to his feet, pulling up his pants, making me look a fool. 'Lola,' he was crying, 'I just had gas pains, is all. I just had to lie down, loosen this goddamned cummerbund.'

Grice came looking for me. A cold wind had sprung up and he thought it was time to implement our Bad Weather Plan.

'Get off my property,' she said to me. 'Get outta here, and take your faggot employee with you.'

Grice said it'd blow over. He said we should carry on like nothing had happened and it'd all be forgotten and who knows, the Dekkers might even settle their account. But I knew what kind of influence a woman like Lola Dekker had. She was Trinity River Tennis Club. She had her hair done at Pierre. And I was right. Two days later Mrs Bonnie Blossburg called to say she'd be making other arrangements for her daughter's marriage to Hart Twisp.

'Relax!' Grice said. 'We didn't want the Blossburg-Twisp wedding anyway. Just *saying* it was hard work.'

I said, 'Well, I think we're ruined. And she referred to you as my "faggot employee". What in tarnation did she mean by that?'

He said, 'Peggy, Lola Dekker is just an ignorant and prejudiced woman. Employee! It is common knowledge that I am your personal assistant and right-hand man.'

76

Spring of '75, Lois got her dearest wish. They moved to New York. They found an apartment in Yonkers, near to Sandie, and Herb went as a supervisor at a sawmill.

'That was what swung it,' she said. 'The smell of wood, plus he can take the dog to work.'

She was driving into the city every day, working out of a rented cupboard, selling West Side co-ops. 'The market's been real slow,' she said, but I'm getting there. I just sold a six-room in the Fairchild, with a park view, and my name's getting around. I've got an exclusive on a seven-room pre-war. West End Avenue. Beautiful. Everything's coming up roses, except for my idiot son.'

Kirk had gotten a girl called Marisa in the family way, and her folks had cast her out. She was staying with Lo and Herb, lying in bed all day, eating sweet pickles and picking out names.

I said, 'Does he have a job?' The last I had heard he was learning butchery.

'Not exactly,' she said. 'That was what I wanted to ask you. You know he's mad on fishing. Ain't a thing he don't know about flies and all that. Would Vern know of anybody might be able to give him a start? He'd be willing to relocate.'

I said, 'What happened to the Institute of Meat?'

'Didn't work out,' she said. 'He didn't like the noise. All those guys hauling beeves around.'

I said, 'Wouldn't they be better off staying put? There has to be more work in the city.'

'No,' she said. 'I think he needs a smaller place. A nice friendly little business somehere. If you could mention to Vern?'

Sounded to me like Lois wanted Kirk and his girl out of her hair. I guessed she didn't want calling on for babysitting, just as her big career was taking off.

I did call Vern. 'For Herb Moon's boy,' he said, 'I'll put the word out.'

Me and Kath hardly ever talked about Lois, but I did tell her there was a grandbaby on the way.

'I see,' she said.

I said, 'Poor Sandie keeps trying, gets to three months then she loses them. Kirk hits the jackpot before he even has a job or a home.'

'How is he?' she said. 'He still a bit of a tearaway?'

I said, 'No, according to Lo he's turned all peaceful and retiring. Likes a quiet night in, tying fishing flies.'

She laughed. 'Well, I'm glad to hear it,' she said, 'that temper he had on him. Still . . . he was a funny little noggin. You just had to handle him right.'

She said she was bored. 'Every day it's the same,' she said. 'Backing round the same old corners time after time. Reminding them to check their mirrors. You can tell some of them till the cows come home and they still won't remember. At least you get a bit of variety in your business.'

But things had gotten so bad in *my* business, I had had to give up my office downtown and work outta my spare bedroom. Lola Dekker had spread poison. Next thing was gonna be having to let Grice go.

We had only one wedding left on our books, then it'd be Labor Day weekend and after that nothing much would be going on, even when the good times were rolling.

Grice said to me, 'Can we talk?' He had been with me eight years and never a cross word.

'Well,' he said, 'we can't continue like this, now, can we? And you're too young to retire.'

I said, 'Honey, I'm too *poor* to retire.'

'That too,' he said. 'So here's an idea. I'll buy you out. Then you can come and work for me.'

I said, 'I don't have anything to sell you.'

He said there was my address book, my contacts. As I pointed out to him, my address book was hardly worth a cent any more. Besides which, he knew the contents of it as well as I did. He could just take it.

'Well, I could,' he said. 'But I wouldn't. Also, I'd be buying your wisdom and experience.'

I said, 'There's something else. I'm sick of weddings.'

'Me too,' he said. 'I'm thinking bigger. I'm ranging wider. I'm thinking sparkle and glitz and fun, fun, fun.'

So that was the start of Swell Parties, the complete party-planning service. Crystal turned up and the three of us went out for Chinese, by way of a celebration. Time was when we'd have gone to the Black Diamond Grill or the Cotillion Room, but we were tightening our belts.

Crystal said, 'How come he can afford to buy you out? You been paying him too much?'

I said, 'No. He has a friend willing to invest.'

'Oh yeah?' she said. 'Would that be a long-time companion kinda friend?'

'Enough of your impertinence, child,' he said. 'Just show a little respect to your mother's new employer. Now tell us, how are things in the pet eternalisation business?'

'Why?' she said. 'You got your eye on my assets too?'

'Never,' he said. 'I cannot abide the smell of acetone.'

Truth was, Crystal was struggling. Most of the enquiries she got was for game heads and fish, and as soon as the customers realised they were dealing with a female they tended to go elsewhere. Then she'd discovered what a cranky bunch pet-owners could be, especially in the throes of grief. If they didn't feel she had exactly captured the personality of their loved one, she had a hard time of it getting them to settle their account. There was a woman claimed her curly-haired retriever had been returned to her looking sly and evil. She never paid a cent.

I said, 'Grice, what will be my vacation entitlement in my new position?'

'I'll need to check with personnel,' he said. 'Okay, I just checked. It'll be the same as before. When we're busy I won't be able to spare you and when we're not I won't be able to pay you. My advice is, take your vacation now, while the going is good.'

And that was how I ended up in Norfolk, England, in the fall of '76.

77

Crystal drove me to the airport.

I said, 'I wish you were coming with me.'

She said, 'Bad enough I'm a thirty years old and outta work. I don't have to go on vacation with my mom to feel like a failure.'

She had finally closed the door of Perpetual Pets, end of September, and she was reconsidering her situation.

I said, 'It was your business failed, not you. Call it a set-back. The only people don't suffer those are the ones who never do anything. And, by the way, you're only twenty-nine.'

I knew what she meant, though, about the vacation. Me and Kath were gonna be sitting around like a pair of old dodos, talking about way back when. Truth was, I was nervous about the trip. Only times I had ever flown international I had had the US Air Force holding my hand.

I said, 'Can you remember Drampton?'

'Sure,' she said. 'I remember the school. Miss Boyle's classroom. Smelled of wax crayons. And I remember having to get my dinner there, and white stuff we had to eat, like glop, and you could have a spoon of red jam to stir into it, help it down.'

I said, 'You remember the base?'

'I think so,' she said. 'Did we live next door to Gayle?'

I said, 'No, that was Wichita. At Drampton we lived opposite Lois and Betty. Me and Betty'd take turns to run y'all to school.'

She said, 'What kinda job did you have over there?'

I said, 'Are you kidding! I was a DW. My duty was to stay home and make pie.'

She laughed. 'You never made pie!' she said.

'I did too make pie. Make pie, wash floors, iron shirts. Defrost the Kelvinator.'

'I can't imagine you,' she said. 'You're too smart for all that.'

I said, 'Smart didn't come into it in those days. Homemaking was what we were raised to do. You kept your home nice. Kept yourself nice. Uncle Sam took care of everything else.'

'Tell you what else I remember,' she said. 'My rabbit-fur mitts from Gramma Dewey. And the high fence. And selling little cups of Kool-Aid with Joey Kurlich, and Sherry's foot dripping blood on the sidewalk.'

She helped me lug my valise on to a trolley.

I said, 'Now I wish I'd never said I'd go. For two pins I'd turn around and come home with you.'

'Well I'm not driving you,' she said. 'So you may as well get yourself on that plane and start acting like a person on vacation.'

I said, 'Did I give you Kath's number?'

'About a hundred times,' she said.

Peggy's Pie

••

Empty a can of carrots and a can of stewed beef into a pie dish. Cover it with a lid of Jus-Rol and bake it in a hot oven in time for friend husband coming from Beer Call. After three beers he'll think he married Betty Crocker.

••

78

I flew into Newark, then onward by red-eye to Heathrow, London, England. Kath was waiting for me at the barrier. She was wearing a beige trenchcoat, same as everyone else standing there. She claimed me while I was still looking for her.

'Peggy,' she said, 'aren't these airyplanes marvellous? Look here, at all these places you can fly to. I've been studying these boards while I was waiting.'

The sky was grey. I was so tired, I just let Kath talk. 'You won't know the old place,' she said. 'We've got supermarkets now and self-service petrol. We've even got different money. That's called decimal. I still think in shillings but I suppose I shall catch on to the new way eventually. And I can't wait for you to see my bungalow. I've got fitted carpet all through, even in the littlest room.'

We'd been on the road about an hour and it commenced to rain. She said, 'That's a welcome sight, Peg. We've had such a dry summer. We've the water rationed, can you believe? Queuing up in the street with a bucket. So I'm not going to complain if we get a bit of rain. And I've got plenty of macs you can borrow. I thought I'd give you a quiet day tomorrow. I've got a lady at nine o'clock, very nervy, so I don't want her going a week without a lesson, else she'll be back to square one. So you can sleep in. Then I'm clear the rest of the week, so we can go on trips out. We can take the train to London one of the days, see all the sights. Go to Marks.'

The Marks and Spencer stores were one of Kath's favourite things. 'They have very reliable knickers,' she said. She was talking about panties.

I said, 'I can remember a time when you laughed at May Gotobed for wearing them. Told me you never bothered with them yourself.'

'That's right,' she said. 'Fancy you remembering that. Well, I feel the cold more than I did. That's what happens when you get heating you can switch on any time you like. It turns you soft. Then I thought, another day we could drive to Ely and Cambridge. You'd like that. All old universities, that go back centuries. And Audrey wants you Friday and Saturday, only you'll have to get a hire car because there's no buses. She said I should go too, but I told her I had lessons booked. I don't like to be unsociable, Peg, but I couldn't take to her new gentleman friend when I met him.'

Audrey had been coaxed back to England by a man she had met. Kath said, 'See, I think that's too soon after Lance. When she was staying with me, she wasn't hardly in her right mind. Going for long walks. Wandering out in the wilds, looking for birds. She could have stumbled and lain there for days. And then she meets this Arthur. Well, it's none of my business, I suppose. I don't know him. I don't think she does properly, neither. You take a long hard look at him, Peggy, when you meet him. See what you think.'

79

I got a rental car and the first thing I did was drive out to Drampton, take a look around the old neighbourhood. Our old base had been turned over to their Royal Air Force in '62. Later on there had been some talk of it being a NATO stand-by base, but nothing ever came of it and it just stood empty. I found a stretch of fence where you could see across to the old facility. Nothing but jack-rabbits and weeds. It was like we never had been there. Then I drove on, past Crystal's old school, which had new buildings and a new name too, Smeeth Combined First and Middle School, then past the railroad crossing where we met Kath the first time, and across to Blackdyke Drove.

She had already told me she had no wish to see what was left of her old place. 'Looking back don't interest me, Peg,' she said. 'Today's what matters. And tomorrow, if we're lucky.'

There wasn't much left to see. The house was just a shell, one end-wall gone completely. And the inside and that terrible outdoors john were all overgrown with nettles. Looking across to Brakey there were new row-houses as far as the eye could see, and the other side there was a tractor at work where me and Audrey had walked across that day, searching for Lois. I blushed, just remembering it.

I drove back by the place Gayle and Aud had been billeted. Their two houses had been renovated, turned into one home with a new tile roof. I never would have recognised it except for that waterway running behind it, higher than the back yard. Someone had made a cute little country home of it, called it 'Willows', and cleared the front yard for parking, but I still wouldn't have spent a night there.

'Well?' she said, when I walked in. 'You see what an eyesore your old base is? I should love to get my hands on it. I'd have it all laid out for driving. You could take the nervy ones on there, first time they get behind the wheel, just let them get the feel of things without traffic tooting at them, getting them flustered. And you could do make-believe tests, you know? Instead of annoying them people up on the Brewer Farm estate, forever reversing round their corners, turning round in their roads, you could do it all up at Drampton. But that just lies there going to waste.'

She made us steak and fries and red wine. 'This is my tipple now,' she said, 'since we've been going to Spain.'

I said, 'There's not much left to see of your old house.'

'So I've heard,' she said. 'Far as I'm concerned they should have knocked down what the sea didn't take. They could have built something new. There's plenty waiting for decent housing.'

I said, 'You think you'd still be there? If the flood hadn't come?'

'I could have been,' she said. 'Our mam lived all her life there. Born there, died there. I could have done. But, of course, other things come along for me. Learning to drive a motor. I don't think you'll ever know what a difference that made to me.'

I said, 'You were a fast study. Left-hand drive an' all.'

'And then John Pharaoh got so poorly,' she said. 'I don't know as we could have stayed up there, not once I needed help with him. Anyway, that great flood did come along and then everything changed.'

There was something I was dying to know. I said, 'Did you and John still share a bed? Right to the end?'

'Course we didn't,' she said. 'We got lovely new divans when we moved to the maisonette. Well, they were old stock. Some bed shop gave them, help people out after the flood. But they were beautiful to sleep on, after that old bed we were used to.'

The red wine had loosened my tongue. I said, 'You know, it's the weirdest thing I ever heard, brother and sister sharing a bed.'

'There was plenty doing the same,' she said. 'May and her sisters were four to a bed, till she went into service. May Gotobed. Gotobed if you can find room, that's what we always said.'

I said, 'Well, *sisters* maybe. But male and female . . . I mean, there could be consequences . . .'

'Oh, I know what you're getting at,' she said, 'but me and John Pharaoh never had consequences. He had his adventures, and maybe he shouldn't have done, but he only had a short life and a man needs that. You only have to look at a dog to see. He smells a bitch, he'll do anything to get to her. Can't stop himself until he's had his consequences.'

I said, 'Neither of you ever think of getting married?'

'No,' she said. 'He had his lady friends. There was one in Brakey. There was one in Kennyhill. Village bikes they used to call them. There was probably others, specially with the war on and men away. But that's as far as it went. He knew not to bring any trouble home. He had enough sense for that.'

I topped up her glass. Topped up mine too. I said, 'What about you?'

But before she could answer, the phone rang. It was Audrey, calling with directions. 'After Witham, watch out for a right turn,' she said. 'It's just a single-track road, so it's easily missed. If you see a general store, with a red mailbox, you've gone too far.'

When I got off the phone, Kath was curled up on her couch, just gazing at her gas-fire flames.

'I had my chances,' she said. 'I did get offers. Specially after my Premium Bond come up. I had offers'd make your hair curl. But what would I want a man for at my time of life? I come home at night, I don't want to have to start peeling spuds. Missing my programmes because there's football on the other side. You know what it's like? You're on your own and you seem happy enough.'

I said, 'Yes, I am. But I wouldn't have missed having Crystal.'

'Course you wouldn't,' she said. 'But that was different for me. I made my mind up a long time ago I wouldn't be having any babies.'

The second bottle was nearly empty. She looked right at me, eyes kinda bright and shining, could have been tears. 'Because of the nerve thing that's in the family. Like our mam had, and then John. That's why he knew to be careful with his consequences. It's in the blood, you see. Only it won't be going any further. I've made sure of that.'

We sat quiet for a minute. 'You ever had a drink called Fundador?' she said. 'It's from Spain. I'll give you a little taster, as a nightcap.'

80

Audrey was right about missing the turn. But I found the general store and the mailbox. I needed to buy Kleenex and throat lozenges anyway. One thing about the English weather. You were guaranteed to get a head cold.

The store-keeper said, 'That'll be the American lady you're visiting. About a mile back they way you come, then sharp left where they leave the milk churns.'

I found it, second time of trying. The track narrowed and dropped, and then I seen the sign, and an old yellow station-wagon, rusty round the wheel arches. Lower Ness.

Now *that* was what I call a house. It had a kinda saltbox look to it, and lots of outbuildings, stables and stuff and the cutest front yard, with ducks running wild on the lawns. And then out came Audrey, with two big red dogs bounding ahead of her.

She looked great, in a natural, English kinda way, just dressed for gardening. I'd have worn pants myself if I had known I was going so deep into the backwoods. If I had known I was gonna have shoulder-high dogs wanting to be my best friends.

I said, 'What's this? You gone native?'

She had allowed her grey hair to grow in. She said, 'Correct. You just drove here. How many hair salons did you pass?'

A man came out of the house. Tall, fair but greying, big droopy moustache.

'Peggy,' she said. 'This is Arthur. We're engaged to be married.'

I guess a good-looking woman like Audrey didn't need to stay a widow for long if she didn't choose.

Arthur was a very polite person. He was very particular about ladies first through doorways and pulling out your chair and all that. I really can't say why I didn't take to him.

We sat straight down to some kinda vegetable soup, then Arthur went off in the station-wagon. Dearest, he called her. 'Back about six, dearest. Leave you girls to chew the fat.'

'Okay,' she said, soon as he was gone. 'Tell me what you think.'

I said, 'He's nice.'

'Nice?' she said. 'Nice! He's a genuine English gentleman. His family goes back hundreds of years.'

I said, 'Honey, *every* family goes back. Question is, where are they headed?'

There was good silver on the table. Not a pattern I knew, but it was quality. The house was shabby, though. Rugs were all faded.

I said, 'Hey, I'm sure he's wonderful. Where'd you find him?'

'I came back from Chicago,' she said, 'couldn't stand the memories. I rented a cottage at Hythe, right by the water here, and started painting. All those years I talked about it. All those paint-boxes Lance gave me for birthdays. I finally got round to it. Painted from breakfast till the cocktail hour. I tell you, Peggy, the day just flies. Then I made a real fool of myself. I took my best efforts into Arthur's little gallery, see if they were good enough to sell. They weren't. One thing there's no shortage of around here is amateur watercolours. He offered me lunch, though. Lunch. Then dinner. Then a job, helping out in his gallery.'

I said, 'And then a wedding band?'

'Well,' she said, 'I'm a foreigner. I can't just come over here and take a job. Getting married kinda regularises things.'

I said, 'You didn't mention falling in love. I suppose that happened, somewhere along the way?'

She laughed. 'Of course!' she said. 'We're just a little long in the tooth for all that romantic stuff.'

Her ring had been in Arthur's family for four generations. When I told Lois, later, back Stateside, she said, 'My God, how cheap can a man get? Was it a big rock?'

I said, 'No. I'd describe it as a modest chip.'

Lo said, 'She's nuts. He's cheap. He's English. Plus, he's old. Soon as the honeymoon's over she's gonna be bankrolling some good American prostate surgery. You heard it here.'

Audrey showed me her paintings, after we had cleared away the soup. They were just sea and sky, mainly, but she had let the different paints mingle while they were still wet, and she seemed to have found a hundred different shades of green. I loved them.

I said, 'Arthur's crazy. I'd buy these.'

'Well, Arthur has a very good eye,' she said. 'He knows good stuff when he sees it. But, if there's something you like, help yourself.'

I picked out one for me and one for Kath, and we both have them still. Anybody asks me I'm always proud to say, 'Yes, this artist is a personal friend of mine. According to some big expert, she didn't understand her medium.'

We went for a walk. There was quite a spread of land around the property. I said, 'What do the boys think? They met Arthur?'

'No,' she said. 'And I don't see it happening. Arthur doesn't care for travelling, and the boys have their own lives.'

It seemed their first act of rebellion, after Lance's demise, was to tear up their papers for the Military Academy. Then they both grew their hair real long. 'Only time they've ever acted like twins,' she said.

So Mikey had stayed on in San Francisco, doing something called concept art, and Lance Jnr was in Providence, Rhode Island, selling clam chowder and sourdough bread.

One side of the garden led on to a grass track. We followed it till we came to water. It was called The Estuary, and there was such a pretty view across to an oyster farm.

I said, 'It's a big step, Aud. Leaving your kids behind. A new country is hard enough. New husband, too . . .'

'I'll take my chance,' she said. 'It has to be better than being a lonely widow, starting over some place nobody knows me.'

I said, 'You only feel that way because it's early days. You're still getting over Lance. Another year or two and you'll turn the corner. That's what they reckon.'

Hell, Audrey was always the strong one. Wherever you dropped her, she'd pick herself up. She'd brush her hair, unpack her good table linen. Next thing you knew, she'd be organising bridge fours at the OWC.

'Twenty-five years, Peggy,' she said. 'I gave it everything I had. Lance got a promotion, I rose with him. He could have made General with me on his team. Now none of it counts for a damn thing.'

One of the red dogs came outta the water, shook itself all over us.

'Know the worst thing?' she said. 'The stupid way it ended. Choking on a stupid piece of beef, arguing . . . and choking . . . three stupid Rudman men . . . and what the hell for? For nothing. Lance is six foot under and the boys have got their stupid no-hope jobs. I'm the one didn't get a fair deal . . .'

Her face was hard and bitter. '. . . wasn't just Lance's life ended,' she said. 'I lost everything. And I can't even say it was a noble sacrifice. Not like Gayle, with Okey . . . and then with her Marine . . .'

I said, 'Aud, you had half a lifetime with Lance. And you have your boys. What do you suppose Gayle would have given for some of that? I don't believe she took much comfort knowing her husbands were killed on active service.'

'Maybe,' she said. She hurled a stick for the dogs. 'But it sure *sounds* better.'

We went inside. It was a cold house. There was a fireplace big enough to walk in and Audrey started up a fire, but move one inch from the hearth and a person could catch their death. We drank tea, like real English ladies, and listened to the ticking of Arthur's old clocks.

I said, 'What do you do all day? I guess you don't paint any more?'

'Help at the gallery,' she said. 'Read. Keep this big house squared away. I'm happy enough.'

I said, 'Okay. Just don't rush into this Arthur thing. Take your time. Know what I'd do? If I could paint pictures like this, I'd go back Stateside, open a little boutique. I guarantee you, fast as you could paint them, they'd be sold.'

'Neat idea,' she said. 'But I've already invested in Arthur's place.'

81

Arthur came home and we had more of the same soup, and then sausages. They weren't big eaters.

I said, 'You sell any pictures today, Arthur.'

'There's more to running a gallery than selling pictures,' he said.

I said, 'Well, Audrey did. I've picked out two of her seascapes and I'm wondering whether to ship a few more.'

He smiled. 'Yes,' he said. 'They're pleasant enough.'

I said, 'I don't know what *pleasant* means. I'm getting them because they look great and she's the first friend I ever had, turned out to be a real live artist.'

'Quite,' he said.

After the sausages they insisted on teaching me mah-jongg. Soon as Arthur realised he had a novice on his hands, he started rushing around, clearing a table by the fireside, setting up the pieces. He was like an excited kid.

'First we twitter the sparrows,' he said. Give you some idea what kinda fool game it was. Main feature of it seemed to be yelling out crazy words.

'Pung!' he'd shout. '*And* I have the wind of the round!'

Scotch whisky's not my usual drink, but I took what was offered. I thought we might have a long night ahead of us.

'Barbarian invasion!' he'd cry. That happened couple of times and it seemed to be a big moment in the game for Arthur.

Audrey had put me in the blue room. It was called that because of the wallpaper and the patchwork quilt, but it could just as well have been because it was so cold, that was the colour you ended up if you slept in there.

'Peg, honey, you're frozen,' she said. 'It's these old English houses. But hang on. I'll fix you up.'

She was gone a while. I think she may have had to fight one of the dogs for that extra blanket she brought me. It had that kinda *animal* smell. Still I was glad of it, and the rubber hot-water bottle and a pair of socks.

'You get used to it,' she said. 'When I'm in the US now, I can't bear how hot they keep their houses. It's not healthy. And Kath keeps her place so warm too, did you notice? I think she's picked up bad American habits.'

She perched on the edge of my bed.

I said, 'Me and Kath have really talked this time. Not having other people around, I guess.'

Aud said, 'She saved my life, Peg. I just turned up and I was probably half out of my mind. She just started frying eggs and finding hangers for my clothes. Didn't ask any questions. I think she realised I didn't have any answers.'

I said, 'They didn't . . . you know . . . her and John? She told me.'

Audrey said, 'You didn't ask her right out about that?'

I said, 'No. She just told me a few things. How their mom and dad used to sleep in that big old bed, and she was in the kitchen with them and John had that other room. The eel-trap store? Then when their mom died, John came in from the cold and slept with their dad. And when their dad died . . . well, you know the rest. It was just about using the furniture they had and staying warm. Kath reckons they weren't the only ones lived that way.'

Aud said, 'Yeah. I've heard stories along those lines.'

I said, 'She told me something else. About why she never married? She says there's a sickness in the family, in the blood, and she didn't want the risk of passing it on.'

Audrey said, 'What's it called?'

I didn't know. I didn't believe Kath had ever told me.

Audrey said, 'John died of pneumonia.'

'Yes,' I said.

A door opened, along the landing. Arthur shouted, 'Audrey? Are you going to be much longer?'

I said, 'Sex before marriage? I didn't think you were that kinda girl.'

She smiled. 'Find out what the disease is,' she said. 'I'd sure like to know what John Pharaoh might have spread around with his wild oats.'

I said, 'Kath swears he knew to be careful.'

'Yeah?' she said. 'Well of course Kath wouldn't believe a bad thing of anybody. But just do something for me. Put together these three words: John, careful and Lois. See what I mean?'

I heard Arthur's door creak again. He shouted, 'Audrey! I am turning out the light!'

It was ten-thirty.

I left next morning with as many of Audrey's paintings as I could carry, plus her solemn promise not to make any hasty decisions about Arthur. The sun struggled through as she was waving me off, and I must say she cut a fine figure standing by the rambling old house, throwing sticks for the dogs.

82

Kath closed the motoring school for five days and the two of us went off on a grand tour of historical England.

We went to Stratford upon Avon, birthplace of William Shakespeare, and Oxford, home of Oxford University, and Cotswold, and Thomas Hardy country, Thomas Hardy being another of their great bards. We also visited the grave of Sir Winston Churchill, the man Kath seemed to believe had won World War II. I kept my opinion to myself.

London was our last destination. We went to Buckingham Palace and there wasn't even a tour we could take. All they allow you to do is look through the perimeter fence. Same story at 10 Downing Street, the closest thing they have to a White House – which is to say, not very close at all. Number 10 doesn't even have a lawn out front.

I noticed many changes for the better, though, since I left England in '52. The people weren't so drab-looking and you could get coffee and cold beer and all kinds of candy bars. But they still didn't seem to me to make the best of what they had. Westminster Abbey was a very good example. It was so cold and damp inside and they could easily have put in a modern furnace. Then we saw the actual throne where all their monarchs have been crowned. Just a shabby old wooden chair, didn't have any jewels on it or a lick of gold. I read somewhere

Queen Elizabeth is one of the wealthiest women in the world, and yet she didn't even have a nice velvet pillow for her throne.

Kath said, 'It's her jubilee next year. Twenty-five years.'

I said, 'Well I hope she splashes out and buys herself a cushion. Is this an Episcopalian church?'

'I don't know about that,' she said. 'Gloomy, isn't it?'

I said, 'Gayle and Lemarr have their own church now. All glass.'

'Is it Methodist?' she said.

I said, 'No, it's the Passy Tabernacle.'

'We're Methodists,' she said. 'Would be, if I ever went. We used to be Church of England. Grandad Pharaoh was a bell-ringer at All Saints in Brakey. We used to have to go every Sunday, necks scrubbed, boots polished. But he got riled about something, one night when they had ringing practice. Had a falling out with the captain and lost his temper. Pulled too hard on his rope and snapped the slider. The rope went up in the air with Grandad on the end of it, cracked his head on the chamber ceiling. After that we were Methodists. Can they do that, then? Gayle and her hubby? Just get up their own church?'

I said, 'Of course they can. They're in the land of the free.'

My last night in England we stayed in a small hotel in Cromwell Road. Small was right. If one of us was getting dressed, the other had to stay on the bed out of the way. I must say, for the money we were paying I'd have expected to have space enough to open the closet doors.

We went out for Italian spaghetti.

Kath said, 'I wish you could have stopped longer. Next time, you want to stop longer. You could come to Benidorm with me and May.'

I said, 'Next time? I have to earn my living now. Don't know I'll ever manage a trip like this again.'

She said, 'In that case, I shall have to start saving up to come to you.'

I said, 'If I had known I'd have to fend for myself all these years, I'd have been a better student when I was in school. I'd have learned how to fix the Disposall and be a lawyer. I don't have a cent to my name.'

'Me neither,' she said. 'As soon as I get it, I spend it. But then, that's what money's for, Peg. There's no pleasure to be had reading a bank-book. Counting out bags of brass. Unless you're some old miser, got a screw loose. Money's there for buying things.'

I said, 'Yeah, like a comfortable old age.'

'Well,' she said, 'we're both grafters. We shall just have to work till we drop. And I'd sooner do that than sit playing housey-housey down the Day Centre.'

83

Grice Terry worked me every bit as hard as I used to work him. December of '76 we never stopped, themed cocktail parties, mainly, and a big fundraiser for a new eye hospital and some cute holiday stuff like a Viennese evening for the Murray Mercks over in Fort Worth, with a string quartet in historical costume and a twelve-foot tree trimmed all in silver.

I was worried about running into some of those fairweather folk who'd blackened the reputation of Peggy Dewey Weddings but, as Grice reminded me, I was an innocent woman.

'Hold your head high, sister,' he said. 'I hear anybody taking your name in vain, there'll be no swell party for them.'

His friend Tucker Hoose was the money behind the scenes. We had a first-floor office on Jefferson Drive but he never showed his face there, which made him the perfect employer. He preferred to stay home and do a little gardening. He was an older man but he kept himself in good shape. Had his mother living with him and, according to Grice, she wore the pants.

Tucker had never married and there was no sign of Grice doing so either so it was nice they had each other's company, as I remarked to Crystal one time. She rolled her eyes. 'Mom, where have you been all your life?' she said. 'Grice and Tucker are an *item*.'

Since 1968 that was the kind of talk you got from the younger generation.

I said, 'I wasn't born yesterday, Crystal. Unnatural behaviour happens in New York, I know, and in California too, but those darling boys are Texans and we don't have anything like that going on round here.'

'Sure,' she said. 'I've noticed how Grice loves those real Texan things, like pink shirts. And guy sleepovers.'

She was going up to Maine for the holidays, see Vern. She said, 'Mom, there might be a job up there. There's a new Museum of American Mammals opening next fall.'

She had sent them her résumé and hadn't even told me.

I said, 'Why didn't you tell me?'

'I just did,' she said, 'and now you're all bent outta shape.'

I was not. I never held Crystal back from doing anything. Not even running off to Bend, Oregon, learning to stuff bobcats.

I said, 'They offer it to you?'

'No,' she said. 'But I think they will when they see my work.' She was taking a mounted otter with her on the plane.

I said, 'Would you move in with dad and Martine?'

'Like hell,' she said. 'Besides, they'll need all the room they've got once the new in-laws start turning up for those long vacations.'

Martine's boy, Eugene, was finally getting married. Must have been nice for her, something to look forward to after all the surgery and ray treatment an' all. She seemed to be doing okay. Got as clean a bill of health as you can get after cancer. And Eugene had found a Oriental girl, picked her out of some kind of pen-pal magazine and all he'd seen of her was two photos before he named the day.

I said, 'The risks a girl will take.'

Crystal said, 'Well, I'm not sure who's taking the biggest risk here. She's getting an airline ticket to the US, plus a worm farmer who doesn't clean under those fingernails too often. He's getting a little woman to do his bidding, plus about a hundred of her nearest friends and relations that are gonna be looking for a new life.'

I said, 'Your dad still liable to call an Oriental a slopehead?'

'Yup,' she said. 'I guess Martine'll be hoping to train him out of that before the big day.'

*   *   *

So Crystal flew off to the frozen north. We were booked to do a surprise fiftieth-birthday party between Christmas and New Year's, out at Lake Arlington, husband wanted everything Russian-style 'cause his wife loved *Doctor Zhivago* so much. We were at December twentieth and I still hadn't located a dog-sled. Grice said maybe the *surprise* should be Hank Biddle's trotting cart and Hank Biddle dressed in furs.

He blew in about ten a.m. 'Behold,' he said, 'I bring you tidings of joy. I have the number of a huskie breeder in Knox County. Also, you are summoned to Tucker's for Christmas dinner. Cocktails at eight. Dress, definitely *up*.'

84

Tucker lived just south of Corinth, in a house called Hickory. It was the loveliest home I ever was in, except as hired help. Grice drove me out there.

I said, 'Nine o'clock is nearly bedtime for me. How come these folks eat so late?'

'Well,' he said, 'Miss Lady doesn't rise till afternoon. Then by the time she's had her hair done and hauled herself into a fresh bed-jacket, time's getting on.'

Lady Hoose was Tucker's mother, ninety-four and going strong, except she reckoned having Jimmy Carter as president'd probably kill her.

I said, 'Am I dressed okay? I don't feel dressed right.' I was wearing my cranberry two-piece from Bloomies, velvet with a jet-bead detail.

He looked me over. 'Take the necklace off,' he said.

I said, 'Take it *off*? I already feel under-dressed.'

'You'll do fine,' he said. 'Just leave off the fake pearls.'

I dropped them in my pocketbook before we went in.

'By the by,' he said 'You're a *widow*. You're my second cousin, recently returned from England. And we don't talk about Swell Parties.'

There was an evergreen garland on the door and a good wood fire burning in the lounge room, and there was help called Etta, serving a Rotel dip and pig eggs and gin-fizz cocktails.

Etta's Pig Eggs

Hard-boil a dozen fresh eggs, cool them in cold running water and peel off their shells.

Mix 2lb of sausage meat with two beaten eggs. Press the mixture around the hard-boiled till they are good and covered. Roll each one in a dish of beaten egg, then in a dish of cornmeal. Fry them in a heavy skillet with plenty of oil turning them often until they are brown all over. Drain them on brown paper, and serve them chilled.

Miss Lady was all in baby blue, including the ribbon in her hair – what there was left of it – and her dog had a ribbon the same colour too. The dog was called Precious, ugliest creature I ever seen, looked like it had collided with a wall at high speed. I could see Lady Hoose weighing me up.

'Dewey?' she said. 'I don't know your people. Are you from out of town?'

Grice jumped right in. 'Peggy's husband was an East-Coaster,' he said. 'Peggy was a Shea, one of the San Antonio Sheas, but of course we're related through her mother's line, the Sherman County Terrys.

'Well, now,' she said, 'I *think* I can place you.'

We had another round of gin fizz, and Grice steered the conversation towards London, England.

'How is Her Majesty?' she asked. 'Will she step aside, do you suppose, when Prince Charles makes a suitable marriage?'

This was a subject I'd heard plenty about from Kath. She was of the opinion those up-coming Silver Jubilee celebrations were just a way of preparing the public for a new monarch, and she was all for it.

'That boy needs a job,' Kath had said. 'A job and a woman. Then he'll be golden.' I repeated this to Miss Lady. Her eyes glittered.

'But he already has a job,' she said, 'serving his mother and Queen. That's job enough for any man.'

Grice had already explained to me that Miss Lady didn't like Tucker going into business, not even as an investor. Still, Grice himself didn't seem afraid to contradict her. He said, 'But, Miss Lady, I believe Tucker's late father had a job, and while his mother still lived. And he was highly respected for it.'

Tucker's pa was Judge James Tucker Hoose.

'That's a different matter,' she said. 'When a family faces ruin, on account of certain events, on account of certain weak links in the chain, a man has to do whatever he can and Tucker's daddy was meant for the law.'

Tucker smiled.

Miss Lady turned to me.

'It was half-brother Jack Hoose was to blame. Blood will out and some of those Shelby County Hooses have very bad hair. My advice is, Queen Elizabeth should not abdicate her throne and the son of Judge James Tucker Hoose should not be dabbling in trade.'

Tucker opened his mouth to say something.

'I decline to discuss it further,' she said. 'Now, I do believe dinner is served.'

The table was set with Repoussé silver and Crown Derby china. We had mock cooter soup, turkey with oyster dressing, creamed peas, strawberry jello fruit-salad and buttermilk pecan pie. Only I hardly ate a mouthful, I was so anxious Miss Lady would get back to the subject of my family.

'Do you hunt?' she asked. 'Judge Hoose and I rode out with the Creek all our married lives.'

Tucker said, 'She was still riding when she was seventy-two. Weren't you, Darling One?' He called her Darling One all the time.

'I was not,' she said. 'I hunted till I was seventy-*three*.'

It was an amazing thing to see how sharp she was. She was old enough to have been the mother of some of the old wrecks I'd seen in State Hospital. But I couldn't take to her. She was a person who had a very high opinion of herself, and all her life nobody had dared to say different.

'Is the Thursday Luncheon Club still going, do you know?' she said. We had withdrawn, back to the wood fire, for port wine and

Grice had discovered the varmint Precious gagging on the remains of my fake pearl necklet which he had stolen out of my bag. Ask me, he was closer kin to a peccary than he was to any make of dog I ever seen. Grice scooped my pearls into his pocket silk and gave it to the help to take away. All my life I was jinxed with jewellery.

'Of course, I was a founder member of the Magnolia Club,' she said. 'We played bridge till there wasn't enough of us left to make a four.'

Tucker said, 'That's because you never let in any new members, Darling One.'

'We didn't want any,' she said. 'After the war, you couldn't get the right kind of people.'

I had really had it with Miss Lady, sitting there at midnight, holding court, quizzing a person on their cousins.

I said, 'I never had time for lunch clubs, nor bridge clubs. I had a daughter to raise and a living to earn. And even if I hadn't had to, I still wouldn't have cared to sit around all day gossiping.'

She gave me a thoughtful look. Grice got to his feet.

I said, 'Thank you for your kind hospitality, ma'am, but I believe I have to get some sleep. Travel is a tiring thing.'

Grice kissed her goodbye. 'Good night, Miss Lady,' he said.

'You're not going?' she said. 'But we haven't played cards yet.'

'Tomorrow,' he said. 'We'll play tomorrow.'

'I could be dead tomorrow,' she said. 'Why do you have to go? Doesn't she have a driver?'

We could still hear her as we left the house. 'Gauche little thing,' she said. 'Precious didn't care for her. Do you suppose she's a Communist?'

8 5

First week of February two things happened, left me feeling like a
big pit opened up under my feet. First off, Crystal called, all excited
'cause they'd hired her at this new wildlife museum.

'I was the only one they interviewed had the sense to bring along
a sample of my work,' she said. 'Soon as they saw the otter, the job
was mine.'

I had to be pleased for her, got no more than she deserved after
all that studying and ruining her hands, but still, it meant she was
settling near Vern and I'd be lucky if I got to see her more than once
a year.

'Don't go all sad on me now,' she said. 'If I can't get down to
you, you can always come up see me here.'

Sure. Go wandering into Vern's territory. I hadn't seen him since
he went home to bury his pa and we split up for good, although we
didn't know, at the time, that's what we were doing. We'd been
cordial, I suppose, specially since his wormery did so good and he
didn't feel like a wash-out any more. But I had no desire to see him.
He had a different life, playing happy families with folk who were
nothing but names to me.

Crystal said Martine was back in harness after her illness, busy
raising baby worms. And Eugene's little wife, Filomena, was helping
out in the yarn store, even though Mom Dewey didn't believe a

person from the Philippine Islands could ever learn about yarn or the English language.

Crystal said, 'You should see Gramma. She has this perfect recall of every piece of knitting any of her customers ever did. They come in trying to match the colour and she's ten steps ahead of them. She's like an old rooster. The older she gets the tougher she grows. Up and down the step-ladder, yanking out bales of yarn, yelling at Filomena in some kind of native talk she seems to think is called for. Good job Filomena's got a nice nature. Only way I can see Gramma ever meeting her Maker is if that ladder gives way.'

I told her about Tucker Hoose's mom. I said, 'She's another one. Have to drop a nucular warhead to get rid of her.'

Crystal didn't care for that kind of talk. She still had a strong streak of red running through her; I hoped her darling daddy realised.

'Mom,' she said, 'I'll call you in a week or two, let you know how the job's going. And . . . well . . . take care and everything . . .'

She was thirty years old. Still, I felt like somebody just stole my baby.

Then I got a package from sister Connie. It contained the walrus-tusk Bambi from Alaska and a short letter.

'Dear Peggy,' she wrote.

Mom passed away January first. We were away to Carrizo Springs visiting with Bobby Earl's boy so the morgue had had to keep her till we come back. They say she went peaceful. I took care of the arrangements, not wanting to drag you down here from your big business and all. I enclose the bill for your attention as I know you will want to do the right thing. The house is left to me. You can see the papers if you don't believe me. Hoping this finds you as it leaves me, your sister Connie.

P.S. We had Mom scattered in the Garden of Rest.

I wrote a cheque for the funeral parlour and a letter to Connie telling her to go steady with her little inheritance, there being no more after that was guzzled away. I mailed them on my way to the office. From that day on, far as I was concerned, the only family I had in San Antonio was my old pal Betty Gillis. And I called her to tell her so, but Betty was too full of her new career to appreciate I had just adopted her as my replacement sister.

'Peggy,' she said, 'I have to tell you about Lipo-Zipp. It's a miracle fat-burning product that has helped me to lose twenty-eight pounds in just three months, and I'm now an authorised distributor for Nutro Labs. We offer all kinds of dietary supplements, but Lipo-Zipp is our flagship product and I'm selling it fast as they can manufacture it. Tell you what, I'm gonna send you a one-week trial pack and you tell me if you don't feel those pounds starting to melt away.'

Seemed I couldn't find anybody to cheer me up, stop me feeling like a lonely old lard-butt. Not even Lois Moon, who must have had some kind of major brain surgery the way she was cooing over her grandbaby.

'Oh, Peggy,' she said, 'he is so cute. He has Kirk's looks and Sandie's nature.'

I said, 'What about his mother? Doesn't he have any of her features?'

I got the feeling Lo didn't rate Marisa. 'Well, I guess he has her eyes,' she said.

They had named him Cory and they were up in Glens Falls, living the country life. Bob Pick, one of Vern's fishing buddies, had given Kirk a start in his reel-and-lure store.

She said, 'I really owe you. And Vern, of course. Since they've been up there, Kirk's really settled down. And they got a good rental. You wouldn't get a closet on Hester Street for that kind of money.'

I said, 'Lois, are you telling me you go up there visiting? You telling me you actually leave the city?'

'Sure, I do,' she said. 'Herb's there more than he's here, and I go when I can. You have to. These babies grown so darned fast. Did I tell you, he knows his name and everything? His little eyes follow you round the room. And he has such a strong grasp, for a kid that's getting nothing but mother's milk. You ever see that stuff? Thin as water. Can't see there's any nourishment in it, but I have to keep my opinions to myself. He's not allowed a bottle. He's not allowed chocolate. He's not even allowed a plain old cookie. That's the modern thinking on how you raise a child. I told Marisa, if she don't start varying his diet somewhat, get him accustomed to meat gravy and Cream of Wheat, she's gonna have a picky eater on her hands. But you can't tell her anything and Kirk just goes right along. I told her, when he starts getting his teeth she'll be sorry she ever opened a milk bar inside her shirt. I told her, when mine were getting their teeth I rubbed bourbon on their gums. Never did them any harm. Probably did them some good. Way I looked at it, anything that guaranteed me my night's sleep knocked on for the whole family. Anything happening with Crystal? Any sign of babies there?'

I said, 'Last I heard she was stuffing a Kodiak bear. Could be a lifetime's work. How about Sandie?'

'No,' she said. 'They say her womb's backward, or something. Her and Gerry are like a pair of old-timers. She plays her cornet. He plays his tuba. And they keep on hoping for babies. Listen, doll, I have to fly. I've got a five-room in a white brick on 60th and 9th and I think I just found a buyer. But I'd just love to see you some time. Shoot the breeze. Why don't you treat yourself to a weekend in the city?'

Sounded great. Trek all the way to New York, spend two days working my way through a pile of baby photos, listening to the Born Again grandmother. Probably get myself mugged, too.

86

It was Grice showed me the story, in the 'Strange But True' section of the *Corinth Register*.

He said, 'Is this your friend?'

And there it was, about Gayle and how her healing powers had taken such a strange turn they were doing a TV special about her.

Licenced Minister Gayle Passy of the Lemarr Passy Tabernacle, Fayetteville, North Carolina, has found an unusual specialty for her powers of healing: dental problems. When the Tabernacle Road Show was in McKenzie, Tennessee, a man reported that while she laid hands on him for the healing of a duodenal ulcer, he had felt his crooked teeth straightening in slow motion.

Pastor Gayle says, 'I went right back to the trailer and prayed on it, and the Lord told me this was to be my new ministry.' A thirty-minute TV program on the Praise God channel, being screened Saturday next at five p.m., features an interview with a woman from Dickson who claims her toothache was cured and a gold cross appeared over an old mercury filling that had been troubling her. No reports of root-canal work so far, but Pastor Gayle dismisses the skeptics. 'The Lord created the universe in six days,' she says. 'Why should He have trouble fixing gum disease or a few cavities?'

I said, 'I wish you'd never showed me.'

I had been inclined to give Gayle the benefit of the doubt, before she turned into some kind of circus act.

Grice said, 'I'm going to record that show. I have to see this fruitcake with my own eyes.'

We were doing a reception Saturday evening, for the opening of the new Weelkes Wing at Trinity River Museum. The theme was meant to be Inca because that was the stuff old man Weelkes collected.

I said to Grice, 'Are you sure margaritas are Inca?'

'Oh, please,' he said.

I phoned Kath to tell her about Gayle. Course, they don't get the Praise God channel over there. They don't get anything much, but I wanted her to know.

She said, 'I see what you mean, Peg. All the suffering there is in the world, that seems funny to be bothering with crooked teeth. But I'll hold my judgement. I should hate to think ill of her without seeing for myself. See, this is the danger, when money changes hands. I mean, we have vicars on the telly here. That's called *Songs of Praise*. But they don't get buckets full of paper money like you saw Gayle getting. Now, listen. Me and May took a run out to Ness last Sunday, thought we'd call in on Audrey and her gentleman friend, but that was all closed up. The picture gallery and the house and the phone just rings out and rings out.'

I said, 'I'll bet they're over here. I told her she shouldn't decide anything till her boys had met Arthur. I hear anything, I'll let you know.'

'Likewise,' she said.

When I called Betty, it was Dawn who picked up. One of Deana's brats.

I said, 'Your gramma there?'

'Out,' she said.

I said, 'How about Carla?' I figured to talk to a member of the Gillis family had its brain connected.

'Carla's gone,' she said. 'We ain't speakin'.'

It was the day before Gayle's TV show before I got to speak to Betty.

I said, 'This Zippa-da-lip you're selling must be hot stuff. You're never home.'

'Lipo-Zipp,' she said. 'Did I send you a sample?'

She didn't even know I'd been calling. Dawn had never said. Hadn't written down my messages or anything.

I said, 'What's the story with Carla?' Then the tears started.

'Peggy,' she said, 'I'm just about to the end of my rope. It's between Carla and Deana really, but course, I'm caught between them.'

What had happened was, Deana's eldest, Delta, had won first prize in a beauty pageant. Holiday for two in Florida. And Deana hadn't been backward at selecting herself to accompany Delta.

Betty said, 'Carla said I should be the one to go with her, and there was a big fight between her and Deana.'

I said, 'Darned right you should be the one to go. You're the one did all those pageants with her, dragging all over the state, sewing her costumes and all. Deana never lifted a finger.'

She said, 'Well, I did it because I wanted to, but I never would have started it if I'd known the trouble it'd bring. Deana and Carla not speaking. Carla hardly even speaking to me because I said Deana should go on the trip. Gosh, Peg, I don't even want to go to Florida. Tell you the truth, I'm so tired I don't want to go anywhere.'

I said, 'You still seeing Slick Bonney?'

'He's my co-distributor,' she said. 'We're out every night demonstrating our products.'

I told her about Gayle. 'My word!' she said. 'Did you ever hear the like?'

I said, 'Ask me, she's taking folk for a ride. I gave her the benefit, but fixing teeth is way too far for me.'

'Well,' she said 'God judges. But imagine us knowing a TV star. I'll get Deana to record it. She has one of these VCRs. Slick wanted to get me one, but I'd never fathom how to work it.'

I said, 'You gonna make up with Carla? She's a good kid, Betty. You shouldn't let Deana freeze her out. Mother and daughter stop talking, that's a terrible thing.'

She sighed, 'I know,' she said. 'And I don't hardly hear from

Sherry neither. She's in New Mexico doing something. Always was the artistic one. Peggy? You still getting your visitor every month?'

I said, 'God, no! I finished all that when I was forty-eight. Didn't you?'

'No,' she said. 'I thought it'd finished. Then it come back.'

I said, 'You take care now. I don't want you getting in the family way. You know Slick'd do just about anything to get you to the altar.'

'Peggy!' she said. 'I don't want to hear that kind of talk!'

I said, 'How did Deana get on in Florida anyhow?'

'Oh, they didn't go yet,' she said. 'There's only certain times you can take up the prize.'

I said, 'Well, promise me you'll make up with Carla.'

'I will,' she said.

'And get some pills, so you don't have that bother no more. Tell the doctor you already had the change. They can give you stuff.'

'I will,' she said.

'And don't forget to watch Gayle.'

'Oh, I won't,' she said. 'I'm gonna buy a tape now and get it round to Deana's.'

The Weelkes Wing opening went off okay. We had pan pipes music and we served jalapeño nachos and bitter chocolate and orange pyramids. The parrots were Grice's idea. He said he was hiring cute little green parakeets, wouldn't be any trouble, but when the woman arrived with them they weren't no parakeets. I'm no expert, but I know a big mean bird when I see one. The guy they hassled was Dr Mitchell Crocker, come all the way from the University of Michigan.

As Grice said, they may have picked on him because his hairpiece looked like some kind of fibrous vegetable matter. Or it could have been because his whiny voice excited them. Either way, we came close to disaster, so the birds got paid off early.

'Okay,' Grice said. 'You were right. I was wrong. We should have gone for the tame llama after all.'

I said, 'Take my advice. Keep all animals out of the equation.'

'Mmm,' he said. 'Know what we overlooked too? Human sacrifice. Damn! Well, there goes our Inca reputation.'

I went home with him to watch Gayle. First time I'd been inside his place, all the years I'd known him. It was neat and clean, no more than you'd expect from a nice boy like Grice. It didn't feel very cosy, though. More like a hotel room than a home, and I said so.

'Well,' he said 'I'm not here too much, you know? It's kind of a place to sleep when I can't get down to Tucker's.'

I said, 'You mean you got a room at his place?' Crystal always reckoned he did.

'Sure I do,' he said. 'I mean, the late hours we work, and you saw Miss Lady. Tucker can't leave her. So I have to keep a place in town.'

I said, 'You make it sound like you're a married couple.'

'If only,' he said. 'If only.' Seemed like Crystal was right all along. Such a know-all.

The show started.

They showed Gayle and Lemarr at one of their healing rallies, like the one me and Betty had seen. Then they showed inside the mouths of some folks claimed God had fixed their teeth through the healing hands of Gayle. Finally we got to see Gayle close up. She was looking good. She was wearing her hair bigger, and she was dressed more tailored than before.

Grice said, 'Is she younger than you?'

I don't know what he meant by that.

Whatever the interviewer asked her, she had a text for it. Romans 8; Isaiah 53. She just knew them all off the top of her head. Just shows what a person can learn if they only put their mind to it.

'Why teeth?' they asked her.

'Many healers are now specialising,' she said. 'Mine is not to reason, but to do whatever work the Lord sends me.'

'And do people have to come to you? Do you have to touch them?'

'All they have to do is believe,' she said. 'People write me and they are healed. People telephone me and they are healed. People even can touch their TV screens and be healed, if they believe. "Himself took our infirmities and bare our sicknesses," Matthew 8:17.'

The interviewer said, 'Do people pay you for this dental work?'

'I'm no dentist,' she said. 'I make no charge for my prayers. But without the generous support of our friends the Lemarr Passy Tabernacle could not continue its work. Every gift, no matter how small, is good in the eyes of the Lord. "The poor widow threw in two mites," Mark 12:42.'

I went out to the bathroom. When I come back, Grice was running the tape again, got his face right up to the TV screen.

I said, 'You'll ruin your eyes.'

'Never mind my eyes,' he said, 'I have a loose crown needs fixing. And I believe, Lord! I believe!'

87

'I've got two things to tell you,' Kath said. 'I've kept trying Audrey's number, see how she's going on, and now she's been cut off. I'd take a drive out there again only I'm chocker with work. And the other thing is, we've got a marvellous programme on the telly now and it's called *Dallas*. I never miss it. I watch it like a hawk, keep thinking I might see you walking past in the street.'

I said, 'They must have moved.'

All the times she had moved when she was married to the airforce, every one of us got a card with her new address.

'Didn't pay their phone bill, more like,' Kath said.

I said, 'Audrey never left a bill unpaid in her life. Something's up.'

'Oh, don't say that,' she said. 'She knows she can always come to me, if she's got troubles. And I will go out there again. I'll look through the letterbox, see if there's bills piling up. But it won't be this week. I'm booked solid.'

Kath wasn't the only one busy that summer. We created an Old-Fashioned party for Moody Pierce up by White Rock Lake and it was so fabulous the whole town wanted one. We decorated the terrace with masses of gardenias. Served fried chicken and potato salad and stuff like that. Everyone ended up in the pool and then we had girls, dressed like Roxy usherettes, bringing round Dixie cups of peach ice cream.

By September I had ate so much leftover ice cream I was having trouble closing my zippers. I called Betty, see about getting some more of her miracle fat-burner. Carla answered.

I said, 'I'm glad to hear you're back.'

'Yeah,' she said, 'I'm back. I guess you heard about Mom?'

Betty was in State, getting tests. Carla said, 'They did a colposcopy and now they're doing a cone biopsy, tomorrow probably. She's got cancer cells and they have to look see how far it's gone.'

I said, 'Is that bad?'

'Could be,' she said. 'Problem is, Aunty Peggy, you can't get any sense out of her, how long this has been going on. You know what she's like, anything below the belt? It might not have come to light yet if Slick hadn't gotten so worried about her back-ache. He just about dragged her to the doctor's office.'

I said, 'I know she was tired. And that family stuff was getting her down. You and Deana work out your differences?'

She laughed. 'Well,' she said, 'that's another story.'

Apparently two nights before Deana and Delta were meant to be going on their prize vacation to Florida, Deana had a road accident. She had gone out to buy a six-pack for Bulldog, got shunted by a car didn't stop at a red, and ended up in the emergency room, neck injuries and suspected fracture of the skull. By the time they let her out of hospital the plane had left for Florida with Bulldog and Delta on it. Last they heard, Delta and Bulldog were living as man and wife in South Miami.

I said, 'But Delta's only a child.'

'No,' she said, 'as a matter of fact, she's sixteen.'

I said, 'So Deana's on the warpath after Bulldog?'

'Oh no,' she said. 'Deana blames Delta. I mean, forty-year-old guy runs off with his girlfriend's sixteen-year-old kid, stands to reason you're gonna blame the kid. So, to answer your question. Me and Deana still don't see eye to eye. It's just the reasons have changed. Meanwhile, Mom's quietly getting cancer.'

I said, 'Know what frightens me? I thought these smear checks we get were meant to show up any problems? It spooks me to think something like this can still creep up on you.'

'Aunty Peggy,' she said, 'you don't think Mom ever took one of those checks, do you? I'll tell you where those appointment cards went: straight in the trash can. You know Mom. She'd sooner get sick than take her clothes off for a doctor.'

I said, 'You take care of yourself, now, Carla. And get your sisters to start pulling their weight.'

'Sure,' she said. 'Only don't let's hold our breath till they do.'

Kath phoned me for my birthday.

'I had a letter from Audrey,' she said. 'No address, not even a telephone number, but I took my magnifying glass to the postmark and I reckon that said Yorkshire. She says, I'll read it to you, "The gallery has been going through lean times, so we're having to tighten our belts. We've been lucky enough to borrow a dear little cottage . . ." See what I mean, Peg? I reckon he's gone bust. They've scarpered. I mean, what about that big house he had? And Audrey's money?'

I felt so depressed.

I said to Grice, 'I'm fifty-two. My friends are all getting sick or taking leave of their senses. I neglected my mother. I hate my sister.'

'Anything else?' he said.

I said, 'Yes. My daughter is too busy stuffing ferrets to remember my birthday.'

'Okay,' he said. 'Here are your options. I can take you out to Mountain Creek now, put heavy rocks in your pants and just throw you in. Or, you can get chop suey with me and Tucker and watch a Judy Garland movie.'

88

June of '79 I got a card announcing that Sandie Moon and her husband Gerry had finally got the little baby they had longed for, named him Patrick Herbert for his two granddaddies; and also a call from Betty to say that Delta had come home in the family way, whereabouts of Daddy Bulldog not known.

Betty was just about back on her feet after her big op. She had been on the table getting a radical hysterectomy.

I said, 'Has she moved in with you?'

'Well, where else is she gonna go?' she said. 'Deana won't have her within a mile of her trailer.'

Then, just as I was thinking I couldn't get left behind much further, Lois now a grandma twice over and Betty gonna be a great-grandma, I heard from Crystal that she was getting married to a boy called Marc Fry. He was the deputy editor of *Cranberry News*.

I said, 'You have made me a very happy woman.'

'Think nothing of it,' she said. 'Just don't ask me to have ten bridesmaids and a three-room gift-display.'

They had fixed on late September, on account of Vern's place having a quiet spell then, while the wild nightcrawlers were being harvested.

I said, 'Spare me the details. I suppose you won't be having it in a church?'

'Correct,' she said.

I said, 'Well, a city-hall wedding can be very nice.'

'It probably can,' she said, 'but we're not getting one of those neither. We're writing our own vows and we're gonna make them on a boat out in Penobscot Bay.'

I said, 'Is that legal?'

'Don't start,' she said.

Grice squealed when I told him. 'Look at it this way,' he said, 'at least you know exactly what to wear. Deck shoes, and something that tones with motion-sickness-green.'

Crystal and Marc were making all their own arrangements, which was kinda hard for me to take, having been in the business and all, but they weren't kids. I couldn't lay down the law. And it was just gonna be a small affair, everybody going for a mess of lobster and beer after this home-made ceremony.

I said to Crystal, 'Can I buy you a washer-drier?'

'Got one, thanks,' she said.

I said, 'How about a dishwasher?'

'Got one of those, too.'

Marc, being a slightly older man, came fully equipped.

I said, 'Well, you're hard to treat. How about some money for your honeymoon?'

'Now you're talking!' she said. 'We're going to South Africa. Seeing rhino, hippo, all the big cats. You sleep in a tent and they take you out in a four-wheel drive and show you everything. And please don't say, "Well, Crystal, if that's what you really want."'

I said, 'Sounds like you've found a soulmate.'

'I have, Mom,' she said. 'And you'll love him too.'

Marc's folks were dead. All he had was a brother, might be coming down from Ottawa for the wedding.

Crystal said, 'Marc's clean. He doesn't have any weird kin or any dark secrets.'

I said, 'You by any chance planning to wear pants for this wedding?'

'Yeah,' she said. 'I'll probably pick something out from L. L. Bean. We'll probably get his 'n' hers waders too.'

I said, 'Is Martine gonna be there?'

'Of course,' she said.

I said, 'Is she pretty?'

'Mom!' she said. 'There's nobody in the world as beautiful as you.'

I was so choked, I couldn't answer her.

I always had wondered about Martine, though. I never had seen any pictures, and when your ex takes another wife, you can't help but be curious. The way Crystal told it, Martine's boy Eugene wasn't no oil-painting. I didn't really care. I'd looked after myself. I'd probably get a few facials the month before I went up there. And I'd definitely give Betty's Lipo-Zipp a try. You get to a certain time of life, don't matter what you eat, your hips spread up and your bosom creeps down and everything just settles round your middle. I was thinking to get a plain sheath dress, not too fitted, and a matching jacket.

I was thinking, whatever I wore I'd probably look like royalty alongside of a worm-farmer's wife.

When I heard Vern's voice, I naturally thought he was calling about the wedding.

'That you, Peg?' he said. Then he started. It came at me like a flash flood. 'You've got some nerve, getting me involved with that Moon kid and not levelling with me. You ask a person a favour, you owe them the full story. That way they know what they're letting theirselves in for.'

I said, 'Vern, I don't know what the hell you're talking about.'

He said, 'Kirk Moon is what I'm talking about. Causing bad feeling between decent folk. You know how many years Bob Pick's been a friend of mine?'

Bottom line was, Kirk was finished at Glens Falls Reel-and-Lure.

I said, 'He have his hand in the till?'

'No,' he said. 'Worse than that. He was fired for lewd and diabolical behaviour, and don't even ask me to tell you. You must have known what he was like.'

He was yelling, just like the bad old days. 'I had my doubts all along,' he said, 'and I should have listened to them. Doing favours. Well, not any more. From now on, I don't ask no favours and I don't do none.'

I said, 'What kind of behaviour did you say?'

'I'm not going into it,' he said. 'You must have known what he's like. You've seen him.'

I said, 'Vern, I haven't seen him since he was a boy. He's a married man now, got a kid of his own.'

'Then ask Lois,' he said. 'Get her to explain why a twenty-five-year-old couldn't find himself a job. Has he been in reformatory? He done time?'

I said, 'Do you think I'd have asked you to help him if I knew he was trouble? All I knew was what Lois told me. Sounded like he'd had a bad run of luck. Then there was a baby on the way.'

'Bad run of luck!' he said. He was still yelling. 'That's real con-talk. Never got an even break neither, I'll bet. Never got straightened out, more like. Never saw enough of Herb's belt. And that's another blow. Was a time I'd have trusted Herb Moon with my life. Now I find out he's spawned a reprobate, behaves like he was never showed right from wrong. You can tell Herb and Lois from me they got some neck dumping a piece of work like that on innocent strangers.' And he slammed down the phone.

I felt sick. I got the shakes. I phoned Lois.

'Yeah,' she said, 'thought I'd be hearing from you.' She made me feel bad before I even started, like I was the one making trouble.

'Look,' she said, 'it just didn't work out, okay? Sometimes things don't. I don't see why folks have to make such a big deal out of it.'

I said, 'What'd he do, Lo? Vern's in a real fit.'

'I swear,' she said, 'these woodchucks oughta get out more, see a little of the world. They spent five minutes in New York they wouldn't get scandalised so easy.'

I asked her again, what he had done.

'All he needs,' she said, 'is for people to show a little patience and understanding. And now he's really down. Marisa's gone home. Her folks won't let him see Cory. I told them they should just butt out. He's pacing around the house. He's even driving Herb nuts.'

I screamed at her. I said, 'Lois, just tell me what he did!' Matter of fact, I said the F-word. First time I ever used it, and I pray it's the last. Made her change her attitude, though.

'Oh Peg,' she said, all soothing and sweet, 'you know Kirk's always had some weird ways. He just made some suggestion to one of the old boys in the store. You know? Like a joke?'

I said, 'He didn't get fired for a joke.'

'Well,' she said. 'He might have done it a few times. He might have given them a flash of his privates or something.'

I said, 'Might have? Did he or didn't he?'

'So they say,' she said. 'But who would you believe? Young married man, got a good-looking wife, or some old hayseed, only action he ever sees is Rosy Palm and her five sisters?'

I said, 'You telling me he didn't do anything? Or he might have done something? What *are* you telling me? Anybody brought charges?'

She said, 'Will you quit the interrogation? I'm sorry if Vern gave out to you, but it's finished now. Me and Herb are dealing with it. Herb'll give Vern a call, smooth things over.'

I said, 'Kirk ever done a thing like that before?'

'Crying out loud, Peg,' she said, 'drop it, will you? What's it to you anyway?'

I said, 'I'll tell you what it is to me. I'm all ready to fly up to Maine, stand beside Vern Dewey and watch our daughter get married, and as of 9 p.m. this evening Vern isn't even speaking to me.'

'Know what I think?' she said. 'You're such a tight-ass, Peggy. No wonder Vern left you. Why don't you just loosen up? And quit picking on my boy.'

I didn't say another word to her. Just put down the telephone. I never expected to speak to her again, not as long as I lived.

I didn't sleep. First thing, I called Crystal.

I said, 'Honey, I don't think I can come to your wedding.'

'Mom,' she said, 'you've been on my case since ever since Trent Weaver. You don't show up, we'll come down there and get you.'

I told her about Kirk and everything, but she already knew.

'You'd think he'd have been more careful,' she said, 'leaving a little thing like that lying around in a bait store.' Crystal always could make me feel better.

Half an hour later Vern phoned. All he said was, 'Idiot! See you next week.'

89

I flew up to Boston, then on to Bangor, and Crystal drove me into town in her old pick-up. I never saw a bride so laid-back in all my days. She hadn't even had her nails done.

'No point,' she said 'First, Marc'd never recognise me if I did. Second, I have a lynx skin in tanning liquor I need to take a look at before I'm through.'

We picked up Marc from his office, so we could all go get something to eat. One thing. He was nothing like her first husband. Matter of fact, you could have gotten two Trent Weavers out of Marc and still had flesh left to spare.

'Y'all finished, then?' she said, as he was climbing into the car. 'Can we go off and get married and go to Africa and everything?'

'Don't pressure me now, Crystal,' he said. 'We've got a big story breaking in there. I shouldn't even be out to dinner.'

He turned to me, gave me a big smile. 'Outbreak of black-headed fireworm in Massachusetts,' he said. 'We're holding the front page.'

Marc was forty-one, same age as Grice, as a matter of fact, and he'd never been married neither. He said Crystal was the first woman he ever met was happier on a mountain trail than she was in a shopping mall.

I liked him, and it was plain to see Crystal was head over heels. The only thing I wished was, she would remember to moisturise at night. A girl spends so much time outdoors she has to think of her skin. It's something, to see your baby turn thirty.

They put me up at the Harbor House Inn. I had a great big canopy bed all to myself and breakfast brought to my room. Blueberry pancakes, hazelnut coffee. I just sent down for a lemon tea. When a person's going out on the ocean they can't be too careful, is what I think.

Ten a.m. the Dewey wagon-train rolled into the car park. I stood inside and watched them pile out. It was the first time I had seen Vern in twenty years. I thought he looked old, and maybe he thought the same about me. He was kinda bashful, though, having me and Martine around. First thing I said to him was, 'I'm real sorry about Kirk.'

'Let's say no more about it,' he said. 'Me and Bob Pick are back on tracks. Main thing is, we make sure Crystal has a great day.'

Martine was a bundle of energy, for a larger woman. She had dyed hair, burgundy red, and a Terylene pants-suit in sky-blue. Took me right by the arm and told me not to worry about a thing. Way I looked at it, it was my daughter's wedding day and it was entirely up to me what I worried about.

Her boy Eugene had a beer gut, and a wispy moustache. I don't believe I heard him speak all day. And his little wife, Filomena, was real homely too, always had her hand over her mouth when she smiled, which she did most of the time, and when I seen her teeth I understood why. Speaking of teeth, Mom Dewey had in new plates, top and bottom. And Crystal was right. She hadn't aged frail. She had gone hard and leathery.

'Well,' she said to me, 'at least she's marrying a white man. She hadn't a been marrying a white man I wouldn't have closed up my store for the day.'

I never saw my girl look so beautiful. She only had a chainstore dress, cream with a chocolate trim, and an ivory wool wrap, but I guess she was wearing her happiness too. Marc was waiting on us down at the quayside, had his shirt buttoned to the neck but no tie. I guess that was the trend. In Texas we don't pay much heed to what the East Coast is doing.

It was a real sail-boat they had hired, a schooner called *Bonaparte* with canvas sails and everything. It even had a lounge downstairs with a soapstone fireplace.

Mom Dewey said, 'Where's the preacher?'

We headed up the coast and I surprised myself. I liked the feel of that old boat dipping through the water. She was so well built, and the colour of the maples, just starting to turn, was so pretty, I didn't even bother thinking about shipwrecks or getting sick or anything.

Mom Dewey said, 'Where's the Justice?'

They stopped the boat by a little granite island and Marc and Crystal made their vows and exchanged rings. Me and Vern both had to wipe a tear, and Mom Dewey heaved her breakfast into the bay and her bottom plate too, which accounts for her face looking kinda caved in in the pictures. There were seals in the water and, as soon as they had finished getting married, the bride and groom were over to the rail checking them out through their field-glasses.

Marc said they were harp seals. Crystal said they were young greys.

'Uh-oh,' he said. 'Our first fight.'

It was the darlingest wedding I ever was at, and I've been to a few.

The boat people had everything ready. Lobsters for baking and all the fixings. They had a pit on the island, lined with firebricks, used it all the time. They'd had it lit since daybreak. Soon as we landed they spread seaweed over the hot bricks and lobsters on top and corn in the husk, pulled a tarp over the top to keep the steam in and served cold beer and Polish sausage while the dinner cooked.

I found myself next to Martine and kinda lost for small talk.

I said, 'Business going okay?' It was the best I could do.

'Going great,' she said. 'Only one outfit bigger'n us now and they're out of state. I do the redworms. Vern and Eugene do the nightcrawlers. Course, I was laid for a while. I expect you heard. I had a cancer in my bosom.'

I said, 'Good friend of mine got cancer of the cervix.'

She sucked in her breath. 'They take it all away? They took all mine away.'

I said, 'They took her womb, took her ovaries. I don't know what else they took,'

'Best thing,' she said. 'She won't be needing it any more. Best they take it all away, give you a clean slate. That's what I got and I never felt better. Did I, Vern?'

He had wandered over to us, after he'd checked those folks knew how to cook lobster. 'Never felt better, never looked better,' he said, and he slipped his arm around her. There was no need for him to do a thing like that, right in front of me.

'Well, Peg,' he said. 'So we finally got her off our hands.'

I said, 'Marc's nice.'

'Yeah,' he said, a bit lukewarm. 'Course, he's white-collar. He's a great one for reading and all that. Can't say I've ever seen him roll up his sleeves. Still, we got Eugene for that. And Crystal's not shy of getting her hands dirty. Takes after her old man, there.'

I said, 'You remember when we were at Drampton? You remember those coney-skin gloves she got? Wouldn't be parted for them, didn't matter how hot she was? I reckon that was the start of this taxidermy thing.'

He said, 'Could be you're right. And that cat we had at Wichita. She was always trying to train him up. Always was good around animals.'

Martine didn't like us reminiscing. 'Vern,' she said. Cut right across me. 'Vern, you think your mom's okay?'

Mom Dewey was just fine. She was sitting on a foldaway chair telling Filomena how corn in the husk was schwartze food. Filomena was nodding and smiling.

Crystal said, 'Did you have insurance on those dentures, Gramma?'

'Only thing I got insurance on is your daddy's life,' she said. 'He goes before I do, I get one thousand dollars. Why didn't you get a preacher, make a proper job of getting married? You looked into the legal side of this? You need to know where you stand in a court of law. You drop dead tomorrow, he might stand to get your worm inheritance. Or he might not. I don't know. A lawyer'd tell you, but he'd send you a bill for doing it. That's a lawyer for you. He'll pocket your hard-earned money just for telling you the time of day.'

Filomena smiled some more.

Crystal said, 'You ready to eat, Gramma?'

'I'll just suck on a little lobster,' she said. 'Don't bother bringing me none of that nigger corn.'

We had applesauce layer-cake and drank their good health in blush wine and then we sailed back to Camden, to wave them off to Africa – first stop, the honeymoon suite at the Lake Alamoosook Sunset Hotel.

'Mom,' she said, when she was hugging me goodbye, 'this was worth waiting for.' And her big bear of a husband put his arm around my shoulder.

'You haven't lost her,' he said. 'You just gained me.'

Read me like a book. I never did like the winding up of a wedding party.

'Well,' Vern said, 'if ever you're Skowhegan way . . .' Like I ever would be.

'Yes,' Martine said. 'Don't be a stranger now. We are family.'

I thought to kiss Vern goodbye and maybe Martine too, once on each cheek. We do that all the time in Dallas. But Vern of course wasn't accustomed to it. We ended up banging noses.

I caught a whiff of him, though, just took me back all those long years. He still smelled of Vitalis. Vitalis and pie.

90

I sent Kath pictures of the wedding.

'What a lovely couple they make,' she wrote back.

I've seen some nice sheepskin rugs on the market I thought they might like, be nice for a bedside mat, but if there's something else you think of let me know. I expect they've already got table mats.

Now, I'm after your money. It's called a sponsored walk, all along the coast road, Hunstanton, Wells, you'd know the route. You can do five miles or ten or fifteen and we have to get people to pay us, so much the mile. Me and May are trying for ten miles, so we're in training. You should see the plimsolls we've got. It's in aid of Huntington's Disease.

I phoned her. I said, 'What's the best offer you've had?'

'Pound a mile,' she said. 'That's from the man I always go to for my motors.'

I said 'Okay, I'll double that. What's Huntington's Disease?'

'That's our family trouble, that I mentioned,' she said. 'In the nerves. They haven't found anything can be done for it so far, but we keep hoping. And of course, that takes money, keeping the scientists going. So there's twenty of us, doing this walk. Dennis Jex is going to try for the fifteen miles. I told him, though, we might need him following behind with his St John bandages. Now, how's Betty going on?'

Betty and Slick were going great guns with their fat-burner product. They had ten distributors working under them, paying them a percentage, and they still did their own selling, out every night, going into people's homes, showing them before and after pictures of satisfied customers.

I'd said to her, 'I hope you're enjoying all that money you're making. I hope you're not giving it all away.'

'Giving it away is what I enjoy,' she said. 'Tell you what, Peg. Doesn't matter how much we make, it can't buy me the two things I want.'

She wanted a new pair of legs and to know that Delta and the great-grandbaby were safe, wherever they might be.

I said 'Have you tried support hose?'

'Tried everything,' she said. 'Makes no difference. And there's still no word from Delta.'

She had had Delta staying with her, carrying Bulldog's child. Then she just took off. Carla's theory was, Bulldog was back on the scene. Deana had said if he was he better watch out because she had a mind to shoot him, and Delta too, and any brats they brought into the world.

I was always glad to hear Carla pick up when I called Betty. She had a wry way about her, reminded me of Crystal.

I said to her, 'Does Deana have a gun?'

'I believe she does,' she said. 'Course, whether she knows how to use it is another question. She could take out half the city before she got a fatal slug into Bulldog. That brain of his is a awful small target.'

I said, 'Carla, that kinda talk makes my blood run cold. Don't Deana have any motherly feelings for Delta? Don't she care she's got a little grandbaby out there?'

'Aunty Peggy,' she said, 'what the hell do I know? I can't even believe I'm related to her. If it wasn't for Mom, I'd have changed my name and gone away long ago. North Dakota sounds about right.'

I asked her what she knew about this Huntington's Disease. She never even heard of it. Neither had Crystal.

'I'll find out for you, though,' she said.

*   *   *

[311]

Our season was easing off somewhat. We had a clear week coming up in June. Grice wanted to go on a trip, but Tucker wouldn't leave Miss Lady because she was predicting to die any minute.

I said, 'If you're looking for someone to keep you company in Key Biscayne, I'm available. If you're looking for someone to babysit Miss Lady, something urgent just came up.'

He said, 'How do you feel about New Mexico?'

I said, 'Long as we avoid Kirtland. I already served my sentence there.'

So we agreed to go take a look at Santa Fe and Albuquerque, and Grice was just starting up, singing about being bound for the Rio Grande, when I took the call from Carla.

'Aunty Peggy?' she said. 'I really need your help.'

Betty's old trouble was back. They had told her at the hospital she had to get ray treatment but that was gonna put her out of action for six weeks and she was refusing.

I said, 'What happens if she don't take the treatment?' Fool question.

I said to Grice, 'Change of plan. I have to go to San Antonio, talk some sense into Betty Gillis.'

His face fell. 'We're not bound for the Rio Grande, then?' he said.

I said, 'Ever been to San Antonio?'

Next thing, he was singing about Davy Crockett, King of the Wild Frontier.

91

Betty said, 'I don't have time for this. We just won Sales Team of the Year and we have to go to Houston, get presented with our certificate. Plus, I promised Danni a Sweet Sixteen party. Plus, my kitchen-dinette hasn't seen a lick of paint in three years and I'm ashamed for anybody to see it.'

'Plus, Mom,' Carla said, 'you have an adenocarcinoma.'

I hated to be in on all this. It didn't seem right. But Carla said, 'You're like family. You're the only one goes all the way back.'

'Well,' Betty said, 'that's what they *say* I have now. They *said* I had a little wart on my insides. Before that they *said* I had a dropping womb. I'm not convinced they know what I do have.'

Carla looked worn out. 'What can I do with her?' she said. 'My own mother has a death wish.'

'Oh, stop that!' Betty said. 'We'll go to Houston, I'll do Danni her party . . .'

Carla said, 'Mom! Danni doesn't want a party. She just wants to go to the mall and hang out . . .'

'. . . do Danni her party, freshen up my dinette and *then* I'll think about ray treatment. If they didn't change their mind in the meanwhile, that is. Peg, who's the friend you're travelling with? Is he your beau?'

Grice was out to the Alamo. 'Don't worry about me,' he said. 'Go do what you have to do. And tomorrow I'm going to the zoo.'

Carla had to go to work. Me and Betty sat out in the yard with iced tea and egg salad. 'I'm fifty-six, Peg,' she said.

'Me too,' I said. 'You think I was getting younger?'

'You feel fifty-six?'

'I dunno,' I said, 'Sometimes, I guess. I felt fifty-two when my mom died.'

'My body feels about hundred and fifty-six,' she said. 'But in my mind I'm no different than when I was in high school. That's what I don't get. How come your head don't keep in step with your insides? And where's all that time gone, that's what I wonder? Fifty-six years. I still haven't finished that quilt I started when Ed got posted to McConnell. That was to be for Deana's hope-chest. I was gonna make a quilt for each of my girls. This rate I won't even have one finished for Destiny Rae.' Destiny Rae was the great-grandbaby. Hadn't been seen since she was six months old and Delta took off with her.

I said, 'I wouldn't give that quilt another thought. Comforters are easier. You can just throw them in the washer.'

'Yeah,' she said. 'Stitching them's hard on the eyes too. Then I'd had in mind to go to college. Get my exams so I could teach elementary school.'

I said, 'Why don't you? You'd be so great at that.' I was getting sick of the sound of my own cheeriness.

'No,' she said. 'It's too late now. I couldn't leave Slick in the lurch after we've built up our Lipo-Zipp sales. Did I ever send you a sample?'

I had Betty's free samples falling outta my bathroom cabinet. I said, 'Well at least take the treatment. How are you gonna keep your sales figures up if you're too sick to work?'

She was quiet for a while. 'Do you know what they did, Peg? When they had me in to find out why my legs were aching so? They put stuff inside me. It lights up, kinda fluorescent on the X-ray. But they put it up my back-passage, Peg. I'd known that's what they were intending to do, I never would have gone.'

I said, 'That why you won't take the treatment?'

She didn't answer.

I said, 'Has Sherry visited lately?'

'No,' she said. 'I don't expect her to trek back here. She has her life.'

I said, 'Ever hear from Ed?'

'No,' she said.

'You and Deana speaking?'

'Deana has her problems,' she said. 'She has her allergies. And she's had nothing but bad luck with men.'

I said, 'Carla's a good kid.'

'I know,' she said. 'She's a darling girl.'

I said, 'She's worried what's gonna happen to you, if you don't listen to the doctors.'

'I'll think about it,' she said. 'And that's all I'm saying. What did you say your beau's name is?'

I said, 'His name is Grice and he's no beau of mine. He's a homosexual. That means he goes with men.'

'Peggy Dewey!' she said. 'I don't want to hear anything about that.'

She liked him, though, when he dropped by. He brought her candy and flowers.

'William Barrett Travis,' he said, 'drew a line in the dust and said every man willing to fight to the death should step over it and Jim Bowie had them carry him over the line, because he was on a stretcher.'

'We know,' I said. 'We grew up here. We heard it all before.'

'Eighteen hundred Mexicans,' he said, 'against two hundred Texans. I got Tucker a Jim Bowie paper-knife from the gift store, but I've a mind to bring him here anyway. He'd love the gardens.'

Betty folded her lips, but I could see Grice was winning.

'Now,' he said, 'I hope you girls are coming with me tomorrow, see the killer whale?'

So Sunday me and Grice, Betty and Slick all rode out to Sea World and when she got too tired to walk she even allowed Grice to push her in a wheelchair after he kidded her it was the only way we'd ever get to see the dolphins without standing in line. He took her fast down a slope, made her squeal, and me and Slick followed behind.

I said, 'She shouldn't be going to Houston, Slick. Running down there just to get some certificate. She should go to State, start the ray treatment.'

He sucked his teeth a little. 'Yup,' he said, 'I know. I wrote to that friend of yours. The one we seen at the Assembly of God. I reckon if there's any miracle healing going begging, Betty should get it.'

When I kissed her goodbye she whispered to me, 'I know he's younger than you, but I still think he'd make a fine beau.'

I said, 'And like I told you a hundred times, he has a beau of his own. This is 1980, you know? That kind of thing is all the rage.'

'Remember the Alamo!' Grice called to her from the car. 'Victory or death!'

92

How fame can change the way a person lives. I called the last home number I had for Gayle and Lemarr but they had changed it. Gone unlisted. Then I called the TV station and didn't even get past first base. The girl said it was impossible for Pastor Gayle to speak personally with the hundreds of callers seeking her help.

I said, 'I'm a friend. Me and Gayle go back more'n twenty-five years.'

'In that case, ma'am,' she said, 'I guess you have her private number.'

I said, 'Can you at least tell me, is she still at the house in White Point?'

All else failed, I figured to write to her.

'I have no information on that,' she said.

I said, 'What kind of information do you have?'

'Tax-effective giving to the Tabernacle Ministry. Also tour-schedules through 1981.'

She told me to have a nice day.

I said, 'Don't tell me what kind of day to have.'

Gayle Jackson. Who'd have thought it? I remember one time at Drampton, England, I had to put that girl to bed she was so wrecked.

Still, and after everything I had said, I fell in behind that old sceptic Slick Bonney. I wrote to her, sent it to the last address I had. I printed

'FROM PEGGY DEWEY, OLD FRIEND, URGENT' all over the envelope, then after I'd mailed it I got to thinking that kind of thing was probably regarded as a guaranteed sign of a mental case, so I sent another copy, in just a plain, typed envelope.

Crystal thought I *was* a mental case. 'You know how much money these TV preachers make?' she said. 'Old ladies sending in dollar bills?'

I said, 'Well, this old lady isn't sending in money. I just want Gayle to know Betty is sick. If she can do anything, that'll be a bonus.'

'Ask me, she shouldn't be encouraged,' she said. 'By the way, are we bringing lobsters?' Crystal and Marc were coming south for Thanksgiving.

I said, 'No. Just cranberries. We're having turkey.'

Give Gayle her due, she called me within the week. 'Peg!' she said. 'It's been too long.'

I told her we'd seen her in San Antonio. Told her I'd seen her on TV.

She said, 'Sometimes I wake in the night, wonder if I just dreamed it all. Don't need to tell you, this isn't what I planned for my life.'

She told me about all the travelling her and Lemarr had to do, the whole year ahead already fixed up and starting to fill dates in early '82. 'It's like a runaway train,' she said. 'And Lemarr is nearly seventy, you know? He don't look it, but he is. He oughta slow down but, like he says, the Lord tells you when to slow down.'

I said, 'I know you kinda specialise now . . .' I was embarrassed to hear myself say it. Crystal was predicting Betty'd get a porcelain crown.

'Not me,' she said. 'Whatever the Lord sends.'

I said, 'Well, I'd sure appreciate it if you could have a word to him about Betty.'

'Already doing it, Peg,' she said, 'already doing it. Now, what about a little human intervention too? She in a good clinic?'

I said, 'She's getting her treatment at State. Carla works there.'

'Okay,' she said. 'But there might be someplace better, you know?

I mean, you know the town, you know Betty's set-up. Whatever you think. Just don't let her go short. I have money.'

Crystal and Marc flew in Wednesday night. She was looking good. Married life seemed to suit her. The latest from Maine was, Mom Dewey had had a couple of dizzy spells. Eugene's wife had said she was happy to go up and down the ladder as required, but so far as Mom Dewey was concerned whoever climbed that ladder ruled the roost and, to her way of thinking, Filomena was closely related to the slant-eyed hordes of China.

Crystal said, 'Yes, the tide of Communism has been checked at the doorway to Clementine Dewey Yarns and Notions. We've been hearing a lot about a guy called Norton Beebe. Got shot in Korea? Any time the subject of ladders and dizzy spells comes up Gramma says, "I let an Oriental run my store, Norton Beebe will have laid down his life for nothing."'

I said, 'So what's the answer?'

'Get rid of the ladder,' she said. 'All the yarn has been brought down from the high shelves and stacked on the floor, on the counter, up along the walls. You can't move. They get any more stuff in there, the customers'll just have to stand outside. Gramma'll be walled up. I reckon Eugene'll have to hack out a hole, to allow the exchange of notions and greenbacks. She may have to rename it. Clementine's Yarn Kiosk.'

Marc and Crystal wanted to watch the football, so we ate at half-time. Felt like we were a real family, first time in years.

Crystal said, 'I found out some stuff for you. Huntington's Disease? How much do you want to know?'

Marc cleared the plates and served the apple pie.

She said, 'It's inherited. First it makes your muscles jerk. Only time they stop is when you're asleep. Then after a few years the jerking stops and the muscles seize up. Last thing is, the mind goes. Does Aunty Kath know somebody has this?'

I said, 'It's in her family. Her mother had it.'

Crystal whistled. She said, 'She probably doesn't have it, though. She'd be sick by now. And she never had kids.'

I said, 'What if she had done? Would they have had it?'

'You got a piece of paper?' she said.

She drew out a load of Xs and Ys to try and explain about genes and stuff, Marc watching her. He said, 'Isn't she something? Brains. Beauty. And she does this great thing with bay scallops.'

I said, 'Crystal, you're making my head spin. Just give me the bottom line.'

'I'm getting there,' she said. 'If you have Huntington's and you have a kid, it's a fifty-fifty chance he'll get it.'

I said, 'Okay, I can grasp that. Like heads or tails.'

'Correct,' she said. 'Problem is, though, it's a slow-developing condition. You wouldn't know for sure if you had it till you were past the time of getting babies. See what I mean? So Aunty Kath did the right thing. I don't know if anybody ever explained her the odds, but she didn't risk it anyhow.'

Friday we met Grice for ribs at the Black Diamond Grill. Crystal wanted Marc and him to meet.

She said, 'He's the nearest I ever had to a brother. No, that's wrong. He's the nearest I ever had to a sister.'

Grice said, 'Well, darling girl, have you mounted anything interesting lately?'

'Wolverine interesting enough for you?' she said.

'No regrets then?' he said. 'I thought you might be missing those white-water thrills of being self-employed.'

'No,' she said. 'Anyway, my life isn't totally safe and dull. I just had a mite-infestation in a case of rodent skins.'

'I hate it when that happens,' he said.

She said, 'It won't happen again. From now on I'm treating all my study skins with arsenic.'

He said, 'You mean you can get your hands on arsenic?'

'Sodium arsenite,' she said. 'Why? Who upset you?'

He had spent Thanksgiving out at Corinth. They didn't get dinner till nine p.m. and then Miss Lady had kept them up, playing cards, till two.

He said to Crystal, 'Some day, if we all live long enough, I may have to ask you to come out of retirement and stuff Miss Lady. If

Tucker doesn't have her around, I know he's just going to go to pieces.'

She said, 'Miss Lady's a human, right?'

'So they claim,' he said. 'She weighs about the same as a German shepherd. But she has some traits of a reptile too, wouldn't you agree, Peggy? I could be putting a unique specimen your way.'

He joked about Miss Lady but sometimes he was really down, the way Tucker always had to put his mother first. Always had to be there to take in her breakfast tray, about two in the afternoon. Always had to sit and read the newspaper with her, tell her who had died. Grice just had to make do with what he could get, and meanwhile him and Tucker weren't getting any younger. 'Good thing we didn't want to have children,' he always said.

Him and Marc got along fine. '*Cranberry News?*' he said. 'Never miss it. In my opinion it stands head and shoulders above the rest of the fruit press. I especially admire the fashion pages.'

Marc said, 'Glad to know that. I write it all myself.'

Grice kept yawning, his late night catching up to him.

I said, 'Are you driving out to Tucker's place tonight?'

'No,' he said. 'I'll just go home. Eat pineapple out of the can. Night, y'all.'

Marc said, 'Tell me something? I always wondered, is there a plural of y'all ?'

'Why, yes, there is,' Grice said. 'It's all y'all. So what I really intended to say was, night-night, all y'all.'

Crystal and Marc started for home Saturday morning. 'Mom,' she said, 'you ever think of retiring?'

I said, 'I doubt I'll ever afford to. Why?'

'Just wondered,' she said. 'I miss you. And Maine's too far for you, while you're working.'

I said, 'Maine's too far. Let's leave it at that. Tell you what, I'll meet you halfway. You guys move to Cincinatti and I'll retire.'

I hated to see her go. Got a first little bit of grey coming into her hair, I noticed.

Crystal's Sour-Cream Scallops

•••

*Splash lemon vodka over ½lb of bay scallops, cover with
sour cream and sweet paprika, and marinate overnight.
Broil for five minutes. Serve with a little freshly chopped
dill weed.*

•••

93

February fifteenth was gonna be Tucker Hoose's sixtieth birthday, and we were throwing a party for him out at Hickory.

Grice said, 'What the heck. Let's call it the fourteenth and go Valentine crazy.'

We started to plan the food. He said, 'First, we must not forget for one instant Hickory is Miss Lady's house, so ... let there be perfect tomato sandwiches, and let there be chicken salad, white meat only. Duty done, respects paid, now we can plan something quite fabulous.'

We ordered salmon sashimi, a baked Virginia ham with a salad of beets, radicchio and walnuts, raspberry palmiers and pink French champagne.

I said, 'You sure Corinth is ready for raw fish?'

'It's a fair question,' he said, 'but I'm going to ignore it. I'm willing to sacrifice everything to my colour scheme. Pink hyacinths everywhere and a net of rose petals to let down at midnight, and everyone has to wear pink. I mean *everyone*.'

I said, 'What about a cake?'

'That,' he said, 'will be dealt with on a need-to-know basis – and you don't need to know.'

About forty people were invited and Grice was on pink patrol, out front, wearing crushed strawberry. Anyone arrived had ignored the dress code, he had a bagful ties and scarves, get them pinked-up before they went in to greet the birthday boy. Miss Lady and Precious already had pale-shell ribbons in their hair, Etta was in bubblegum gingham and the hired help were all in carnation vests. I was in fuchsia and so was the woman playing the harp. It never was an instrument I cared for.

Tucker seemed happy, pushing Miss Lady around in her bathchair. You'd have thought it was her birthday the way she was holding court. He didn't look sixty, I will say. Then, he never really did a day's work, except run around after his mother. I liked him, though. Whatever else she may have done to ruin his life, Miss Lady had raised him to have perfect manners.

It was a perfect party for a perfect gentleman. I can't say I enjoyed it. Fact was, I didn't really know my place that night. I was there to make sure we did a good job, but I was there because he was a friend too. I couldn't mix with the hunting crowd because they knew I wasn't one of them. And I couldn't hang out with the help because I was wearing a dress from Neiman Marcus. One thing: I was right about the sashimi.

I nearly slipped away after the buffet was cleared and the sax combo were setting up ready for dancing, but I couldn't find Grice anywhere and I had to be sure the rose petals got released on cue. Just before midnight there was a long drum-roll, three of the waiters wheeled in a cardboard cake, size of a tank, and Grice come bursting out of the middle, singing 'You're the Top' in the style of Ethel Merman. Precious yipped and growled all the way through.

'Tell me truly,' he kept asking me all the next week. 'How was I?'

We were doing some corporate stuff for Bosque Oil, lunches, receptions. It was just grunt work. I said, 'You were a star, same as you were last time you asked me.'

'You don't sound very sincere,' he said. 'What's bugging you, anyway?'

I didn't know what was bugging me.

He said, 'What a party! Though I do say so myself. All the best people were there.'

I said, 'What in tarnation does that mean? The *best* people.' There was that side to him.

He said, 'You losing your sense of humour, Peggy Dewey? You feeling lacklustre? Disinclined to get out of your bed in the morning?'

'Yes,' I said. 'I'm gonna be fifty-seven next birthday.'

'I know an outfit does great parties,' he said.

I said, 'I don't want a party. I don't even like parties.'

He said, 'You just like making lists.'

It was true. I liked dotting every 'i' and crossing every 't' and making sure everyhing came out perfect. I hated the schmoozing. I said, 'All I do is work and go home. And I don't have a damn thing to show for it. Pay the rent. Find people their stupid party favours. What's the point of it? My friend Audrey can paint pictures good enough to hang on the wall. And Betty makes beautiful things with her sewing. I don't have the gift for anything like that.'

Then he said the nicest thing. He said, 'You have a gift for friendship, Peggy. Sitting there spinning your web, sending out letters, calling people up. Heck, you're still up with folk from high school. I mean, you could be creative too, if you really wanted. Make things out of dried seed-heads or something. But your best thing is being a good friend.'

We sent out for Singapore noodles and finished off the Bosque schedules. He said, 'Hey, friend, wanna play hookey? Wanna go to Ripley's Believe It Or Not?'

94

The next thing that happened was, State told Carla and Slick they couldn't do anything more for Betty. It was time for her to go home.

I hadn't spoken with Lois since our falling out over Kirk and the reel store job, but I had the strongest feeling I had to talk to her.

'Hey!' she said. 'How ya been?' Lois never did brood over cross words.

I said, 'I've been good. Wish I could say the same for Betty. She's on her last legs, Lo. They've done everything they can for her and now they're just keeping her comfortable.'

'Shit!' she said. 'How'd a thing like that happen?'

I said, 'Would you think of visiting? I know it's a long way, but it'd sure make Betty happy.'

'Oh, I dunno about that, Peg,' she said. 'I'm not much good around a sick room. I'd probably knock something over or pull out a tube or something.'

I said, 'There aren't any tubes.'

'Other thing is,' she said, 'I don't know that I can get away. I'm working all hours as it is.'

I really didn't want to hear about Lois's hard life. I said, 'How're the brats?'

'Yeah . . .' she said, 'Patrick's cute. Cory we don't see, but we keep hoping.'

I said, 'Kirk and Sandie?'

'Sandie's okay,' she said. 'Kirk's . . . kinda between jobs. How long do you reckon Betty has?'

I said, 'Weeks. I dunno. I'm going down there. Carla's nursing her, plus they have an agency nurse at night. But they need company, Lo, and nice surprises, to get them through the days.'

'I'll will think about it,' she said. 'I promise.'

I called Kath next. She said, 'I thought that didn't sound too good, when she had to have more of the rays. Will you get her some flowers, from me? Tell her I'm thinking of her.'

I said, 'Lois might visit.'

'Well that'll kill her or cure her!' she said. 'And how's she going on, being a gran?'

I said, 'She likes it. Must be mellowing at long last. Kirk's back home, though. Vern fixed him up with a job, but he left that under a kinda cloud. Well, you know what a temper he had when he was a kid. Lo reckons he's got arthritis of the joints, but I don't know. She's always made excuses for him. I'm starting to think he's just plum work-shy.'

Kath didn't say anything for a second or two. Then she said, 'Has he got it all over?'

I said, 'I don't know, Kath. Seems young for arthritis.'

Six a.m. my phone went. Kath said, 'Did I waken you? Only I've lain here all night thinking and I've decided, I'm coming.'

I said, 'Betty wouldn't expect you to do that.'

'I know she wouldn't,' she said, 'but if I can come, I will. You have to say your goodbyes in life. I shall just need a few days to make arrangements for my ladies.'

I closed up my apartment and drove down. Grice said, 'Go. I'll manage. Time Tucker found out what the worker ants do, anyway.'

Carla had explained to me, they were giving Betty another blast of rays but this time it was just to help with the pain. Palliative, they called it. I was dreading what I was gonna find. But I heard her voice as soon as I came through the door.

'Let her come in,' she said. 'I'm not a bit tired.'

Some places she was all blown out, some places, like her arms, she had dropped a lot of weight. Her belly looked like she was expecting. She had the drapes closed because the sun had been bothering her. We sat in the shadows and I gave her iced water, like Carla had told me. She had one of Audrey's sea views on the wall opposite her bed.

'Peggy,' she said, 'I just don't know what's gone wrong. I had the treatment like everyone said, but I just go from bad to worse. Carla never leaves my side hardly, and now they have a person come in at ten, sits here through the night. I don't like having a stranger sitting in my room.'

I said, 'Well, Carla has to get her sleep. Maybe now I'm here we can get by without strangers. You settle for me sitting here?'

'Why,' she said 'how long are you here for? Are you staying over?'

I was staying at the Pan American Motel, took the cheapest deal they had. I said, 'I'll be around for a while. If you'll have me.'

'I'd love it,' she said. 'And when I'm over this bad patch, we can go to the parks together. I haven't been to Southside Lions in the longest time. There's just the fifth I have to keep clear. What date is it today?'

It was July tenth. 'Plenty of time, then,' she said. 'Opportunity Day is August fifth.'

It was some recruiting event for Nutro Labs. 'Me and Slick have to get presented, up on the platform,' she said. 'It's to encourage people to sign on, when they hear our success story.'

I talked to Carla, after Betty had fallen asleep. I said, 'You realise she's talking about going to Houston on August fifth?'

'Sure,' she said. 'That's okay.'

I said, 'But she's not gonna be there.'

'Gives her something to aim for, though,' she said.

I said, 'It's just, we have Kath Pharaoh arriving next week, and maybe even Lois, and I don't see how we're gonna explain to your mom why folks are gathering to her bedside when she thinks she's getting well enough to star at Opportunity Day.'

'Mom's playing it both ways,' she said. 'Last week she had Slick checking out hotel prices for Christmas dinner, said she was through slaving for everybody and never getting a word of thanks. Next thing, she made me go through all her ten-cent necklaces and stuff with her, had to be done there and then, deciding how the family jewels get divided up. She knows the score. She just doesn't always want to talk about it.'

I said, 'Your dad been told?'

'Yeah,' she said. 'I don't know what his intentions are.'

Gayle had sent a note that prayer teams had been mobilised, and a cheque for five hundred dollars.

Carla said, 'We don't need money. Slick's generous, and anyways, night nurses don't cost that much. It'd just be nice for Mom if Deana'd take a turn once in a while or Delta'd show her face, bring the baby. It's eating her up she don't even know where Destiny Rae is. That's why I'm glad English Kath is coming. Have people around her. Save her having to look at my face all day long. No disrespect to Gayle, but a visit would have been worth more than any cheque.'

I said, 'Do you know how you got your name?'

She said, 'I have a horrible feeling it's connected with Princess Margaret or Jackie Kennedy Onassis.'

'Not at all,' I said. 'You were named for Gayle's first husband. We only ever knew him as Okey till he got killed in a B-47, crashed on landing at McConnell. Then everybody referred to him as First Lieutenant Carl Jackson. Your mom was expecting you and your dad was so cut up about Okey, you were named for him. He was a nice guy. Ask your dad about him, if he ever shows up.'

When Betty woke, she wasn't in such good shape. The treatment upset her insides and sometimes she had to have her sheets changed.

I tried to soothe her. I said, 'Honey, it's nothing. That washer-drier you have out there, looks like you could send a man to the moon in it.'

I sat with her for an hour and we looked through some of her albums. 'I want you to have these,' she said, 'when I'm gone. You can keep them, or you can let Crystal have them. She used to love them.'

I hated that kind of talk.

'Know what I'm really looking forward to?' she said. 'Seeing Prince

Charles a married man. I've waited long enough. And she's such a precious darling.'

I phoned Kath that night. I said, 'Can you bring something with Charles and Lady Di on it? They got any souvenir mugs or anything?'

'How many dozen would you like?' she said. 'Whole country's turned soft in the head. By the way, when you start looking for me at the airport, I've gone lilac.'

95

Lilac was right.

'That's meant to be a blue rinse,' she said, 'only they've got a new youngster at Pam's and she was so busy nattering about her boyfriend, I think she put the wrong shade on me. Still, I quite like it. Makes a nice change. Jolly Dame, they've got the salon called now. It's French. That's been Pam's Place as long as I've been going there, but now she's gone all continental. Next thing she'll be going unisex. I'll tell you one good thing, though. I reckon Mrs Thatcher's going to get us out of that Common Market mess.'

Betty was having a good day. Kath sat with her all afternoon, talking about the old days back at Drampton.

Kath said, 'Remember that time we all went to Ely market and they had tinned goods reduced, no labels?'

Herb Moon got a few surprise dinners outta that little excursion.

Betty said, 'And you tried on a pair of men's pants, right there in public. There was hardly even a curtain to go behind.'

Kath said, 'That was Dutch Redd's stall. He's still there. Course, that's all T-shirts and blue jeans now. He's still a dirty old bugger, though. Spying on you in your knickers.'

'So long ago,' Betty said. 'And to us it was a foreign country. You didn't even speak the same language. And the weather! Oh Peggy, driving in that fog. And then there was the monster, was supposed to be hiding in the fens. My babies used to have such nightmares. What was it called, Peggy? We used to hear it booming, even when we were safe inside the base.'

Kath winked at me. She said, 'I know the one you mean. I'll think what it was called in a minute. When it was out on the rampage, everybody stopped indoors, kept the bolt across. Terrible mouth they said it had on it. Lois! That was it! The Lois Moon. They reckoned by the time she was finished with you there'd be nothing left only a little pile of bones.'

Betty laughed. 'Shame on you, Kath,' she said. 'Lois is a changed person. When she heard I had to go into hospital again, she sent me a satin peignoir set from Bergdorf Goodman, all in a box and tissue paper and ribbons and all. So beautiful. Get Carla to show you. I made her put it away. It's too good to wear.'

That evening, Deana showed up with three of her brats. Dawn and Danni and Dixie, the baby, as everyone thought of her, but she was going on fifteen and there was nothing babylike about her. They were driving an old rust-bucket. Deana was still in a neck-brace from the time she totalled her vehicle, lost a boyfriend and a trip to Florida and gained a son-in-law. Carla reckoned the neck-brace had gone from being a medical necessity to a fashion habit.

They kinda filled up the apartment. Betty sitting in an armchair in a nice fresh robe.

'See all my lovely visitors?' she said. 'Now y'all tell Kath and Peggy here who you are and how old, because they don't know you.'

I seen Dixie rolling her eyes. Dawn and Danni were flipping through the TV channels.

I said, 'Your neck still troubling you, Deana?'

'It's the nerve in the bone,' she said. 'They say it'll never be right again.'

Betty said, 'Kath has come all the way from Norfolk, England. You remember when we lived in England, Deana? You remember that cute little school you went to?'

Dixie said, 'I'm getting a soda.'

Deana said, 'Yeah. Get me one too.'

'And Peggy's girl, Crystal, you remember her, Deana? She used to play dollies with you and Sherry. Crystal got married on a sail-boat. You ever hear of anybody doing that?'

Deana said, 'I'm getting the VCR fixed, ready for Lady Diana's wedding.'

Betty said, 'Why don't y'all come round here, watch it live, keep me company?'

Deana said, 'I ain't getting up in the middle of the night.'

'Well,' Betty said, 'that's a pity, because I'd be able to tell you who all the royals are. I know them all. How about you, Dixie? You gonna come and watch the royal wedding with Gramma?'

Dixie sighed. 'Dunno,' she said. 'What is it?'

I said, 'You working, Deana?'

She gave me the evil eye.

Betty said, 'Deana does great crochet. Carla, show Kath and Peggy the toaster-cover Deana crocheted.'

I said, 'How about you girls?' Dawn was nineteen, Danni was seventeen. They were old enough to be doing something more'n sit around all day chewing gum.

Betty said, 'Danni wants to be a beauty therapist, if she can just get a start someplace. And Dawn was at Piggly-Wiggly, only they had to lay people off. Any news there, Dawn? Any sign of them setting on again?'

I never heard anything like it. A person is willing to work, they'll find something.

Carla said, 'Deana, you gonna help out with the shopping this week? I wrote a list.'

Deana said, 'Don't know that I have enough gas.'

I said, 'I'll do it.'

'Yes,' Betty said. 'Peggy could take Kath. She'd love to see what wonderful supermarkets we have here.'

'Well,' Carla said, giving me a meaningful look, 'that'd be very kind of Peggy. I'd just hate Deana to feel she wasn't being allowed to help out. I'd really hate for her to feel I was running the whole show here, keeping her from making her contribution.'

Kath said, 'That's right. And anyway, we've got supermarkets. We've got one in Lynn has ten checkouts.'

'I'll do it next time,' Deana said. 'I'm waiting on a cheque.'

When they were leaving, Betty started scrabbling in her pocket-book. She put a roll of bills in Dawn's hand.

'You give this to your mom, now,' she said. 'I can't see her going short.'

We walked out front to say goodbye. Deana had made chenille slip-covers for the car seats. Looked like she had used an old bed-spread.

Kath whispered, 'Watch that suspension when they all get in.' It was something to see. The car nearly bottomed.

'What a crew,' she said, as they pulled away. 'There's not a spark of life in them.'

I said, 'You're right. And yet when they were kids, when they used to come and stay with Betty, she used to do all kinds of stuff with them. Sewing for their dolls, having fairy tea-parties. I don't know what went wrong.'

'Now, another thing I wonder about is,' she said, 'legs on them like that, why do they wear them shiny leggings that cling so? Don't they ever take a look in a mirror?'

I said to Carla, later, 'Deana and her girls don't appear to understand how sick your mom is.'

'Well, they've been told,' she said. She looked so tired.

I said, 'Now, me and Kath'll take your shopping list. I don't mean to let Deana off light, but Betty's right, Kath'd love to do it. Ten checkouts! Wait till she sees MajorMart.'

'Thanks, Aunty Peggy,' she said. 'Deana would have wriggled out of doing it one way or another. She always waits till we're out of milk. Then she calls to say her engine's overheating.'

I said, 'When do you expect Sherry?'

'Don't know,' she said. 'Soon as the dream-catcher season slows down, I guess.'

Sherry had a small business in Santa Fe, selling blankets and Indian stuff.

Kath did love MajorMart. I lost her one time. Found her back in the breakfast-product canyon with a box of Froot Loops in her hand.

'I shall have to bring my camera in here,' she said. 'If I don't take a picture, May'll never believe it.'

PERFECT!

Balcony scene at Buckingham Palace : To huge cheers from the crowd, Prince Charles kisses his beautiful bride
One little bridesmaid watches, two others clinging to Princess Diana are too tired after their long day

INSIDE: More news and pictures 2, 3, 4, 7, 9, 10, 11; Femail—The Dress 13-15; Party Time 16-17; The TV Battle 19; Nigel Dempster 23; Going Away 24-25

96

Slick had bought Betty a new TV, so she wouldn't miss the least thing of the wedding or be disappointed if she couldn't get a good picture. She wouldn't have a video recorder in the house, even though it would have meant she could watch the wedding over and over. She thought it might give out harmful rays. So Slick got her the widest-screen set he could find. Took two men to carry it in and fix it up, and Betty had a chair put in the bathroom so she could hide in there and they wouldn't see her in night-attire, as she put it.

'You spoil me, Slick Bonney,' she said when she saw the size of that sucker.

'I do my best,' he said.

I felt so for Slick, watching Betty fade away. I said to him one time, 'You won't stay away, just 'cause me and Kath are in town? Any time you want to take a turn at her bedside, you just say and we'll make ourselves scarce.'

'Thanks all the same,' he said, 'but I think she's happier having a woman around. I'd do something wrong. Get yelled at.'

We strung Union flag pennants round the room, that Kath had brought with her, and Betty drank her iced water out of the Charles and Diana commemorative mug. She had a pink carnation pinned to her robe, so she'd feel more like a guest than a mere spectator.

We watched the whole thing. Never bothered going to bed. They showed people camping out on the streets of London, ready to see the procession. Kath said, 'That's what me and May done for the Coronation. May brought a Lilo bed for us to sit on, only she forgot the pump and we didn't have enough puff to blow it up the hard way. I wouldn't do it now. You get a better view watching it on the telly. You can get up and make a brew when you want one, without losing your place.'

Betty was our expert commentator. She knew all the names. Who was cousins to who. Bottom line was, they were all kin. Royals from Norway and Greece and places I didn't even know had any. Ronald and Nancy Reagan. Kath remarked it was a shame we had to ruin a great country, having people running amok with guns.

I said, 'Great country is right. The land of the free. Free to bear arms.'

'Free to shoot the president,' she said.

But, as I pointed out to her, our president was alive and well and attending St Paul's cathedral in the company of crowned heads. Took more than a drifter like Hinckley to finish Ronnie Reagan.

Betty said, 'I agree with Peggy. He's my kind of president. And I just loved him in *The Hasty Heart*.'

There was a long build-up, waiting to see Lady Diana's dress. Then we only caught a flash of it and she was bundled up inside a little horse-drawn carriage with her father, the Earl of Spencer. Why they didn't use a stretch limousine, I shall never understand. By the time she got to the church that dress looked like it could have used a steam-iron. Betty wouldn't hear any criticism, though.

'It's meant to look that way,' she said. 'Top designers have been working on it for months. Clouds of billowing silk. Deana wore a similar style herself when she married Dwayne.'

Of course, when Deana Gillis married Dwayne it wasn't just the dress that was billowing.

We all felt so flat after it was through.

Betty said, 'I wish they'd let us see the greeting line and everything. I'd love to see what gifts they got.'

She watched the edited highlights until she fell asleep and I took Kath for a drive around the old neighbourhood. Took her past Topperwein High.

'Well, that looks like a fancy place,' she said. 'You must have had a sight more schooling than I did, Peg. Me and John Pharaoh went to Smeeth Elementary, but half the time we didn't even get there. If the weather was bad or Dad needed John to help him with the eels, or Mam could get me a turn at the beet singling, we just didn't go. And that wasn't just us. If you were needed at home, for washday or anything, that's where you stayed. Then the Chaplin girls, there was nine of them, and they only had three or four pair of boots between them, so they had to take turns going to school. Nobody thought anything of it. Now you'd have an inspector knocking at your door, telling you your business. If they'd have come round in our day, they'd have found theirselves on the wrong end of an eel glave. Our mam didn't think much of book-learning. Tell you the truth, John Pharaoh never did get the hang of reading and writing. He could add up, though. He was handy that way.'

I said, 'But you had magazines in your house. First time we came there, I remember you showing us.'

'Yes, but I always had to read them out to him. Pick bits out he'd like to hear. I cottoned on to things like that faster than he did. I'd have liked a bit more schooling if I could have had it, but I've managed all right.'

I told her about high school. I said, 'See, me and Betty were never friends back then. Those Future Homemaker girls were always getting up cupcake sales. I thought they were pretty dull. If I wasn't outside pitching a softball, I was inside playing volleyball. And I was prom queen in my junior year. Senior year we had a Sadie Hawkins Hop.'

Kath didn't know what that was. I said, 'It's a dance, where the girls get to ask the boys. I guess we had Women's Liberation and we didn't even realise it.'

She said, 'So who did you ask?'

I asked Larry Mace, Class President. I said, 'We'll have to ask Betty who was her drag. It sure wasn't Slick Bonney.'

Kath hadn't realised Slick went right back to our school days.

I said, 'He was a Future Farmer of America. Won prizes for his bantams, and I think he was on the track team too, though you wouldn't have thought it, size of his waistline before he started on these Lipo pills.'

She said, 'Tickles me how he tiptoes around Betty, trying to please her. Like she'd ever say boo to a goose. He does love her so. How come they never got wed?'

'Not for Slick's want of asking,' I said. 'Fact is, she's still married to Ed.'

We drove back past Mom's old house, so I could show Kath where I grew up. I had told her how things lay between me and my sister Connie.

'I know you've had a falling out,' she said. 'But if you want to see if she's at home, I can sit outside in the motor. I don't mind waiting. Now you're here, that seems a pity not to bury the hatchet.'

I said, 'I don't want to, Kath. It's a closed chapter. I don't even know why I brought you here. There's nothing worth showing you.'

The old place looked closed up anyhow. Maybe her and Bobby Earl won the lottery.

'Well, now we're quits,' she said. 'You've seen where I was dragged up and I've seen where you were. Tell you what, Peg, we've both moved on.'

When we got back, the doctor was making a house call. Betty had had a kind of a seizure and Carla had thought it was the end. It wasn't, though. They gave her a shot, made her sleep some more, and when she woke, about seven, she wanted iced tea, lime jello and company.

'I don't know what all that was about,' she said. 'All my life I never got sick. Now everything's going wrong.'

I said, 'You want to see if they're still showing re-runs of the wedding?'

'No,' she said. 'Yes. Why? Did I miss it?'

I said to Carla, 'Now what?'

'I'm getting her back into State tomorrow,' she said. 'Time has come to move some family ass.' She got on to Ed, and to Sherry. Then Lois called. Carla put me on.

Lo said, 'I'm coming. I decided. Carla says she don't have long.'

I said, 'I don't know. She was talking us through Lady Di's wedding this morning. She just had a setback this afternoon is all.'

'I'm out of the door,' she said. 'I just have a board package to deliver, then I'm on my way. Will you pick me up? I'll get Herb to call, tell you what time my plane gets in.'

I said, 'Will do. We're at the Pan American, got their weekly rate. You want me to get you a room?'

'Yeah,' she said, 'and, Peg? Is Betty all hooked up to stuff? She got machines keeping her alive?'

I said, 'You've seen too many hospital shows.'

'Okay,' she said. 'So definitely no machines and no tubes?'

'Definitely,' I said.

'I'm on my way,' she said.

I looked in on Betty before we left. I said, 'Time to break out that fancy New York negligée. The Lois Moon Experience is heading your way.'

97

I left Kath taking turns with Carla and Slick, went to pick up Lois up from the airport. I could see her big red hair bobbing towards me as she came through Arrivals, weaving in and out, trying to get past the slow movers. She was carrying more weight than she used to, but nothing else had changed. She never stopped talking, even when she was filling her mouth with candy, which was most of the time.

'Christ, they've taken the joy out of flying,' she said. 'All that time on the freeway. Then all that time waiting in line to check your bag. Least when we were Dependants we could just climb aboard the transport and go. Wasn't always my destination of choice, but at least you didn't have to get felt-up by some security dyke before they'd let you near a plane. And those cabin girls! Why do they have to talk to you like you're five years old? What kind of moron do they think can't work out a seat belt? I tell you. They giving Betty stuff for the pain?'

I said, 'Yes. She's going peaceful. We're just hoping she doesn't have no more seizures. Every time she gets one, she's confused afterwards. It's because the cancer has gone into her brain.'

Lo said, 'Oh my God, Peg. Don't tell me any more.'

I said, 'She knows you're coming though. She's so excited. You ever considered, Lo, the only time people make a real effort for you is when you're dying?'

'I guess,' she said 'This is the weirdest trip I ever took, no two ways. And I've been working right up to the last minute. I've had this divine eight-room in the Wyatt, it's a co-op, pre-war, view across to the lake, fireplaces, two maids' rooms, it's the dog's cojones, found a buyer and then the board turned him down, so I had to start over, showing it again. I mean, I knew I could sell it, it's such a gem. It's just they're so goddamned particular. Anyway, I found them an Arab. He's happy. They're happy. I have to be back for the closing. Then I'll be happy. He'll probably bring the money in cash. In his Louis Vuitton.'

I said, 'Ed's on his way. And you know Kath's here?'

'Yeah?' she said. 'Imagine that. You think there'll be a gathering of the clans when my time comes? There won't 'cause there'll be none of you left. I'll see you all out. How about Gayle and Mrs Full-Bird Colonel?'

I said, 'Gayle and Lemarr are doing a healing tour of Kentucky and Missouri. But they're saying prayers for Betty. Audrey's disappeared. Last we heard, she was baling out her English gentleman. He had troubles of a financial nature.'

'No shit?' she said. 'You think she had to give back that diamond splinter?'

I said, 'We're nearly there. You want to go right in, or get a coffee or something?'

'I'll see her first,' she said, 'while my courage is up. Does she look real sick?'

I said, 'I guess. I've been around her so much this week, I'm not sure any more. Sometimes she wants to lie there quiet, but she still likes to have people sit with her. Then she perks up, wants to talk. She talks about stuff I don't think I'd be bothered with if I was dying.'

'Yeah?' she said. 'What, like meatloaf recipes?'

They were just changing her sheets when we got there. That was always a signal for her to get upset. I hadn't thought to warn Lois about that. She just barged right in.

'Okay, Gillis,' she said. 'What are you doing in the sack this time of day? Call yourself a homemaker? I want you out of that cot, get these floors waxed, get this gear squared away.'

Then she saw Betty was crying. 'Betty, darling,' she said, 'don't cry now! I didn't mean it!'

Betty was going through that great bag of hers, looking for Kleenex. 'Oh, Lois,' she said. 'I'm in such a fix. I had a little accident. They keep on happening and I feel so bad, these poor nurses having to clean up after me.'

'Will you stop that!' Lo said. 'Just quit being so goddarned considerate. It's what they do. They get paid. And all they have to do is drop the stuff in the hamper. Jeez, Betty. Listen to you anybody'd think they had to haul those sheets down to the river or something. Bash them with rocks to get them clean. You ever hear of a thing called a hospital laundry? There are people down there waiting for your sheets. You are keeping people in employment. Think of that. You could be the difference between some little beaner going home with a paycheque, feeding his family, paying his dues, or getting laid off. You keep those dirty sheets coming, girl. You are helping keep some nose-miner off welfare.'

She kept it up for a full hour till Slick come back to take another turn. He musta wondered what the heck was going on, as he came back along the corridor, Lois's voice booming away and Betty squealing for mercy.

I said, 'It's okay. She's laughing, not crying. The comedy act has arrived.'

But when we got out of there, left Slick to it, Lo looked shattered.

We drove to the motel and Lois checked in while I showered. Kath was resting. She had been with Betty, reading, all morning – reading her the papers, about the royal honeymoon.

I said, 'Lo's arrived. You coming out for fajitas?'

So the three of us drove to Bravo Bravo, and the first beer didn't touch the sides.

Lois said, 'Jeez, I don't know if I can go through that again.'

I said, 'You don't have to. Betty just wants folk around. Doesn't have to be non-stop cabaret.'

'Well,' she said, 'seems to me she has enough visitors can do *gloom*.

It's like a chapel of rest in there already. Hell, at least I got a laugh out of her.'

I said, 'Lois, I'm just trying to help. You tired yourself out in there, and you probably tired Betty too.'

'*Tired* her?' she said. 'She's about to rest for all eternity. What's wrong with *tiring* her, as you put it? Besides, it's a known fact that laughter is good for the health. I need another beer. And who was the sadsack in the white socks?'

I said, 'That was Slick.'

She roared. 'Slick! Somebody with a big sense of irony give him that, or did he just get the wrong name? He ever think of changing it to Hump? Or Stump.'

Kath said, 'I don't see why you have to pick on him. He's a kind man. And he loves Betty.'

I said, 'Yes, anybody else you'd care to take a poke at? I mean, I know you only just got here, but you're a fast study . . .'

'I know,' she said. 'Let's have a row. I'll go out, come in again, do something that really frosts you, like *smile* or say something *carefree*, and then we can have it all out. You can rub my nose in everything I ever did wrong . . .'

I said, 'Not enough time.'

'. . . we can have a full and frank. Where is that moron waitress with my beer? Clear the air about all the ways I ever offended your tight-ass sensibilities. You up for that, Kath?'

Kath said, 'You really want to fight with me, Lois?' She said it so calm and even, but there was something dangerous in it. Lois quieted down.

The girl had brung a mountain of nachos and we sat in silence for a while. Not a one of us was hungry, but we still kept pecking at them. Then Lois caught hold of my hand, on the way to the dish. 'I'm sorry,' she said.

I looked across to Kath. So far from home, caught up in stupid arguing. I grabbed her hand. Lois grabbed the other one. We looked like we were trying to make contact with the dead.

Lois said, 'I'm sorry, I'm sorry, I'm sorry.'

The fajitas arrived.

'You must admit, though, girls,' she said. 'Betty's guy is definitely more like a Stump than a Slick.'

Kath just shook her lilac head.

98

I stopped knowing what day of the week it was. I hardly even knew the time of day. We just rotated back and forth, motel, hospital, Betty's place, coffee shop.

I left Kath at the mall, getting a few things for Betty, and I drove across to State. First thing I saw when I stepped out of the elevator was Lois, standing by the ice machine, talking to an old guy. It was only when he spoke I realised it was Ed.

He still wore a crewcut. He was still kinda hard and square. Only he had grown wider, same as the rest of us, and his face had deep, deep lines. He looked like a real old boy who still liked to stay in shape. An old grandpop who did push-ups.

Lo said, 'You know who this is, Ed?'

He shook his head.

She said, 'It's Peggy Dewey. From 96th. You remember Vern?'

He chuckled. 'Vern Dewey!' he said. 'That young son of a gun. Well, I'll be darned.'

I said, 'How're you doing, Ed?'

'Good,' he said. 'I'm doing good. Vern okay?'

I didn't trouble him with the details.

Lois said, 'I was just saying to Ed, us girls have kept up all these years. It's a pity the boys didn't do the same. Herb's always wondering where everyone got to.'

Let him wonder, was what I thought. I knew Vern wouldn't give a pig's patootie to know where Ed was at. Nor Herb neither, after the business with Kirk.

Sherry had arrived too. Her and Carla were sitting in with Betty.

I said, 'You still in Warsaw, Ed?'

'Still in Warsaw,' he said.

I said, 'Long-distance driving? Is that what I heard?'

'Pretty much,' he said.

'Oh,' Lois said, digging me in the ribs, 'there's Mr Stump. I'll just go and have a word to him.'

I hadn't even noticed Slick come in.

I said, 'Well, it's a sad thing to see you under these circumstances, Ed.' I was talking like I was at the wake already.

'Yup,' he said. 'I come down on Route 65, far as Nashville, crossed into Arkansas at Memphis, slept in the rig.'

I said, 'I'm in Dallas now. Crystal's in Maine.'

'Yup,' he said, like he already knew. 'Could have gone right on down to the Pontchartrain interchange and then come across on Route 10 . . .'

Lois was flagging me to walk with him a while, away from where she was standing with Slick.

'. . . I come the Fort Worth way, though. Come round on the Lyndon B. Johnson Freeway and then south on 35.'

When Sherry come out of Betty's room, snuffling into a Kleenex, Ed figured it was his turn and Slick was right behind him. Carla came to the door, gave me a tired wave.

'Dad,' she said. 'I'd appreciate it if you'd wait a while and let Slick come on through. Mom's asking for him.'

Ed went back to his seat, never said anything. I was cat-napping, Lo was flicking through the property pages. Suddenly she said, 'Uh-oh. There's some kinda Spandex Freak Show just tumbled outta the elevator.'

It was Deana, with Dawn and Dixie. They went into a huddle with Ed, never even spoke to us. A nurse went in to Betty. Then another one. I was just starting to wonder what was keeping Kath when she appeared. She had brought cut flowers and cologne.

I walked across to Betty's room. Thought I'd wave to her at least. Let her know we were there. I couldn't really see her, though. Just Carla standing there and Slick hunched over in his chair. A nurse come and shut the door in my face.

I heard Deana say, 'It's not right. We're family. We shouldn't be waiting out here.'

Dixie went to get a soda from the machine. Lois started clearing candy-wrappers out of her bag. Ed was cracking the visor of his Wooster Cement baseball cap back and forth. Kath just sat there, gazing into space.

Then she started to gather her things together. 'There's no sense just sitting,' she said. 'Why don't I come back later? You give her the flowers. And just dab a bit of cologne on her pillow. That's got a nice refreshing smell. Tell her I'll be back later.'

I said, 'Don't go, Kath.' And I heard something inside Betty's room. Maybe it was just somebody moving a chair. Or a voice. Something, though. And Lois heard it too. She looked at me and looked away again fast.

It was a while before Carla come out. 'She's gone,' she said. 'Five minutes ago. She's gone.'

Deana started howling. Dawn followed suit.

I heard Lois say, 'Shit!'

Carla said we could go in and see her, if we wanted, after Slick and the family.

I said, 'You all right, honey?'

'No, Aunty Peggy,' she said. 'I'm not one bit all right.'

We waited in line. Slick come out eventually, didn't look anywhere except down and there was a nurse had hold of his arm, taking him somewhere private I suppose. Then Deana and her brats and Sherry went in, keening and holding each other up, and Ed, shuffling in behind them. He looked kind of bashful. That just left us, plus a domestic pushing a floor-polisher around.

Lois said, 'Would it be really bad form if I didn't go in and see her?'

I said, 'No. Idiot.'

She said, 'You going in?'

I said, 'I guess.'

She said, 'You going, Kath?'

'Oh yes,' she said. 'I believe in it. That's all part of it. That's how you start getting used to the idea they're really gone.'

We all went together.

'See?' I said to Lo. 'It's only Betty. There's nothing to be afraid of.'

There was, though. It was the first time I ever had seen a dead person.

Lois whispered, 'It's like getting in to see the Pope or something. It's like meeting somebody who's done something really amazing.'

That was about right. Betty had upped and left us. Little Betty, who never went anywhere or did anything.

Kath kissed her goodbye, so I did too, but really we'd said goodbye the night before. Only we didn't know it at the time. Lo stayed far back from the bed.

She said, 'Is she cold?'

She wasn't. But she was definitely gone. There was no arguing against it. I guess that was what I didn't like about it. We couldn't play it again.

Just as we were leaving, Lo changed her mind and went right over to her. She touched her hand, fluffed her hair.

'Bye, Pie-Crust Queen,' she said. 'Rest in peace. God knows you earned it.'

Once every twenty-five years or so Lois does something makes you realise why you love her.

When we come out, Ed was down the hall, breaking his knuckles on the soda machine. There was no sign of Carla and the rest of them.

Kath said, 'Drop of the hard stuff. That's what I need.'

So we drove round to O'Malley's, to drink Betty God speed.

Lo said, 'Peg, I noticed she had a couple of whiskers under her chin. Will they get rid of them? Will the mortician get rid of them, before people come viewing her?'

I said, '*What?*'

'Whiskers,' she said. 'You have to promise me now, if I do go before you, you'll make sure I'm tidied up before they put me on display. Bring your tweezers. It's no use leaving it to Herb. He'll be too busy picking out the wood for my casket.'

I said, 'You are nuts.'

'Very possibly,' she said. 'But I still don't want people knowing I have facial hair.'

Kath said, 'The fourth of August – it's the Queen Mother's birthday.'

Lo said, 'Well there you go. Betty always looked for a royal tie-in.'

It sure beat dying on Nutro Labs Opportunity Day.

99

Twenty-four hours after Betty passed over, all hell broke loose.

Sherry wanted her cremated. She said she'd take the urn back to New Mexico, scatter the ashes in the desert, dust to dust and all that. Slick said Betty would want a plain Christian burial with a sitting-up and a Methodist preacher. Ed said why didn't Slick Bonney butt out of what only concerned family and if that was too hard for him to understand, he'd be happy to take him outside and make it real clear. He said this even though he had his explaining hand bound up. I guess the soda machine had won.

Then there was Lois, worried about getting back for the closing on the Wyatt apartment. Danni got in a fight with another girl and came home with three teeth knocked out. It was over a guy. And Deana announced that her mom was getting nothing short of a top-line sealer casket, limousines, notices in the paper, everything, and she was willing to go into debt the rest of her life to pay for it.

'Let her,' Carla said. 'Soon as Mom's laid to rest, I'm outta here, address unknown.'

I said, 'Not unknown to me, I hope.'

'No,' she said. 'Just to all these misfits, claim to be my kin.'

I was on the peace-keeping team. Me and Kath were negotiating with Slick; Lois and Carla were trying to get Ed to see reason. By the time we struck a deal, Deana had already picked out a mahogany casket and a black knit two-piece from Barney's Big 'n' Beautiful.

So they got a plot in the Live Oak Garden of Rest. Just a single. Slick conceded it wasn't the right time to discuss whether she'd have liked space kept for her de facto or for her lawful wedded. As Lois said, 'Once Ed climbs back into his rig, he'll soon forget. Let a little more cement dust settle between his ears and he won't care if you bury Mickey Mouse on top of her.

They booked the Converse Assembly of God for two-thirty, with viewing of the body the evening before. None of us went for that.

Kath said, 'I did it with John Pharaoh, but only 'cause there wasn't anybody else to do it. I'd already took my leave. I like things to be done properly, but I don't like to see a meal made of it.'

Lois said, 'S'okay, Kath. You can leave that to Deana. I think she may be planning to throw herself into the grave.'

I phoned the Passy Tabernacle. They played 'Morning Has Broken' while you held. Gayle and Lemarr were on the road, of course, but the girl on the switchboard said my message would be passed along.

Lois said, 'I bet it will, too. Gayle'll need to stand down the prayer squad. Reassign it where it's still needed.'

Two days later we got a package delivered by FedEx. A Bible cake, for the funeral tea, selected from the Passy Tabernacle Gift Catalogue, and a video cassette containing a personal tribute from Pastor Gayle.

Carla called Deana. She said, 'Can you bring your VCR round?'

'No,' she said. 'It's broke.'

Dixie come around soon after, meant to be helping make sandwiches.

Carla said, 'Since when has your mom been living with a broken VCR?'

Dixie said, 'It ain't broke. The repo man took it.'

Me and Kath and Lois got our hair done, then we went for pasta. They were having funeral meats back at Betty's after the burying, but I had to drive Lois straight out to the airport.

She said, 'Well, I guess we should be eating chicken pot-pie and drinking iced tea, in memory of Betty, but I'm having red wine in the biggest glass they have.'

We got a jug.

I said, 'You getting collected at the other end?'

'No,' she said, 'I left my run-about parked at Kennedy. I'm going straight to my office, put in some catch-up time.'

Kath said, 'How are your nippers going on? I still haven't seen any pictures.'

Lo brung out a little wallet with photos of Cory. He was just a baby when they were taken.

'I don't have anything recent,' she said. 'He's two years old and I don't have a good picture of him. But that's Marisa for you. She's a bitch. Just 'cause things didn't work out between her and Kirk, don't mean she has to punish us. It breaks Herb's heart. All the stuff he'd like to be doing with Cory.'

I said, 'Doesn't Kirk get access?'

'No,' she said. 'Well, he probably could if he hired an attorney but so far he didn't.'

Kath was studying the photos. 'And how about Kirk?' she said. 'Peg tells me he's not been well.'

Lo said, 'He's getting physio, help loosen him up. He'll be okay.'

Kath said, 'And what's his temper like these days? He still got a paddy on him?'

Lois said, 'He's twenty-eight, Kath. You're talking about him like he's still a brat.'

She drained her glass. Kath drained hers.

Kath said, 'No, well, I just wondered . . . He seems to have trouble keeping in work. I just wondered.'

Slick came to the house just before two, wearing the identical same jacket as Ed. They were both sweating, neither of them being jacket kinda men. I was at the window, watching for the limos. A car I recognised pulled up and Grice Terry climbed out, carrying a cushion wreath of yellow rosebuds. I ran out to him. I said, 'I couldn't believe my eyes. You drove all this way for a person you only knew for five minutes? You're such a darling boy.'

I hadn't shed many tears since the afternoon we said farewell to Betty, but I sure made up for it when I seen Grice. He gave me a handkerchief, never been used.

I said, 'And you're wearing mourning, too. It suits you.'

'Thank you,' he said. 'I'm having a dry run, ready for Miss Lady.'

I said, 'Why? Is she fading?'

'No,' he said. 'She's got the yard people working all hours. She's re-designing the flower beds.'

Just then the hearse and cars turned on to Gibb.

Grice said, 'I'll move my car. I'll follow behind when you move off.'

Everybody had come out front for the arrival of the casket.

Lois whispered, 'Dewey, who's the arm candy?'

There were carnations from the gang, and roses from Carla and Ed and Slick. Then, one side of the casket, there was a solid slab chrysanthemums with 'MOM' picked out in white, and other side there was one said 'GRAMMA'.

There were a few there from the old days. Arlene Pickett, née Wilday, used to be in Sewing Club with Betty. The Siro twins. Mrs Siro always checked the death notices. She loved a funeral. I guess it ran in the family.

The preacher called Betty 'Elizabeth'. He said her life was a fine example of the worthiness of modest achievements and devotion to family. He asked us to remember Edward in his bereavement.

Somebody near to me said, 'And Slick. Don't forget Slick.'

It was Kath. She had said it loud enough that folks turned and looked at her.

The preacher said, 'Let us also remember at this time Deana, Sherry, Carla, Dawn, Danni and Dixie.'

It seemed like Delta and Destiny Rae had been air-brushed out of the picture.

They played 'The Lord Is My Shepherd' and 'Lead, Kindly Light'. Then we followed the bier round to Live Oak. I found myself standing beside Sherry when we got to the graveside.

I said, 'It was a lovely service, honey.'

'Intense,' she said.

After they lowered the casket, Ed and the girls went up to say a final farewell. Ed saluted with his busted hand, chewing away at the inside of his cheek. After family, we went up, with Slick. Me one side of him, Kath the other. He was holding himself so hard against breaking down he felt like he was armour-plated.

Lois was the last to leave the graveside.

I said, 'If you're gonna catch that plane . . .'

I took the Loop to the airport, but there was still traffic. We were running things close.

I said, 'I'm glad you came, Lo. I hope you're glad too.'

She was crying. She said, 'I wish to God it was me they just lowered into that hole.'

I could hardly believe my ears. I said, 'Lo? What kinda talk is that?'

She just shook her head.

I said, 'Are you sick?' I knew she wasn't sick.

I said, 'Flying home to Herb and Sandie's little baby and all. You realise, out of all of us, you're the only one left still got your airman? You're the only one left has grandbabies and a real family.'

Still the tears kept coming.

I said, 'Do you have depression? You might have. Could be your diet, or something. Running around, cutting these deals. You probably don't eat right.'

'My life's shit,' was all she would say.

I said, 'You *are* depressed. You should see a doctor. Tell him you just had a bereavement. He'll give you something.'

I pulled round to the drop-off point. She looked in the vanity mirror. 'Now I even look shit,' she said.

She pulled her valise out of the trunk and we hugged.

I said, 'Will you see a doctor?'

'It ain't a doctor thing,' she said.

She started to go, but she came back for another hug. 'Hey!' she said. 'I'm okay. Forget my stupid crying. Forget I ever spoke.'

She walked backward into the terminal building, shouting all the way. 'And tell that infant you're dating *he is cute*. Tell him, any time he wants to come to New York . . .'

I yelled, 'He is *not* my date. He is a one hundred per cent homosexual gay faggot.'

There was a couple walking by, lost control of their luggage cart.

'Can't hear you,' she yelled back, 'you'll have to speak up.'

•••

Blend two tablespoons Amos, 4:5 with two cups Jeremiah, 6:20. Cream with one cup Judges, 5:25. Gradually beat in four cups First Kings, 4:22 and six medium Jeremiah. 17:11. Add two tablespoons First Samuel, 14:13, three cups Numbers, 17:18, three cups First Samuel, 30:12, half cup of Judges, 4:19 , good teaspoon of Second Chronicles, 9:9 and a pinch of Leviticus, 2:13

Bake at 300 degrees until a skewer comes out clean.

•••

100

The evening after we buried Betty, Ed started his long drive back to Indiana and Grice was heading home too. The rest of us gathered at Slick's place so we could hear Pastor Gayle's recorded eulogy.

'My dear friends,' she said. 'How it grieves me I can't be with you today. You who were so often there for me . . .'

Dawn said, 'You see the size of that diamond?'

'. . . Betty has been taken from us so young. I know you'll be asking, Why? I know you'll be asking if God hasn't made some big mistake taking a good soul like Betty from her loved ones, while sinners live to see another day. I don't have an answer. But I do have a wonderful message of hope. The word of God and its message of good news. The witness of Scripture is that even at this dark hour, nothing can separate us from the love of God . . .'

Dixie said, 'Can I get a soda?'

'. . . For I am persuaded that neither death nor life, nor angels nor principalities nor powers, nor things present nor things to come, nor height nor depth, nor any other created thing, shall be able to separate us from the love of God, which is in Christ Jesus our Lord. Romans, 8:38. Let me tell you the story of the disciples on the road to Emmaus . . .'

Deana said, 'Crying out loud. Can't you fast-forward through this stuff?'

[359]

'. . . Two disciples were on the road to Emmaus. They had seen Lord Jesus die on the cross. They were discouraged and afraid. They were running away from their pain. But as they walked along, the Risen Lord came and walked beside them. And they didn't even know it was Him. They poured out their sorrows to Him and still they didn't know Him, until He took bread with them and blessed it and broke it and gave it to them. Then they recognised Him. He vanished from their sight. But He left them with new hope. He showed them his victory over death and filled them with hope . . . May the Risen Lord walk with you, Deana and Sherry and Carla. Lean on Jesus! Whoever believes in Him should not perish but have eternal life. John, 3:15.'

Then an electric piano started up and she sang 'The Old Rugged Cross'.

Deana said, 'I've had enough of this.'

Carla said, 'Why don't you button your lip and show some respect?'

Deana said, 'You speak to me like that. I'm the one owed respect. I'm the eldest.'

'Then act like it,' Carla said. 'Hell, Deana, you can't even watch a five-minute tape without griping. And your brats are as bad. Can't even turn up to Mom's burying dressed respectful.' Danni had worn a jeans skirt, didn't cover more than the bare necessities.

Sherry said, 'This a really bad scene.'

'Yeah?' Deana said. 'Who asked you? Why don't you hit the road? We've been managing just fine around here without you. No reason for you to stay. There ain't nothing for you.'

Carla said, 'You're something, Deana. You forget those manners Mom taught you? We're guests here, in Slick's house.'

Deana was on her feet. 'And there's nothing for you neither,' she yelled at Slick. His eyes were burning.

Kath grabbed her by her jersey. She said, 'I've a mind to wash your mouth out with soap. I don't care how old you are.'

Dawn said, 'Come on, Mom. Let's go.'

Deana said, 'When I'm ready. When I've put this English retard straight. Come over here, hogging Mom's last days, keeping us from her. And you!' She started jabbing at me. 'Turning Mom against us.'

I said, 'Deana, even you couldn't manage that.'

'Pair of old lesbos,' she said, 'hanging around my mom. And that other one. I know about her. She went with the Devil and got a baby!'

Kath swung at her, but she missed. Deana was out the door with all the other Ds. Carla had her head in her hands.

Kath said, 'When she was a nipper, I used to think she got paddled too much. Now I'm not so sure. She could do with a good hiding today.'

'Intense,' Sherry said.

Slick was looking like a tank just rolled over him.

I looked outside. Deana and her girls were standing beside that heap of junk they drove, staring under the hood.

I went out. I said, 'Problem?'

Dawn said, 'Yeah. Battery's flat.'

I got jump-leads from Slick and Deana came sidling along, trying to make up.

She said, 'I didn't mean that about you being a lesbo.'

I said, 'I'm glad to hear it. I'm not sure I even know what one is.'

She sniggered.

I said, 'Slick, you know, he loved your mom? He was always there for her. And now she's gone, he don't have person left in the world.'

'Yeah,' she said.

I said, 'I know he's not kin, but your mom'd expect you to treat him decent. Show him a little kindness and consideration. That's what your mom was. Kind and considerate.'

'Yeah,' she said.

Dixie yelled from inside the car. 'Mom! We're nearly outta gas too.'

I said, 'Do you have money for gas?'

'Well . . .' she said.

I gave her a few bucks.

'Tell you what,' she said. 'That Gayle must be a big earner. She's probably a millionaire or something by now.'

I guess I knew right then who was going to pay for Betty's mahogany casket.

101

Me and Kath drove back to Dallas in ninety degrees.

I said, 'You'll be glad to get back to grey Norfolk skies.'

'I'm not going,' she said. 'Not yet. I'm thinking of going to New York.'

I knew Lois never invited her. I said, 'You can't go there in August. It'll be hotter than hell. If you want to see New York, you should come in the fall sometime.'

She was quiet for a while. Then she said, 'What happened? After Vern got Kirk that job. What went wrong?'

I said, 'There was a falling out.'

I pulled into the Georgetown rest area and we bought sodas. I said, 'Okay, let's talk about New York.'

'I want to see Lois's boy,' she said. 'I want to see him for myself.'

I said, 'Did you broach this with Lois?'

'You know I didn't,' she said. 'All she does is lark around. You can't pin her down. Specially not what I've got in mind.'

She looked at me. The traffic was swishing by on the Interstate. 'You know what I mean?' she said.

I said, 'Why now, Kath?'

She said, 'Because I've got a bad feeling. It come to me when you told me Kirk had the arthritis. And it come to me again when I saw the snaps of his little baby. Can you tell me any more, Peg? Do you know if John Pharaoh went with Lois?'

I said, 'Yes. He did.'

She said, 'And is Kirk his boy?'

I said, 'I have no idea.'

A guy parked alongside of us, playing his radio so loud it made your ears hurt. We continued on our way.

'I might have done a terrible thing,' she said. 'If Kirk's got John Pharaoh's bad blood, that's a thing that can't be undone. And I had my chance . . .'

I said, 'You couldn't have stopped Lois. Nothing ever stopped her if she was looking for fun.'

'Oh, I know that,' she said. 'But I might have stopped Kirk. Do you see what I'm saying? But I didn't speak up, and now it might be too late. Now there's another little baby come along might have it. And so it goes on.'

I said, 'You have to talk to Lois. We can call her tonight.'

'If you like,' she said, 'but I'm still going there, whatever she says, because I don't trust her, not as far as I can spit. And if I don't go now and see for myself, I might not get another chance.'

I talked with Grice, after we got home.

He said, 'You can't let her go alone. She'll get robbed and murdered.'

I said, 'I don't want her to go at all. Herb's up there, quietly getting on with his life, and Kath walks in and drops a bomb. Say what you like about Lois, but she's stayed a married woman longer than almost anybody I know. Kath could blow the whole thing apart, and we don't even know if she's right.'

Grice said, 'What do you think?'

I said, 'I think I have to go to New York.'

102

We flew to La Guardia. Got a Midtown hotel, had all kinds of extras. Bad carpet. Neon sign for a car-rental office flashing just level with our window. Slowest elevator in the civilised world. Only things it didn't have were views and ventilation.

I called Lois. I said, 'Kath didn't want to leave without visiting.'

She said, 'Are you crazy? We only just said goodbye.'

I said, 'Maybe so, but she has her heart set on seeing Sandie and everybody.'

'I'm busy,' she said. 'We're leaving for the Jersey shore.' And she slammed down the phone.

Kath was watching me. 'Well, then,' she said.

Neither of us slept. There was an air-conditioning unit just outside the window. Amount of noise it was making, I hope somebody was feeling the benefit of it. We lay in the dark. Listened to the police sirens and talked.

Kath said, 'I know what Frank Sinatra meant now. The city that never sleeps.'

I said, 'Do I phone Herb, in the morning?'

She said, 'I'm sorry for the trouble I'm bringing you. I know you're fond of Lois. And I'm sorry for the trouble I'll be bringing her.'

I said, 'I think her troubles already arrived. After the burying, when I drove her to get her plane, she told me she wished she was dead. She was crying, and Lois never cries.'

I heard Kath sit up in her bed. 'What else?' she said.

'Nothing,' I said. 'She wouldn't explain herself. I thought it coulda been the red wine and the grieving. If you've got your health and your family, you don't wish yourself dead.'

'I did,' she said. 'There were times I did, Peg, and I'm not a person to get down-hearted easy. But there were times with John Pharaoh. I'd got my little job at the laundry and I didn't want to lose that. I didn't want to end up on the social. But I couldn't get people to sit with him, and he couldn't be left . . .'

Every thirty seconds or so the Kwik Kars sign lit her up, orange.

'I had a lot of people offered, but they'd do it once and they didn't want to be asked again. He was a handful. Sometimes he'd sleep. That was the best you could hope for. Sometimes he'd get in such a paddy, you could tell he'd have wrecked the place if he could have got across the room. He couldn't do it, but you could feel him seething. That was a frightening thing. And he'd say nasty things. I can't blame people for not coming back. I don't think he knew what he was saying, half the time, but nobody wants to hear that kind of talk. Some days I'd be at the end of my rope. I'd tell him he'd have to go away, have a nurse to look after him. That was a terrible cruel thing for me to say because I was all he had in the world and we'd never been apart.

'People said he was trouble. Some people said he was born bad. But he wasn't, Peg. When we were nippers he was no more trouble than any other lad. It wasn't him that was bad, it was his blood, and I could have had it too, only I got a better roll of the dice. If I could have him back for five minutes, I would. Tell him I'm sorry I taunted him like that, about being put away. It didn't come to it, of course, because the pneumonia got him. One of the doctors said to me, if he'd been in the hospital, like everybody said, he could have had exercises, stop his chest filling up. He might have lived longer. But he slipped away peaceful and he did it in his own bed, so I've no regrets there. I just wish I'd had more patience with him before he went.

'I used to feel that sorry for myself, I used to think if I was dead he'd be somebody else's worry and they probably wouldn't have it for long because he wouldn't last five minutes without me. I did think of it. He had these pills, meant to keep him calmed down. I'd look at them sometimes. Wonder how many it'd take. Only I didn't have the gumption. But I could understand anybody who did. It's a funny thing about human nature. Nobody ever wonders why they've got a healthy brother or a perfect kiddie. Anything goes wrong, though, we soon start asking why, oh why . . .'

We were both quiet for a while, but I knew she was still awake. She said, 'What happened? When the fishing shop sacked him?'

I said, 'He started acting weird. Dropped his pants a couple of times.'

'Oh, God help us,' I heard her whisper.

I said, 'Kath, I only got this from Vern. I don't know for sure,'

'God help us all,' she said. 'He promised me, Peg. John promised me he'd be careful.'

I said, 'Kath, do you think it would be really out of line for me to call Sandie?'

'Well,' she said, 'I was hoping you'd offer.'

103

Sandie was married to Gerry Carroll. I got their number from information while Kath was having coffee and donuts in the lobby.

I was nervous. I used to push that kid around in her stroller, but my heart was pounding like I was calling up the president himself.

'Aunty Peggy!' she said. 'I didn't know you were coming to town.' I could hear her little one prattling in the background.

I said, 'Sandie, I'm gonna cut to the chase. I'm here with English Kath, and your mom's real busy with work and going on vacation and everything . . .'

She said, 'Vacation? First I heard. Where are you?'

I said, 'We're in a hotel, Midtown.'

She said, 'Well come up and see me. And Dad too. He could use some company.'

I said, 'Ain't he working?'

She didn't answer right away. Then she said, 'He had to quit, stay home with Kirk. Well, somebody had to, and Mom was earning a lot more than Dad.'

I said, 'I didn't know.'

'Okay,' she said. 'So will you come and see my little boy? You can get the Liberty bus on Madison and I'll pick you up when you get to the end of the line.'

I said, 'I don't want to make trouble between you and your mom.'

'Aunty Peggy,' she said, 'we can make our own trouble. Makes no difference whether we get outside help or not. And you can't come to New York and not see me. Heck, I just wish I'd known you were coming. I'd have loved for you to meet my Gerry, but he's working.'

Kath hardly spoke, all the way up through Harlem and the Bronx. 'This is a big place,' she said. 'That just goes on and on. And they've got every colour under the sun living here. We've got a few Pakistanis in Lynn, now, but they've got flavours here I've never seen. Look at that! Men with ringlets. Smart black overcoats, and yet they've got ringlets.' We were passing a yeshiva.

I said, 'They're a type of Hebrew, I believe.'

'Well,' she said, 'they must be stifled, whoever they are, wearing big coats and hats, this time of year.'

I said, 'Have you worked out what you're gonna say to Sandie?'

'No,' she said. 'But I shall do what I have to do.'

Patrick was a darling child, never stopped smiling, just like I remembered Sandie. He took Kath's hand and toddled right along with her to the apartment.

Kath said, 'I reckon I've got a new pal.'

Sandie had a fan going inside, just stirring the heat. She brung out iced coffee and we sat on lawn chairs in their little patch of back yard, watched Patrick playing with his pull-along train.

I said, 'We didn't know Kirk was so sick.'

She said, 'Mom doesn't care to talk about it. I mean, she loves him so. He always was the blue-eyed boy. But now he's sick, she can't stand being around him. She hates anything to do with disease. You could have knocked me down when she took off and visited Betty. But Kirk . . . Some days she doesn't even go in to see him. She gets home late, Dad's already put him to bed, and she's gone before he's up in the morning. I don't think she's feeling too proud of herself. And you know what she's like. If she's not happy, it's the end of the world. She's all for herself. Doesn't occur to her how Dad's struggling.'

I said, 'And what exactly is wrong with Kirk?'

'Well,' she said, 'it's a kinda nervous thing. It's a kinda degeneration of the brain.'

Kath was playing with the baby, but she was listening.

Sandie said, 'He's seen nerve doctors. He's seen shrinks. All they do is give him pills, keep him tranquillised. They can't tell us if it's catching. They can't tell us if it's inherited. And you know . . . we waited so long to get Patrick . . . Anything ever happened to him : . . We don't let Patrick too near him any more. It's a pity. He doesn't see his own kid, and now we can't even let him be an uncle. But we daren't. Not till we know . . . Dad's good with Kirk. Plays him nice music and gets the dog to sit by him. He loves the dog. And I take a turn when I can. When Gerry can look after Patrick, I go over. Give Dad a break. But Mom . . .'

Kath stood up.

'Sandie,' she said, 'your Kirk, does he go like this?' And she started moving around the yard. One leg jolted and juddered. As her foot touched the ground it jerked up again. Her hands writhed and her face twitched. She was like a hanged man, dancing on a rope. Little Patrick was laughing. But all the colour had drained away from Sandie's rosy cheeks

'How did you know?' she whispered. 'How did you know a thing like that?'

Kath said, 'I know because I've seen it. I know what's wrong with him. And I can tell you something else. Your little un's all right. He won't get it. He's different blood from Kirk, bless his heart.'

She sat down again.

I said, 'Kath. I know what you're saying, but Sandie don't. You can't start a story and not finish it. Tell her about John Pharaoh.'

'I'm going to,' she said. 'But I got other fish to fry first. I've got to see Lois, and Herb. I've got to see Kirk. That's the main thing. I shall have to go round there now, see him for myself.'

Sandie hadn't moved.

Kath said, 'We shall have to do it, Peg. That's what we're here for. Get Herb on the phone. Tell him I've got to go round there, get a few things straight.'

I said, 'I can't do it, Kath. I can't go behind Lois's back.'

Sandie said, 'Will you just tell me what's going on? I'll take you to Dad. If you know anything about what's wrong with Kirk, Dad'll want to hear it. But I have to know before I take you.'

I couldn't look at her. She started yelling, made the baby cry. 'Tell me, damn it!' she said. 'Mom and Dad aren't the only ones suffering. I do my share.'

I said, 'Kirk's not Herb's child.'

She picked up Patrick. Tried to soothe him.

I said, 'Kath had a brother, John. Your mom went with him, and then she had Kirk. And John had this twitching and jerking. It's inherited. It's called Huntington's chorea.'

She said, 'Never heard of it. Kirk's seen plenty of doctors. I never heard of that.'

Kath said, 'Well, they're only doctors. If they don't know what they're looking for they don't always see it. We knew with John Pharaoh, see? We'd seen it in our mam and our Uncle Dancer.'

Sandie said, 'You know for sure she went with him? How do you know?'

Neither of us answered.

She said, 'Can they fix it? If that's what he has?'

Kath said, 'No. They can't.'

'So you're asking me,' she said, 'to take you to Dad. Walk in out of the blue and tell him there's nothing can be done for Kirk and oh, by the way, he's not even your kid. Is that right?'

I said, 'Kath, we can't do it.'

Sandie said, 'Why are you hitting us with this now? You don't have to do this to him. Mom's the one. If you're right, she's caused all this. Anyone has to tell Dad, it should be her.'

Kath's face was set hard. 'She's had twenty-eight years to do that,' she said. 'And she knows I'm here. She knows why I've come, and still she won't do it. Telling us she's going on holiday. I'm not leaving, Sandie, not till I've done it. I should have spoke up years ago and look what's happened because I didn't. Now there's another little baby out there. Lois showing her photos around. "Look at my little grandson." That little boy could have it. Nobody ever says anything, he'll grow up then *he* could pass it on. That'll go on and on, causing misery, all because Lois won't own up. Well, it's half out of the bag now, so let's get it over and done with. I dread it. I'm sick to my stomach thinking of it. Your poor dad. But I tell you what, he's suffering already and he's got worse to come. At least he'll know. At least he won't go around dreaming Kirk's going to get better.'

Sandie said, 'I wish you'd never come.'

Kath said, 'I know that.'

Sandie said, 'What's gonna happen, when Dad finds out? What's gonna happen if he walks out on Mom? She won't stay home with Kirk. Who does that leave? Me. I can see it. My own baby taking a back seat so I can nurse Mom's . . . bastard. I hate him. I always hated him. I hate her. She never does the right thing. Never.'

We just stood there. Little Patrick checking out our faces, trying to work out what was going on. Like we knew.

Eventually Kath said, 'I'll go, Peg. You don't have to come. If you can put me in a taxi, set me right. I'll go. I should have done that anyway.'

'Aunty Kath?' Sandie said. 'I'm sorry.'

Kath gave her a funny old smile.

'So am I, sweetheart,' she said. 'Sorry I've dithered all this time. Sorry I didn't keep John Pharaoh on a shorter rope.'

Sandie said, 'Here's what I'm gonna do. I'm gonna call Mom. Give her one more chance. If she doesn't cancel her appointments, come home right away, I'm taking to you to Dad.'

104

Lois hung up on Sandie.

I said, 'What does that mean?'

She said, 'It means we're going to see Dad.'

Kath sat in the back of the station-wagon, next to the baby. I rode up front with Sandie.

She said, 'It's only ten minutes.'

I said, 'I haven't seen Herb since we left McConnell.'

She said, 'You think he's *my* Dad?'

I said, 'Sure I do.' What did I know?

It was a nice building, nothing fancy.

Sandie said, 'I'm going up, tell Dad you're here. I'll leave Patrick here with you. If there's gonna be a scene, I don't want him around.'

We sat in the parking lot. Had the doors open, try and get a breath of air. Kath was playing Incey Spider with the baby. Sandie was gone a while. Then I saw Herb.

He didn't have much hair left. Was wearing one of those knit T-shirts. He always did love the louder shades of green.

I climbed out of the car. Back of my shirt was stuck to me with sweat. 'Peggy?' he said. He darned near lifted me off my feet. Then he ducked inside the car, to give his little grandbaby a kiss.

Kath climbed out. She said, 'You won't remember me.'

'Oh, but I do,' he said. 'Fourth of July, 1952. You hit a home run first time you ever faced a ball.'

She said, 'I'm here about your boy, Herb.'

'Yeah,' he said. 'I guess you heard, he's not well?'

Kath said, 'Can I come and see him?'

'Kinda question is that?' he said. 'Come right up, get a cold beer.'

I said, 'You want me to stay here? Mind the baby?'

But he was already unstrapping Patrick from his little car seat. 'I do not,' he said. 'You're all to come right on in. I have to warn you, though, place is a mess. I wasn't expecting company.'

Sandie was rinsing off a few dishes when we walked in. Herb wasn't wrong about the mess. He hurried around, though, trying to find glasses and potato chips and a cookie for Patrick. There was no sign of Kirk.

'Dad,' Sandie said. 'Quit flapping around. Sit down. Kath wants to talk to you.'

He looked so tired. He looked an old man compared to Vern. I spotted Lo's old Hawaiian hula doll on the shelf.

Kath said, 'I had a brother, you know? John. Now, when he was twenty, he started up with the twitching. He didn't get it all the time. Only if he got worked up over something. After the big flood, though, he was never the same. The twitching got worse, and his mind started to go. He'd shout out bad words. He'd fall over. Everybody thought he was drunk, but he never took drink. Well, we knew what was wrong, because it was in the family. Our mam had had it the very same. Only time she didn't twitch was when she fell asleep. But later on it did stop, and then she seized up. She couldn't move about nor even talk properly. Then she couldn't swallow. And that's how she went. She choked. All we were giving her was porridge or mash, but her throat was all seized up, and the reason I'm telling you all this is I think your lad has the same thing . . .'

I heard a cry from somewhere in the apartment. Sounded like a baying creature.

'. . . and the reason is, Lois used to drive out and see my John sometimes. It was one of them daft things. Looking for a bit of excitement I suppose. She was only young . . .'

An old spaniel came padding in, went straight to Herb.

Kath said, 'I'm sorry, Herb. I think your boy has John Pharoah's blood.'

'Okay,' Herb said to the dog. 'Tell him I'm coming.' He looked at Kath. Then he reached over and patted her hand. He couldn't seem to say anything.

She said, 'Can I see him?'

Herb said to the dog, 'Tell him he has a visitor.' And the mutt padded back where it'd come from.

'Dad?' Sandie said. 'You okay?'

'Sure,' he said. 'Hey, I still didn't find a cookie for my little guy here.'

He jumped up.

'Dad!' she cried. 'I'm sorry. Did I do wrong, bringing them here?'

'No,' he said. He was rattling around in the kitchen. 'No, you did right. All of you did right.'

Herb brought beer to the table. Took Patrick on his knee. Put his arm around Sandie.

'Dad?' she said. 'I can't be here, when Mom gets home. I can't be here if there's gonna be yelling.'

'There won't be,' he said. 'Not from me, anyhow.'

Kath had followed the dog, gone looking for Kirk.

Herb gave me a resigned kinda smile. 'How's Vern?' he said.

'He's good,' I said.

'Kirk's in the first room,' he said. 'If you want to see him. He won't harm you or anything.'

I crossed the landing and looked in through the open door. Kath was down on her knees, scratching the old dog behind its ears, talking in a real quiet voice. Kirk was sitting in a high-back armchair. Such a fine-looking man, with Lois's red hair. But he had someone else's curls, someone else's dimples. Someone else's hands, twitching, twitching. It was John Pharoah, back from the grave.

'. . . and then we went for boiled shrimps,' she was saying. 'Do you remember? After Gayle's wedding? We went for a dinner, and we sat outside, right down near the water, and you told me you were going to be a Marine when you grew up . . .'

She heard me move. 'Kirk,' she said. 'Here's your Aunty Peggy come to see you as well. Two visitors in one day. Aren't you the VIP.'

I heard an outside door slam, real hard.

I whispered, 'Kath, I think Lois is home.'

Herb and Sandie and the baby were still sitting at the table. And there stood Lo, in her business suit, face tight and pale. Her eyes blazed at me. 'You happy now, Peggy?' she said. 'You seen him? Had your way? Barged into my home. Sticking your nose into my life. Anything else you'd care to do before you leave?'

Behind me I heard Kath came into the room. 'Hello, Lois,' she said. 'Well, now . . . I was just saying to Kirk, I suppose this makes us family. Don't it?'

105

It was Lois took things the worst, for a while at any rate. Herb said he had guessed all along Kirk wasn't his boy. He said he might not be the sharpest knife in the box, but then he didn't need to be. Fact was, it had took him about five minutes to fall in love with the little fella and he sure didn't want anybody else raising him. This seemed to hit Lois harder than if he only just found out. I suppose it made her feel foolish as well as guilty.

She moved out for a while, stayed in town. But she missed the sound of his whittling and he missed her banging about and cussing, so they patched things up. They knew they had a tough row to hoe with Kirk. He was thirty-eight when he died, same age as his other daddy, John Pharaoh.

Kath's first worry was how she was gonna stay on and help Herb and Lois. 'That's not like I can prove we're flesh and blood,' she kept saying. 'Your immigration people catch me, they'll throw me on the first boat that's leaving. I could end up in Panama.'

But it never happened, because Slick Bonney chased her all the way to New York and asked her to be his bride. She said, 'All right, then, but I can't live in Texas. I've got to be near my boy.'

'My boy' was how she referred to Kirk.

Slick said, 'Well, I let one good woman get away. I'm not losing another.'

They were married in City Hall, San Antonio, in the spring of '82. Slick sold up Bonney's Farm Vehicles, and Kath sold her School of Motoring, and then they moved to Westchester County, New York, to be on the Kirk Moon support team.

Nineteen ninety-three there was a big breakthrough from the scientists studying Huntington's chorea. It meant they could take a blood sample of a person and tell them if they had the gene. Course, not everybody would want to know this, because if you have the gene, sure as the sun rises, you are going to get the disease. Still, Kath and Slick and Herb made it their business to track down Marisa and lay the matter before her. Cory was only fourteen years old at that time but, given his good looks and the human failing of closing stable doors after the event, Kath dedicated herself to helping him face the terrible facts. As she said to me, 'It's a curse. That's like living with a time bomb. But that'd be a worse thing to find out after you'd had nippers and passed it on. It's all you can do. Just stop it doing any more harm.'

Herb and Lois tried retiring to Florida but Lo said it was one long bad-hair day, what with the humidity and all. They ended up back near White Plains, New York.

Lois said, 'I have to look at it this way, Peg. This is as near the city as Herb Moon is willing to be, and I owe him a few. If it turns out I can't stand it, I don't have far to go to hurl myself into the Hudson, put an end to it all.'

In 1999 Cory took the predictive test and got a clean bill of health. He's a fine young man. Good with his hands. Herb says he'd be a good wood-carver if he'd quit sitting at his computer all night long – and Sandie's boy too, ruining their eyes and ignoring the gifts God gave them.

Speaking of God's gifts, Gayle cut right down on her public appearances after Lemarr passed over. She said to me, 'Peggy, I always thought it was Lemarr had the healing gift, not me. I thought it just rubbed off on me somehow. I can't explain. When I found out I could still do it, after he was gone, I was terrified. I nearly went back to the bourbon bottle. Actually, I did go back to it, and the first shot I poured, I tripped over the rug, and the whole lot went flying, brand-new bottle and everything. I took that as a sign. So I'm carrying on. I'm through with television, though.'

I said, 'Honey, I got to tell you, I had the biggest trouble believing that stuff you did with teeth.'

'Yeah?' she said. 'Well, God loves, is all I can tell you. God loves, I deliver.'

Just as Gayle was quitting show business, Deana was starting up. I had kinda lost touch with Betty's girls. Carla moved to Bethesda, Maryland, to be a cancer nurse, and I always get a Christmas card from her, but she never mentioned the rest of the family. Then I tuned into *Rikki Lake* one day and there was Deana. The show was called 'My Daughter Stole My Man' and Deana was the star exhibit because it had happened to her twice. Delta running off with Bulldog I knew about. But lightning had struck again and Dixie had stolen the heart of an ageing biker called TeeJay, meant to be Deana's one and only.

Deana put her bad luck hanging on to husbands down to an unsettled childhood as a military brat and a long series of tragedies in her life, from car-crash injuries to nursing her dying mother night and day. Then they brought on Dixie and TeeJay and Deana offered to break Dixie's neck for her, then and there.

I said to Crystal, 'I wished I known she was gonna be on. I'd have taped it.'

'Mom,' she said. 'Just keep watching those shows. I'll bet you a dime to a dollar Deana's gonna appear of every last one of them.' She was right.

Crystal and Marc decided they were too old to have a family the regular way so they adopted. They started with a white Labrador-retriever, been abandoned on the road between Waterville and Bangor. Then they got a pair of cross-breeds, only had seven legs between them. They had belonged to an old boy who had to go into a rest home. Also a low-slung terrier type of dog, needed insulin injections twice a day.

I said, 'Crystal, what is it with you and cripples? Why do you have to fill your life with trouble?'

'Because Marc doesn't give me enough of it,' she said. 'And by the way, I don't care for the word "cripple".'

I said, 'Sometimes I think you saddle yourself with all these creatures just so you won't be able to visit me.'

'No comment,' she said.

They stayed on in Maine. I guess they'll be there for ever. Marc had the opportunity to edit *Fruit Digest*, the non-citrus section, but he turned it down. Said he wanted to sleep nights. Wanted time to go bird-watching and all that stuff him and Crystal like to do.

Audrey I haven't seen since 1976, but we write. She stayed with Arthur until he found another widow with money, then she came back Stateside and we picked up where we left off. She does her little paintings, birds and ocean views and stuff. She even sold a few. Mikey told her she could ruin his credibility in the world of installation art, whatever that might be. He has the HIV disease. Lance Jnr has a chain of juice bars, gone national, thinking to franchise them or something. I guess he's practically a millionaire.

Vern and Martine retired up to Belgrade Lakes. They thought they'd be taking Mom Dewey with them but she decided to stay on and plague Eugene a while longer, make sure that foreign wife of his didn't allow the yellow peril to infiltrate Vern's Vermiculture. She died in her ninety-second year, from complications of a broken hip.

Of course, she was a juvenile compared to Miss Lady. She hung on to one hundred and three and she didn't give in till the very end. Her last day she had Tucker wheeling her round her flower beds, then kept him up till 2 a.m., playing piquet. She went in her sleep.

After that, Grice moved to Corinth, all above board. I was out there one Sunday. They had invited me for afternoon tea and a new game they had, called darts. Just throwing arrows at a target. I had seen it before, in England. Turned out I was pretty good at it.

We were sitting out, under one of those tall old hickories. Tucker was complaining the tomato sandwiches were cut too thick. Grice was complaining they had to have them at all, except as some kind of memorial to Miss Lady.

I said, 'You two are like a regular married couple. Arguing about a sandwich. I'll be glad when it's the cocktail hour.'

Grice sighed. 'Me too,' he said. 'I'm so bored. I'm a prisoner in paradise.'

He got up, started running up and down the lawn, stripped off his shirt.

'A prisoner, I tell you! I'm stifled! It's all just too damned perfect. I need knots in my wood. I need grit in my shell. I need somebody to coach me at darts.'

The help was carrying out a fresh jug of iced tea. Never missed a beat.

Tucker smiled at me. 'I don't know if you ever thought of moving from the city?' he said. 'But we do miss the womanly tapping of a walking stick around here.'

Miss Lady's Correct Tomato Sandwiches

••

Have your help cut fresh white bread into rounds the same size as the tomatoes. The bread must be spread thinly with Hellmann's mayonnaise. The tomato must be sliced thin and allowed to drain before the sandwich is assembled. I detest a soggy sandwich. The Shelby County Hooses have been known to add cayenne pepper. This is the kind of behavior gets a family discussed.

••

ONE

I t was just as well I had ripped off my Ear Correcting Bandages. Had I been bound up in my usual bedtime torture-wear, I would never have heard my mother's screams.

The bandages were part of my preparation for the great husband hunt. I was only fifteen years old, but my mother recognized a difficult case when she saw one. She had taken up the challenge the day after my twelfth birthday and never spared herself since.

'The early bird, Poppy,' she always said, when I complained. 'The early bird.'

And so, assisted by my aunt, she began an all-fronts campaign to catch me a worm.

I was forbidden candy and other waist-thickening substances. I was enrolled for classes in piano, singing and cotillion dancing, and spent an hour every day in a backboard, during which I practiced French pronunciation whilst a series of Irish maids tried to straighten my hair, or at least, defeat its natural wiriness into the kind of soft loose curls preferred by husbands.

On alternate days my neck was painted with Gomper's Patent Skin Whitener, to coax out of it a certain oriental tinge. The label advised using the paste no oftener than once a week. But as my mother said, what did they know? They hadn't seen my neck.

As to my nose, she knew the limits of home improvements. I was to go to a beauty doctor in Cincinnati, as soon as I was sixteen, and have a little cartilage shaved off.

Meanwhile she applied herself to the correction of my protruding ears. She designed an adjustable bandeau to hold them flat against my skull while I slept and had the Irish girl make them up for me in a selection of nightwear colours.

'So you can choose, you see?' Ma explained. 'According to your frame of mind.'

And, gauging my frame of mind all too well, my aunt informed me that some day, when I had grown in wisdom, I would be grateful for their efforts.

The alternative to all this was that I would be left an old maid.

I knew what an old maid was. My cousin Addie was being one up in Duluth, Minnesota, riding around all day with her dogs and not wearing corsets. And I knew what marriage was too. My sister Honey had recently married Harry Glaser and as soon as the marrying was done she had to leave home and put up her hair. As far as I could see she wasn't allowed to play with her dolls anymore, and she had hardly any time for cutting out pretty things for her scrapbook. She had to go to tea parties all the time, but never appear too eager about cake, and whenever she came to call Ma would make mysterious inquiries.

'Honey,' she'd whisper, 'how are Things? Are you still using the Lysol?'

To avoid the fate that had befallen Honey, I decided on stealthy sabotage rather than outright rebellion. As long as things *appeared* to be satisfactory my mother took them to *be* satisfactory. Surface was her preferred level. Hidden depths were unattractive to her, therefore she behaved as though they did not exist. So, every night, I took off my ear correctors, but only after the house had fallen dark and silent.

Then, that night, someone came to the front door and rang the bell with great persistence. I thought it had to be a stranger. Anyone who knew us knew the hours we kept. They knew our disapproval of night life and lobster suppers and men who rolled home incapable of putting a key neatly in a keyhole.

I heard the Irish slide back the bolt, eventually, and voices. And then, leaning up on my elbow, holding my breath so as not to miss anything, I heard my Ma scream. This signaled excitement. The late visitors were Aunt Fish and Uncle Israel Fish, come straight from the opera, still in their finery, because they had seen newsboys selling a late extra edition with reports of a tragedy at sea. 'At sea' was where my Pa was, sailing home from Europe.

Aunt Fish was my mother's sister and she always seemed as at home in our parlor as she did in her own. By the time I had pulled on my wrapper and run downstairs she had already arranged Ma on a couch and was administering sal volatile.

'Are you sure he sailed, Dora?' she kept asking, but my mother wasn't sure of anything. 'Maybe he didn't sail. Maybe business kept him in London.'

My father had been in Berlin and London, inspecting his subsidiaries.

'Israel will go to the shipping offices,' Aunt Fish said. 'Israel, go to the shipping offices.'

Uncle Israel was stretched out with a cigarette.

'Nothing to be done at this hour,' he said. Aunt Fish turned and looked at him.

He left immediately. And my mother, released from the constraints of being seen by her brother-in-law dressed only in her nightgown, collapsed anew.

'Poppy,' said Aunt Fish, 'don't just stand there. Be a comfort to your mother.' And so while she plagued the Irish for a facecloth soaked in vinegar, and more pillows, and a jug of hot chocolate, I stood by my mother's side and wondered what kind of comforting to do.

I tried stroking her arm, but this appeared to irritate her. I looked at her, with my head set at a compassionate angle, but that didn't please her either. I was altogether relieved when Aunt Fish returned from harassing our help and resumed her post as couch-side comforter.

I said, 'Aunt Fish, is Pa lost at sea?' and Ma resumed her wailing.

'Poppy!' said Aunt Fish. 'Don't you have even an ounce of sense? Your poor mother has received a terrible shock. If you can't be quiet and sensible, then please return to your bed.'

I'm sure it wasn't me that had rung the doorbell in the middle of the night with news of shipwrecks.

'And send the Irish in, to build up the fire,' she shouted after me.

We had stopped bothering with names for our Irish maids. They never stayed long enough to make it worth learning a new one.

'And Poppy,' my mother called weakly, from her couch, 'don't forget to strap down your ears.'

I lay awake, waiting to hear Uncle Israel's return, but eventually I must have dozed, and then it was morning. But it was not like any other morning. Our family was suddenly part of a great drama. The first edition of the *Herald* reported that though Pa's ship had been in a collision, all hands were saved and she was now being towed into Halifax, Nova Scotia.

Aunt Fish returned, having changed into a morning gown, and then Uncle Israel, with news that the White Star Line was chartering a train to take relatives up to Halifax to be reunited with their loved ones.

I said, 'I'll go. Let me go.' This provided my aunt with further reasons to despair of me.

'For heaven's sakes, child!' she sighed, and Uncle Israel winked at me.

'Out of the question, Pops,' he said. 'Too young, you see. But why not write a little note? I'll see he gets it as soon he sets foot on land.'

'There's no need for you to go, Israel,' my mother said. The morning's brighter news had restored her appetite and she was eating a pile of toast and jam. 'I can always send Harry, if it isn't convenient to you.'

'Of course, it's convenient,' said Aunt Fish. 'It's Israel's place to go.'

I went to the escritoire and started composing my letter to Pa, but I was still more haunted by the idea that he might have drowned than I was uplifted by the prospect that he was safe. I had no sooner written the words 'Please, never go away again' than I burst into inappropriate and inconsiderate tears and was sent to my room.

Soon after, my sister arrived with her husband. Honey came up to my room and lay on my bed beside me.

'Don't cry, Pops,' she said. 'Pa's safe. And you don't want to get swollen eyes.'

I said, 'Why did he have to go across an ocean, anyhow?'

'Why, because that's what men do,' she said.

I said, 'Would you allow Harry?'

'Allow?' she said. 'It isn't my place to allow. Besides, I know everything Harry does is for the very best.'

I had often suspected that marrying had caused a softening of Honey's brain.

Uncle Israel left that afternoon on the special train to Halifax. And Harry went downtown, first to his broker with instructions to buy stock in the Marconi wireless company whose wonderful shipboard radio had helped save so many lives and bring comforting news to the waiting families. Then he went to the White Star offices to inquire when the passengers might be expected back in New York.

Honey and I were pasting scraps, just like old times, when Harry walked in, looking smaller and flatter and grayer than usual. He scratched his head.

'It's gone,' he said. 'The *Titanic* has sunk, with heavy losses. A boat called the *Carpathia* is bringing the survivors home.'

It was eight o'clock. Up in Massachusetts Uncle Israel's train was stopped, directed into a siding and reversed. There had been, he was told, a change of plan.

My cheeks were hot from the fire, but something deathly cold touched me. My mother fainted onto a couch. My sister uttered a terrible little cry. And Harry studied the pattern on the parlor rug.

'Marconi stock closed up one hundred and twenty points,' he said, to no one in particular.

TWO

My Grandpa Minkel and his brother Meyer arrived in Great Portage, Minnesota, in 1851 intending to set up as fur traders, but they were too late. The beaver pelt business was finished. They stayed on though and changed their plans and did well enough trading in lumber to build a fine house on top of a hill in Duluth. From Grandpa Minkel's house you could see clear to Wisconsin. So they said.

Meyer and his wife were never blessed with children. This was somehow due to the accidental firing of a Winchester '73, but I was never allowed to know the details. So when Grandpa headed south, looking to buy a spread and turn farmer, he left behind one of his own boys, Jesse, as a kind of second-hand son. Gave him away near enough, though he was a grown man and might well have had plans of his own. Grandpa took his other boy, Abe, to Iowa to be a mustard farmer. And that was my Pa.

Uncle Jesse stayed where he was put, married one of the Zukeman girls and had a number of obedient children, plus Cousin Addie, the one who refused to knuckle down to marriage. Grandpa Minkel grew so much mustard he had to buy a factory. Grandma Minkel told him he should make mustard that had a fine flavor but a short life, and she was right. Folks just had to keep coming back for more and Minkel's Mighty Fine Mustard did so well Grandma and Grandpa had to send Pa to New York City, to invest the profits and keep his finger on the quickening pulse of finance.

My mother's people were Plotzes. They sold feathers and goose down, in Cedar Rapids. She married Pa in 1890 and came with him